GATES OF EMPIRE
AND OTHER TALES OF THE CRUSADES

ALSO BY ROBERT E. HOWARD

The Complete Action Stories
Graveyard Rats and Others
Waterfront Fists and Others

GATES OF EMPIRE

AND OTHER TALES OF THE CRUSADES

ROBERT E. HOWARD

Edited by
Paul Herman

Introduction by
Fred Blosser

WILDSIDE PRESS

To Dena, for believing in me.

GATES OF EMPIRE AND OTHER TALES OF THE CRUSADES

"Red Blades of Black Cathay" first appeared in *Oriental Stories*, February-March 1931. "Hawks of Outremer" first appeared in *Oriental Stories*, Spring (April-May-June) 1931. "The Blood of Belshazzar" first appeared in *Oriental Stories*, Fall 1931. "Lord of Samarcand" first appeared in *Oriental Stories*, Spring 1932. "The Sowers of the Thunder" first appeared in *Oriental Stories*, Winter 1932. "The Lion of Tiberias" first appeared in *Magic Carpet Magazine*, July 1933. "The Shadow of the Vulture" first appeared in *Magic Carpet Magazine*, January 1934. "Gates of Empire" first appeared in *Golden Fleece*, January 1939.

Published by:
Wildside Press
P.O. Box 301
Holicong, PA 18928-0301
www.wildsidepress.com

First Wildside Press edition: 2004

CONTENTS

INTRODUCTION

Fantasy and adventure fans were once advised not to plumb Robert E. Howard's Conan stories for "hidden philosophical meanings." Why not? Because "they aren't there," pioneer Conan enthusiast John D. Clark told us with fervid but misguided certainty. I don't know if this same opinion colored Dr. Clark's perspective on Howard's other fiction, but I suspect it did.

And then there was L. Sprague de Camp, who said with equally heartfelt but short-sighted critical acumen that it was easy to rewrite some of Howard's then-unpublished historical adventure yarns into Conan stories in the 1950s. Why? Because "Howard's heroes were mostly cut from the same cloth," he declared.

De Camp and Clark were influential in the movement that returned Howard to print in the '50s and '60s, leading to the tremendous popularity that stamped Howard's name onto millions of paperback covers in the 1970s. As a result, their opinions carried weight with readers, editors, and critics. Thus was fostered an unfortunate misperception that still persists, even though some aficionados more recently have tried to sway the argument with a fairer assessment. According to the misperception, Howard's fiction, being empty of "meanings," was bereft of literary value, and was characterized by hard-muscled but thick-headed, mindlessly macho protagonists who all looked and thought alike, at least as far as the act of drawing and wielding a sword might constitute a mental process.

As you will soon see once you begin to read the stories in this collection, de Camp and Clark were both wrong. At his best—and story for story, the tales gathered in this volume show the author working at the top of his form—Howard rivals virtually any other U.S. fiction writer of the 20th Century for literary quality. As for the allegations that his works were lacking in "philosophical meanings" (for the sake of argument, I will infer that the charge implies an absence of substance and artistry) and that his protagonists were more or less interchangeable—well, let's review the evidence.

"Red Blades of Black Cathay" finds a 12th Century Norman Crusader on the Eastern frontiers of the world as it was known to his European contemporaries, rallying a rich but militarily weak splinter kingdom against the invading hordes of Genghis Khan. Disillusioned and violent, Godric de Villehard recognizes that greed and exploitation underpin the lofty ideals of the Crusade; he learns that the empire of Prester John, which he seeks, is "a dream and a fantasy." Nevertheless, he comes to the chivalric defense of Black Cathay and its requisitely beautiful princess. Some critics have found the ending of the story improbable (I won't spoil it by going into details here). As is often the case, the critics are wrong. The denouement flows logically from the situation and the personalities of the characters; Howard is not guilty of slipshod plotting—the critics are guilty of not reading the story closely enough.

The next two stories in this volume revolve around another hard-bitten knight, the half-Irish Cormac FitzGeoffrey. In "Hawks of Outremer," as in "Red Blades of Black Cathay," Howard sets his protagonist on a collision course with an actual historical character, in this case the Islamic hero Saladin who commanded the Moslem armies in the Third Crusade. Howard's portrayal of Saladin perhaps reflects the influence of Sir Walter Scott's *The Talisman*, and whereas in "Red Blades" the treachery and double-dealing of the European Crusaders are alluded to, in this story they are vividly dramatized. In "Blood of Belshazzar," Howard drops Cormac into a bandit stronghold where outlaws scheme against each other for a fabulous jewel. This was a favorite plot device of Howard's; outnumbered and surrounded by enemies, his hero must survive and prevail. Here, the means of survival is somewhat arbitrary, and one senses that Howard was still mastering his craft. Later, in similar straits in "The Black Stranger," under Howard's more experienced hand, Conan of Cimmeria would engineer his own victory.

Howard once told a correspondent that Cormac was "the most somber character I have yet attempted," but then he trumped himself with Donald McDeesa, a wandering Highland Scot who exacts bloody revenge against two towering tyrants of history in "Lord of Samarcand." This story is a marvel of compression, packing into a few thousand words what most writers would spin into a couple of bloated novels. The mood that Howard conveys is so bleak, so comfortless, that the novelette almost begs to be taken with an anti-depressant. One error mars the tale—or does it? McDeesa makes fateful use of a pistol a century before handguns were developed. Critics who get upset over anachronisms may cry carelessness, but I think Howard knew exactly what he was doing; read the story carefully for Howard's ironies and see if you don't agree.

"The Sowers of the Thunder" pits two evenly matched characters against one another; in fact, they are mirror images of each other in many ways. The Crusader Red Cahal is an exiled Irish prince who has been cheated out of kingship. The red-haired Baibars the Panther is a former slave who will one day seize a throne. Figuratively, one man will be the death of the other, and in a sense this is Howard's version of Poe's classic "William Wilson," played out against the turbulent background of the 13th Century in which the Holy Land is savaged by warring Europeans, Moslems, and nomads from the distant steppes. The spirit of Scott manifests itself in the presence of a mysterious Masked Knight who rides through the story, identity hidden until the end, like the Black Knight in *Ivanhoe.*

In "The Lion of Tiberias," two storylines diverge and then converge. In one, a gigantic British Dane named John Norwald is sent to the galleys by the warlord Zenghi, there to toil for more than twenty years as a cold, hard core of hate keeps him alive. The other storyline concerns Miles Du Courcey, a Crusader who invades Zenghi's stronghold to rescue his kidnapped sweetheart. Again, the story bears close study to appreciate its dramatic unity as one storyline reflects and enriches the other. Do you think that Howard was a brutish purveyor of simple-minded blood 'n' guts, as he has been stereotyped by the mavens of popular culture? Then read the brief, wrenching passage where he reflects on the devastating effects of abused power, as Miles flees from Zenghi's camp with his traumatized sweetheart: "So through the night they rode, the broken woman and the embittered man, handiworks of the Lion who dealt in swords and souls and human hearts, and whose victims, living and dead, filled the land like a blight of sorrow, agony, and despair." Many names in the story—Irak, Bagdad, Mosul, Ousama—remind us that history's catastrophes tend to repeat themselves endlessly.

"The Shadow of the Vulture" and "Gates of Empire" reveal a lighter side of Howard; yet here too, darkness lurks underneath the light. Although "The Shadow of the Vulture" is best known as the story in which Howard introduced Red Sonya of Rogatino, the prototype for Roy Thomas' Red Sonja of the comics and Sam Raimi's Xena, Warrior Princess, the male protagonist is Gottfried Von Kalmbach, a dauntless but somewhat oblivious German knight. Gottfried's behavior, from scene to scene, causes the reader to wonder if he's dumb like a fox, or simply dumb and dumber. Giles Hobson in "Gates of Empire" is an even unlikelier hero, a corpulent drunkard whom Howard surely modeled on Shakespeare's Sir John Falstaff. Enjoy Howard's jokes but don't overlook the serious themes that give dramatic weight to both stories—the elegiac lament implicit in the scene in which Gottfried in "rusty chain mail" watches a "newer, brighter generation" of gun-toting infantry march past—Giles' instinctive plea to an enemy to redeem their baser natures, his cowardice and his enemy's consuming hate, when their sword-arms are needed to bolster a last stand of the Crusaders against an overwhelming force of Saracens.

Historical fiction tends to have a limited shelf life. Who today reads the charming but long-winded epics of Rafael Sabatini, or those ponderous bestsellers of our parents' and grandparents' generation, *Prince of Foxes* and *Captain from Castile*? To be commercially successful as historical fiction, the trappings of the past must be "translated into the manners as well as the language of the age we live in," as the redoubtable Walter Scott once observed. Consequently, as reading tastes change, so wanes the popularity of those authors who try too strenuously to appeal to the fashion of the day.

Robert E. Howard was fortunate, perhaps—or more likely, instinctively prescient—in capturing a certain American mood of cynicism and despair that has never quite gone out of style since the sombrous days of the Great Depression, when the stories in this volume first appeared in *Oriental Stories* and *Golden Fleece*. Writing about political expediency, tarnished honor, and physical violence with unflinching realism and irony, he anticipates the Samurai epics of Kurosawa and Kobayashi (Donald McDeesa's fate prefigures that of Tatsuya Nakadai's vengeful ronin in Kobayashi's 1962 drama *Harakiri*), the westerns of Sam Peckinpah and Sergio Leone, and the nihilistic carnage of today's extreme video games. Let's hope that this reprinting of his Crusader masterpieces, containing the unedited texts of the original magazine stories, furthers a greater appreciation of Howard's genius.

RED BLADES OF BLACK CATHAY

Trumpets die in the loud parade,
The gray mist drinks the spears;
Banners of glory sink and fade
In the dust of a thousand years.
Singers of pride the silence stills,
The ghost of empire goes,
But a song still lives in the ancient hills,
And the scent of a vanished rose.
Ride with us on a dim, lost road
To the dawn of a distant day,
When swords were bare for a guerdon rare—
The Flower of Black Cathay.

Chapter 1

The singing of the swords was a deathly clamor in the brain of Godric de Villehard. Blood and sweat veiled his eyes and in the instant of blindness he felt a keen point pierce a joint of his hauberk and sting deep into his ribs. Smiting blindly, he felt the jarring impact that meant his sword had gone home, and snatching an instant's grace, he flung back his vizor and wiped the redness from his eyes. A single glance only was allowed him: in that glance he had a fleeting glimpse of huge, wild black mountains; of a clump of mail-clad warriors, ringed by a howling horde of human wolves; and in the center of that clump, a slim, silk-clad shape standing between a dying horse and a dying swordsman. Then the wolfish figures surged in on all sides, hacking like madmen.

"Christ and the Cross!" the old Crusading shout rose in a ghastly croak from Godric's parched lips. As if far away he heard voices gaspingly repeat the words. Curved sabers rained on shield and helmet. Godric's eyes blurred to the sweep of frenzied dark faces with bristling, foam-flecked beards. He fought like a man in a dream. A great weariness fettered his limbs. Somewhere—long ago it seemed—a heavy axe, shattering on his helm, had bitten through an old dent to rend the scalp beneath. He heaved his curiously weighted arm above his head and split a bearded face to the chin.

"*En avant*, Montferrat!" We must hack through and shatter the gates, thought the dazed brain of Godric; we can not long stand this press, but once within the city—no—these walls were not the walls of Constantinople: he was mad; he dreamed—these towering heights were the crags of a lost and nameless land and Montferrat and the Crusade lay lost in leagues and years.

Godric's steed reared and pitched headlong, throwing his rider with a clash of armor. Under the lashing hoofs and the shower of blades, the knight struggled clear and rose, without his shield, blood starting from every joint in his armor. He reeled, bracing himself; he fought not these foes alone, but the long grinding days behind—the days and days of hard riding and ceaseless fighting.

Godric thrust upward and a man died. A scimitar shivered on his crest, and the wielder, torn from his saddle by a hand that was still iron, spilled his entrails at Godric's feet. The rest reined in around howling, seeking to overthrow the giant Frank by sheer weight of numbers. Somewhere in the hellish din a woman's scream knifed the air. A clatter of hoofs burst like a sudden whirlwind and the press was cleared. Through a red mist the dulling eyes of the knight saw the wolfish, skin-clad assailants swept away by a sudden flood of mailed riders who hacked them down and trampled them under.

Then men were dismounting around him, men whose gaudy silvered armor, high fur kaftans and two-handed scimitars he saw as in a dream. One with thin drooping mustaches adorning his dark face spoke to him in a Turkish tongue the knight could faintly understand, but the burden of the words was unintelligible. He shook his head.

"I can not linger," Godric said, speaking slowly and with growing difficulty, "De Montferrat awaits my report and I must—ride—East—to—find—the—kingdom—of—Prester—John—bid—my—men—mount—"

His voice trailed off. He saw his men; they lay about in a silent, sword-gashed cluster, dead as they had lived—facing the foe. Suddenly the strength flowed from Godric de Villehard in a great surge and he fell as a blasted tree falls. The red mist closed about him, but ere it engulfed him utterly, he saw bending near him two great dark eyes, strangely soft and luminous, that filled him with formless yearning; in a world grown dim and unreal they were the one tangible reality and this vision he took with him into a nightmare realm of shadows.

Godric's return to waking life was as abrupt as his departure. He opened his eyes to a scene of exotic splendor. He was lying on a silken couch near a wide window whose sill and bars were of chased gold. Silken cushions littered the marble floor and the walls were of mosaics where they were not worked in designs of gems and silver, and were hung with heavy tapestries of silk, satin and cloth-of-gold. The ceiling was a single lofty dome of lapis lazuli from which was suspended on golden chains a censer that shed a faint alluring scent over all. Through the window a faint breeze wafted scents of spices, roses and jasmine, and beyond Godric could see the clear blue of the Asian skies.

He tried to rise and fell back with a startled exclamation. Whence this strange weakness? The hand he lifted to his gaze was thinner than should be, and its bronze was faded. He gazed in perplexity at the silken, almost feminine garments which clothed him, and then he remembered—the long wandering, the battle, the slaughter of his men-at-arms. His heart turned sick within him as he remembered the staunch faithfulness of the men he had led to the shambles.

A tall, thin yellow man with a kindly face entered and smiled to see that he was awake and in his right mind. He spoke to the knight in several languages unknown to Godric, then used one easy to understand—a rough Turkish dialect much akin to the bastard tongue used by the Franks in their contacts with the Turanian peoples.

"What place is this?" asked Godric. "How long have I lain here?"

"You have lain here many days," answered the other. "I am You-tai, the emperor's man-of-healing. This is the heaven-born empire of Black Cathay. The princess Yulita has attended you with her own hands while you lay raving in delirium. Only through her care and your own marvelous natural strength have you survived. When she told the emperor how you with your small band recklessly charged and delivered her from the hands of the Hian bandits who had slain her guard and taken her prisoner, the heavenly one gave command that naught be spared to preserve you. Who are you, most noble lord? While you raved you spoke of many unknown peoples, places and battles and your appearance is such as to show that you come from afar."

Godric laughed, and bitterness was in his laughter.

"Aye," quoth he, "I have ridden far; the deserts have parched my lips and the mountains have wearied my feet. I have seen Trebizond in my wanderings, and Teheran and Bokhara and Samarcand. I have looked on the waters of the Black Sea and the Sea of Ravens. From Constantinople far to the west I set forth more than a year agone, riding eastward. I am a knight of Normandy, Sir Godric de Villehard."

"I have heard of some of the places you name," answered You-tai, "but many of them are unknown to me. Eat now, and rest. In time the princess Yulita will come to you."

So Godric ate the curiously spiced rice, the dates and candied meats, and drank the colorless rice wine brought him by a flat-faced girl slave who wore golden bangles on her ankles, and soon slept, and sleeping, his unquenchable vitality began to assert itself.

When he awoke from that long sleep he felt refreshed and stronger, and soon the pearl-inlaid doors opened and a slight, silk-clad figure entered. Godric's heart suddenly pounded as he again felt the soft, tender gaze of those great dark eyes upon him. He drew himself together with an effort; was he a boy to tremble before a pair of eyes, even though they adorned the face of a princess?

Long used was he to the veiled women of the Moslems, and Yulita's creamy cheeks with her full ruby lips were like an oasis in the waste.

"I am Yulita," the voice was soft, vibrant and musical as the silvery tinkle of the fountain in the court outside. "I wish to thank you. You are brave as Rustum. When the Hians rushed from the defiles and cut down my guard, I was afraid. You answered my screams as unexpectedly and boldly as a hero sent down from paradise. I am sorry your brave men died."

"And I likewise," the Norman answered with the bluntness of his race, "but it was their trade: they would not have had it otherwise and they could not have died in a better cause."

"But why did you risk your life to aid me, who am not of your race and whom you never saw before?" she pursued.

Godric might have answered as would nine out of any ten knights in his position—with the repeating of the vow of chivalry, to protect all weaker things. But being Godric de Villehard, he shrugged his shoulders.

"God knows. I should have known it was death to us all to charge that horde. I have seen too much rapine and outrage since I turned my face east to have thus thrown away my men and expedition in the ordinary course of events. Perhaps I saw at a glance you were of regal blood and followed the knight's natural instinct to rush to the aid of royalty."

She bowed her head. "I am sorry."

"I am not," he growled. "My men would have died anyhow today or tomorrow—now they are at rest. We have ridden through hell for more than a year. Now they are beyond the sun's heat and the Turk's saber."

She rested her chin on her hands and her elbows on her knees, leaning forward to gaze deep into his eyes. His senses swam momentarily. Her eyes traversed his mighty frame to return to his face. Thin-lipped, with cold gray eyes, Godric de Villehard's sun-darkened, clean-shaven face inspired trust and respect in men but there was little in his appearance to stir the heart of a woman. The Norman was not past thirty, but his hard life had carved his face into inflexible lines. Rather than the beauty that appeals to women, there was in his features the lean strength of the hunting wolf. The forehead was high and broad, the brow of a thinker, and once the mouth had been kindly, the eyes those of a dreamer. But now his eyes were bitter and his whole appearance that of a man with whom life has dealt hardly—who has ceased to look for mercy or to give it.

"Tell me, Sir Godric," said Yulita, "whence come you and why have you ridden so far with so few men?"

"It's a long tale," he answered. "It had its birth in a land halfway across the world. I was a boy and full of high ideals of chivalry and knighthood—and I hated that Saxon-French pig, King John. A wine-bibber named Fulk of Neuilly began ranting and screaming death and damnation because the Holy Land was still in the possession of the Paynim. He howled until he stirred the blood of such young fools as myself, and the barons began recruiting men—forgetting how the other Crusades had ended.

"Walter de Brienne and that black-faced cut-throat Simon de Montfort fired us young Normans with promises of salvation and Turkish loot, and we set forth. Boniface and Baldwin were our leaders and they plotted against each other all the way to Venice.

"There the mercenary Venetians refused us ships and it sickened my very entrails to see our chiefs go down on their knees to those merchant swine. They promised us ships at last but they set such a high price we could not pay. None of us had any money, else we had never started on that mad venture. We wrenched the jewels from our hilts and the gold from our buckles and raised part of the money, bargaining to take various cities from the Greeks and give them over to Venice for the rest of the price. The Pope—Innocent III—raged, but we went our ways and quenched our swords in Christian blood instead of Paynim.

"Spalato we took, and Ragusa, Sebenico and Zara. The Venetians got the cities and we got the glory." Here Godric laughed harshly. A quick glance told him the girl was sitting spellbound, eyes aglow. Somehow he felt ashamed.

"Well," he continued, "young Alexius who had been driven from Constantinople persuaded us that it would be doing God's work to put old Angelus back on the throne, so we fared forth.

"We took Constantinople with no great difficulty, but only a scant time had elapsed before the maddened people strangled old Angelus and we were forced to take the city again. This time we sacked it and split the empire up. De Montfort had long returned to England and I fought under Boniface of Montferrat, who was made King of Macedonia. One day he called me to him, and said he: 'Godric, the Turkomans harry the caravans and the trade of the East dries up because of constant war. Take a hundred men-at-arms and find me this kingdom of Prester John. He too is a Christian and we may establish a route of trade between us, guarded by both of us, and thus safeguard the caravans.'

"Thus he spoke, being a natural-born liar and unable to tell the truth on a wager. I saw through his design and understood his wish for me to conquer this fabulous kingdom for him.

"'Only a hundred men?' quoth I.

"'I can not spare you more,' said he, 'lest Baldwin and Dandolo and the Count of Blois come in and cut my throat. These are enow. Gain ye to Prester John and abide with him awhile—aid him in his wars for a space, then send riders to report your progress to me. Mayhap then I can send you more men.' And his eyelids drooped in a way I knew.

"'But where lies this kingdom?' said I.

"'Easy enough,' said he; 'to the east—any fool can find it if he fares far enough.'

"So," Godric's face darkened, "I rode east with a hundred heavily armed horsemen—the pick of the Norman warriors. By Satan, we hacked our way through! Once past Trebizond we had to fight almost every mile.

We were assailed by Turks, Persians and Kirghiz, as well as by our natural foes of heat, thirst and hunger. A hundred men—there were less than a score with me when I heard your screams and rode out of the defiles. Their bodies lie scattered from the hills of Black Cathay to the shores of the Black Sea. Arrows, spears, swords, all took their toll, but still I forged eastward."

"And all for your liege lord!" cried Yulita, her eyes sparkling, as she clasped her hands. "Oh, it is like the tales of honor and chivalry; of Iran and those You-tai has told me of the heroes of ancient Cathay. It makes my blood burn! You too are a hero such as all men were once in the days of our ancestors, with your courage and loyalty!"

The sting of his healing wounds bit into Godric.

"Loyalty?" he snarled. "To that devious-minded assassin, Montferrat? Bah! Do you think I intended giving up my life to carve out a kingdom for him? He had naught to lose and all to gain. He gave me a handful of men, expecting to receive the rewards of what I did. If I failed, he was still winner, for he would be rid of a turbulent vassal. The kingdom of Prester John is a dream and a fantasy. I have followed a will-o'-the-wisp for a thousand miles. A dream that receded farther and farther into the mazes of the East, leading me to my doom."

"And had you found it, what then?" asked the girl, grown suddenly quiet.

Godric shrugged his shoulders. It was not the Norman way to flaunt secret ambitions to any chance-met man or woman, but after all, he owed his life to this girl. She had paid her debt to him and there was something in her eyes. . . .

"Had I found Prester John's kingdom," said Godric, "I had made shift to conquer it for myself."

"Look," Yulita took Godric's arm and pointed out a gold-barred window, whose sheer silken curtains, blowing inward, disclosed the rugged peaks of distant mountains, shouldering against the blazing blue of the skies.

"Beyond those mountains lies the kingdom of him you call Prester John."

Godric's eyes gleamed suddenly with the conquering spirit of the true Norman—the born empire-maker, whose race had carved out kingdoms with their swords in every land of the West and Near East.

"And does he dwell in purple-domed palaces of gold and glittering gems?" he asked eagerly. "Do, as I have heard, learned philosophers and magi sit at either hand, doing wonders with stars and suns and ghosts of the mighty dead? Does his city loom among the clouds with golden spires thrusting among the stars? And does the deathless monarch, who learned at the feet of our fair Lord Christ, sit on an ivory throne in a room whose walls are carved of one great sapphire dispensing justice?"

She shook her head.

"Prester John—Wang Khan we name him—is very old, but he is not deathless nor has he ever been beyond the confines of his own kingdom. His people are the Keraits—Krits—Christians; they dwell in cities, true, but the houses are mud huts and goatskin tents, and the palace of Wang Khan is as a hut itself compared to this palace."

Godric fell back and his eyes went dull.

"My dream is vanished," he muttered. "You should have let me die."

"Dream again, man," she answered; "only dream something more attainable."

Shaking his head, he looked into her eyes.

"Dreams of empire have haunted my life," said he, "yet even now the shadow of a dream lingers in my soul, ten times less attainable than the kingdom of Prester John."

Chapter 2

"Scrawled screens and secret gardens
And insect-laden skies—
Where fiery plains stretch on and on
To the purple country of Prester John
And the walls of Paradise."

—Chesterton

The days passed and slowly the giant frame of the Norman knight regained its accustomed vigor. In those days he sat in the chamber with the lapis lazuli dome, or walked in the outer courts where fountains tinkled musically beneath the shade of cherry trees, and soft petals fell in a colorful rain about him. The battle-scarred warrior felt strangely out of place in this setting of exotic luxury but was inclined to rest there and lull the restlessness of his nature for a time. He saw nothing of the city, Jahadur, for the walls about the courts were high, and he presently understood that he was practically a prisoner. He saw only Yulita, the slaves and

You-tai. With the thin yellow man he talked much. You-tai was a Cathayan—a member of the race who lived in Greater Cathay, some distance to the south. This empire, Godric soon realized, had given rise to many of the tales of Prester John; it was an ancient, mighty but now loosely knit empire, divided into three kingdoms—the Khitai, the Chin and the Sung. You-tai was learned beyond any man Godric had ever known and he spoke freely.

"The emperor inquires often after your health," said he, "but I tell you frankly, it were best that you not be presented to him for a time at least. Since your great battle with the Hian bandits, you have captured the fancy of the soldiers, especially old Roogla, the general who loves the princess like his own since he bore her as a babe on his saddle-bow from the ruins of Than when the Naimans raided over the border. Chamu Khan fears anyone the army loves. He fears you might be a spy. He fears most things, does the emperor, even his niece, the princess Yulita."

"She does not took like the Black Cathayan girls I have seen" commented Godric; "her face is not flat, nor do her eyes slant as much."

"She has Iranian blood," answered You-tai. "She is the daughter of a royal Black Cathayan and a Persian woman."

"I see sadness in her eyes, at times," said Godric.

"She remembers that she is soon to leave her mountain home," answered You-tai, eyeing Godric closely. "She is to marry prince Wang Yin of the Chin emperors. Chamu Khan has promised her to him, for he is anxious to gain favor with Cathay. The emperor fears Genghis Khan."

"Who is Genghis Khan?" Godric asked idly.

"A chief of the Yakka Mongols. He has grown greatly in power for the last decade. His people are nomads—fierce fighters who have so little to live for in their barren deserts that they do not mind dying. Long ago their ancestors, the Hiong-nu, were driven into the Gobi by my ancestors, the Cathayans. They are divided into many tribes and fight against one another, but Genghis Khan seems to be uniting them by conquest. I even hear wild tales that he plans to shake off the liege-ship of Cathay and even make war on his masters. But that is foolish. This small kingdom is different. Though Hia and the Keraits lie between Chamu Khan and the Yakkas, Genghis Khan is a real threat to this mountain empire.

"Black Cathay has grown to be a kingdom apart, pent in the fastness where no strong foe has come against them for ages. They are neither Turks nor Chinese any longer, but constitute a separate nation of their own, with separate traditions. They have never needed any alliances for protection, but now since they have grown soft and degenerate from long years of peace, even Chamu realizes their weaknesses and seeks to ally his house with that of the Chins of Cathay."

Godric mused a space. "It would seem Jahadur is the key to Black Cathay. These Mongols must first take this city to make sure of their conquests. No doubt the walls throng with archers and spearmen?"

You-tai spread his hands helplessly. "No man knows the mind of Chamu Khan. There are scarce fifteen hundred warriors in the city. Chamu has even sent our strongest detachment—a troop of hard-riding western Turks—to another part of the empire. Why, no one knows. I beg you, stir not from the court until I tell you. Chamu Khan deems you a spy of Genghis Khan, I fear, and it were best if he did not send for you."

But Chamu Khan did call for Godric before many days had drifted by. The emperor gave him audience, not in the great throne room, but in a small chamber where Chamu Khan squatted like a great fat toad on a silken divan attended by a huge black mute with a two-handed scimitar. Godric veiled the contempt in his eyes and answered Chamu Khan's questions regarding his people and his country with patience. He wondered at the absurdity of most of these questions, and at the emperor's evident ignorance and stupidity. Old Roogla, the general, a fiercely mustached, barrel-chested savage, was present and he said nothing. But his eyes strayed in comparison from the fat, helpless mass of flesh and arrogance on the cushions to the erect, broad-shouldered figure and hard, scarred face of the Frank. From the corner of his eye Chamu Khan observed this but he was not altogether a fool. He spoke pleasantly to Godric, but the wary Norman, used to dealing with rulers, sensed that dislike was mixed with the khan's feeling of obligation, and that this dislike was mingled with fear. Chamu asked him suddenly of Genghis Khan and watched him narrowly. The sincerity of the knight's reply evidently convinced Chamu, for a shadow of relief passed over his fat face. After all, decided Godric, it was but natural that an emperor should be suspicious of a stranger in his realm, especially one of such war-like aspects as the Norman knew himself to be.

At the end of the interview, Chamu fastened a heavy golden chain about Godric's neck with his own pudgy hands. Then Godric went back to his chamber with the lapis lazuli dome, to the cherry blossoms drifting in gay-colored clouds from the breeze-shaken trees, and to lazy strolls and talks with Yulita.

"It seems strange," said he abruptly one day, "that you are to leave this land and go to another. Somehow I can not think of you save as a slim girl forever under these blossom-heavy trees, with the dreamy fountains singing and the mountains of Black Cathay rising against the skies."

She caught her breath and turned away her face as if from an inner hurt.

"There are cherry trees in Cathay," said she, without looking at him, "and fountains too—and finer palaces than I have ever seen."

"But there are no such mountains," returned the knight.

"No," her voice was low, "there are no such mountains—nor—"

"Nor what?"

"No Frankish knight to save me from bandits," she laughed suddenly and gayly.

"Nor will there be here, long," he said somberly. "The time approaches when I must take the trail again. I come of a restless breed and I have dallied here overlong."

"Whither will you go, oh Godric?" Did she catch her breath suddenly as she spoke?

"Who knows?" In his voice was the ancient bitterness that his heathen Viking ancestors knew. "The world is before me—but not all the world with its shining leagues of sea or sand can quench the hunger that is in me. I must ride—that is all I know. I must ride till the ravens pluck my bones. Perchance I will ride back to tell Montferrat that his dream of an Eastern empire is a bubble that has burst. Perhaps I will ride east again."

"Not east," she shook her head. "The ravens are gathering in the east and there is a red flame there that pales the night. Wang Khan and his Keraits have fallen before the riders of Genghis Khan and Hia reels before his onslaught. Black Cathay too, I fear, is doomed, unless the Chins send them aid."

"Would you care if I fell?" he asked curiously.

Her clear eyes surveyed him.

"Would I care? I would care if a dog died. Surely then I would care if a man who saved my life, fell."

He shrugged his mighty shoulders. "You are kind. Today I ride. My wounds are long healed. I can lift my sword again. Thanks to your care I am strong as I ever was. This has been paradise—but I come of a restless breed. My dream of a kingdom is shattered and I must ride—somewhere.

I have heard much from the slaves and You-tai of this Genghis Khan and his chiefs. Aye, of Subotai and Chepe Noyon. I will lend my sword to him—"

"And fight against my people?" she asked.

His gaze fell before her clear eyes. "'Twere the deed of a dog," he muttered. "But what would you have? I am a soldier—I have fought for and against the same men since I rode east. A warrior must pick the winning side. And Genghis Khan, from all accounts, is a born conqueror."

Her eyes flashed. "The Cathayans will send out an army and crush him. He can not take Jahadur—what do his skin-clad herders know of walled cities?"

"We were but a naked horde before Constantinople," muttered Godric, "but we had hunger to drive us on and the city fell. Genghis and his men are hungry. I have seen men of the same breed. Your people are fat and indolent. Genghis Khan will ride them down like sheep."

"And you will aid him," she blazed.

"War is a man's game," he said roughly; shame hardened his tone; this slim, clear-eyed girl, so ignorant and innocent of the world's ways, stirred old dreams of idealistic chivalry in his soul—dreams he thought long lost in the fierce necessity of life. "What do you know of war and men's perfidy? A warrior must better himself as he may. I am weary of fighting for lost causes and getting only hard blows in return."

"What if I asked you—begged you?" she breathed, leaning forward.

A sudden surge of madness swept him off his feet.

"For you," he roared suddenly, like a wounded lion, "I would ride down on the Mongol yurts alone and crush them into the red earth and bring back the heads of Genghis and his khans in a cluster at my saddle-bow!"

She recoiled, gasping before the sudden loosing of his passion, but he caught her in an unconsciously rough embrace. His race loved as they hated, fiercely and violently. He would not have bruised her tender skin for all the gold in Cathay, but his own savagery swept him out of himself.

Then a sudden voice brought him to himself and he released the girl and whirled, ready to battle the whole Black Cathayan army. Old Roogla stood before them, panting.

"My princess," he gasped; "the courtiers from Greater Cathay—they have just arrived—"

She went white and cold as a statue.

"I am ready, oh Roogla," she whispered.

"Ready the devil!" roared the old soldier. "Only three of them got through to the gates of Jahadur and they're bleeding to death! You are not going to Cathay to marry Wang Yin. Not now, at least. And you'll be lucky if you're not dragged by the hair to Subotai's yurt. The hills are swarming with Mongols. They cut the throats of the watchers in the passes, and ambushed the courtiers from Cathay. An hour will bring them—the whole horde of howling devils—to the very gates of Jahadur. Chamu Khan is capering about like a devil with a hornet in his khalat. We can't send you out now—Genghis holds all the outer passes. The western Turks might give you sanctuary—but we can not reach them. There's only one thing to do—and that's hold the city! But with these fat, perfume-scented, wine-bibbing dogs that call themselves soldiery we'll be lucky if we get to strike a single blow in our defense—"

Yulita turned to Godric with level eyes.

"Genghis Khan is at our gates," said she. "Go to him." And turning she walked swiftly into a nearby doorway.

"What did she mean?" asked old Roogla wonderingly.

Godric growled deep in his throat. "Bring my armor and my sword. I go to seek Genghis Khan—but not as she thought."

Roogla grinned and his beard bristled. He smote Godric a blow that had rendered a lesser man senseless.

"Hai, wolf-brother!" he roared; "we'll give Genghis a fight yet! We'll send him back to the desert to lick his wounds if we can only keep three men in the army from fleeing! They can stand behind us and hand us weapons when we break our swords and axes, while we pile up Mongol dead so high that the women on the battlements will look up at them!"

Godric smiled thinly.

Chapter 3

"To grow old cowed in a conquered land,
        With the sun itself discrowned,
To see trees crouch and cattle slink—
Death is a better ale to drink,
And by high Death on the fell brink,
        That flagon shall go round."

—Chesterton

Godric's armor had been mended cleverly, he found, the rents in hauberk and helmet fused with such skill that no sign of a gash showed. The knight's armor was unusually strong, anyway, and of a weight few men could have borne. The blades that had wounded him in the battle of the defiles had hacked through old dents. Now that these were mended, the armor was like new. The heavy mail was reinforced with solid plates of steel on breast, back and shoulders and the sword belt was of joined steel plates a hand's breadth wide. The helmet, instead of being merely a steel cap with a long nasal, worn over a mail hood, as was the case of most Crusaders, was made with a vizor and fitted firmly into the steel shoulder-pieces. The whole armor showed the trend of the times—chain and scale mail giving way gradually to plate armor.

Godric experienced a fierce resurge of power as he felt the familiar weight of his mail and fingered the worn hilt of his long, two-handed sword. The languorous illusive dreaminess of the past weeks vanished; again he was a conqueror of a race of conquerors. With old Roogla he rode to the main gates, seeing on all hands the terror that had seized the people. Men and women ran distractedly through the streets, crying that the Mongols were upon them; they tied their belongings into bundles, loaded them on donkeys and jerked them off again, shouting reproaches at the soldiers on the walls, who seemed as frightened as the people.

"Cowards!" old Roogla's beard bristled. "What they need is war to stiffen their thews. Well, they've got war now and they'll have to fight."

"A man can always run," answered Godric sardonically.

They came to the outer gates and found a band of soldiery there, handling their pikes and bows nervously. They brightened slightly as Roogla and Godric rode up. The tale of the Norman's battle with the Hian bandits had lost nothing in the telling. But Godric was surprized to note their fewness.

"Are these all your soldiers?"

Roogla shook his head.

"Most of them are at the Pass of Skulls," he growled. "It's the only way a large force of men can approach Jahadur. In the past we've held it easily against all comers—but these Mongols are devils. I left enough men here to hold the city against any stray troops that might climb down the cliffs."

They rode out of the gates and down the winding mountain trail. On one side rose a sheer wall, a thousand feet high. On the other side the cliff fell away three times that distance into a fathomless chasm. A mile's ride brought them to the Pass of Skulls. Here the trail debouched into a sort of upland plateau, passing between two walls of sheer rock.

A thousand warriors were encamped there, gaudy in their silvered mail, long-toed leather boots and gold-chased weapons. With their peaked helmets with mail drops, their long spears and wide-bladed scimitars, they seemed war-like enough. They were big men, but they were evidently nervous and uncertain.

"By the blood of the devil, Roogla," snapped Godric, "have you no more soldiers than these?"

"Most of the troops are scattered throughout the empire," Roogla answered. "I warned Chamu Khan to collect all the warriors in the empire here, but he refused to do so. Why, Erlik alone knows. Well, a man can always die."

He rose in his saddle and his great voice roared through the hills:

"Men of Black Cathay, you know me of old! But here beside me is one you know only by word of mouth; a chief out of the West who will fight beside you today. Now take heart, and when Genghis comes up the defile, show him Black Cathayans can still die like men!"

"Not so fast," growled Godric. "This pass looks impregnable to me. May I have a word as to the arranging of the troops?"

Roogla spread his hands. "Assuredly."

"Then set men to work rebuilding that barricade," snapped Godric, pointing to the wavering lines of stone, half tumbled down, which spanned the pass.

"Build it high and block that gate. There'll be no caravans passing through today. I thought you were a soldier; it should have been done long ago. Put your best bowmen behind the first line of stone. Then the spearmen, and the swordsmen and ax-fighters behind the spearmen—"

The long hot day wore on. At last far away sounded the deep rattle of many kettledrums, then a thunder of myriad hoofs. Then up the deep defile and out onto the plateau swept a bizarre and terrible horde. Godric had expected a wild, motley mass of barbarians, like a swarm of locusts without order or system. These men rode in compact formation, of such as he had never before seen; in well ordered ranks, divided into troops of a thousand each.

The tugh, the yak-tail standards, were lifted above them. At the sight of their orderly array and hard-bitten appearance, Godric's heart sank. These men were used to fierce warfare; they outnumbered his own soldiers by seven times. How could he hope to hold the pass against them even for a little while? Godric swore deeply and fervently and put the hope of survival from him; thereafter during the whole savage fight, his one idea was to do as much damage to the enemy as he possibly could before he died.

Now he stood on the first line of fortifications and gazed curiously at the advancing hosts, seeing stocky, broad-built men mounted on wiry horses, men with square flat faces, devoid of humor or mercy, whose armor was plain stuff of hardened leather, lacquer, or iron plates laced together. With a wry face he noted the short, heavy bows and long arrows. From the look of those bows he knew they would drive shafts through ordinary mail as if it were paper. Their other weapons consisted of spears, short-handled axes, maces and curved sabers, lighter and more easily handled than the huge two-handed scimitars of the Black Cathayans.

Roogla, standing at his shoulder, pointed to a giant riding ahead of the army.

"Subotai," he growled, "a Uriankhi—from the frozen tundras, with a heart as cold as his native land. He can twist a spear shaft in two between his hands. The tall fop riding beside him is Chepe Noyon; note his silvered mail and heron plumes. And by Erlik, there is Kassar the Strong, sword-bearer to the khan. Well—if Genghis himself is not here now, he soon will be, for he never allows Kassar long out of his sight—the Strong One is a fool, useful only in actual combat."

Godric's cold gray eyes were fixed on the giant form of Subotai; a growing fury stirred in him, not a tangible hatred of the Uriankhi but the fighting rage one strong man feels when confronted by a foe his equal in prowess. The knight expected a parley but evidently the Mongols were of a different mind. They came sweeping across the boulder-strewn plateau like a wind from Hell, a swarm of mounted bowmen preceding them.

"Down!" roared Godric, as shafts began to rain around him. "Down behind the rocks! Spearmen and swordsmen lie flat! Archers return their fire."

Roogla repeated the shout and arrows began to fly from the barricades. But the effort was half-hearted. The sight of that onrushing horde had numbed the men of Jahadur. Godric had never seen men ride and shoot from the saddle as these Mongols did. They were barely within arrow flight, yet men were falling along the lines of stone. He felt the Jahadurans wavering—realized with a flood of blind rage that they would break before the Mongol heavy cavalry reached the barricade.

A bowman near him roared and fell backward with an arrow through his throat and a shout went up from the faltering Black Cathayans.

"Fools!" raged Godric, smiting right and left with clenched fists. "Horsemen can never take this pass if you stand to it! Bend your bows and throw your shoulders into it! Fight, damn you!"

The bowmen had split to either side, and through the gap the flying swordsmen swept. Now if ever was the time to break the charge, but the Jahaduran bowmen loosed wildly or not at all and behind them the spearmen were scrambling up to flee. Old Roogla was screaming and tearing his hair, cursing the day he was born, and not a man had fallen on the Mongols' side. Even at that distance Godric, standing upright on the barricade, saw the broad grin on Subotai's face. With a bitter curse he tore a spear from the hand of a warrior near by and threw every ounce of his mighty-thewed frame into the cast.

It was too far for an ordinary spearcast even to carry—but with a hum the spear hissed through the air and the Mongol next to Subotai fell headlong, transfixed. From the Black Cathayan ranks rose a sudden roar. These riders could be slain after all! And surely no mortal man could have made that cast! Godric, towering above them on the barricade, like a man of iron, suddenly assumed supernatural proportions in the eyes of the warriors behind him. How could they be defeated when such a man led them? The quick fire of Oriental battle-lust blazed up and sudden courage surged through the veins of the wavering warriors.

With a shout they pulled shaft to ear and loosed, and a sudden hail of death smote the charging Mongols. At that range there was no missing. Those long shafts tore through buckler and hauberk, transfixing the wearers. Flesh and blood could not stand it. The charge did not exactly break, but in the teeth of that iron gale the squadrons wheeled and circled away out of range. A wild yell of triumph rose from the Jahadurans and they waved their spears and shouted taunts.

Old Roogla was in ecstasies, but Godric snarled a mirthless laugh. At least he had whipped courage into the Black Cathayans. But here, he knew, he and Roogla and all the others would leave their corpses before the day was over. And Yulita—he would not allow himself to think of her. At least, he swore, a red mist waving in front of his eyes, Subotai would not take her.

The yak tails were waving, the kettledrums beating for another charge. This time the bowmen rode out more warily, loosing a perfect rain of shafts. At Godric's order his men did not return the fire, but sheltered themselves behind their barricade; he himself stood contemptuously upright, trusting to the strength of his half-plate armor. He became the center of the fire, but the long shafts glanced harmlessly from his shield or splintered on his hauberk.

The horsemen wheeled closer, drawing harder on their heavy bows, and at Godric's word the Jahadurans answered them. In a short fierce exchange the men in the open had the worst of it. They galloped out of range with several empty saddles, but Godric had not let his attention stray from the real menace—the heavily armed cavalry. These had approached at a rapid trot while the arrow fire was being exchanged, and now they struck in the spurs and came like a bolt from a crossbow.

Again the sweeping rain of arrows met and broke them, though this time their momentum carried them to within a hundred feet of the barricades. One rider broke through to the lines and Godric saw a wild figure, spurting blood and hewing madly at him. Then as the Mongol rose in his stirrups to reach the knight's head, a dozen spears, thrusting over the backs of the bowmen, pierced him and hurled him headlong.

Again the Mongols retreated out of range, but this time their losses had been severe. Riderless horses ranged the plateau, which was dotted with still or writhing forms.

Already the Jahadurans had inflicted more damage on the men of Genghis Khan than the Mongols were accustomed to. But from the way the nomads ranged themselves for the third charge, Godric knew that this time no flight of arrows would stop them. He spared a moment's admiration for their courage.

The supply of arrows was running low. Black Cathay, as in all things pertaining to war, had neglected the manufacture of war-arrows. A large number of shafts remaining in the quivers of the archers were hunting-arrows, good only at short range.

This time there was no great exchange between the bowmen. The archers of Subotai mingled themselves among the front ranks of the swordsmen, and when the charge came, a sheet of arrows preceded it.

"Save your shafts!" roared Godric, gripping the ax he had chosen from the arms of Jahadur. "Back, archers—spearmen, on the wall!"

The next moment the headlong horde broke like a red wave on the barricade. Evidently they had misjudged the strength of those stone lines, not knowing them newly reinforced—had expected to shatter them by sheer weight and velocity and to ride through the ruins. But the strengthened walls held.

Horses hit the barricade with a splintering of bones, and men's brains were dashed out by the shock. Doubtless they had expected to sacrifice the first line, but the slaughter was greater than they could have reckoned. The second line, hot on the heels of the first, plunged against the wall over its writhing remnants, and the third line piled up on both. The whole line of the barricade was a red welter of dying, screaming horses, lashing hoofs and writhing men, while the blood-maddened Jahadurans yelled like wolves, hacking and stabbing down at the crimson shambles.

The rear lines ruthlessly trampled down their dying comrades to strike at the defenders, but the ground was thick with dead and wounded and the plunging, writhing horses fouled the hoofs that swept over them.

Still, some of the Mongols did gain through to the lines and made a desperate effort to clamber over the wall. They died like rats in a trap beneath the lunging spears of the inspired Black Cathayans.

One, a huge brutal-faced giant, rode over a writhing welter of red torn flesh, reined in close to the barricade and an iron mace in his hands dashed out the brains of a spearman. From both hosts rose a shout of: "Kassar!"

"Kassar, eh?" growled Godric, stepping forward on the precarious top of the barricade. The giant rose in his stirrups, the clotted mace swung back and at that instant the twenty-pound battle-ax in Godric's right hand crashed down on the peaked helmet. Ax and helmet shattered together and the steed went to his knees under the shock. Then it reared and plunged wildly away, Kassar's crumpled body lolling and swaying in the saddle, held by the deep stirrups.

Godric tossed away the splintered ax-haft and picked up the mace that had fallen on the stones. He heard old Roogla shouting: "Bogda! Bogda! Bogda! Gurgaslan!"

The whole host of Jahadur took up the shout; thus Godric gained his new name, which means the Lion, and crimson was the christening.

The Mongols were again in slow, stubborn retreat and Godric brandished the mace and shouted: "Ye be men! Stand to it boldly! Already have you slain more than half your own number!"

But he knew that now the real death grip was about to be. The Mongols were dismounting. Horsemen by nature and choice, they had realized however that cavalry charges could never take those solid walls, manned by inspired madmen. They held their round, lacquered bucklers before them and swung solidly onward in much the same formation as they had maintained mounted.

They rolled like a black tide over the corpse-strewn plain and like a black flood they burst on the spear-bristling wall. Few arrows were loosed on either side. The Black Cathayans had emptied their quivers and the Mongols wished only to come to hand-grips.

The line of barricades became a red line of Hell. Spears jabbed downward, curved blades broke on lances. In the very teeth of the girding steel, the Mongols strove to climb the wall, piling heaps of their own dead for grim ladders. Most of them were pierced by the spears of the defenders, and the few who did win over the barriers were cut down by the swordsmen behind the spearmen.

The nomads perforce fell back a few yards, then surged on again. The terrific shocks of their impact shook the whole barricade. These men needed no shouts or commands to spur them on. They were fired with an indomitable will which emanated from within as well as from without. Godric saw Chepe Noyon fighting silently on foot with the rest of the warriors. Subotai sat his horse a few yards back of the mass, directing the movements.

Charge after charge crashed against the barriers. The Mongols were wasting lives like water and Godric wondered at their unquenchable resolve to conquer this relatively unimportant mountain kingdom. But he realized that Genghis Khan's whole future as a conqueror depended on his stamping out all opposition, no matter what the cost.

The wall was crumbling. The Mongols were tearing it to pieces. They could not climb it, so they thrust their spears between the stones and loosened them, tearing them away with bare hands. They died as they toiled, but their comrades trampled their corpses and took up their work.

Subotai leaped from his horse, snatched a heavy curved sword from his saddle and joined the warriors on foot. He gained to the center of the wall and tore at it with his naked hands, disdaining the down-lunging spears which broke on his helmet and armor. A breach was made and the Mongols began to surge through.

Godric yelled fiercely and leaped to stem the sudden tide, but a wash of the black wave over the wall hemmed him in with howling fiends. A crashing sweep of his mace cleared a red way and he plunged through. The Mongols were coming over the ruins of the barriers and through the great breach Subotai had made. Godric shouted for the Jahadurans to fall back, and even as he did, he saw Roogla parrying the whistling strokes of Chepe Noyon's curved scimitar.

The old general was bleeding already from a deep gash in the thigh, and even as the Norman sprang to aid him, the Mongol's blade cut through Roogla's mail and blood spurted. Roogla slumped slowly to the earth and Chepe Noyon wheeled to meet the knight's furious charge. He flung up his sword to parry the whistling mace, but the giant Norman in his berserk rage dealt a blow that made nothing of skill or tempered steel. The scimitar flew to singing sparks, the helmet cracked and Chepe Noyon was dashed to earth like a pole-axed steer.

"Bear Roogla back!" roared Godric, leaping forward and swinging his mace up again to dash out the prostrate Mongol's brains as a man kills a wounded snake. But even as the mace crashed downward, a squat warrior leaped like a panther, arms wide, shielding the fallen chieftain's body with his own and taking the stroke on his own head. His shattered corpse fell across Chepe Noyon and a sudden determined rush of Mongols bore Godric back. Even as the Jahadurans bore the desperately wounded Roogla back across the next line of stone, the Mongols lifted the stunned Chepe Noyon and carried him out of the battle.

Fighting stubbornly, Godric retreated, half-ringed by the squat shapes that fought so silently and thrust so fiercely for his life. He reached the next wall, over which the Jahadurans had already gone, and for a moment stood at bay, back against the stones, while spears flashed at him and curved sabers hacked at him. His armor had saved him thus far, though a shrewd thrust had girded deep into the calf of his leg and a heavy blow on his hauberk had partly numbed the shoulder beneath.

Now the Black Cathayans leaned over the wall, cleared a space with their spears and seizing their champion under the armpits, lifted him bodily over. The fight rolled on. Life became to the men on the walls one red continuance of hurtling bodies and lunging blades. The spears of the defenders were bent or splintered. The arrows were gone. Half the Black Cathayans were dead. Most of the rest were wounded. But possessed of a fanatical fervor they fought on, swinging their notched axes and blunted scimitars as fiercely as if the fight had but started. The full fighting fury of their Turkish ancestors was roused and only death could quench it. After all, they were of the same blood as these unconquerable demons from the Gobi.

The second barricade crumbled and the Jahadurans began to fall back to the last line of barricades. But this time the Mongols were over the falling stones and upon them before they could make good their escape. Godric and fifty men, covering the withdrawal of the rest, were cut off. Then the others would have come back over the wall to aid them, but a solid mass of Mongols were between that balked their fiercest efforts.

Godric's men died about him like hunted wolves, slaying and dying without a groan or whimper. Their last gasps were snarls of deathless fury. Their heavy two-handed scimitars wrought fearful destruction among their stocky foes but the Mongols ran in under the sweep of the blades and ripped upward with their shorter sabers.

Godric's plated mail saved him from chance blows and his enormous strength and amazing quickness made him all but invincible. His shield he had long discarded. He gripped the heavy mace in both hands and it smashed like a black god of death through the battle rout. Blood and brains splashed like water as shields, helmets and corselets gave way.

Across the heads of the hacking warriors Godric saw the giant frame of Subotai, looming head and shoulders above his men. With a curse the Norman hurled the mace, which spattered blood as it hummed through the air. Men cried out at the long cast, but Subotai ducked swiftly. Godric whipped out his two-handed sword for the first time during the fight, and the long straight blade which the Pope had blessed years ago shimmered like a living thing—like the blue waves of the western sea.

It was a heavy blade, forged to cut through thick mail and strong plates, armor many times heavier than that worn by most Orientals, who usually preferred shirts of light chain mail. Godric wielded it in one hand as lightly as most men could swing it with both. His left hand held a dirk, point upward, and they who ducked beneath the sword to grapple, died from the thrust of the shorter blade. The Norman set his back against a heap of dead, and in a red haze of battle madness, split skulls to the teeth, cleft bosoms to the spine, severed shoulder bones, hewed through neck cords, hacked off legs at the hip and arms at the shoulder until they gave back in sudden, unaccustomed fear and stood panting and eyeing him as hunters eye a wounded tiger.

And Godric laughed at them, taunted them, spat in their faces. Centuries of civilizing French influence were wiped away; it was a berserk Viking who faced his paling foes.

He was wounded, he faintly sensed, but unweakened. The fire of fury left no room in his brain for any other sensation. A giant form surged through the ranks, flinging men right and left as spray is flung by a charging galley. Subotai of the frozen tundras stood before his foe at last.

Godric took in the height of the man, the mighty sweep of chest and shoulder, and the massive arms which wielded the sword that had more than once, during the fight, sheared clear through the torso of a mailed Jahaduran.

"Back!" roared Subotai, his fierce eyes alight—those eyes were blue, Godric noted, and the Mongol's hair red; surely somewhere in that frozen land of tundras a wandering Aryan strain had mingled with the Turanian blood of Subotai's tribe—"Back, and give us room! None shall slay this chief but Subotai!"

Somewhere down the deep defile there sounded a rally of kettle-drums and the tramp of many hoofs, but Godric was hardly aware he heard. He saw the Mongols fall back, leaving a space clear. He heard Chepe Noyon, still slightly groggy, and with a new helmet, shouting orders at the men who surged about the wall. Fighting ceased altogether and all eyes turned on the chiefs, who swung up their blades and rushed together like two maddened bulls.

Godric knew that his armor would never stand against the full sweep of the great sword Subotai was swinging in his right hand. The Norman leaped and struck as a tiger strikes, throwing every ounce of his body behind the blow and nerving himself to superhuman quickness. His heavy, straight blade sheared through the lacquered buckler Subotai flung above his head, and crashing full on the peaked helmet, bit through to the scalp beneath. Subotai staggered, a jet of blood trickling down his dark face, but almost instantly swung a decapitating stroke that whistled harmlessly through the air as Godric bent his knees quickly.

The Frank thrust viciously but Subotai evaded the lunging point with a twist of his huge frame and hacked in savagely. Godric sprang away but could not entirely avoid the blow. The great blade struck under his armpit, crunched through the mail and bit deep into his ribs. The impact numbed his whole left side, and in an instant his hauberk was full of blood.

Stung to renewed madness, Godric sprang in, parrying the scimitar, then dropped his sword and grappled Subotai. The Mongol returned the fierce embrace, drawing a dagger. Close-locked they wrestled and strained, staggering on hard-braced legs, each seeking to break the other's spine or to drive home his own blade. Both weapons were reddened in an instant as they girded through the crevices in the armor or were driven straight through solid mail, but neither could free his hand enough to drive in a death thrust.

Godric was gasping for breath; he felt that the pressure of the Mongol's huge arms was crushing him. But Subotai was in no better way. The Norman saw sweat thickly beading the Mongol's brow, heard his breath coming in heavy pants, and a savage joy shook him.

Subotai lifted his foe bodily to dash him headlong, but Godric's grip held them together so firmly this was impossible. With both feet braced on the blood-soaked earth again, Godric suddenly ceased trying to free his dirk wrist from Subotai's iron grip, and releasing the Mongol's dagger arm, drove his left fist into Subotai's face.

With the full power of mighty arm and broad shoulders behind it, the blow was like that of a club. Blood spattered and Subotai's head snapped back as if on hinges—but at that instant he drove his dagger deep in Godric's breast muscles.

The Norman gasped, staggered, and then in a last burst of strength he flung the Mongol from him. Subotai fell his full length and rose slowly, dazedly, like a man who has fought out the last red ounce of his endurance. His mighty frame sagged back on the arms of the ringing warriors and he shook his head like a bull, striving to nerve himself again for the combat.

Godric recovered the sword he had dropped and now he faced his foes, feet braced wide against his sick dizziness. He groped a moment for support and felt firm stones at his back. The fight had carried them almost to the last barricades. There he faced the Mongols like a wounded lion at bay, head lowered on his mighty, mailed breast, terrible eyes glittering through the bars of his vizor, both hands gripping his red sword.

"Come on," he challenged as he felt his life waning in thick red surges. "Mayhap I die—but I will slay seven of you before I die. Come in and make an ending, you pagan swine!"

Men thronged the plateau behind the tattered horde—thousands of them. A powerful, bearded chieftain on a white horse rode forward and surveyed the silent, battle-weary Mongols and the stone bulwark with its thin ranks of bloody defenders. This, Godric knew in a weary way, was the great Genghis Khan and he wished he had enough life left in him to charge through the ranks and hew the khan from his saddle; but weakness began to steal over him.

"A good thing I came with the Horde," said Genghis Khan sardonically. "It seems these Cathayans have been drinking some wine that makes men of them. They have slain more Mongols already than the Keraits and the Hians did. Who spurred these scented women to battle?"

"He." Chepe Noyon pointed to the bloodstained knight. "By Erlik, they have drunk blood this day. The Frank is a devil; my head still sings from the blow he dealt me; Kassar is but now recovering his senses from an ax the Frank shattered on his helmet, and he has but now fought Subotai himself to a standstill."

Genghis reigned his horse forward and Godric tensed himself. If the khan would only come within reach—a sudden spring, a last, desperate blow—if he could but take this paynim lord with him to the realm of death, he would die content.

The great, deep gray eyes of Genghis were upon the knight and he felt their full power.

"You are of such steel as my chiefs are forged from," said Genghis. "I would have you for friend, not foe. You are not of the race of those men; come and serve under me."

"My ears are dull with blows on my helmet," answered Godric, tightening his grip on his hilt and tensing his weary muscles; "I can not understand you. Come closer that I may hear you."

Instead Genghis reigned his steed back a few paces and grinned with tolerant understanding.

"Will you serve me?" he persisted. "I will make you a chief."

"And what of these?" Godric indicated the Black Cathayans.

Genghis shrugged his shoulders. "What am I to do with them? They must die."

"Go to your brother the Devil," Godric growled. "I come of a race that sell their swords for gold—but we are no jackals to turn on men that have bled beside us. These warriors and I have already killed more than our own number and wounded many more of your warriors. There are still three hundred of us left and the strongest of the barricades. We have slain over a thousand of your wolves—if you enter Jahadur you ride over our corpses. Charge in now and see how desperate men can die."

"But you owe no allegiance to Jahadur," argued Genghis.

"I owe my life to Chamu Khan," snapped Godric. "I have thrown in my lot with him and I serve him with as much fealty as if he were the Pope himself."

"You are a fool," Genghis said frankly. "I have long had my spies among the Jahadurans. Chamu planned to sacrifice Jahadur and all therein to save his own hide. That is why he refused to bring more soldiers to the city. His main force he gathered on the western border. He planned to flee by a secret way through the cliffs as soon as I attacked the pass.

"Well, he did, but some of my warriors came upon him. They only asked a gift of him," Genghis chuckled. "Then they made no effort to hinder him. He might then go where he would. Would you see the gift they took from Chamu Khan?"

And a Mongol behind the khan held up a ghastly, grinning head. Godric cursed: "Liar, traitor and coward though he was, he was yet a king. Come in and make an ending. I swear to you that before you ride over this wall, your horses will tread fetlock-deep in a carpet of your dead."

Still Genghis sat his horse and pondered. Subotai came up to him, and grinning broadly, spoke in his ear. The Khan nodded.

"Swear to serve me and I will spare the lives of your men; I will take Black Cathay unharmed into my empire."

Godric turned to his men. "You heard—I would rather die here on a heap of Mongol dead—but it is for you to say."

They answered with a shout: "The emperor is dead! Why should we die, if Genghis Khan will grant us peace? Give us Gurgaslan for ruler and we will serve you."

Genghis raised his hand. "So be it!"

Godric shook the blood and sweat out of his eyes and snarled a bitter laugh.

"A puppet king on a tinsel throne, to dance on your string, Mongol? No! Get another for the task."

Genghis scowled and suddenly swore. "By the yellow face of Erlik! I have already made more concessions today than I ever made in my life before! What want ye, Gurgaslan—shall I give you my scepter for a war-club?"

"If he wishes it you may as well give it to him," grinned Subotai, who was no more awed by his khan than if Genghis had been a horse-boy. "These Franks are built of iron without and within. Reason with him, Genghis!"

The khan glared at his general for a moment as if he were of a mind to brain him, then grinned suddenly. These men of the steppes were a frank, open race greatly different from the devious-minded peoples of Asia

Minor.

"To have you and your warriors fighting beside me," said Genghis calmly, "I will do that which I never expected to do. You are fit to tread the crimson road of empire. Take Black Cathay and rule it as you will; I ask only that you aid me in my wars, as an equal ally. We will be two kings, reigning side by side and aiding each other against all enemies."

Godric's thin lips smiled. "It is fair enough."

The Mongols sent up a thunderous roar and the bloody Jahadurans swarmed over the barricades to kiss the hands of their new ruler. He did not hear Genghis say to the warrior who bore the grisly severed head of Chamu Khan: "See that the skull is prepared and sheathed in silver, and set among the rest that were khans of tribes; when I fall I would wish my own skull treated with the same respect."

Godric felt a firm grasp on his hand and looked into the steady eyes of Subotai, feeling a rush of friendship for the man that equaled his former rage.

"Erlik, what a man!" growled the chief. "We should be good comrades, Gurgaslan! Here—by the gods, man, you are sorely wounded! He swoons—get off his armor and see to his hurts, you thick-headed fools, do you want him to die?"

"Scant chance," grinned Chepe Noyon, feeling his head tenderly. "Such men as he are not made to die from steel. Wait, you big buffalo, you'll kill him with your clumsiness. I'll bring one more fitted to attend him—one that was found being forcibly escorted out of Jahadur by the palace eunuchs. I saw her only five minutes agone and I am almost ready to cut your throat for her, Gurgaslan. Genghis, will you bid them bring the girl?"

Again Godric saw, as in a closing mist, two great dark eyes bend over him—he felt soft arms go about his neck and heard a sobbing in his ear.

"Well, Yulita," he said as in a dream, "I went to Genghis Khan after all!"

"You saved Black Cathay, my king," she sobbed, pressing her lips against his. Then while his dull head swam those soft lips were withdrawn and a goblet took their place, filled with a stinging wine that jerked him back into consciousness.

Genghis was standing over him.

"You have already found your queen, eh?" he smiled. "Well—rest of your wounds; I will not need your aid for some months yet. Marry your queen, organize your kingdom—there is a great army drawn up on the western border ready to your hand now that there is to be no invasion of your kingdom. It may be the western Turks will dispute your liegeship—you have but to send the word and I will send you as many riders as you need. When the desert grass deepens for spring, we ride in to Greater Cathay."

The khan turned on his heel and strode away and Godric gathered the slim form of Yulita into his weary arms.

"Wang Yin will wait long for his bride," said he, and the laughter of Yulita was like the tinkle of the silvery fountains in the cherry blossom courts of Jahadur. And so the dream that had haunted Godric de Villehard of an Eastern empire woke to life.

HAWKS OF OUTREMER

"The still, white, creeping road slips on,
Marked by the bones of man and beast.
What comeliness and might have gone
To pad the highway of the East!
Long dynasties of fallen rose,
The glories of a thousand wars,
A million lovers' hearts compose
The dust upon the road to Fars."
—Vansittart

1. A Man Returns

"Halt!" The bearded man-at-arms swung his pike about, growling like a surly mastiff. It paid to be wary on the road to Antioch. The stars blinked redly through the thick night and their light was not sufficient for the fellow to make out what sort of man it was who loomed so gigantically before him.

An iron-clad hand shot out suddenly and closed on the soldier's mailed shoulder in a grasp that numbed his whole arm. From beneath the helmet the guardsman saw the blaze of ferocious blue eyes that seemed lambent, even in the dark.

"Saints preserve us!" gasped the frightened man-at-arms, "Cormac FitzGeoffrey! Avaunt! Back to Hell with ye, like a good knight! I swear to you, sir—"

"Swear me no oaths," growled the knight. "What is this talk?"

"Are you not an incorporeal spirit?" mouthed the soldier. "Were you not slain by the Moorish corsairs on your homeward voyage?"

"By the accursed gods!" snarled FitzGeoffrey. "Does this hand feel like smoke?"

He sank his mailed fingers into the soldier's arm and grinned bleakly at the resultant howl.

"Enough of such mummery; tell me who is within that tavern."

"Only my master, Sir Rupert de Vaile, of Rouen."

"Good enough," grunted the other. "He is one of the few men I count friends, in the East or elsewhere."

The big warrior strode to the tavern door and entered, treading lightly as a cat despite his heavy armor. The man-at-arms rubbed his arm and stared after him curiously, noting, in the dim light, that FitzGeoffrey bore a shield with the horrific emblem of his family—a white grinning skull. The guardsman knew him of old—a turbulent character, a savage fighter and the only man among the Crusaders who had been esteemed stronger than Richard the Lion-hearted. But FitzGeoffrey had taken ship for his native isle even before Richard had departed from the Holy Land. The Third Crusade had ended in failure and disgrace; most of the Frankish knights had followed their kings homeward. What was this grim Irish killer doing on the road to Antioch?

Sir Rupert de Vaile, once of Rouen, now a lord of the fast-fading Outremer, turned as the great form bulked in the doorway. Cormac FitzGeoffrey was a fraction of an inch above six feet, but with his mighty shoulders and two hundred pounds of iron muscle, he seemed shorter. The Norman stared in surprized recognition, and sprang to his feet. His fine face shone with sincere pleasure.

"Cormac, by the saints! Why, man, we heard that you were dead!"

Cormac returned the hearty grip, while his thin lips curved slightly in what would have been, in another man, a broad grin of greeting. Sir Rupert was a tall man, and well knit, but he seemed almost slight beside the huge Irish warrior who combined bulk with a sort of dynamic aggressiveness that was apparent in his every movement.

FitzGeoffrey was clean-shaven and the various scars that showed on his dark, grim face lent his already formidable features a truly sinister aspect. When he took off his plain visorless helmet and thrust back his mail coif, his square-cut, black hair that topped his low broad forehead contrasted strongly with his cold blue eyes. A true son of the most indomitable and savage race that ever trod the bloodstained fields of battle, Cormac FitzGeoffrey looked to be what he was—a ruthless fighter, born to the game of war, to whom the ways of violence and bloodshed were as natural as the ways of peace are to the average man.

Son of a woman of the O'Briens and a renegade Norman knight, Geoffrey the Bastard, in whose veins, it is said, coursed the blood of William the Conqueror, Cormac had seldom known an hour of peace or ease in all his thirty years of violent life. He was born in a feud-torn and blood-drenched land, and raised in a heritage of hate and savagery. The ancient culture of Erin had long crumbled before the repeated onslaughts of Norsemen and Danes. Harried on all sides by cruel foes, the rising civilization of the Celts had faded before the fierce necessity of incessant conflict, and the merciless struggle for survival had made the Gaels as savage as the heathens who assailed them.

Now, in Cormac's time, war upon red war swept the crimson isle, where clan fought clan, and the Norman adventurers tore at one another's throats, or resisted the attacks of the Irish, playing tribe against tribe, while from Norway and the Orkneys the still half-pagan Vikings ravaged all impartially.

A vague realization of all this flashed through Sir Rupert's mind as he stood staring at his friend.

"We heard you were slain in a sea-fight off Sicily," he repeated.

Cormac shrugged his shoulders. "Many died then, it is true, and I was struck senseless by a stone from a ballista. Doubtless that is how the rumor started. But you see me, as much alive as ever."

"Sit down, old friend." Sir Rupert thrust forward one of the rude benches which formed part of the tavern's furniture. "What is forward in the West?"

Cormac took the wine goblet proffered him by a dark-skinned servitor, and drank deeply.

"Little of note," said he. "In France the king counts his pence and squabbles with his nobles. Richard—if he lives—languishes somewhere in Germany, 'tis thought. In England Shane—that is to say, John—oppresses the people and betrays the barons. And in Ireland—Hell!" He laughed shortly and without mirth. "What shall I say of Ireland but the same old tale? Gael and foreigner cut each other's throat and plot together against the king. John De Coursey, since Hugh de Lacy supplanted him as governor, has raged like a madman, burning and pillaging, while Donal O'Brien lurks in the west to destroy what remains. Yet, by Satan, I think this land is but little better."

"Yet there is peace of a sort now," murmured Sir Rupert.

"Aye—peace while the jackal Saladin gathers his powers," grunted

Cormac. "Think you he will rest idle while Acre, Antioch and Tripoli remain in Christian hands? He but waits an excuse to seize the remnants of Outremer."

Sir Rupert shook his head, his eyes shadowed.

"It is a naked land and a bloody one. Were it not akin to blasphemy I could curse the day I followed my King eastward. Betimes I dream of the orchards of Normandy, the deep cool forests and the dreaming vineyards. Methinks my happiest hours were when a page of twelve years—"

"At twelve," grunted FitzGeoffrey, "I was running wild with shock-head kerns on the naked fens—I wore wolf skins, weighed near to fourteen stone, and had killed three men."

Sir Rupert looked curiously at his friend. Separated from Cormac's native land by a width of sea and the breadth of Britain, the Norman knew but little of the affairs in that far isle. But he knew vaguely that Cormac's life had not been an easy one. Hated by the Irish and despised by the Normans, he had paid back contempt and ill-treatment with savage hate and ruthless vengeance. It was known that he owned a shadow of allegiance only to the great house of Fitzgerald, who, as much Welsh as Norman, had even then begun to take up Irish customs and Irish quarrels.

"You wear another sword than that you wore when I saw you last."

"They break in my hands," said Cormac. "Three Turkish sabers went into the forging of the sword I wielded at Joppa—yet it shattered like glass in that sea-fight off Sicily. I took this from the body of a Norse sea-king who led a raid into Munster. It was forged in Norway—see the pagan runes on the steel?"

He drew the sword and the great blade shimmered bluely, like a thing alive in the candle light. The servants crossed themselves and Sir Rupert shook his head.

"You should not have drawn it here—they say blood follows such a sword."

"Bloodshed follows my trail anyway," growled Cormac. "This blade has already drunk FitzGeoffrey blood—with this that Norse sea-king slew my brother, Shane."

"And you wear such a sword?" exclaimed Sir Rupert in horror. "No good will come of that evil blade, Cormac!"

"Why not?" asked the big warrior impatiently. "It's a good blade—I wiped out the stain of my brother's blood when I slew his slayer. By Satan, but that sea-king was a grand sight in his coat of mail with silvered scales.

His silvered helmet was strong too—ax, helmet and skull shattered together."

"You had another brother, did you not?"

"Aye—Donal. Eochaidh O'Donnell ate his heart out after the battle at Coolmanagh. There was a feud between us at the time, so it may be Eochaidh merely saved me the trouble—but for all that I burned the O'Donnell in his own castle."

"How came you to first ride on the Crusade?" asked Sir Rupert curiously. "Were you stirred with a desire to cleanse your soul by smiting the Paynim?"

"Ireland was too hot for me," answered the Norman-Gael candidly. "Lord Shamus MacGearailt—James Fitzgerald—wished to make peace with the English king and I feared he would buy favor by delivering me into the hands of the king's governor. As there was feud between my family and most of the Irish clans, there was nowhere for me to go. I was about to seek my fortune in Scotland when young Eamonn Fitzgerald was stung by the hornet of Crusade and I accompanied him."

"But you gained favor with Richard—tell me the tale."

"Soon told. It was on the plains of Azotus when we came to grips with the Turks. Aye, you were there! I was fighting alone in the thick of the fray and helmets and turbans were cracking like eggs all around when I noted a strong knight in the forefront of our battle. He cut deeper and deeper into the close-ranked lines of the heathen and his heavy mace scattered brains like water. But so dented was his shield and so stained with blood his armor, I could not tell who he might be.

"But suddenly his horse went down and in an instant he was hemmed in on all sides by the howling fiends who bore him down by sheer weight of numbers. So hacking a way to his side I dismounted—"

"Dismounted?" exclaimed Sir Rupert in amazement.

Cormac's head jerked up in irritation at the interruption. "Why not?" he snapped. "I am no French she-knight to fear wading in the muck—anyway, I fight better on foot. Well, I cleared a space with a sweep or so of my sword, and the fallen knight, the press being lightened, came up roaring like a bull and swinging his blood-clotted mace with such fury he nearly brained *me* as well as the Turks. A charge of English knights swept the heathen away and when he lifted his visor I saw I had succored Richard of England.

"'Who are you and who is your master?' said he.

"'I am Cormac FitzGeoffrey and I have no master,' said I. 'I followed young Eamonn Fitzgerald to the Holy Land and since he fell before the walls of Acre, I seek my fortune alone.'

"'What think ye of me as a master?' asked he, while the battle raged half a bow-shot about us.

"'You fight reasonably well for a man with Saxon blood in his veins,' I answered, 'but I own allegiance to no English king.'

"He swore like a trooper. 'By the bones of the saints,' said he, 'that had cost another man his head. You saved my life, but for this insolence, no prince shall knight you!'

"'Keep your knighthoods and be damned,' said I. 'I am a chief in Ireland—but we waste words; yonder are pagan heads to be smashed.'

"Later he bade me to his royal presence and waxed merry with me; a rare drinker he is, though a fool withal. But I distrust kings—I attached myself to the train of a brave and gallant young knight of France—the Sieur Gerard de Gissclin, full of insane ideals of chivalry, but a noble youth.

"When peace was made between the hosts, I heard hints of a renewal of strife between the Fitzgeralds and the Le Boteliers, and Lord Shamus having been slain by Nial Mac Art, and I being in favor with the king anyway, I took leave of Sieur Gerard and betook myself back to Erin. Well—we swept Ormond with torch and sword and hanged old Sir William le Botelier to his own barbican. Then, the Geraldines having no particular need of my sword at the moment, I bethought myself once more of Sieur Gerard, to whom I owed my life and which debt I have not yet had opportunity to pay. How, Sir Rupert, dwells he still in his castle of Ali-El-Yar?"

Sir Rupert's face went suddenly white, and he leaned back as if shrinking from something. Cormac's head jerked up and his dark face grew more forbidding and fraught with somber potentialities. He seized the Norman's arm in an unconsciously savage grip.

"Speak, man," he rasped. "What ails you?"

"Sieur Gerard," half-whispered Sir Rupert. "Had you not heard? Ali-El-Yar lies in smoldering ruins and Gerard is dead."

Cormac snarled like a mad dog, his terrible eyes blazing with a fearful light. He shook Sir Rupert in the intensity of his passion.

"Who did the deed? He shall die, were he Emperor of Byzantium!"

"I know not!" Sir Rupert gasped, his mind half-stunned by the blast of the Gael's primitive fury. "There be foul rumors—Sieur Gerard loved a girl in a sheik's harem, it is said. A horde of wild riders from the desert assailed his castle and a rider broke through to ask aid of the baron Conrad Von Gonler. But Conrad refused—"

"Aye!" snarled Cormac, with a savage gesture. "He hated Gerard because long ago the youngster had the best of him at sword-play on shipboard before old Frederick Barbarossa's eyes. And what then?"

"Ali-El-Yar fell with all its people. Their stripped and mutilated bodies lay among the coals, but no sign was found of Gerard. Whether he died before or after the attack on the castle is not known, but dead he must be, since no demand for ransom has been made."

"Thus Saladin keeps the peace!"

Sir Rupert, who knew Cormac's unreasoning hatred for the great Kurdish sultan, shook his head. "This was no work of his—there is incessant bickering along the border—Christian as much at fault as Moslem. It could not be otherwise with Frankish barons holding castles in the very heart of Muhammadan country. There are many private feuds and there are wild desert and mountain tribes who owe no lordship even to Saladin, and wage their own wars. Many suppose that the sheik Nureddin El Ghor destroyed Ali-El-Yar and put Sieur Gerard to death."

Cormac caught up his helmet.

"Wait!" exclaimed Sir Rupert, rising. "What would you do?"

Cormac laughed savagely. "What would I do? I have eaten the bread of the de Gissclins. Am I a jackal to sneak home and leave my patron to the kites? Out on it!"

"But wait," Sir Rupert urged. "What will your life be worth if you ride on Nureddin's trail alone? I will return to Antioch and gather my retainers; we will avenge your friend together."

"Nureddin is a half-independent chief and I am a masterless wanderer," rumbled the Norman-Gael, "but you are Seneschal of Antioch. If you ride over the border with your men-at-arms, the swine Saladin will take advantage to break the truce and sweep the remnants of the Christian kingdoms into the sea. They are but weak shells, as it is, shadows of the glories of Baldwin and Bohemund. No—the FitzGeoffreys wreak their own vengeance. I ride alone."

He jammed his helmet into place and with a gruff "Farewell!" he turned and strode into the night, roaring for his horse. A trembling servant brought the great black stallion, which reared and snorted with a flash of wicked teeth. Cormac seized the reins and savagely jerked down the rearing steed, swinging into the saddle before the pawing front hoofs touched earth.

"Hate and the glutting of vengeance!" he yelled savagely, as the great stallion whirled away, and Sir Rupert, staring bewilderedly after him, heard the swiftly receding clash of the brazen-shod hoofs. Cormac FitzGeoffrey was riding east.

2. The Cast of an Ax

White dawn surged out of the Orient to break in rose-red billows on the hills of Outremer. The rich tints softened the rugged outlines, deepened the blue wastes of the sleeping desert.

The castle of the baron Conrad Von Gonler frowned out over a wild and savage waste. Once a stronghold of the Seljuk Turks, its metamorphosis into the manor of a Frankish lord had abated none of the Eastern menace of its appearance. The walls had been strengthened and a barbican built in place of the usual wide gates. Otherwise the keep had not been altered.

Now in the dawn a grim, dark figure rode up to the deep, waterless moat which encircled the stronghold, and smote with iron-clad fist on hollow-ringing shield until the echoes reverberated among the hills. A sleepy man-at-arms thrust his head and his pike over the wall above the barbican and bellowed a challenge.

The lone rider threw back his helmeted head, disclosing a face dark with a passion that an all-night's ride had not cooled in the least.

"You keep rare watch here," roared Cormac FitzGeoffrey. "Is it because you're so hand-in-glove with the Paynim that you fear no attack? Where is that ale-guzzling swine you call your liege?"

"The baron is at wine," the fellow answered sullenly, in broken English.

"So early?" marveled Cormac.

"Nay," the other gave a surly grin, "he has feasted all night."

"Wine-bibber! Glutton!" raged Cormac. "Tell him I have business with him."

"And what shall I say your business is, Lord FitzGeoffrey?" asked the carl, impressed.

"Tell him I bring a passport to Hell!" yelled Cormac, gnashing his teeth, and the scared soldier vanished like a puppet on a string.

The Norman-Gael sat his horse impatiently, shield slung on his shoulders, lance in its stirrup socket, and to his surprize, suddenly the barbican door swung wide and out of it strutted a fantastic figure. Baron Conrad Von Gonler was short and fat; broad of shoulder and portly of belly, though still a young man. His long arms and wide shoulders had gained him a reputation as a deadly broadsword man, but just now he looked little of the fighter. Germany and Austria sent many noble knights to the Holy Land. Baron Von Gonler was not one of them.

His only arm was a gold-chased dagger in a richly brocaded sheath. He wore no armor, and his costume, flaming with gay silk and heavy with gold, was a bizarre mingling of European gauds and Oriental finery. In one hand, on each finger of which sparkled a great jewel, he held a golden wine goblet. A band of drunken revelers reeled out behind him—minnesingers, dwarfs, dancing girls, wine-companions, vacuous-faced, blinking like owls in the daylight. All the boot-kissers and hangers-on that swarm after a rich and degenerate lord trooped with their master—scum of both races. The luxury of the East had worked quick ruin on Baron Von Gonler.

"Well," shouted the baron, "who is it wishes to interrupt my drinking?"

"Any but a drunkard would know Cormac FitzGeoffrey," snarled the horseman, his lip writhing back from his strong teeth in contempt. "We have an account to settle."

That name and Cormac's tone had been enough to sober any drunken knight of the Outremer. But Von Gonler was not only drunk; he was a degenerate fool. The baron took a long drink while his drunken crew stared curiously at the savage figure on the other side of the dry moat, whispering to one another.

"Once you were a man, Von Gonler," said Cormac in a tone of concentrated venom; "now you have become a groveling debauchee. Well, that's your own affair. The matter I have in mind is another—why did you refuse aid to the Sieur de Gissclin?"

The German's puffy, arrogant face took on new hauteur. He pursed his thick lips haughtily, while his bleared eyes blinked over his bulbous nose like an owl. He was an image of pompous stupidity that made Cormac grind his teeth.

"What was the Frenchman to me?" the baron retorted brutally. "It was his own fault—out of a thousand girls he might have taken, the young fool tried to steal one a sheik wanted himself. He, the purity of honor! Bah!"

He added a coarse jest and the creatures with him screamed with mirth, leaping and flinging themselves into obscene postures. Cormac's sudden and lion-like roar of fury gave them pause.

"Conrad Von Gonler!" thundered the maddened Gael, "I name you liar, traitor and coward—dastard, poltroon and villain! Arm yourself and ride out here on the plain. And haste—I can not waste much time on you—I must kill you quick and ride on lest another vermin escape me."

The baron laughed cynically, "Why should I fight you? You are not even a knight. You wear no knightly emblem on your shield."

"Evasions of a coward," raged FitzGeoffrey. "I am a chief in Ireland and I have cleft the skulls of men whose boots you are not worthy to touch. Will you arm yourself and ride out, or are you become the swinish coward I deem you?"

Von Gonler laughed in scornful anger.

"I need not risk my hide fighting you. I will not fight you, but I will have my men-at-arms fill your hide with crossbow bolts if you tarry longer."

"Von Gonler," Cormac's voice was deep and terrible in its brooding menace, "will you fight, or die in cold blood?"

The German burst into a sudden brainless shout of laughter.

"Listen to him!" he roared. "He threatens me—he on the other side of the moat, with the drawbridge lifted—I here in the midst of my henchmen!"

He smote his fat thigh and roared with his fool's laughter, while the debased men and women who served his pleasures laughed with him and insulted the grim Irish warrior with shrill anathema and indecent gestures. And suddenly Cormac, with a bitter curse, rose in his stirrups, snatched his battle-ax from his saddle-bow and hurled it with all his mighty strength.

The men-at-arms on the towers cried out and the dancing girls screamed. Von Gonler had thought himself to be out of reach—but there is no such thing as being out of reach of Norman-Irish vengeance. The heavy ax hissed as it clove the air and dashed out Baron Conrad's brains.

The fat, gross body buckled to the earth like a mass of melted tallow, one fat, white hand still gripping the empty wine goblet. The gay silks and cloth-of-gold were dabbled in a deeper red than ever was sold in the bazaar, and the jesters and dancers scattered like birds, screaming at the sight of that blasted head and the crimson ruin that had been a human face.

Cormac FitzGeoffrey made a fierce, triumphant gesture and voiced a deep-chested yell of such ferocious exultation that men blenched to hear. Then wheeling his black steed suddenly, he raced away before the dazed soldiers could get their wits together to send a shower of arrows after him.

He did not gallop far. The great steed was weary from a hard night's travel. Cormac soon swung in behind a jutting crag, and reining his horse up a steep incline, halted and looked back the way he had come. He was out of sight of the keep, but he heard no sounds of pursuit. A wait of some half-hour convinced him that no attempt had been made to follow him. It was dangerous and foolhardy to ride out of a safe castle into these hills. Cormac might well have been one of an ambushing force.

At any rate, whatever his enemies' thoughts were on the subject, it was evident that he need expect no present attempt at retaliation, and he grunted with angry satisfaction. He never shunned a fight, but just now he had other business on hand.

Cormac rode eastward.

3. The Road to El Ghor

The way to El Ghor was rough indeed. Cormac wound his way between huge jagged boulders, across deep ravines and up treacherous steeps. The sun slowly climbed toward the zenith and the heat waves began to dance and shimmer. The sun beat fiercely on Cormac's helmeted head, and glancing back from the bare rocks, dazzled his narrowed eyes. But the big warrior gave no heed; in his own land he learned to defy sleet and snow and bitter cold; following the standard of Coeur de Lion, before the shimmering walls of Acre, on the dusty plains of Azotus, and before Joppa, he had become inured to the blaze of the Oriental sun, to the glare of naked sands, to the slashing dust winds.

At noon he halted long enough to allow the black stallion an hour's rest in the shade of a giant boulder. A tiny spring bubbled there, known to him of old, and it slaked the thirst of the man and the horse. The stallion cropped eagerly at the scrawny fringe of grass about the spring and Cormac ate of the dried meats he carried in a small pouch. Here he had watered his steed in the old days, when he rode with Gerard. Ali-El-Yar lay to the west; in the night he had swung around it in a wide circle as he rode to the castle of Von Gonler. He had had no wish to gaze on the moldering ruins. The nearest Moslem chief of any importance was Nureddin El Ghor, who with his brother-at-arms, Kosru Malik, the Seljuk, held the castle of El Ghor, in the hills to the east.

Cormac rode on stolidly through the savage heat. As mid-afternoon neared he rode up out of a deep, wide defile and came onto the higher levels of the hills. Up this defile he had ridden aforetime to raid the wild tribes to the east, and on the small plateaus at the head of the defile stood a gibbet where Sieur Gerard de Gissclin had once hanged a red-handed Turkoman chief as a warning to those tribes.

Now, as FitzGeoffrey rode up on the plateau, he saw the old tree again bore fruit. His keen eyes made out a human form suspended in midair, apparently by the wrists. A tall warrior in the peaked helmet and light mail shirt of a Moslem stood beneath, tentatively prodding at the victim with a spear, making the body sway and spin on the rope. A bay Turkoman horse stood near. Cormac's cold eyes narrowed. The man on the rope—his naked body glistened too white in the sun for a Turk. The Norman-Gael touched spurs to the black stallion and swept across the plateau at a headlong run.

At the sudden thunder of hoofs the Muhammadan started and whirled. Dropping the spear with which he had been tormenting the captive, he mounted swiftly, stringing a short heavy bow as he did so. This done, and his left forearm thrust through the straps of a small round buckler, he trotted out to meet the onset of the Frank.

Cormac was approaching at a thundering charge, eyes glaring over the edge of his grim shield. He knew that this Turk would never meet him as a Frankish knight would have met him—breast to breast. The Moslem would avoid his ponderous rushes, and circling him on his nimbler steed, drive in shaft after shaft until one found its mark. But he rushed on as recklessly as if he had never before encountered Saracen tactics.

Now the Turk bent his bow and the arrow glanced from Cormac's shield. They were barely within javelin cast of each other, but even as the Moslem laid another shaft to string, doom smote him. Cormac, without checking his headlong gait, suddenly rose in his stirrups and gripping his long lance in the middle, cast it like a javelin. The unexpectedness of the move caught the Seljuk off guard and he made the mistake of throwing up his shield instead of dodging. The lance-head tore through the light buckler and crashed full on his mail-clad breast. The point bent on his hauberk without piercing the links, but the terrific impact dashed the Turk from his saddle and as he rose, dazed and groping for his scimitar, the great black stallion was already looming horrific over him, and under those frenzied hoofs he went down, torn and shattered.

Without a second glance at his victim Cormac rode under the gibbet and rising in the saddle, stared into the face of he who swung therefrom.

"By Satan," muttered the big warrior, "'tis Micaul na Blaos—Michael de Blois, one of Gerard's squires. What devil's work is this?"

Drawing his sword he cut the rope and the youth slid into his arms. Young Michael's lips were parched and swollen, his eyes dull with suffering. He was naked except for short leathern breeks, and the sun had dealt cruelly with his fair skin. Blood from a slight scalp wound caked his yellow hair, and there were shallow cuts on his limbs—marks left by his tormentor's spear.

Cormac laid the young Frenchman in the shade cast by the motionless stallion and trickled water through the parched lips from his canteen. As soon as he could speak, Michael croaked: "Now I know in truth that I am dead, for there is but one knight ever rode in Outremer who could cast a long lance like a javelin—and Cormac FitzGeoffrey has been dead for many months. But I be dead, where is Gerard—and Yulala?"

"Rest and be at ease," growled Cormac. "You live—and so do I."

He loosed the cords that had cut deep into the flesh of Michael's wrists and set himself to gently rub and massage the numb arms. Slowly the delirium faded from the youth's eyes. Like Cormac, he too came of a race that was tough as spring steel; an hour's rest and plenty of water, and his intense vitality asserted itself.

"How long have you hung from this gibbet?" asked Cormac.

"Since dawn." Michael's eyes were grim as he rubbed his lacerated wrists. "Nureddin and Kosru Malik said that since Sieur Gerard once hanged one of their race here, it was fitting that one of Gerard's men should grace this gibbet."

"Tell me how Gerard died," growled the Irish warrior. "Men hint at foul tales—"

Michael's fine eyes filled with tears. "Ah, Cormac, I who loved him, brought about his death. Listen—there is more to this than meets the casual eye. I think that Nureddin and his comrade-at-arms have been stung by the hornet of empire. It is in my mind that they, with various dog-knights among the Franks, dream of a mongrel kingdom among these hills, which shall hold allegiance neither to Saladin nor any king of the West.

"They begin to broaden their holdings by treachery. The nearest Christian hold was that of Ali-El-Yar, of course. Sieur Gerard was a true knight, peace be upon his fair soul, and he must be removed. All this I learned later—would to God I had known it beforehand! Among Nureddin's slaves is a Persian girl named Yulala, and with this innocent tool of their evil wishes, the twain sought to ensnare my lord—to slay at once his body and his good name. And God help me, through me they succeeded where otherwise they had failed.

"For my lord Gerard was honorable beyond all men. When in peace, and at Nureddin's invitation, he visited El Ghor, he paid no heed to Yulala's blandishments. For according to the commands of her masters, which she dared not disobey, the girl allowed Gerard to look on her, unveiled, as if by chance, and she pretended affection for him. But Gerard gave her no heed. But I—I fell victim to her charms."

Cormac snorted in disgust. Michael clutched his arm.

"Cormac," he cried, "bethink you—all men are not iron like you! I swear I loved Yulala from the moment I first set eyes on her—and she loved me! I contrived to see her again—to steal into El Ghor itself—"

"Whence men got the tale that it was Gerard who was carrying on an affair with Nureddin's slave," snarled FitzGeoffrey.

Michael hid his face in his hands. "Mine the fault," he groaned. "Then one night a mute brought a note signed by Yulala—apparently—begging me to come with Sieur Gerard and his men-at-arms and save her from a frightful fate—our love had been discovered, the note read, and they were about to torture her. I was wild with rage and fear. I went to Gerard and told him all, and he, white soul of honor, vowed to aid me. He could not break the truce and bring Saladin's wrath upon the Christian's cities, but he donned his mail and rode forth alone with me. We would see if there was any way whereby we might steal Yulala away, secretly; if not, my lord would go boldly to Nureddin and ask the girl as a gift, or offer to pay a great ransom for her. I would marry her.

"Well, when we reached the place outside the wall of El Ghor, where I was wont to meet Yulala, we found we were trapped. Nureddin, Kosru Malik and their warriors rose suddenly about us on all sides. Nureddin first spoke to Gerard, telling him of the trap he had set and baited, hoping to entice my lord into his power alone. And the Moslem laughed to think that the chance love of a squire had drawn Gerard into the trap where the carefully wrought plan had failed. As for the missive—Nureddin wrote that himself, believing, in his craftiness, that Sieur Gerard would do just as indeed he did.

"Nureddin and the Turk offered to allow Gerard to join them in their plan of empire. They told him plainly that his castle and lands were the price a certain powerful nobleman asked in return for his alliance, and they offered alliance with Gerard instead of this noble. Sieur Gerard merely answered that so long as life remained in him, he would keep faith with his king and his creed, and at the word the Moslems rolled on us like a wave.

"Ah, Cormac, Cormac, had you but been there with our men-at-arms! Gerard bore himself right manfully as was his wont—back to back we fought and I swear to you that we trod a knee-deep carpet of the dead before Gerard fell and they dragged me down. 'Christ and the Cross!' were his last words, as the Turkish spears and swords pierced him through and through. And his fair body—naked and gashed, and thrown to the kites and the jackals!"

Michael sobbed convulsively, beating his fists together in his agony. Cormac rumbled deep in his chest like a savage bull. Blue lights burned and flickered in his eyes.

"And you?" he asked harshly.

"Me they flung into a dungeon for torture," answered Michael, "but that night Yulala came to me. An old servitor who loved her, and who had dwelt in El Ghor before it fell to Nureddin, freed me and led us both through a secret passage that leads from the torture chamber, beyond the wall. We went into the hills on foot and without weapons and wandered there for days, hiding from the horsemen sent forth to hunt us down. Yesterday we were recaptured and brought back to El Ghor. An arrow had struck down the old slave who showed us the passageway, unknown to the present masters of the castle, and we refused to tell how we had escaped though Nureddin threatened us with torture. This dawn he brought me forth from the castle and hanged me to this gibbet, leaving that one to guard me. What he has done to Yulala, God alone knows."

"You knew that Ali-El-Yar had fallen?"

"Aye," Michael nodded dully. "Kosru Malik boasted of it. The lands of Gerard now fall heir to his enemy, the traitor knight who will come to

Nureddin's aid when the Moslem strikes for a crown."

"And who is this traitor?" asked Cormac softly.

"The baron Conrad Von Gonler, whom I swear to spit like a hare—"

Cormac smiled thinly and bleakly. "Swear me no oaths. Von Gonler has been in Hell since dawn. I knew only that he refused to come to Gerard's aid. I could have slain him no deader had I known his whole infamy."

Michael's eyes blazed. "A de Gissclin to the rescue!" he shouted fiercely. "I thank thee, old war-dog! One traitor is accounted for—what now? Shall Nureddin and the Turk live while two men wear de Gissclin steel?"

"Not if steel cuts and blood runs red," snarled Cormac. "Tell me of this secret way—nay, waste no time in words—show *me* this secret way. If you escaped thereby, why should we not enter the same way? Here—take the arms from that carrion while I catch his steed which I see browses on the moss among the rocks. Night is not far away; mayhap we can gain through to the interior of the castle—there—"

His big hands clenched into iron sledges and his terrible eyes blazed; in his whole bearing there was apparent a plain tale of fire and carnage, of spears piercing bosoms and swords splitting skulls.

4. The Faith of Cormac

When Cormac FitzGeoffrey took up the trail to El Ghor again, one would have thought at a glance that a Turk rode with him. Michael de Blois rode the bay Turkoman steed and wore the peaked Turkish helmet. He was girt with the curved scimitar and carried the bow and quiver of arrows, but he did not wear the mail shirt; the hammering hoofs of the plunging stallion had battered and brayed it out of all usefulness.

The companions took a circuitous route into the hills to avoid outposts, and it was dusk before they looked down on the towers of El Ghor which stood, grim and sullen, girt on three sides by scowling hills. Westward a broad road wound down the steeps on which the castle stood. On all other sides ravine-cut slopes straggled to the beetling walls. They had made such a wide circle that they now stood in the hills almost directly east of the keep, and Cormac, gazing westward over the turrets, spoke suddenly to his friend.

"Look—a cloud of dust far out on the plain—"

Michael shook his head: "Your eyes are far keener than mine. The hills are so clouded with the blue shadows of twilight I can scarcely make out the blurred expanse that is the plain beyond, much less discern any movement upon it."

"My life has often depended on my eyesight," growled the Norman-Gael. "Look closely—see that tongue of plainsland that cleaves far into the hills like a broad valley, to the north? A band of horsemen, riding hard, are just entering the defiles, if I may judge by the cloud of dust they raise. Doubtless a band of raiders returning to El Ghor. Well—they are in the hills now where going is rough and it will be hours before they get to the castle. Let us to our task—stars are blinking in the east."

They tied their horses in a place hidden from sight of any watcher below down among the gullies. In the last dim light of dusk they saw the turbans of the sentries on the towers, but gliding among boulders and defiles, they kept well concealed. At last Michael turned into a deep ravine.

"This leads into the subterranean corridor," said he. "God grant it has not been discovered by Nureddin. He had his warriors searching for something of the sort, suspecting its existence when we refused to tell how we had escaped."

They passed along the ravine, which grew narrower and deeper, for some distance, feeling their way; then Michael halted with a groan. Cormac, groping forward, felt iron bars, and as his eyes grew accustomed to the darkness, made out an opening like the mouth of a cave. Solid iron sills had been firmly bolted into the solid rock, and into these sills were set heavy bars, too close together to allow the most slender human to slip through.

"They have found the tunnel and closed it," groaned Michael. "Cormac, what are we to do?"

Cormac came closer and laid hands tentatively on the bars. Night had fallen and it was so dark in the ravine even his catlike eyes could hardly make out objects close at hand. The big Norman-Celt took a deep breath, and gripping a bar in each mighty hand, braced his iron legs and slowly exerted all his incredible strength. Michael, watching in amazement, sensed rather than saw the great muscles roll and swell under the pliant mail, the veins swell in the giant's forehead and sweat burst out. The bars groaned and creaked, and even as Michael remembered that this man was stronger than King Richard himself, the breath burst from Cormac's lips in an explosive grunt and simultaneously the bars gave way like reeds in his iron hands. One came away, literally torn from its sockets, and the others bent deeply. Cormac gasped and shook the sweat out of his eyes, tossing the bar aside.

"By the saints," muttered Michael, "are you man or devil, Cormac FitzGeoffrey? That is a feat I deemed even beyond your power."

"Enough words," grunted the Norman. "Let us make haste, if we can squeeze through. It's likely that we'll find a guard in this tunnel, but it's a chance we must take. Draw your steel and follow me."

It was as dark as the maw of Hades in the tunnel. They groped their way forward, expecting every minute to blunder into a trap, and Michael, stealing close at the heels of his friend, cursed the pounding of his own heart and wondered at the ability of the giant to move stealthily and with no rattling of arms.

To the comrades it seemed that they groped forward in the darkness for an eternity, and just as Michael leaned forward to whisper that he believed they were inside the castle's outer walls, a faint glow was observed ahead. Stealing warily forward they came to a sharp turn in the corridor around which shone the light. Peering cautiously about the corner they saw that the light emanated from a flickering torch thrust into a niche in the wall, and beside this stood a tall Turk, yawning as he leaned on his spear. Two other Moslems lay sleeping on their cloaks nearby. Evidently Nureddin did not lay too much trust in the bars with which he had blocked the entrance.

"The guard," whispered Michael, and Cormac nodded, stepping back and drawing his companion with him. The Norman-Gael's wary eyes had made out a flight of stone steps beyond the warriors, with a heavy door at the top.

"These seem to be all the weapon-men in the tunnel," muttered Cormac. "Loose a shaft at the waking warrior—and do not miss."

Michael fitted notch to string, and leaning close to the angle of the turn, aimed at the Turk's throat, just above the hauberk. He silently cursed the flickering, illusive light. Suddenly the drowsy warrior's head jerked up and he glared in their direction, suspicion flaring his eyes. Simultaneously came the twang of the loosed string and the Turk staggered and went down, gurgling horribly and clawing at the shaft that transfixed his bull neck.

The other two, awakened by their comrade's death throes and the sudden swift drum of feet on the ground, started up—and were cut down as they rubbed at sleep-filled eyes and groped for weapons.

"That was well done," growled Cormac, shaking the red drops from his steel. "There was no sound that should have carried through yonder door. Still, if it be bolted from within, our work is useless and we undone."

But it was not bolted, as the presence of the warriors in the tunnel suggested. As Cormac gently opened the heavy iron door, a sudden pain-fraught whimper from the other side electrified them.

"Yulala!" gasped Michael, whitening. "'Tis the torture chamber, and that is her voice! In God's name, Cormac—in!"

And the big Norman-Gael recklessly flung the door wide and leaped through like a charging tiger, with Michael at his heels. They halted short. It was the torture chamber, right enough, and on the floor and the walls stood or hung all the hellish appliances that the mind of man has invented for the torment of his brother. Three people were in the dungeon and two of these were bestial-faced men in leathern breeches, who looked up, startled, as the Franks entered. The third was a girl who lay bound to a sort of bench, naked as the day she was born. Coals glowed in braziers nearby, and one of the mutes was in the very act of reaching for a pair of white-hot pinchers. He crouched now, glaring in amazement, his arm still outstretched.

From the white throat of the captive girl burst a piteous cry.

"Yulala!" Michael cried out fiercely and leaped forward, a red mist floating before his eyes. One of the beast-faced mutes was before him, lifting a short sword, but the young Frank, without checking his stride, brought down his scimitar in a sweeping arc that drove the curved blade through scalp and skull. Wrenching his weapon free, he dropped to his knees beside the torture bench, a great sob tearing his throat.

"Yulala! Yulala! Oh girl, what have they done to you?"

"Michael, my beloved!" Her great dark eyes were like stars in the mist. "I knew you would come. They have not tortured me—save for a whipping—they were just about to begin—"

The other mute had glided swiftly toward Cormac as a snake glides, knife in hand.

"Satan!" grunted the big warrior. "I won't sully my steel with such blood—"

His left hand shot out and caught the mute's wrist and there was a crunch of splintering bones. The knife flew from the mute's fingers, which spread wide suddenly like an inflated glove. Blood burst from the fingertips and the creature's mouth gaped in silent agony. And at that instant Cormac's right hand closed on his throat and through the open lips burst a red deluge of blood as the Norman's iron fingers ground flesh and vertebrae to a crimson pulp.

Flinging aside the sagging corpse, Cormac turned to Michael, who had freed the girl and now was nearly crushing her in his arms as he gripped her close in a very passion of relief and joy. A heavy hand on his shoulder brought him back to a realization of their position. Cormac had found a cloak and this he wrapped about the naked girl.

"Go, at once," he said swiftly. "It may not be long before others come to take the place of the guards in the tunnel. Here—you have no armor—take my shield—no, don't argue. You may need it to protect the girl from arrows if you—if we, are pursued. Haste now—"

"But you, Cormac?" Michael lingered, hesitant.

"I will make fast that outer door," said the Norman. "I can heap benches against it. Then I will follow you. But don't wait for me. This is a command, do you understand? Hasten through the tunnel and go to the horses. There, instantly mount the Turkoman horse and ride! I will follow by another route—aye, by a road none but I can ride! Ride ye to Sir Rupert de Vaile, Seneschal of Antioch. He is our friend; hasten now."

Cormac stood a moment in the doorway at the head of the stairs and watched Michael and the girl hurry down the steps, past the place where the silent sentries lay, and vanish about the turn in the tunnel. Then he turned back into the torture chamber and closed the door. He crossed the room, threw the bolt on the outer door and swung it wide. He gazed up a winding flight of stairs. Cormac's face was immobile. He had voluntarily sealed his doom.

The giant Norman-Celt was an opportunist. He knew that such chance as had led him into the heart of his foe's stronghold was not likely to favor him again. Life was uncertain in Outremer; if he waited for another opportunity to strike at Nureddin and Kosru Malik, that opportunity might not come. This was his best opportunity for the vengeance for which his barbaric soul lusted.

That he would lose his own life in the consummating of that vengeance made no difference. Men were born to die in battle, according to his creed, and Cormac FitzGeoffrey secretly leaned toward the belief of his Viking ancestors in a Valhalla for the souls loosed gloriously in the clash of swords. Michael, having found the girl, had instantly forgotten the original plan of vengeance. Cormac had no blame for him; life and love were sweet to the young. But the grim Irish warrior owed a debt to the murdered Gerard and was prepared to pay with his own life. Thus Cormac kept faith with the dead.

He wished that he could have bade Michael ride the black stallion, but he knew that the horse would allow none but himself to bestride it. Now it would fall into Moslem hands, he thought with a sigh. He went up the stairs.

5. The Lion of Islam

At the top of the stairs, Cormac came into a corridor and along this he strode swiftly but warily, the Norse sword shimmering bluely in his hand. Going at random he turned into another corridor and here came full on a Turkish warrior, who stopped short, agape, seeing a supernatural horror in this grim slayer who strode like a silent phantom of death through the castle. Before the Turk could regain his wits, the blue sword shore through his neck cords.

Cormac stood above his victim for a moment, listening intently. Somewhere ahead of him he heard a low hum of voices, and the attitude of this Turk, with shield and drawn scimitar, had suggested that he stood guard before some chamber door. An irregular torch faintly illumined the wide corridor, and Cormac, groping in the semidarkness for a door, found instead a wide portal masked by heavy silk curtains. Parting them cautiously he gazed through into a great room thronged with armed men.

Warriors in mail and peaked helmets, and bearing wide-pointed, curved swords, lined the walls, and on silken cushions sat the chieftains—rulers of El Ghor and their satellites. Across the room sat Nureddin El Ghor, tall, lean, with a high-bridged, thin nose and keen dark eyes; his whole aspect distinctly hawk-like. His Semitic features contrasted with the Turks about him. His lean strong hand continually caressed the ivory hilt of a long, lean saber, and he wore a shirt of mesh-mail. A renegade chief from southern Arabia, this sheik was a man of great ability; his dream of an independent kingdom in these hills was no mad hashish hallucination. Let him win the alliance of a few Seljuk chiefs, of a few Frankish renegades like Von Gonler, and with the hordes of Arabs, Turks and Kurds that would assuredly flock to his banner, Nureddin would be a menace both to Saladin and the Franks who still clung to the fringes of Outremer. Among the mailed Turks Cormac saw the sheepskin caps and wolf skins of wild chiefs from beyond the hills—Kurds and Turkomans. Already the Arab's fame was spreading, if such unstable warriors as these were rallying to him.

Near the curtain-hung doorway sat Kosru Malik, known to Cormac of old, a warrior typical of his race, strongly built, of medium height, with a dark cruel face. Even as he sat in council he wore a peaked helmet and a gilded mail hauberk and held across his knees a jeweled-hilted scimitar. It seemed to Cormac that these men argued some matter just before setting out on some raid, as they were all fully armed. But he wasted no time on speculation. He tore the hangings aside with a mailed hand and strode into the room.

Amazement held the warriors frozen for an instant, and in that instant the giant Frank reached Kosru Malik's side. The Turk, his dark features paling, sprang to his feet like a steel spring released, raising his scimitar, but even as he did so, Cormac braced his feet and smote with all his power. The Norse sword shivered the curved blade and, rending the gilded mail, severed the Turk's shoulder-bone and cleft his breast.

Cormac wrenched the heavy blade free from the split breastbone and with one foot on Kosru Malik's body, faced his foes like a lion at bay. His helmeted head was lowered, his cold blue eyes flaming from under the heavy black brows, and his mighty right hand held ready the stained sword. Nureddin had leaped to his feet and stood trembling in rage and astonishment. This sudden apparition came as near to unmanning him as anything had ever done. His thin, hawk-like features lowered in a wrathful snarl, his beard bristled and with a quick motion he unsheathed his ivory-hilted saber. Then even as he stepped forward and his warriors surged in behind him, a startling interruption occurred.

Cormac, a fierce joy surging in him as he braced himself for the charge, saw, on the other side of the great room, a wide door swing open and a host of armed warriors appear, accompanied by sundry of Nureddin's men, who wore empty scabbards and uneasy faces.

The Arab and his warriors whirled to face the newcomers. These men, Cormac saw, were dusty as if from long riding, and his memory flashed to the horsemen he had seen riding into the hills at dusk. Before them strode a tall, slender man, whose fine face was traced with lines of weariness, but whose aspect was that of a ruler of men. His garb was simple in comparison with the resplendent armor and silken attendants. And Cormac swore in amazed recognition.

Yet his surprize was no greater than that of the men of El Ghor.

"What do you in my castle, unannounced?" gasped Nureddin.

A giant in silvered mail raised his hand warningly and spoke sonorously: "The Lion of Islam, Protector of the Faithful, Yussef Ibn Eyyub, Salah-ud-din, Sultan of Sultans, needs no announcement to enter yours or any castle, Arab."

Nureddin stood his ground, though his followers began salaaming madly; there was iron in this Arabian renegade.

"My lord," said he stoutly, "it is true I did not recognize you when you first came into the chamber; but El Ghor is mine, not by virtue of right or aid or grant from any sultan, but the might of my own arm. Therefore, I make you welcome but do not beg your mercy for my hasty words."

Saladin merely smiled in a weary way. Half a century of intrigue and warring rested heavily on his shoulders. His brown eyes, strangely mild for so great a lord, rested on the silent Frankish giant who still stood with his mail-clad foot on what had been the chief Kosru Malik.

"And what is this?" asked the Sultan.

Nureddin scowled: "A Nazarene outlaw has stolen into my keep and assassinated my comrade, the Seljuk. I beg your leave to dispose of him. I will give you his skull, set in silver—"

A gesture stopped him. Saladin stepped past his men and confronted the dark, brooding warrior.

"I thought I had recognized those shoulders and that dark face," said the Sultan with a smile. "So you have turned your face east again, Lord Cormac?"

"Enough!" The deep voice of the Norman-Irish giant filled the chamber. "You have me in your trap; my life is forfeit. Waste not your time in taunts; send your jackals against me and make an end of it. I swear by my clan, many of them shall bite the dust before I die, and the dead will be more than the living!"

Nureddin's tall frame shook with passion; he gripped his hilt until the knuckles showed white. "Is this to be borne, my Lord?" he exclaimed fiercely. "Shall this Nazarene dog fling dirt into our faces—"

Saladin shook his head slowly, smiling as if at some secret jest: "It may be his is no idle boast. At Acre, at Azotus, at Joppa I have seen the skull on his shield glitter like a star of death in the mist, and the Faithful fall before his sword like garnered grain."

The great Kurd turned his head, leisurely surveying the ranks of silent warriors and the bewildered chieftains who avoided his level gaze.

"A notable concourse of chiefs, for these times of truce," he murmured, half to himself. "Would you ride forth in the night with all these warriors to fight genii in the desert, or to honor some ghostly sultan, Nureddin? Nay, nay, Nureddin, thou hast tasted the cup of ambition, meseemeth—and thy life is forfeit!"

The unexpectedness of the accusation staggered Nureddin, and while he groped for reply, Saladin followed it up: "It comes to me that you have plotted against me—aye, that it was your purpose to seduce various Moslem and Frankish lords from their allegiances, and set up a kingdom of your own. And for that reason you broke the truce and murdered a good knight, albeit a Caphar, and burned his castle. I have spies, Nureddin."

The tall Arab glanced quickly about, as if ready to dispute the question with Saladin himself. But when he noted the number of the Kurd's warriors, and saw his own fierce ruffians shrinking away from him, awed, a smile of bitter contempt crossed his hawk-like features, and sheathing his blade, he folded his arms.

"God gives," he said simply, with the fatalism of the Orient.

Saladin nodded in appreciation, but motioned back a chief who stepped forward to bind the sheik. "Here is one," said the Sultan, "to whom you owe a greater debt than to me, Nureddin. I have heard Cormac FitzGeoffrey was brother-at-arms to the Sieur Gerard. You owe many debts of blood, oh Nureddin; pay one, therefore, by facing the lord Cormac with the sword."

The Arab's eyes gleamed suddenly. "And if I slay him—shall I go free?"

"Who am I to judge?" asked Saladin. "It shall be as Allah wills it. But if you fight the Frank you will die, Nureddin, even though you slay him; he comes of a breed that slays even in their death-throes. Yet it is better to die by the sword than by the cord, Nureddin."

The sheik's answer was to draw his ivory-hilted saber. Blue sparks flickered in Cormac's eyes and he rumbled deeply like a wounded lion. He hated Saladin as he hated all his race, with the savage and relentless hatred of the Norman-Celt. He had ascribed the Kurd's courtesy to King Richard and the Crusaders to Oriental subtlety, refusing to believe that there could be ought but trickery and craftiness in a Saracen's mind. Now he saw in the Sultan's suggestion but the scheming of a crafty trickster to match two of his foes against each other, and a feline-like gloating over his victims. Cormac grinned without mirth. He asked no more from life than to have his enemy at sword-points. But he felt no gratitude toward Saladin, only a smoldering hate.

The Sultan and the warriors gave back, leaving the rivals a clear space in the center of the great room. Nureddin came forward swiftly, having donned a plain round steel cap with a mail drop that fell about his shoulders.

"Death to you, Nazarene!" he yelled, and sprang in with the pantherish leap and headlong recklessness of an Arab's attack. Cormac had no shield. He parried the hacking saber with upflung blade, and slashed back. Nureddin caught the heavy blade on his round buckler, which he turned slightly slantwise at the instant of impact, so that the stroke glanced off. He returned the blow with a thrust that rasped against Cormac's coif, and leaped a spear's length backward to avoid the whistling sweep of the Norse sword.

Again he leaped in, slashing, and Cormac caught the saber on his left forearm. Mail links parted beneath the keen edge, and blood spattered, but almost simultaneously the Norse sword crashed under the Arab's arm, bones cracked and Nureddin was flung his full length to the floor. Warriors gasped as they realized the full power of the Irishman's tigerish strokes.

Nureddin's rise from the floor was so quick that he almost seemed to rebound from his fall. To the onlookers it seemed that he was not hurt, but the Arab knew. His mail had held; the sword edge had not gashed his flesh, but the impact of that terrible blow had snapped a rib like a rotten twig, and the realization that he could not long avoid the Frank's rushes filled him with a wild beast determination to take his foe with him to Eternity.

Cormac was looming over Nureddin, sword high, but the Arab nerving himself to a dynamic burst of superhuman quickness, sprang up as a cobra leaps from its coil, and struck with desperate power. Full on Cormac's bent head the whistling saber clashed, and the Frank staggered as the keen edge bit through steel cap and coif links into his scalp. Blood jetted down his face, but he braced his feet and struck back with all the power of arm and shoulders behind the sword. Again Nureddin's buckler blocked the stroke, but this time the Arab had no time to turn the shield, and the heavy blade struck squarely. Nureddin went to his knees beneath the stroke, bearded face twisted in agony. With tenacious courage he reeled up again, shaking the shattered buckler from his numbed and broken arm, but even as he lifted the saber, the Norse sword crashed down, cleaving the Moslem helmet and splitting the skull to the teeth.

Cormac set a foot on his fallen foe and wrenched free his gory sword. His fierce eyes met the whimsical gaze of Saladin.

"Well, Saracen," said the Irish warrior challengingly, "I have killed your rebel for you."

"And your enemy," reminded Saladin.

"Aye," Cormac grinned bleakly and ferociously. "I thank you—though well I know it was no love of me or mine that prompted you to send the Arab against me. Well—make an end, Saracen."

"Why do you hate me, Lord Cormac?" asked the Sultan curiously.

Cormac snarled. "Why do I hate any of my foes? You are no more and no less than any other robber chief, to me. You tricked Richard and the rest with courtly words and fine deeds, but you never deceived me, who well knew you sought to win by deceit where you could not gain by force of arms."

Saladin shook his head, murmuring to himself. Cormac glared at him, tensing himself for a sudden leap that would carry the Kurd with him into the Dark. The Norman-Gael was a product of his age and his country; among the warring chiefs of blood-drenched Ireland, mercy was unknown and chivalry an outworn and forgotten myth. Kindness to a foe was a mark of weakness; courtesy to an enemy a form of craft, a preparation for treachery; to such teachings had Cormac grown up, in a land where a man took every advantage, gave no quarter and fought like a blood-mad devil if he expected to survive.

Now at a gesture from Saladin, those crowding the door gave back.

"Your way is open, Lord Cormac."

The Gael glared, his eyes narrowing to slits: "What game is this?" he growled. "Shall I turn my back to your blades? Out on it!"

"All swords are in their sheaths," answered the Kurd. "None shall harm you."

Cormac's lion-like head swung from side to side as he glared at the Moslems.

"You honestly mean I am to go free, after breaking the truce and slaying your jackals?"

"The truce was already broken," answered Saladin. "I find in you no fault. You have repaid blood for blood, and kept your faith to the dead. You are rough and savage, but I would fain have men like you in mine own train. There is a fierce loyalty in you, and for this I honor you."

Cormac sheathed his sword ungraciously. A grudging admiration for this weary-faced Moslem was born in him and it angered him. Dimly he realized at last that this attitude of fairness, justice and kindliness, even to foes, was not a crafty pose of Saladin's, not a manner of guile, but a natural nobility of the Kurd's nature. He saw suddenly embodied in the Sultan, the ideals of chivalry and high honor so much talked of—and so little practiced—by the Frankish knights. Blondel had been right then, and Sieur Gerard, when they argued with Cormac that high-minded chivalry was no mere romantic dream of an outworn age, but had existed, and still existed and lived in the hearts of certain men. But Cormac was born and bred in a savage land where men lived the desperate existence of the wolves whose hides covered their nakedness. He suddenly realized his own innate barbarism and was ashamed. He shrugged his lion's shoulders.

"I have misjudged you, Moslem," he growled. "There is fairness in you."

"I thank you, Lord Cormac," smiled Saladin. "Your road to the west is clear."

And the Moslem warriors courteously salaamed as Cormac FitzGeoffrey strode from the royal presence of the slender noble who was Protector of the Califs, Lion of Islam, Sultan of Sultans.

THE BLOOD OF BELSHAZZAR

It shone on the breast of the Persian king,
    It lighted Iskander's road;
It blazed where the spears were splintering,
    A lure and a maddening goad.
And down through the crimson, changing years
    It draws men, soul and brain;
They drown their lives in blood and tears,
    And they break their hearts in vain.
Oh, it flames with the blood of strong men's hearts
    Whose bodies are clay again.

—The Song of the Red Stone.

CHAPTER 1

Once it was called Eski-Hissar, the Old Castle, for it was very ancient even when the first Seljuks swept out of the east, and not even the Arabs, who rebuilt that crumbling pile in the days of Abu Bekr, knew what hands reared those massive bastions among the frowning foothills of the Taurus. Now, since the old keep had become a bandit's hold, men called it Bab-el-Shaitan, the Gate of the Devil, and with good reason.

That night there was feasting in the great hall. Heavy tables loaded with wine pitchers and jugs, and huge platters of food, stood flanked by crude benches for such as ate in that manner, while on the floor large cushions received the reclining forms of others. Trembling slaves hastened about, filling goblets from wineskins and bearing great joints of roasted meat and loaves of bread.

Here luxury and nakedness met, the riches of degenerate civilizations and the stark savagery of utter barbarism. Men clad in stenching sheepskins lolled on silken cushions, exquisitely brocaded, and guzzled from solid golden goblets, fragile as the stem of a desert flower. They wiped their bearded lips and hairy hands on velvet tapestries worthy of a shah's palace.

All the races of western Asia met here. Here were slim, lethal Persians, dangerous-eyed Turks in mail shirts, lean Arabs, tall ragged Kurds, Lurs and Armenians in sweaty sheepskins, fiercely mustached Circassians, even a few Georgians, with hawk-faces and devilish tempers.

Among them was one who stood out boldly from all the rest. He sat at a table drinking wine from a huge goblet, and the eyes of the others strayed to him continually. Among these tall sons of the desert and mountains his height did not seem particularly great, though it was above six feet. But the breadth and thickness of him were gigantic. His shoulders were broader, his limbs more massive than any other warrior there.

His mail coif was thrown back, revealing a lion-like head and a great corded throat. Though browned by the sun, his face was not as dark as those about him and his eyes were a volcanic blue, which smoldered continually as if from inner fires of wrath. Square-cut black hair like a lion's mane crowned a low, broad forehead.

He ate and drank apparently oblivious to the questioning glances flung toward him. Not that any had as yet challenged his right to feast in Bab-el-Shaitan, for this was a lair open to all refugees and outlaws. And this Frank was Cormac FitzGeoffrey, outlawed and hunted by his own race. The ex-Crusader was armed in close-meshed chain mail from head to foot. A heavy sword hung at his hip, and his kite-shaped shield with the grinning skull wrought in the center lay with his heavy vizorless helmet, on the bench beside him. There was no hypocrisy of etiquette in Bab-el-Shaitan. Its occupants went armed to the teeth at all times and no one questioned another's right to sit down to meat with his sword at hand.

Cormac, as he ate, scanned his fellow-feasters openly. Truly Bab-el-Shaitan was a lair of the spawn of Hell, the last retreat of men so desperate and bestial that the rest of the world had cast them out in horror. Cormac was no stranger to savage men; in his native Ireland he had sat among barbaric figures in the gatherings of chiefs and reavers in the hills. But the wild-beast appearance and utter inhumanness of some of these men impressed even the fierce Irish warrior.

There, for instance, was a Lur, hairy as an ape, tearing at a half-raw joint of meat with yellow fangs like a wolf's. Kadra Muhammad, the fellow's name was, and Cormac wondered briefly if such a creature could have a human soul. Or that shaggy Kurd beside him, whose lip, twisted back by a sword scar into a permanent snarl, bared a tooth like a boar's tusk. Surely no divine spark of soul-dust animated these men, but the merciless and soulless spirit of the grim land that bred them. Eyes, wild and cruel as the eyes of wolves, glared through lank strands of tangled hair, hairy hands unconsciously gripped the hilts of knives even while the owners gorged and guzzled.

Cormac glanced from the rank and file to scrutinize the leaders of the band—those whom superior wit or war-skill had placed high in the confidence of their terrible chief, Skol Abdhur, the Butcher. Not one but had a whole volume of black and bloody history behind him. There was that slim Persian, whose tone was so silky, whose eyes were so deadly, and whose small, shapely head was that of a human panther—Nadir Tous, once an emir high in the favor of the Shah of Kharesmia. And that Seljuk Turk, with his silvered mail shirt, peaked helmet and jewel-hilted scimitar—Kai Shah; he had ridden at Saladin's side in high honor once, and it was said that the scar which showed white in the angle of his jaw had been made by the sword of Richard the Lion-hearted in that great battle before the walls of Joppa. And that wiry, tall, eagle-faced Arab, Yussef el Mekru—he had been a great sheikh once in Yemen and had even led a revolt against the Sultan himself.

But at the head of the table at which Cormac sat was one whose history for strangeness and vivid fantasy dimmed them all. Tisolino di Strozza, trader, captain of Venice's warships, Crusader, pirate, outlaw— what a red trail the man had followed to his present casteless condition! Di Strozza was tall and thin and saturnine in appearance, with a hook-nosed, thin-nostriled face of distinctly predatory aspect. His armor, now worn and tarnished, was of costly Venetian make, and the hilt of his long narrow sword had once been set with gems. He was a man of restless soul, thought Cormac, as he watched the Venetian's dark eyes dart continually from point to point, and the lean hand repeatedly lifted to twist the ends of the thin mustache.

Cormac's gaze wandered to the other chiefs—wild reavers, born to the red trade of pillage and murder, whose pasts were black enough, but lacked the varied flavor of the other four. He knew these by sight or reputation—Kojar Mirza, a brawny Kurd; Shalmar Khor, a tall swaggering Circassian; and Jusus Zehor, a renegade Georgian who wore half a dozen knifes in his girdle.

There was one not known to him, a warrior who apparently had no standing among the bandits, yet who carried himself with the assurance born of prowess. He was of a type rare in the Taurus—a stocky, strongly built man whose head would come no higher than Cormac's shoulder. Even as he ate, he wore a helmet with a lacquered leather drop, and Cormac caught the glint of mail beneath his sheepskins; through his girdle was thrust a short wide-bladed sword, not curved as much as the Moslem scimitars. His powerful bowed legs, as well as the slanting black eyes set in an inscrutable brown face, betrayed the Mongol.

He, like Cormac, was a newcomer; riding from the east he had arrived at Bab-el-Shaitan that night at the same time that the Irish warrior had ridden in from the south. His name, as given in guttural Turki, was Toghrul Khan.

A slave whose scarred face and fear-dulled eyes told of the brutality of his masters, tremblingly filled Cormac's goblet. He started and flinched as a sudden scream faintly knifed the din; it came from somewhere above, and none of the feasters paid any attention. The Norman-Gael wondered at the absence of women-slaves. Skol Abdhur's name was a terror in that part of Asia and many caravans felt the weight of his fury. Many women had been stolen from raided villages and camel-trains, yet now there were apparently only men in Bab-el-Shaitan. This, to Cormac, held a sinister implication. He recalled dark tales, whispered under the breath, relating to the cryptic inhumanness of the robber chief—mysterious hints of foul rites in black caverns, of naked white victims writhing on hideously ancient altars, of blood-chilling sacrifices beneath the midnight moon. But that cry had been no woman's scream.

Kai Shah was close to di Strozza's shoulder, talking very rapidly in a guarded tone. Cormac saw that Nadir Tous was only pretending to be absorbed in his wine cup; the Persian's eyes, burning with intensity, were fixed on the two who whispered at the head of the table. Cormac, alert to intrigue and counter-plot, had already decided that there were factions in Bab-el-Shaitan. He had noticed that di Strozza, Kai Shah, a lean Syrian scribe named Musa bin Daoud, and the wolfish Lur, Kadra Muhammad, stayed close to each other, while Nadir Tous had his own following among the lesser bandits, wild ruffians, mostly Persians and Armenians, and Kojar Mirza was surrounded by a number of even wilder mountain Kurds. The manner of the Venetian and Nadir Tous toward each other was of a wary courtesy that seemed to mask suspicion, while the Kurdish chief wore an aspect of truculent defiance toward both.

As these thoughts passed through Cormac's mind, an incongruous figure appeared on the landing of the broad stairs. It was Jacob, Skol Abdhur's majordomo—a short, very fat Jew attired in gaudy and costly robes which had once decked a Syrian harem master. All eyes turned toward him, for it was evident he had brought word from his master—not often did Skol Abdhur, wary as a hunted wolf, join his pack at their feasts.

"The great prince, Skol Abdhur," announced Jacob in pompous and sonorous accents, "would grant audience to the Nazarene who rode in at dusk—the lord Cormac FitzGeoffrey."

The Norman finished his goblet at draft and rose deliberately, taking up his shield and helmet.

"And what of me, Yahouda?" It was the guttural voice of the Mongol. "Has the great prince no word for Toghrul Khan, who has ridden far and hard to join his horde? Has he said naught of an audience with me?"

The Jew scowled. "Lord Skol said naught of any Tartar," he answered shortly. "Wait until he sends for you, as he will do—if it so pleases him."

The answer was as much an insult to the haughty pagan as would have been a slap in the face. He half-made to rise then sank back, his face, schooled to iron control, showing little of his rage. But his serpent-like eyes glittering devilishly, took in not only the Jew but Cormac as well, and the Norman knew that he himself was included in Toghrul Khan's black anger. Mongol pride and Mongol wrath are beyond the ken of the Western mind, but Cormac knew that in his humiliation, the nomad hated him as much as he hated Jacob.

But Cormac could count his friends on his fingers and his personal enemies by the scores. A few more foes made little difference and he paid no heed to Toghrul Khan as he followed the Jew up the broad stairs, and along a winding corridor to a heavy, metal-braced door before which stood, like an image carven of black basalt, a huge naked Nubian who held a two-handed scimitar whose five-foot blade was a foot wide at the tip.

Jacob made a sign to the Nubian, but Cormac saw that the Jew was trembling and apprehensive.

"In God's name," Jacob whispered to the Norman, "speak him softly; Skol is in a devilish temper tonight. Only a little while ago he tore out the eyeball of a slave with his hands."

"That was that scream I heard then," grunted Cormac. "Well, don't stand there chattering; tell that black beast to open the door before I knock it down."

Jacob blenched; but it was no idle threat. It was not the Norman-Gael's nature to wait meekly at the door of any man—he who had been cup-companion to King Richard. The majordomo spoke swiftly to the mute, who swung the door open. Cormac pushed past his guide and strode across the threshold.

And for the first time he looked on Skol Abdhur the Butcher, whose deeds of blood had already made him a semi-mythical figure. The Norman saw a bizarre giant reclining on a silken divan, in the midst of a room hung and furnished like a king's. Erect, Skol would have towered half a head taller than Cormac, and though a huge belly marred the symmetry of his figure, he was still an image of physical prowess. His short, naturally black beard had been stained to a bluish tint; his wide black eyes blazed with a curious wayward look not altogether sane at times.

He was clad in cloth-of-gold slippers whose toes turned up extravagantly, in voluminous Persian trousers of rare silk, and a wide green silken sash, heavy with golden scales, was wrapt about his waist. Above this he wore a sleeveless jacket, richly brocaded, open in front, but beneath this his huge torso was naked. His blue-black hair, held by a gemmed circlet of gold, fell to his shoulders, and his fingers were gleaming with jewels, while his bare arms were weighted with heavy gem-crusted armlets. Women's earrings adorned his ears.

Altogether his appearance was of such fantastic barbarism as to inspire in Cormac an amazement which in an ordinary man would have been a feeling of utmost horror. The apparent savagery of the giant, together with his fantastic finery which heightened rather than lessened the terror of his appearance, lent Skol Abdhur an aspect which set him outside the pale of ordinary humanity. The effect of an ordinary man, so garbed, would have been merely ludicrous; in the robber chieftain it was one of horror.

Yet as Jacob salaamed to the floor in a very frenzy of obeisance, he was not sure that Skol looked any more formidable than the mail-clad Frank with his aspect of dynamic and terrible strength directed by a tigerish nature.

"The lord Cormac FitzGeoffrey, oh mighty prince," proclaimed Jacob, while Cormac stood like an iron image not deigning even to incline his lion-like head.

"Yes, fool, I can see that," Skol's voice was deep and resonant. "Take yourself hence before I crop your ears. And see that those fools downstairs have plenty of wine."

From the stumbling haste with which Jacob obeyed, Cormac knew the threat of cropping ears was no empty one. Now his eyes wandered to a shocking and pitiful figure—the slave standing behind Skol's divan ready to pour wine for his grim master. The wretch was trembling in every limb as a wounded horse quivers, and the reason was apparent—a ghastly gaping socket from which the eye had been ruthlessly ripped. Blood still oozed from the rim to join the stains which blotched the twisted face and spotted the silken garments. Pitiful finery! Skol dressed his miserable slaves in apparel rich merchants might envy. And the wretch stood shivering in agony, yet not daring to move from his tracks, though with the pain-misted half-sight remaining him, he could scarcely see to fill the gem-crusted goblet Skol lifted.

"Come and sit on the divan with me, Cormac," hailed Skol. "I would speak to you. Dog! Fill the lord Frank's goblet, and haste, lest I take your other eye."

"I drink no more this night," growled Cormac, thrusting aside the goblet Skol held out to him. "And send that slave away. He'll spill wine on you in his blindness."

Skol stared at Cormac a moment and then with a sudden laugh waved the pain-sick slave toward the door. The man went hastily, whimpering in agony.

"See," said Skol, "I humor your whim. But it was not necessary. I would have wrung his neck after we had talked, so he could not repeat our words."

Cormac shrugged his shoulders. Little use to try to explain to Skol that it was pity for the slave and not desire for secrecy that prompted him to have the man dismissed.

"What think you of my kingdom, Bab-el-Shaitan?" asked Skol suddenly.

"It would be hard to take," answered the Norman.

Skol laughed wildly and emptied his goblet.

"So the Seljuks have found," he hiccupped. "I took it years ago by a trick from the Turk who held it. Before the Turks came the Arabs held it and before them—the devil knows. It is old—the foundations were built in the long ago by Iskander Akbar—Alexander the Great. Then centuries later came the Roumi—the Romans—who added to it. Parthians, Persians, Kurds, Arabs, Turks—all have shed blood on its walls. Now it is mine, and while I live, mine it shall remain! I know its secrets—and its secrets," he cast the Frank a sly and wicked glance full of sinister meaning, "are more than most men reckon—even those fools Nadir Tous and di Strozza, who would cut my throat if they dared."

"How do you hold supremacy over these wolves?" asked Cormac bluntly.

Skol laughed and drank once more.

"I have something each wishes. They hate each other; I play them against one another. I hold the key to the plot. They do not trust each other enough to move against me. I am Skol Abdhur! Men are puppets to dance on my strings. And women"—a vagrant and curious glint stole into his eyes—"women are food for the gods," he said strangely.

"Many men serve me," said Skol Abdhur, "emirs and generals and chiefs, as you saw. How came they here to Bab-el-Shaitan where the world ends? Ambition—intrigues—women—jealousy—hatred—now they serve the Butcher. And what brought you here, my brother? That you are an outlaw I know—that your life is forfeit to your people because you slew a certain emir of the Franks, one Count Conrad von Gonler. But only when hope is dead do men ride to Bab-el-Shaitan. There are cycles within cycles, outlaws beyond the pale of outlawry, and Bab-el-Shaitan is the end of the world."

"Well," growled Cormac, "one man can not raid the caravans. My friend Sir Rupert de Vaile, Seneschal of Antioch, is captive to the Turkish chief Ali Bahadur, and the Turk refuses to ransom him for the gold that has been offered. You ride far, and fall on the caravans that bring the treasures of Hind and Cathay. With you I may find some treasure so rare that the Turk will accept it as a ransom. If not, with my share of the loot I will hire enough bold rogues to rescue Sir Rupert."

Skol shrugged his shoulders. "Franks are mad," said he, "but whatever the reason, I am glad you rode hither. I have heard you are faithful to the lord you follow, and I need such a man. Just now I trust no one but Abdullah, the black mute that guards my chamber."

It was evident to Cormac that Skol was fast becoming drunk. Suddenly he laughed wildly.

"You asked me how I hold my wolves in leash? Not one but would slit my throat. But look—so far I trust you I will show you why they do not!"

He reached into his girdle and drew forth a huge jewel which sparkled like a tiny lake of blood in his great palm. Even Cormac's eyes narrowed at the sight.

"Satan!" he muttered. "That can be naught but the ruby called—"

"The Blood of Belshazzar!" exclaimed Skol Abdhur. "Aye, the gem Cyrus the Persian ripped from the sword-gashed bosom of the great king on that red night when Babylon fell! It is the most ancient and costly gem in the world. Ten thousand pieces of heavy gold could not buy it.

"Hark, Frank," again Skol drained a goblet, "I will tell you the tale of the Blood of Belshazzar. See you how strangely it is carved?"

He held it up and the light flashed redly from its many facets. Cormac shook his head, puzzled.

The carving was strange indeed, corresponding to nothing he had ever seen, east or west. It seemed that the ancient carver had followed some plan entirely unknown and apart from that of modern lapidary art. It was basically *different* with a difference Cormac could not define.

"No mortal cut that stone!" said Skol, "but the djinn of the sea! For once in the long, long ago, in the very dawn of happenings, the great king, even Belshazzar, went from his palace on pleasure bent and coming to the Green Sea—the Persian Gulf—went thereon in a royal galley, golden-prowed and rowed by a hundred slaves. Now there was one Naka, a diver of pearls, who desiring greatly to honor his king, begged the royal permission to seek the ocean bottom for rare pearls for the king, and Belshazzar granting his wish, Naka dived. Inspired by the glory of the king, he went far beyond the depth of divers, and after a time floated to the surface, grasping in his hand a ruby of rare beauty—aye, this very gem.

"Then the king and his lords, gazing on its strange carvings, were amazed, and Naka, nigh to death because of the great depth to which he had gone, gasped out a strange tale of a silent, seaweed-festooned city of marble and lapis lazuli far below the surface of the sea, and of a monstrous mummied king on a jade throne from whose dead taloned hand Naka had wrested the ruby. And then the blood burst from the diver's mouth and ears and he died.

"Then Belshazzar's lords entreated him to throw the gem back into the sea, for it was evident that it was the treasure of the djinn of the sea, but the king was as one mad, gazing into the crimson deeps of the ruby, and he shook his head.

"And lo, soon evil came upon him, for the Persians broke his kingdom, and Cyrus, looting the dying monarch, wrested from his bosom the great ruby which seemed so gory in the light of the burning palace that the soldiers shouted: 'Lo, it is the heart's blood of Belshazzar!' And so men came to call the gem the Blood of Belshazzar.

"Blood followed its course. When Cyrus fell on the Jaxartes, Queen Tomyris seized the jewel and for a time it gleamed on the naked bosom of the Scythian queen. But she was despoiled of it by a rebel general; in a battle against the Persians he fell and it went into the hands of Cambyses, who carried it with him into Egypt, where a priest of Bast stole it. A Numidian mercenary murdered him for it, and by devious ways it came back to Persia once more. It gleamed on Xerxes' crown when he watched his army destroyed at Salamis.

"Alexander took it from the corpse of Darius and on the Macedonian's corselet its gleams lighted the road to India. A chance sword blow struck it from his breastplate in a battle on the Indus and for centuries the Blood of Belshazzar was lost to sight. Somewhere far to the east, we know, its gleams shone on a road of blood and rapine, and men slew men and dishonored women for it. For it, as of old, women gave up their virtue, men their lives and kings their crowns.

"But at last its road turned to the west once more, and I took it from the body of a Turkoman chief I slew in a raid far to the east. How he came by it, I do not know. But now it is mine!"

Skol was drunk; his eyes blazed with inhuman passion; more and more he seemed like some foul bird of prey.

"It is my balance of power! Men come to me from palace and hovel, each hoping to have the Blood of Belshazzar for his own. I play them against each other. If one should slay me for it, the others would instantly cut him to pieces to gain it. They distrust each other too much to combine against me. And who would share the gem with another?"

He poured himself wine with an unsteady hand.

"I am Skol the Butcher!" he boasted, "a prince in my own right! I am powerful and crafty beyond the knowledge of common men. For I am the most feared chieftain in all the Taurus, I who was dirt beneath men's feet, the disowned and despised son of a renegade Persian noble and a Circassian slave-girl.

"Bah—these fools who plot against me—the Venetian, Kai Shah, Musa bin Daoud and Kadra Muhammad—over against them I play Nadir Tous, that polished cutthroat, and Kojar Mirza. The Persian and the Kurd hate me and they hate di Strozza, but they hate each other even more. And Shalmar Khor hates them all."

"And what of Seosamh el Mekru?" Cormac could not twist his Norman-Celtic tongue to the Arabic of Joseph.

"Who knows what is in an Arab's mind?" growled Skol. "But you may be certain he is a jackal for loot, like all his kind, and will watch which way the feather falls, to join the stronger side—and then betray the winners.

"But I care not!" the robber roared suddenly. "I am Skol the Butcher! Deep in the deeps of the Blood have I seen misty, monstrous shapes and read dark secrets! Aye—in my sleep I hear the whispers of that dead, half-human king from whom Naka the diver tore the jewel so long ago. Blood! That is a drink the ruby craves! Blood follows it; blood is drawn to it! Not the head of Cyrus did Queen Tomyris plunge into a vessel of warm blood as the legends say, but the gem she took from the dead king! He who wears it must quench its thirst or it will drink his own blood! Aye, the heart's flow of kings and queens have gone into its crimson shadow!

"And I have quenched its thirst! There are secrets of Bab-el-Shaitan none knows but I—and Abdullah whose withered tongue can never speak of the sights he has looked upon, the shrieks his ears have heard in the blackness below the castle when midnight holds the mountains breathless. For I have broken into secret corridors, sealed up by the Arabs who rebuilt the hold, and unknown to the Turks who followed them."

He checked himself as if he had said too much. But the crimson dreams began to weave again their pattern of insanity.

"You have wondered why you see no women here? Yet hundreds of fair girls have passed through the portals of Bab-el-Shaitan. Where are they now? Ha ha ha!" the giant's sudden roar of ghastly laughter thundered in the room.

"Many went to quench the ruby's thirst," said Skol, reaching for the wine jug, "or to become the brides of the Dead, the concubines of ancient demons of the mountains and deserts, who take fair girls only in death throes. Some I or my warriors merely wearied of, and they were flung to the vultures."

Cormac sat, chin on mailed fist, his dark brows lowering in disgust.

"Ha!" laughed the robber. "You do not laugh—are you thin-skinned, lord Frank? I have heard you spoken of as a desperate man. Wait until you have ridden with me for a few moons! Not for nothing am I named the Butcher! I have built a pyramid of skulls in my day! I have severed the necks of old men and old women, I have dashed out the brains of babes, I have ripped up women, I have burned children alive and sat them by scores on pointed stakes! Pour me wine, Frank."

"Pour your own damned wine," growled Cormac, his lip writhing back dangerously.

"That would cost another man his head," said Skol, reaching for his goblet. "You are rude of speech to your host and the man you have ridden so far to serve. Take care—rouse me not." Again he laughed his horrible laughter.

"These walls have re-echoed to screams of direst agony!" his eyes began to burn with a reckless and maddened light. "With these hands have I disemboweled men, torn out the tongues of children and ripped out the eyeballs of girls—thus!"

With a shriek of crazed laughter his huge hand shot at Cormac's face. With an oath the Norman caught the giant's wrist and bones creaked in that iron grip. Twisting the arm viciously down and aside with a force that nearly tore it from its socket, Cormac flung Skol back on the divan.

"Save your whims for your slaves, you drunken fool," the Norman rasped.

Skol sprawled on the divan, grinning like an idiotic ogre and trying to work his fingers which Cormac's savage grasp had numbed. The Norman rose and strode from the chamber in fierce disgust; his last backward glance showed Skol fumbling with the wine jug, with one hand still grasping the Blood of Belshazzar, which cast a sinister light all over the room.

The door shut behind Cormac and the Nubian cast him a sidelong, suspicious glance. The Norman shouted impatiently for Jacob, and the Jew bobbed up suddenly and apprehensively. His face cleared when Cormac brusquely demanded to be shown his chamber. As he tramped along the bare, torch-lighted corridors, Cormac heard sounds of revelry still going on below. Knives would be going before morning, reflected Cormac, and some would not see the rising of the sun. Yet the noises were neither as loud nor as varied as they had been when he left the banquet hall; no doubt many were already senseless from strong drink.

Jacob turned aside and opened a heavy door, his torch revealing a small cell-like room, bare of hangings, with a sort of bunk on one side; there was a single window, heavily barred, and but one door. The Jew thrust the torch into a niche of the wall.

"Was the lord Skol pleased with you, my lord?" he asked nervously.

Cormac cursed. "I rode over a hundred miles to join the most powerful raider in the Taurus, and I find only a wine-bibbing, drunken fool, fit only to howl bloody boasts and blasphemies to the roof."

"Be careful, for God's sake, sir," Jacob shook from head to foot. "These walls have ears! The great prince has these strange moods, but he is a mighty fighter and a crafty man for all that. Do not judge him in his drunkenness. Did—did—did he speak aught of me?"

"Aye," answered Cormac at random, a whimsical grim humor striking him. "He said you only served him in hopes of stealing his ruby some day."

Jacob gasped as if Cormac had hit him in the belly and the sudden pallor of his face told the Norman his chance shot had gone home. The majordomo ducked out of the room like a scared rabbit and it was in somewhat better humor that his tormentor turned to retire.

Looking out the window, Cormac glanced down into the courtyard where the animals were kept, at the stables wherein he had seen that his great black stallion had been placed. Satisfied that the steed was well sheltered for the night, he lay down on the bunk in full armor, with his shield, helmet and sword beside him, as he was wont to sleep in strange holds. He had barred the door from within, but he put little trust in bolts and bars.

CHAPTER 2

Cormac had been asleep less than an hour when a sudden sound brought him wide awake and alert. It was utterly dark in the chamber; even his keen eyes could make out nothing, but someone or something was moving on him in the darkness. He thought of the evil reputation of Bab-el-Shaitan and a momentary shiver shook him—not of fear but of superstitious revulsion.

Then his practical mind asserted itself. It was that fool Toghrul Khan who had slipped into his chamber to cleanse his strange nomadic honor by murdering the man who had been given priority over him. Cormac cautiously drew his legs about and lifted his body until he was sitting on the side of the bunk. At the rattle of his mail, the stealthy sounds ceased, but the Norman could visualize Toghrul Khan's slant eyes glittering snake-like in the dark. Doubtless he had already slit the throat of Jacob the Jew.

As quietly as possible, Cormac eased the heavy sword from its scabbard. Then as the sinister sounds recommenced, he tensed himself, made a swift estimate of location, and leaped like a huge tiger, smiting blindly and terribly in the dark. He had judged correctly. He felt the sword strike solidly, crunching through flesh and bone, and a body fell heavily in the darkness.

Feeling for flint and steel, he struck fire to tinder and lighted the torch, then turning to the crumpled shape in the center of the room, he halted in amazement. The man who lay there in a widening pool of crimson was tall, powerfully built and hairy as an ape—Kadra Muhammad. The Lur's scimitar was in his scabbard, but a wicked dagger lay by his right hand.

"He had no quarrel with me," growled Cormac, puzzled. "What—" He stopped again. The door was still bolted from within, but in what had been a blank wall to the casual gaze, a black opening gaped—a secret doorway through which Kadra Muhammad had come. Cormac closed it and with sudden purpose pulled his coif in place and donned his helmet. Then taking up his shield, he opened the door and strode forth into the torch-lighted corridor. All was silence, broken only by the tramp of his iron-clad feet on the bare flags. The sounds of revelry had ceased and a ghostly stillness hung over Bab-el-Shaitan.

In a few minutes he stood before the door of Skol Abdhur's chamber and saw there what he had half-expected. The Nubian Abdullah lay before the threshold, disemboweled, and his woolly head half severed from his body. Cormac thrust open the door; the candles still burned. On the floor, in the blood-soaked ruins of the torn divan lay the gashed and naked body of Skol Abdhur the Butcher. The corpse was slashed and hacked horribly, but it was evident to Cormac that Skol had died in drunken sleep with no chance to fight for his life. It was some obscure hysteria or frantic hatred that had led his slayer or slayers to so disfigure his dead body. His garments lay near him, ripped to shreds. Cormac smiled grimly, nodding.

"So the Blood of Belshazzar drank your life at last, Skol," said he.

Turning toward the doorway he again scanned the body of the Nubian.

"More than one slew these men," he muttered, "and the Nubian gave scathe to one, at least."

The black still gripped his great scimitar, and the edge was nicked and bloodstained.

At that moment a quick rattle of steps sounded on the flags and the affrighted face of Jacob peered in at the door. His eyes flared wide and he opened his mouth to the widest extent to give vent to an ear-piercing screech.

"Shut up, you fool," snarled Cormac disgusted, but Jacob gibbered wildly.

"Spare my life, most noble lord! I will not tell anyone that you slew Skol—I swear—"

"Be quiet, Jew," growled Cormac. "I did not slay Skol and I will not harm you."

This somewhat reassured Jacob, whose eyes narrowed with sudden avarice.

"Have you found the gem?" he chattered, running into the chamber. "Swift, let us search for it and begone—I should not have shrieked but I feared the noble lord would slay me—yet perchance it was not heard—"

"It was heard," growled the Norman. "And here are the warriors."

The tramp of many hurried feet was heard and a second later the door was thronged with bearded faces. Cormac noted the men blinked and gaped like owls, more like men roused from deep sleep than drunken men. Bleary-eyed, they gripped their weapons and ogled, a ragged, bemused horde. Jacob shrank back, trying to flatten himself against the wall, while Cormac faced them, bloodstained sword still in his hand.

"Allah!" ejaculated a Kurd, rubbing his eyes. "The Frank and the Jew have murdered Skol!"

"A lie," growled Cormac menacingly. "I know not who slew this drunkard."

Tisolino di Strozza came into the chamber, followed by the other chiefs. Cormac saw Nadir Tous, Kojar Mirza, Shalmar Khor, Yussef el Mekru and Justus Zenor. Toghrul Khan, Kai Shah and Musa bin Daoud were nowhere in evidence, and where Kadra Muhammad was, the Norman well knew.

"The jewel!" exclaimed an Armenian excitedly. "Let us look for the gem!"

"Be quiet, fool," snapped Nadir Tous, a light of baffled fury growing in his eyes. "Skol has been stripped; be sure who slew him took the gem."

All eyes turned toward Cormac.

"Skol was a hard master," said Tisolino. "Give us the jewel, lord Cormac, and you may go your way in peace."

Cormac swore angrily; had not, he thought, even as he replied, the Venetian's eyes widened when they first fell on him?

"I have not your cursed jewel; Skol was dead when I came to his room."

"Aye," jeered Kojar Mirza, "and blood still wet on your blade." He pointed accusingly at the weapon in Cormac's hand, whose blue steel, traced with Norse runes, was stained a dull red.

"That is the blood of Kadra Muhammad," growled Cormac, "who stole into my cell to slay me and whose corpse now lies there."

His eyes were fixed with fierce intensity on di Strozza's face but the Venetian's expression altered not a whit.

"I will go to the chamber and see if he speaks truth," said di Strozza, and Nadir Tous smiled a deadly smile.

"You will remain here," said the Persian, and his ruffians closed menacingly around the tall Venetian. "Go you, Selim." And one of his men went grumbling. Di Strozza shot a swift glance of terrible hatred and suppressed wrath at Nadir Tous, then stood imperturbably; but Cormac knew that the Venetian was wild to escape from that room.

"There have been strange things done tonight in Bab-el-Shaitan," growled Shalmar Khor. "Where are Kai Shah and the Syrian—and that pagan from Tartary? And who drugged the wine?"

"Aye!" exclaimed Nadir Tous, "who drugged the wine which sent us all into the sleep from which we but a few moments ago awakened? And how is it that you, di Strozza, were awake when the rest of us slept?"

"I have told you, I drank the wine and fell asleep like the rest of you," answered the Venetian coldly. "I awoke a few moments earlier, that is all, and was going to my chamber when the horde of you came along."

"Mayhap," answered Nadir Tous, "but we had to put a scimitar edge to your throat before you would come with us."

"Why did you wish to come to Skol's chamber anyway?" countered di Strozza.

"Why ," answered the Persian, "when we awoke and realized we had been drugged, Shalmar Khor suggested that we go to Skol's chamber and see if he had flown with the jewel—"

"You lie!" exclaimed the Circassian. "That was Kojar Mirza who said that—"

"Why this delay and argument!" cried Kojar Mirza. "We know this Frank was the last to be admitted to Skol this night. There is blood on his blade—we found him standing above the slain! Cut him down!"

And drawing his scimitar he stepped forward, his warriors surging in behind him. Cormac placed his back to the wall and braced his feet to meet the charge. But it did not come; the tense figure of the giant Norman-Gael was so fraught with brooding menace, the eyes glaring so terribly above the skull-adorned shield, that even the wild Kurd faltered and hesitated, though a score of men thronged the room and many more than that number swarmed in the corridor outside. And as he wavered the Persian Selim elbowed his way through the band, shouting: "The Frank spoke truth! Kadra Muhammad lies dead in the lord Cormac's chamber!"

"That proves nothing," said the Venetian quietly. "He might have slain Skol after he slew the Lur."

An uneasy and bristling silence reigned for an instant. Cormac noted that now Skol lay dead, the different factions made no attempt to conceal their differences. Nadir Tous, Kojar Mirza and Shalmar Khor stood apart from each other and their followers bunched behind them in glaring, weapon-thumbing groups. Yussef el Mekru and Justus Zehor stood aside, looking undecided; only di Strozza seemed oblivious to this cleavage of the robber band.

The Venetian was about to say more, when another figure shouldered men aside and strode in. It was the Seljuk, Kai Shah, and Cormac noted that he lacked his mail shirt and that his garments were different from those he had worn earlier in the night. More, his left arm was bandaged and bound close to his chest and his dark face was somewhat pale.

At the sight of him di Strozza's calm for the first time deserted him; he started violently.

"Where is Musa bin Daoud?" he exclaimed.

"Aye!" answered the Turk angrily. "Where is Musa bin Daoud?"

"I left him with you!" cried di Strozza fiercely, while the others gaped, not understanding this byplay.

"But you planned with him to elude me," accused the Seljuk.

"You are mad!" shouted di Strozza, losing his self-control entirely.

"Mad?" snarled the Turk. "I have been searching for the dog through the dark corridors. If you and he are acting in good faith, why did you not return to the chamber, when you went forth to meet Kadra Muhammad whom we heard coming along the corridor? When you came not back I stepped to the door to peer out for you, and when I turned back, Musa had darted through some secret opening like a rat—"

Di Strozza almost frothed at the mouth. "You fool!" he screamed, "keep silent!"

"I will see you in Gehennum and all our throats cut before I let you cozen me!" roared the Turk, ripping out his scimitar. "What have you done with Musa?"

"You fool of Hell," raved di Strozza, "I have been in this chamber ever since I left you! You knew that Syrian dog would play us false if he got the opportunity and—"

And at that instant when the air was already supercharged with tension, a terrified slave rushed in at a blind, stumbling run, to fall gibbering at di Strozza's feet.

"The gods!" he howled. "The black gods! Aie! The cavern under the floors and the djinn in the rock!"

"What are you yammering about, dog?" roared the Venetian, knocking the slave to the floor with an open-handed blow.

"I found the forbidden door open," screeched the fellow. "A stair goes down—it leads into a fearful cavern with a terrible altar on which frown gigantic demons—and at the foot of the stairs—the lord Musa—"

"What!" di Strozza's eyes blazed and he shook the slave as a dog shakes a rat.

"Dead!" gasped the wretch between chattering teeth.

Cursing terribly, di Strozza knocked men aside in his rush to the door; with a vengeful howl Kai Shah pelted after him, slashing right and left to clear a way. Men gave back from his flashing blade, howling as the keen edge slit their skins. The Venetian and his erstwhile comrade ran down the corridor, di Strozza dragging the screaming slave after him, and the rest of the pack gave tongue in rage and bewilderment and took after them. Cormac swore in amazement and followed, determined to see the mad game through.

Down winding corridors di Strozza led the pack, down broad stairs, until he came to a huge iron door that now swung open. Here the horde hesitated.

"This is in truth the forbidden door," muttered an Armenian. "The brand is on my back that Skol put there merely because I lingered too long before it once."

"Aye," agreed a Persian. "It leads into places once sealed up by the Arabs long ago. None but Skol ever passed through that door—he and the Nubian and the captives who came not forth. It is a haunt of devils."

Di Strozza snarled in disgust and strode through the doorway. He had snatched a torch as he ran and he held this high in one hand. Broad steps showed, leading downward, and cut out of solid rock. They were on the lower floor of the castle; these steps led into the bowels of the earth. As di Strozza strode down, dragging the howling, naked slave, the high-held torch lighting the black stone steps and casting long shadows into the darkness before them, the Venetian looked like a demon dragging a soul into Hell.

Kai Shah was close behind him with his drawn scimitar, with Nadir Tous and Kojar Mirza crowding him close. The ragged crew had, with unaccustomed courtesy, drawn back to let the lord Cormac through and now they followed, uneasily and casting apprehensive glances to all sides.

Many carried torches, and as their light flowed into the depths below a medley of affrighted yells went up. From the darkness huge evil eyes glimmered and titanic shapes loomed vaguely in the gloom. The mob wavered, ready to stampede, but di Strozza strode stolidly downward and the pack called on Allah and followed. Now the light showed a huge cavern in the center of which stood a black and utterly abhorrent altar, hideously stained, and flanked with grinning skulls laid out in strangely systematic lines. The horrific figures were disclosed to be huge images, carved from the solid rock of the cavern walls, strange, bestial, gigantic gods, whose huge eyes of some glassy substance caught the torchlight.

The Celtic blood in Cormac sent a shiver down his spine. Alexander built the foundations of this fortress? Bah—no Grecian ever carved such gods as these. No; an aura of unspeakable antiquity brooded over this grim cavern, as if the forbidden door were a mystic threshold over which the adventurer stepped into an elder world. No wonder mad dreams were here bred in the frenzied brain of Skol Abdhur. These gods were grim vestiges of an older, darker race than Roman or Hellene—a people long faded into the gloom of antiquity. Phrygians—Lydians—Hittites? Or some still more ancient, more abysmal people?

The age of Alexander was as dawn before these ancient figures, yet doubtless he bowed to these gods, as he bowed to many gods before his maddened brain made himself a deity.

At the foot of the stairs lay a crumpled shape—Musa bin Daoud. His face was twisted in horror. A medley of shouts went up: "The djinn have taken the Syrian! Let us begone! This is an evil place!"

"Be silent, you fools!" roared Nadir Tous. "A mortal blade slew Musa—see, he has been slashed through the breast and his bones are broken. See how he lies. Someone slew him and flung him down the stairs—"

The Persian's voice trailed off, as his gaze followed his own pointing fingers. Musa's left arm was outstretched and his fingers had been hacked away.

"He held something in that hand," whispered Nadir Tous. "So hard he gripped it that his slayer was forced to cut off his fingers to obtain it—"

Men thrust torches into niches on the wall and crowded nearer, their superstitious fears forgotten.

"Aye!" exclaimed Cormac, having pieced together some of the bits of the puzzle in his mind. "It was the gem! Musa and Kai Shah and di Strozza killed Skol, and Musa had the gem. There was blood on Abdullah's sword and Kai Shah has a broken arm—shattered by the sweep of the Nubian's great scimitar. Whoever slew Musa has the gem."

Di Strozza screamed like a wounded panther. He shook the wretched slave.

"Dog, have you the gem?"

The slave began a frenzied denial, but his voice broke in a ghastly gurgle as di Strozza, in a very fit of madness, jerked his sword edge across the wretch's throat and flung the blood-spurting body from him. The Venetian whirled on Kai Shah.

"You slew Musa!" he screamed. "He was with you last! You have the gem!"

"You lie!" exclaimed the Turk, his dark face an ashy pallor. "You slew him yourself—"

His words ended in a gasp as di Strozza, foaming at the mouth and all sanity gone from his eyes, ran his sword straight through the Turk's body. Kai Shah swayed like a sapling in the wind; then as di Strozza withdrew the blade, the Seljuk hacked through the Venetian's temple, and as Kai Shah reeled, dying on his feet but clinging to life with the tenacity of the Turk, Nadir Tous leaped like a panther and beneath his flashing scimitar Kai Shah dropped dead across the dead Venetian.

Forgetting all else in his lust for the gem, Nadir Tous bent over his victim, tearing at his garments—bent further as if in a deep salaam and sank down on the dead men, his own skull split to the teeth by Kojar Mirza's stroke. The Kurd bent to search the Turk, but straightened swiftly to meet the attack of Shalmar Khor. In an instant the scene was one of ravening madness, where men hacked and slew and died blindly. The flickering torches lit the scene, and Cormac, backing away toward the stairs, swore amazedly. He had seen men go mad before, but this exceeded anything he had ever witnessed.

Kojar Mirza slew Selim and wounded a Circassian, but Shalmar Khor slashed through his arm-muscles, Justus Zehor ran in and stabbed the Kurd in the ribs, and Kojar Mirza went down, snapping like a dying wolf, to be hacked to pieces.

Justus Zehor and Yussef el Mekru seemed to have taken sides at last; the Georgian had thrown in his lot with Shalmar Khor, while the Arab rallied to him the Kurds and Turks. But besides these loosely knit bands of rivals, various warriors, mainly the Persians of Nadir Tous, raged through the strife, foaming at the mouth and striking all impartially. In an instant a dozen men were down, dying and trampled by the living. Justus Zehor fought with a long knife in each hand and he wrought red havoc before he sank, skull cleft, throat slashed and belly ripped up.

Even while they fought, the warriors had managed to tear to shreds the clothing of Kai Shah and di Strozza. Finding naught there, they howled like wolves and fell to their deadly work with new frenzy. A madness was on them; each time a man fell, others seized him, ripping his garments apart in search for the gem, slashing at each other as they did so.

Cormac saw Jacob trying to steal to the stairs, and even as the Norman decided to withdraw himself, a thought came to the brain of Yussef el Mekru. Arab-like, the Yemenite had fought more coolly than the others, and perhaps he had, even in the frenzy of combat, decided on his own interests. Possibly, seeing that all the leaders were down except Shalmar Khor, he decided it would be best to reunite the band, if possible, and it could be best done by directing their attention against a common foe. Perhaps he honestly thought that since the gem had not been found, Cormac had it. At any rate, the Sheikh suddenly tore away and pointing a lean arm toward the giant figure at the foot of the stairs, screamed: *"Allahu akbar! There stands the thief! Slay the Nazarene!"*

It was good Moslem psychology. There was an instant of bewildered pause in the battle, then a bloodthirsty howl went up and from a tangled battle of rival factions, the brawl became instantly a charge of a solid compact body that rushed wild-eyed on Cormac howling: "Slay the Caphar!"

Cormac snarled in disgusted irritation. He should have anticipated that. No time to escape now; he braced himself and met the charge. A Kurd, rushing in headlong, was impaled on the Norman's long blade, and a giant Circassian, hurling his full weight on the kite-shaped shield, rebounded as from an iron tower. Cormac thundered his battle cry, *"Cloigeand abu,"* (Gaelic: "The skull to victory.") in a deep-toned roar that drowned the howls of the Moslems; he freed his blade and swung the heavy weapon in a crashing arc. Swords shivered to singing sparks and the warriors gave back. They plunged on again as Yussef el Mekru lashed them with burning words. A big Armenian broke his sword on Cormac's helmet and went down with his skull split. A Turk slashed at the Norman's face and howled as his wrist was caught on the Norse sword, and the hand flew from it.

Cormac's defense was his armor, the unshakable immovability of his stance, and his crashing blows. Head bent, eyes glaring above the rim of his shield, he made scant effort to parry or avoid blows. He took them on his helmet or his shield and struck back with thunderous power. Now Shalmar Khor smote full on his helmet with every ounce of his great rangy body behind the blow, and the scimitar bit through the steel cap, notching on the coif links beneath. It was a blow that might have felled an ox, yet Cormac, though half-stunned, stood like a man of iron and struck back with all the power of arm and shoulders. The Circassian flung up his round buckler but it availed not. Cormac's heavy sword sheared through the buckler, severed the arm that held it and crashed full on the Circassian's helmet, shattering both steel cap and the skull beneath.

But fired by fanatical fury as well as greed, the Moslems pressed in. They got behind him. Cormac staggered as a heavy weight landed full on his shoulders. A Kurd had stolen up the stairs and leaped from them full on to the Frank's back. Now he clung like an ape, slavering curses and hacking wildly at Cormac's neck with his long knife.

The Norman's sword was wedged deep in a split breastbone and he struggled fiercely to free it. His hood was saving him so far from the knife strokes of the man on his back, but men were hacking at him from all sides and Yussef el Mekru, foam on his beard, was rushing upon him. Cormac drove his shield upward, catching a frothing Moslem under the chin with the rim and shattering his jawbone, and almost at the same instant the Norman bent his helmeted head forward and jerked it back with all the strength of his mighty neck, and the back of his helmet crushed the face of the Kurd on his back. Cormac felt the clutching arms relax; his sword was free, but a Lur was clinging to his right arm—they hemmed him in so he could not step back, and Yussef el Mekru was hacking at his face and throat. He set his teeth and lifted his sword-arm, swinging the clinging Lur clear of the floor. Yussef's scimitar rasped on his bent helmet—his hauberk—his coif links—the Arab's swordplay was like the flickering of light and in a moment it was inevitable that the flaming blade would sink home. And still the Lur clung, ape-like, to Cormac's mighty arm.

Something whispered across the Norman's shoulder and thudded solidly. Yussef el Mekru gasped and swayed, clawing at the thick shaft that protruded from his heavy beard. Blood burst from his parted lips and he fell dying. The man clinging to Cormac's arm jerked convulsively and fell away. The press slackened. Cormac, panting, stepped back and gained the stairs. A glance upward showed him Toghrul Khan standing on the landing bending a heavy bow. The Norman hesitated; at that range the Mongol could drive a shaft through his mail.

"Haste, *bogatyr,*" came the nomad's gutturals. "Up the stairs!"

At that instant Jacob started running fleetly for the darkness beyond the flickering torches; three steps he took before the bow twanged. The Jew screamed and went down as though struck by a giant's hand; the shaft had struck between his fat shoulders and gone clear through him.

Cormac was backing warily up the stairs, facing his foes who clustered at the foot of the steps, dazed and uncertain. Toghrul Khan crouched on the landing, beady eyes a-glitter, shaft on string, and men hesitated. But one dared—a tall Turkoman with the eyes of a mad dog. Whether greed for the gem he thought Cormac carried, or fanatical hate sent him leaping into the teeth of sword and arrow, he sprang howling up the stairs, lifting high a heavy iron-braced shield. Toghrul Khan loosed, but the shaft glanced from the metal work, and Cormac, bracing his legs again, struck downward with all his power. Sparks flashed as the down-crashing sword shattered the shield and dashed the onrushing Turkoman headlong to lie stunned and bloodied at the foot of the stairs.

Then as the warriors fingered their weapons undecidedly, Cormac gained the landing, and Norman and Mongol backed together out of the door which Toghrul Khan slammed behind them. A wild medley of wolfish yells burst out from below and the Mongol, slamming a heavy bolt in place, growled: "Swiftly, *bogatyr*! It will be some minutes before those dog-brothers can batter down the door. Let us begone!"

He led the way at a swift run along a corridor, through a series of chambers, and flung open a barred door. Cormac saw that they had come into the courtyard, flooded now by the gray light of dawn. A man stood near, holding two horses—the great black stallion of Cormac's and the Mongol's wiry roan. Leaning close Cormac saw that the man's face was bandaged so that only one eye showed.

"Haste," Toghrul Khan was urging. "The slave saddled my mount, but yours he could not saddle because of the savagery of the beast. The serf is to go with us."

Cormac made haste to comply; then swinging into the saddle he gave the fellow a hand and the slave sprang up behind him. The strangely assorted companions thundered across the courtyard just as raging figures burst through the doorway through which they had come.

"No sentries at the gates this night," grunted the Mongol.

They pulled up at the wide gates and the slave sprang down to open them. He swung the portals wide, took a single step toward the black stallion and went down, dead before he struck the ground. A crossbow bolt had shattered his skull, and Cormac, wheeling with a curse, saw a Moslem kneeling on one of the bastions, aiming his weapon. Even as he looked, Toghrul Khan rose in his stirrups, drew a shaft to the head and loosed. The Moslem dropped his arbalest and pitched headlong from the battlement.

With a fierce yell the Mongol wheeled away and charged through the gates, Cormac close at his heels. Behind them sounded a wild and wolfish babble as the warriors rushed about the courtyard, seeking to find and saddle mounts.

CHAPTER 3

"Look!" The companions had covered some miles of wild gorges and treacherous slopes, without hearing any sound of pursuit. Toghrul Khan pointed back. The sun had risen in the east, but behind them a red glow rivaled the sun.

"The Gate of Erlik burns," said the Mongol. "They will not hunt us, those dog-brothers. They stopped to loot the castle and fight one another; some fool has set the hold on fire."

"There is much I do not understand," said Cormac slowly. "Let us sift truth from lies. That di Strozza, Kai Shah and Musa killed Skol is evident, also that they sent Kadra Muhammad to slay me—why, I know not. But I do not understand what Kai Shah meant by saying that they heard Kadra Muhammad coming down the corridor, and that di Strozza went forth to meet him, for surely at that moment Kadra Muhammad lay dead on my chamber floor. And I believe that both Kai Shah and the Venetian spoke truth when they denied slaying Musa."

"Aye," acknowledged the Mongol. "Harken, lord Frank: scarcely had you gone up to Skol's chamber last night, when Musa the scribe left the banquet hall and soon returned with slaves who bore a great bowl of spiced wine—prepared in the Syrian way, said the scribe, and the steaming scent of it was pleasant.

"But I noted that neither he nor Kadra Muhammad drank of it, and when Kai Shah and di Strozza plunged in their goblets, they only pretended to drink. So when I raised my goblet to my lips, I sniffed long and secretly and smelled therein a very rare drug—aye, one I had thought was known only to the magicians of Cathay. It makes deep sleep and Musa must have obtained a small quantity in some raid on a caravan from the East. So I did not drink of the wine, but all the others drank saving those I have mentioned, and soon men began to grow drowsy, though the drug acted slowly, being weak in that it was distributed among so many.

"Soon I went to my chamber which a slave showed me, and squatting on my bunk, devised a plan of vengeance in my mind, for because that dog of a Jew put shame upon me before the lords, hot anger burned in my heart so that I could not sleep. Soon I heard one staggering past my door as a drunkard staggers, but this one whined like a dog in pain. I went forth and found a slave whose eye, he said, his master had torn out. I have some knowledge of wounds, so I cleansed and bandaged his empty socket, easing his pain, for which he would have kissed my feet.

"Then I bethought me of the insult which had been put upon me, and desired the slave to show me where slept the fat hog, Jacob. He did so, and marking the chamber in my mind, I turned again and went with the slave into the courtyard where the beasts were kept. None hindered us, for all were in the feasting-hall and their din was growing lesser swiftly. In the stables I found four swift horses, ready saddled—the mounts of di Strozza and his comrades. And the slave told me, furthermore, that there were no guards at the gates that night—di Strozza had bidden all to feast in the great hall. So I bade the slave saddle my steed and have it ready, and also your black stallion which I coveted.

"Then I returned into the castle and heard no sound; all those who had drunk of the wine slept in the sleep of the drug. I mounted to the upper corridors, even to Jacob's chamber, but when I entered to slit his fat throat, he was not sleeping there. I think he was guzzling wine with the slaves in some lower part of the castle.

"I went along the corridors searching for him, and suddenly saw ahead of me a chamber door partly open, through which shone light, and I heard the voice of the Venetian speak: 'Kadra Muhammad is approaching; I will bid him hasten.'

"I did not desire to meet these men, so I turned quickly down a side corridor, hearing di Strozza call the name of Kadra Muhammad softly and as if puzzled. Then he came swiftly down the corridor, as if to see whose footfalls it was he heard, and I went hurriedly before him, crossing the landing of a wide stair which led up from the feasting-hall, and entered another corridor where I halted in the shadows and watched.

"Di Strozza came to the landing and paused, like a man bewildered, and at that moment an outcry went up from below. The Venetian turned to escape but the waking drunkards had seen him. Just as I had thought, the drug was too weak to keep them sleeping long, and now they realized they had been drugged and stormed bewilderedly up the stairs and laid hold on di Strozza, accusing him of many things and making him accompany them to Skol's chamber. Me they did not spy.

"Still seeking Jacob, I went swiftly down the corridor at random and coming onto a narrow stairway, came at last to the ground floor and a dark tunnel-like corridor which ran past a most strange door. And then sounded quick footsteps and as I drew back in the shadows, there came one in panting haste—the Syrian Musa, who gripped a scimitar in his right hand and something hidden in his left.

"He fumbled with the door until it opened; then lifting his head, he saw me and crying out wildly he slashed at me with his scimitar. Erlik! I had no quarrel with the man, but he was as one maddened by fear. I struck with the naked steel, and he, being close to the landing inside the door, pitched headlong down the stairs.

"Then I was desirous of learning what he held so tightly in his left hand, so I followed him down the stairs. Erlik! That was an evil place, dark and full of glaring eyes and strange shadows. The hair on my head stood up but I gripped my steel, calling on the Lords of Darkness and the high places. Musa's dead hand still gripped what he held so firmly that I was forced to cut off the fingers. Then I went back up the stairs and out the same way by which we later escaped from the castle, and found the slave ready with my mount, but unable to saddle yours.

"I was loath to depart without avenging my insult, and as I lingered I heard the clash of steel within the hold. And I stole back and came to the forbidden stair again while the fighting was fiercest below. All were assailing you, and though my heart was hot against you, because you had been given preference over me, I warmed to your valor. Aye, you are a hero, *bogatyr*!"

"Then it was thus, apparently," mused the Frank, "di Strozza and his comrades had it well planned out—they drugged the wine, called the guards from the walls, and had their horses ready for swift flight. As I had not drunk the drugged wine, they sent the Lur to slay me. The other three killed Skol and in the fight Kai Shah was wounded—Musa took the gem doubtless because neither Kai Shah nor the Venetian would trust it to the other.

"After the murder, they must have retired into a chamber to bandage Kai Shah's arm, and while there they heard you coming along the corridor and thought it the Lur. Then when di Strozza followed he was seized by the waking bandits, as you say—no wonder he was wild to be gone from Skol's chamber! And meanwhile Musa gave Kai Shah the slip somehow, meaning to have the gem for himself. But what of the gem?"

"Look!" the nomad held out his hand in which a sinister crimson glow throbbed and pulsed like a living thing in the early sun.

"The Blood of Belshazzar," said Toghrul Khan. "Greed for this slew Skol and fear born of this evil thing slew Musa; for, escaping from his comrades, he thought the hand of all men against him and attacked me, when he could have gone on unmolested. Did he think to remain hidden in the cavern until he could slip away, or does some tunnel admit to outer air?

"Well, this red stone is evil—one can not eat it or drink it or clothe himself with it, or use it as a weapon, yet many men have died for it. Look—I will cast it away." The Mongol turned to fling the gem over the verge of the dizzy precipice past which they were riding. Cormac caught his arm.

"Nay—if you do not want it, let me have it."

"Willingly," but the Mongol frowned. "My brother would wear the gaud?"

Cormac laughed shortly and Toghrul Khan smiled.

"I understand; you will buy favor from your sultan."

"Bah!" Cormac growled, "I buy favor with my sword. No." He grinned, well pleased. "This trinket will pay the ransom of Sir Rupert de Vaile to the chief who now holds him captive."

LORD OF SAMARCAND

The roar of battle had died away; the sun hung like a ball of crimson gold on the western hills. Across the trampled field of battle no squadrons thundered, no war-cry reverberated. Only the shrieks of the wounded and the moans of the dying rose to the circling vultures whose black wings swept closer and closer until they brushed the pallid faces in their flight.

On his rangy stallion, in a hillside thicket, Ak Boga the Tatar watched, as he had watched since dawn, when the mailed hosts of the Franks, with their forest of lances and flaming pennons, had moved out on the plains of Nicopolis to meet the grim hordes of Bayazid.

Ak Boga, watching their battle array, had chk-chk'd his teeth in surprize and disapproval as he saw the glittering squadrons of mounted knights draw out in front of the compact masses of stalwart infantry, and lead the advance. They were the flower of Europe—cavaliers of Austria, Germany, France and Italy; but Ak Boga shook his head.

He had seen the knights charge with a thunderous roar that shook the heavens, had seen them smite the outriders of Bayazid like a withering blast and sweep up the long slope in the teeth of a raking fire from the Turkish archers at the crest. He had seen them cut down the archers like ripe corn, and launch their whole power against the oncoming spahis, the Turkish light cavalry. And he had seen the spahis buckle and break and scatter like spray before a storm, the light-armed riders flinging aside their lances and spurring like mad out of the mêlée. But Ak Boga had looked back, where, far behind, the sturdy Hungarian pikemen toiled, seeking to keep within supporting distance of the headlong cavaliers.

He had seen the Frankish horsemen sweep on, reckless of their horses' strength as of their own lives, and cross the ridge. From his vantage-point Ak Boga could see both sides of that ridge and he knew that there lay the main power of the Turkish army—sixty-five thousand strong—the janizaries, the terrible Ottoman infantry, supported by the heavy cavalry, tall men in strong armor, bearing spears and powerful bows.

And now the Franks realized, what Ak Boga had known, that the real battle lay before them; and their horses were weary, their lances broken, their throats choked with dust and thirst.

Ak Boga had seen them waver and look back for the Hungarian infantry; but it was out of sight over the ridge, and in desperation the knights hurled themselves on the massed enemy, striving to break the ranks by sheer ferocity. That charge never reached the grim lines. Instead a storm of arrows broke the Christian front, and this time, on exhausted horses, there was no riding against it. The whole first rank went down, horses and men pincushioned, and in that red shambles their comrades behind them stumbled and fell headlong. And then the janizaries charged with a deep-toned roar of "Allah!" that was like the thunder of deep surf.

All this Ak Boga had seen; had seen, too, the inglorious flight of some of the knights, the ferocious resistance of others. On foot, leaguered and outnumbered, they fought with sword and ax, falling one by one, while the tide of battle flowed around them on either side and the blood-drunken Turks fell upon the infantry which had just toiled into sight over the ridge.

There, too, was disaster. Flying knights thundered through the ranks of the Wallachians, and these broke and retired in ragged disorder. The Hungarians and Bavarians received the brunt of the Turkish onslaught, staggered and fell back stubbornly, contesting every foot, but unable to check the victorious flood of Moslem fury.

And now, as Ak Boga scanned the field, he no longer saw the serried lines of the pikemen and ax-fighters. They had fought their way back over the ridge and were in full, though ordered, retreat, and the Turks had come back to loot the dead and mutilate the dying. Such knights as had not fallen or broken away in flight, had flung down the hopeless sword and surrendered. Among the trees on the farther side of the vale, the main Turkish host was clustered, and even Ak Boga shivered a trifle at the screams which rose where Bayazid's swordsmen were butchering the captives. Nearer at hand ran ghoulish figures, swift and furtive, pausing briefly over each heap of corpses; here and there gaunt dervishes with foam on their beards and madness in their eyes plied their knives on writhing victims who screamed for death.

"Erlik!" muttered Ak Boga. "They boasted that they could hold up the sky on their lances, were it to fall, and lo, the sky has fallen and their host is meat for the ravens!"

He reined his horse away through the thicket; there might be good plunder among the plumed and corseleted dead, but Ak Boga had come hither on a mission which was yet to be completed. But even as he emerged from the thicket, he saw a prize no Tatar could forego—a tall Turkish steed with an ornate high-peaked Turkish saddle came racing by. Ak Boga spurred quickly forward and caught the flying, silver-worked rein. Then, leading the restive charger, he trotted swiftly down the slope away from the battlefield.

Suddenly he reined in among a clump of stunted trees. The hurricane of strife, slaughter and pursuit had cast its spray on this side of the ridge. Before him Ak Boga saw a tall, richly clad knight grunting and cursing as he sought to hobble along using his broken lance as a crutch. His helmet was gone, revealing a blond head and a florid choleric face. Not far away lay a dead horse, an arrow protruding from its ribs.

As Ak Boga watched, the big knight stumbled and fell with a scorching oath. Then from the bushes came a man such as Ak Boga had never seen before, even among the Franks. This man was taller than Ak Boga, who was a big man, and his stride was like that of a gaunt gray wolf. He was bareheaded, a tousled shock of tawny hair topping a sinister scarred face, burnt dark by the sun, and his eyes were cold as gray icy steel. The great sword he trailed was crimson to the hilt, his rusty scale-mail shirt hacked and rent, the kilt beneath it torn and slashed. His right arm was stained to the elbow, and blood dripped sluggishly from a deep gash in his left forearm.

"Devil take all!" growled the crippled knight in Norman French, which Ak Boga understood; "this is the end of the world!"

"Only the end of a horde of fools," the tall Frank's voice was hard and cold, like the rasp of a sword in its scabbard.

The lame man swore again. "Stand not there like a blockhead, fool! Catch me a horse! My damnable steed caught a shaft in its cursed hide, and though I spurred it until the blood spurted over my heels, it fell at last, and I think, broke my ankle."

The tall one dropped his sword-point to the earth and stared at the other somberly.

"You give commands as though you sat in your own fief of Saxony, Lord Baron Frederik! But for you and divers other fools, we had cracked Bayazid like a nut this day."

"Dog!" roared the baron, his intolerant face purpling; "this insolence to me? I'll have you flayed alive!"

"Who but you cried down the Elector in council?" snarled the other, his eyes glittering dangerously. "Who called Sigismund of Hungary a fool because he urged that the lord allow him to lead the assault with his infantry? And who but you had the ear of that young fool High Constable of France, Philip of Artois, so that in the end he led the charge that ruined us all, nor would wait on the ridge for support from the Hungarians? And now you, who turned tail quicker than any when you saw what your folly had done, you bid me fetch you a horse!"

"Aye, and quickly, you Scottish dog!" screamed the baron, convulsed with fury. "You shall answer for this—"

"I'll answer here," growled the Scotsman, his manner changing murderously. "You have heaped insults on me since we first sighted the Danube. If I'm to die, I'll settle one score first!"

"Traitor!" bellowed the baron, whitening, scrambling up on his knee and reaching for his sword. But even as he did so, the Scotsman struck, with an oath, and the baron's roar was cut short in a ghastly gurgle as the great blade sheared through shoulder-bone, ribs and spine, casting the mangled corpse limply upon the blood-soaked earth.

"Well struck, warrior!" At the sound of the guttural voice the slayer wheeled like a great wolf, wrenching free the sword. For a tense moment the two eyed each other, the swordsman standing above his victim, a brooding somber figure terrible with potentialities of blood and slaughter, the Tatar sitting his high-peaked saddle like a carven image.

"I am no Turk," said Ak Boga. "You have no quarrel with me. See, my scimitar is in its sheath. I have need of a man like you—strong as a bear, swift as a wolf, cruel as a falcon. I can bring you to much you desire."

"I desire only vengeance on the head of Bayazid," rumbled the Scotsman.

The dark eyes of the Tatar glittered.

"Then come with me. For my lord is the sworn enemy of the Turk."

"Who is your lord?" asked the Scotsman suspiciously.

"Men call him the Lame," answered Ak Boga. "Timour, the Servant of God, by the favor of Allah, Amir of Tatary."

The Scotsman turned his head in the direction of the distant shrieks which told that the massacre was still continuing, and stood for an instant like a great bronze statue. Then he sheathed his sword with a savage rasp of steel.

"I will go," he said briefly.

The Tatar grinned with pleasure, and leaning forward, gave into his hands the reins of the Turkish horse. The Frank swung into the saddle and glanced inquiringly at Ak Boga. The Tatar motioned with his helmeted head and reined away down the slope. They touched in the spurs and cantered swiftly away into the gathering twilight, while behind them the shrieks of dire agony still rose to the shivering stars which peered palely out, as if frightened by man's slaughter of man.

CHAPTER 2

"Had we twa been upon the green,
And never an eye to see,
I wad hae had you, flesh and fell;
But your sword shall gae wi' me."
—*The Ballad of Otterbourne.*

Again the sun was sinking, this time over a desert, etching the spires and minarets of a blue city. Ak Boga drew rein on the crest of a rise and sat motionless for a moment, sighing deeply as he drank in the familiar sight, whose wonder never faded.

"Samarcand," said Ak Boga.

"We have ridden far," answered his companion. Ak Boga smiled. The Tatar's garments were dusty, his mail tarnished, his face somewhat drawn, though his eyes still twinkled. The Scotsman's strongly chiseled features had not altered.

"You are of steel, bogatyr," said Ak Boga. "The road we have traveled would have wearied a courier of Genghis Khan. And by Erlik, I, who was bred in the saddle, am the wearier of the twain!"

The Scotsman gazed unspeaking at the distant spires, remembering the days and nights of apparently endless riding, when he had slept swaying in the saddle, and all the sounds of the universe had died down to the thunder of hoofs. He had followed Ak Boga unquestioning: through hostile hills where they avoided trails and cut through the blind wilderness, over mountains where the chill winds cut like a sword-edge, into stretches of steppes and desert. He had not questioned when Ak Boga's relaxing vigilance told him that they were out of hostile country, and when the Tatar began to stop at wayside posts where tall dark men in iron helmets brought fresh steeds. Even then there was no slacking of the headlong pace: a swift guzzling of wine and snatching of food; occasionally a brief interlude of sleep, on a heap of hides and cloaks; then again the drum of racing hoofs. The Frank knew that Ak Boga was bearing the news of the battle to his mysterious lord, and he wondered at the distance they had covered between the first post where saddled steeds awaited them and the blue spires that marked their journey's end. Wide-flung indeed were the boundaries of the lord called Timour the Lame.

They had covered that vast expanse of country in a time the Frank would have sworn impossible. He felt now the grinding wear of that terrible ride, but he gave no outward sign. The city shimmered to his gaze, mingling with the blue of the distance, so that it seemed part of the horizon, a city of illusion and enchantment. Blue: the Tatars lived in a wide magnificent land, lavish with color schemes, and the prevailing motif was blue. In the spires and domes of Samarcand were mirrored the hues of the skies, the far mountains and the dreaming lakes.

"You have seen lands and seas no Frank has beheld," said Ak Boga, "and rivers and towns and caravan trails. Now you shall gaze upon the glory of Samarcand, which the lord Timour found a town of dried brick and has made a metropolis of blue stone and ivory and marble and silver filigree."

The two descended into the plain and threaded their way between converging lines of camel-caravans and mule-trains whose robed drivers shouted incessantly, all bound for the Turquoise Gates, laden with spices, silks, jewels, and slaves, the goods and gauds of India and Cathay, of Persia and Arabia and Egypt.

"All the East rides the road to Samarcand," said Ak Boga.

They passed through the wide gilt-inlaid gates where the tall spearmen shouted boisterous greetings to Ak Boga, who yelled back, rolling in his saddle and smiting his mailed thigh with the joy of homecoming. They rode through the wide winding streets, past palace and market and mosque, and bazaars thronged with the people of a hundred tribes and races, bartering, disputing, shouting. The Scotsman saw hawk-faced Arabs, lean apprehensive Syrians, fat fawning Jews, turbaned Indians, languid Persians, ragged swaggering but suspicious Afghans, and more unfamiliar forms; figures from the mysterious reaches of the north, and the far east; stocky Mongols with broad inscrutable faces and the rolling gait of an existence spent in the saddle; slant-eyed Cathayans in robes of watered silk; tall quarrelsome Vigurs; round-faced Kipchaks;

narrow-eyed Kirghiz; a score of races whose existence the West did not guess. All the Orient flowed in a broad river through the gates of Samarcand.

The Frank's wonder grew; the cities of the West were hovels compared to this. Past academies, libraries and pleasure-pavilions they rode, and Ak Boga turned into a wide gateway, guarded by silver lions. There they gave their steeds into the hands of silk-sashed grooms, and walked along a winding avenue paved with marble and lined with slim green trees. The Scotsman, looking between the slender trunks, saw shimmering expanses of roses, cherry trees and waving exotic blossoms unknown to him, where fountains jetted arches of silver spray. So they came to the palace, gleaming blue and gold in the sunlight, passed between tall marble columns and entered the chambers with their gilt-worked arched doorways, and walls decorated with delicate paintings of Persian and Cathayan artists, and the gold tissue and silver work of Indian artistry.

Ak Boga did not halt in the great reception room with its slender carven columns and frieze-work of gold and turquoise, but continued until he came to the fretted gold-adorned arch of a door which opened into a small blue-domed chamber that looked out through gold-barred windows into a series of broad, shaded, marble-paved galleries. There silk-robed courtiers took their weapons, and grasping their arms, led them between files of giant black mutes in silken loincloths, who held two-handed scimitars upon their shoulders, and into the chamber, where the courtiers released their arms and fell back, salaaming deeply. Ak Boga knelt before the figure on the silken divan, but the Scotsman stood grimly erect, nor was obeisance required of him. Some of the simplicity of Genghis Khan's court still lingered in the courts of these descendants of the nomads.

The Scotsman looked closely at the man on the divan; this, then, was the mysterious Tamerlane, who was already becoming a mythical figure in Western lore. He saw a man as tall as himself, gaunt but heavy-boned, with a wide sweep of shoulders and the Tatar's characteristic depth of chest. His face was not as dark as Ak Boga's, nor did his black magnetic eyes slant; and he did not sit cross-legged as a Mongol sits. There was power in every line of his figure, in his clean-cut features, in the crisp black hair and beard, untouched with gray despite his sixty-one years. There was something of the Turk in his appearance, thought the Scotsman, but the dominant note was the lean wolfish hardness that suggested the nomad. He was closer to the basic Turanian rootstock than was the Turk; nearer to the wolfish, wandering Mongols who were his ancestors.

"Speak, Ak Boga," said the Amir in a deep powerful voice. "Ravens have flown westward, but there has come no word."

"We rode before the word, my lord," answered the warrior. "The news is at our heels, traveling swift on the caravan roads. Soon the couriers, and after them the traders and the merchants, will bring to you the news that a great battle has been fought in the west; that Bayazid has broken the hosts of the Christians, and the wolves howl over the corpses of the kings of Frankistan."

"And who stands beside you?" asked Timour, resting his chin on his hand and fixing his deep somber eyes on the Scotsman.

"A chief of the Franks who escaped the slaughter," answered Ak Boga. "Single-handed he cut his way through the mêlée, and in his flight paused to slay a Frankish lord who had put shame upon him aforetime. He has no fear and his thews are steel. By Allah, we passed through the land out-racing the wind to bring thee news of the war, and this Frank is less weary than I, who learned to ride ere I learned to walk."

"Why do you bring him to me?"

"It was my thought that he would make a mighty warrior for thee, my lord."

"In all the world," mused Timour, "there are scarce half a dozen men whose judgment I trust. Thou art one of those," he added briefly, and Ak Boga, who had flushed darkly in embarrassment, grinned delightedly.

"Can he understand me?" asked Timour.

"He speaks Turki, my lord."

"How are you named, oh Frank?" queried the Amir. "And what is your rank?"

"I am called Donald MacDeesa," answered the Scotsman. "I come from the country of Scotland, beyond Frankistan. I have no rank, either in my own land or in the army I followed. I live by my wits and the edge of my claymore."

"Why do you ride to me?"

"Ak Boga told me it was the road to vengeance."

"Against whom?"

"Bayazid the Sultan of the Turks, whom men name the Thunderer."

Timour dropped his head on his mighty breast for a space and in the silence MacDeesa heard the silvery tinkle of a fountain in an outer court and the musical voice of a Persian poet singing to a lute.

Then the great Tatar lifted his lion's head.

"Sit ye with Ak Boga upon this divan close at my hand," said he. "I will instruct you how to trap a gray wolf."

As Donald did so, he unconsciously lifted a hand to his face, as if he felt the sting of a blow eleven years old. Irrelevantly his mind reverted to another king and another, ruder court, and in the swift instant that elapsed as he took his seat close to the Amir, glanced fleetingly along the bitter trail of his life.

Young Lord Douglas, most powerful of all the Scottish barons, was headstrong and impetuous, and like most Norman lords, choleric when he fancied himself crossed. But he should not have struck the lean young Highlander who had come down into the border country seeking fame and plunder in the train of the lords of the marches. Douglas was accustomed to using both riding-whip and fists freely on his pages and esquires, and promptly forgetting both the blow and the cause; and they, being also Normans and accustomed to the tempers of their lords, likewise forgot. But Donald MacDeesa was no Norman; he was a Gael, and Gaelic ideas of honor and insult differ from Norman ideas as the wild uplands of the North differ from the fertile plains of the Lowlands. The chief of Donald's clan could not have struck him with impunity, and for a Southron to so venture—hate entered the young Highlander's blood like a black river and filled his dreams with crimson nightmares.

Douglas forgot the blow too quickly to regret it. But Donald's was the vengeful heart of those wild folk who keep the fires of feud flaming for centuries and carry grudges to the grave. Donald was as fully Celtic as his savage Dalriadian ancestors who carved out the kingdom of Alba with their swords.

But he hid his hate and bided his time, and it came in a hurricane of border war. Robert Bruce lay in his tomb, and his heart, stilled forever, lay somewhere in Spain beneath the body of Black Douglas, who had failed in the pilgrimage which was to place the heart of his king before the Holy Sepulcher. The great king's grandson, Robert II, had little love for storm and stress; he desired peace with England and he feared the great family of Douglas.

But despite his protests, war spread flaming wings along the border and the Scottish lords rode joyfully on the foray. But before the Douglas marched, a quiet and subtle man came to Donald MacDeesa's tent and spoke briefly and to the point.

"Knowing that the aforesaid lord hath put despite upon thee, I whispered thy name softly to him that sendeth me, and sooth, it is well known that this same bloody lord doth continually embroil the kingdoms and stir up wrath and woe between the sovereigns—" he said in part, and he plainly spoke the word, "Protection."

Donald made no answer and the quiet person smiled and left the young Highlander sitting with his chin on his fist, staring grimly at the floor of his tent.

Thereafter Lord Douglas marched right gleefully with his retainers into the border country and "burned the dales of Tyne, and part of Bambroughshire, and three good towers on Reidswire fells, he left them all on fire," and spread wrath and woe generally among the border English, so that King Richard sent notes of bitter reproach to King Robert, who bit his nails with rage, but waited patiently for news he expected to hear.

Then after an indecisive skirmish at Newcastle, Douglas encamped in a place called Otterbourne, and there Lord Percy, hot with wrath, came suddenly upon him in the night, and in the confused mêlée which ensued, called by the Scottish the Battle of Otterbourne and by the English Chevy Chase, Lord Douglas fell. The English swore he was slain by Lord Percy, who neither confirmed nor denied it, not knowing himself what men he had slain in the confusion and darkness.

But a wounded man babbled of a Highland plaid, before he died, and an ax wielded by no English hand. Men came to Donald and questioned him hardly, but he snarled at them like a wolf, and the king, after piously burning many candles for Douglas' soul in public, and thanking God for the baron's demise in the privacy of his chamber, announced that "we have heard of this persecution of a loyal subject and it being plain in our mind that this youth is innocent as ourselves in this matter we hereby warn all men against further hounding of him at pain of death."

So the king's protection saved Donald's life, but men muttered in their teeth and ostracized him. Sullen and embittered, he withdrew to himself and brooded in a hut alone, till one night there came news of the king's sudden abdication and retirement into a monastery. The stress of a monarch's life in those stormy times was too much for the monkish sovereign. Close on the heels of the news came men with drawn daggers to Donald's hut, but they found the cage empty. The hawk had flown, and though they followed his trail with reddened spurs, they found only a steed that had fallen dead at the seashore, and saw only a white sail dwindling in the growing dawn.

Donald went to the Continent because, with the Lowlands barred to him, there was nowhere else to go; in the Highlands he had too many blood-feuds; and across the border the English had already made a noose for him. That was in 1389. Seven years of fighting and intriguing in European wars and plots. And when Constantinople cried out before the irresistible onslaught of Bayazid, and men pawned their lands to launch a new Crusade, the Highland swordsman had joined the tide that swept eastward to its doom. Seven years—and a far cry from the border marches to the blue-domed palaces of fabulous Samarcand, reclining on a silken divan as he listened to the measured words which flowed in a tranquil monotone from the lips of the lord of Tatary.

CHAPTER 3

"If thou'rt the lord of this castle,
Sae well it pleases me:
For, ere I cross the border fells,
The tane of us shall dee."

—*Battle of Otterbourne.*

Time flowed on as it does whether men live or die. The bodies rotted on the plains of Nicopolis, and Bayazid, drunk with power, trampled the scepters of the world. The Greeks, the Serbs and the Hungarians he ground beneath his iron legions, and into his spreading empire he molded the captive races. He laved his limbs in wild debauchery, the frenzy of which astounded even his tough vassals. The women of the world flowed whimpering between his iron fingers and he hammered the golden crowns of kings to shoe his war-steed. Constantinople reeled beneath his strokes, and Europe licked her wounds like a crippled wolf, held at bay on the defensive. Somewhere in the misty mazes of the East moved his arch-foe Timour, and to him Bayazid sent missives of threat and mockery. No response was forthcoming, but word came along the caravans of a mighty marching and a great war in the south; of the plumed helmets of India scattered and flying before the Tatar spears. Little heed gave Bayazid; India was little more real to him than it was to the Pope of Rome. His eyes were turned westward toward the Caphar cities. "I will harrow

Frankistan with steel and flame," he said. "Their sultans shall draw my chariots and the bats lair in the palaces of the infidels."

Then in the early spring of 1402 there came to him, in an inner court of his pleasure-palace at Brusa, where he lolled guzzling the forbidden wine and watching the antics of naked dancing girls, certain of his emirs, bringing a tall Frank whose grim scarred visage was darkened by the suns of far deserts.

"This Caphar dog rode into the camp of the janizaries as a madman rides, on a foam-covered steed," said they, "saying he sought Bayazid. Shall we flay him before thee, or tear him between wild horses?"

"Dog," said the Sultan, drinking deeply and setting down the goblet with a satisfied sigh, "you have found Bayazid. Speak, ere I set you howling on a stake."

"Is this fit welcome for one who has ridden far to serve you?" retorted the Frank in a harsh unshaken voice. "I am Donald MacDeesa and among your janizaries there is no man who can stand up against me in swordplay, and among your barrel-bellied wrestlers there is no man whose back I can not break."

The Sultan tugged his black beard and grinned.

"Would thou wert not an infidel," said he, "for I love a man with a bold tongue. Speak on, oh Rustum! What other accomplishments are thine, mirror of modesty?"

The Highlander grinned like a wolf.

"I can break the back of a Tatar and roll the head of a Khan in the dust."

Bayazid stiffened, subtly changing, his giant frame charged with dynamic power and menace; for behind all his roistering and bellowing conceit was the keenest brain west of the Oxus.

"What folly is this?" he rumbled. "What means this riddle?"

"I speak no riddle," snapped the Gael. "I have no more love for you than you for me. But more I hate Timour-il-leng who has cast dung in my face."

"You come to me from that half-pagan dog?"

"Aye. I was his man. I rode beside him and cut down his foes. I climbed city walls in the teeth of the arrows and broke the ranks of mailed spearmen. And when the honors and gifts were distributed among the emirs, what was given me? The gall of mockery and the wormwood of insult. 'Ask thy dog-sultans of Frankistan for gifts, Caphar,' said

Timour—may the worms devour him—and the emirs roared with laughter. As God is my witness, I will wipe out that laughter in the crash of falling walls and the roar of flames!"

Donald's menacing voice reverberated through the chamber and his eyes were cold and cruel. Bayazid pulled his beard for a space and said, "And you come to me for vengeance? Shall I war against the Lame One because of the spite of a wandering Caphar vagabond?"

"You *will* war against him, or he against you," answered MacDeesa. "When Timour wrote asking that you lend no aid to his foes, Kara Yussef the Turkoman, and Ahmed, Sultan of Bagdad, you answered him with words not to be borne, and sent horsemen to stiffen their ranks against him. Now the Turkomans are broken, Bagdad has been looted and Damascus lies in smoking ruins. Timour has broken your allies and he will not forget the despite you put upon him."

"Close have you been to the Lame One to know all this," muttered Bayazid, his glittering eyes narrowing with suspicion. "Why should I trust a Frank? By Allah, I deal with them by the sword! As I dealt with those fools at Nicopolis!"

A fierce uncontrollable flame leaped up for a fleeting instant in the Highlander's eyes, but the dark face showed no sign of emotion.

"Know this, Turk," he answered with an oath, "I can show you how to break Timour's back."

"Dog!" roared the Sultan, his gray eyes blazing, "think you I need the aid of a nameless rogue to conquer the Tatar?"

Donald laughed in his face, a hard mirthless laugh that was not pleasant.

"Timour will crack you like a walnut," said he deliberately. "Have you seen the Tatars in war array? Have you seen their arrows darkening the sky as they loosed, a hundred thousand as one? Have you seen their horsemen flying before the wind as they charged home and the desert shook beneath their hoofs? Have you seen the array of their elephants, with towers on their backs, whence archers send shafts in black clouds and the fire that burns flesh and leather alike pours forth?"

"All this I have heard," answered the Sultan, not particularly impressed.

"But you have not seen," returned the Highlander; he drew back his tunic sleeve and displayed a scar on his iron-thewed arm. "An Indian tulwar kissed me there, before Delhi. I rode with the emirs when the whole world seemed to shake with the thunder of combat. I saw Timour trick the Sultan of Hindustan and draw him from the lofty walls as a serpent is drawn from its lair. By God, the plumed Rajputs fell like ripened grain before us!

"Of Delhi Timour left a pile of deserted ruins, and without the broken walls he built a pyramid of a hundred thousand skulls. You would say I lied were I to tell you how many days the Khyber Pass was thronged with the glittering hosts of warriors and captives returning along the road to Samarcand. The mountains shook with their tread and the wild Afghans came down in hordes to place their heads beneath Timour's heel—as he will grind *thy* head underfoot, Bayazid!"

"This to me, dog?" yelled the Sultan. "I will fry you in oil!"

"Aye, prove your power over Timour by slaying the dog he mocked," answered MacDeesa bitterly. "You kings are all alike in fear and folly."

Bayazid gaped at him. "By Allah!" he said, "thou'rt mad to speak thus to the Thunderer. Bide in my court until I learn whether thou be rogue, fool, or madman. If spy, not in a day or three days will I slay thee, but for a full week shalt thou howl for death."

So Donald abode in the court of the Thunderer, under suspicion, and soon there came a brief but peremptory note from Timour, asking that "the thief of a Christian who hath taken refuge in the Ottoman court" be given up for just punishment. Whereat Bayazid, scenting an opportunity to further insult his rival, twisted his black beard gleefully between his fingers and grinned like a hyena as he dictated a reply, "Know, thou crippled dog, that the Osmanli are not in the habit of conceding to the insolent demands of pagan foes. Be at ease while thou mayest, oh lame dog, for soon I will take thy kingdom for an offal-heap and thy favorite wives for my concubines."

No further missives came from Timour. Bayazid drew Donald into wild revels, plied him with strong drink and even as he roared and roistered, he keenly watched the Highlander. But even his suspicions grew blunter when at his drunkest Donald spoke no word that might hint he was other than he seemed. He breathed the name of Timour only with curses. Bayazid discounted the value of his aid against the Tatars, but contemplated putting him to use, as Ottoman sultans always employed foreigners for confidants and guardsmen, knowing their own race too well. Under close, subtle scrutiny the Gael indifferently moved, drinking all but the Sultan onto the floor in the wild drinking-bouts and bearing himself with a reckless valor that earned the respect of the hard-bitten Turks, in forays against the Byzantines.

Playing Genoese against Venetian, Bayazid lay about the walls of Constantinople. His preparations were made: Constantinople, and after that, Europe; the fate of Christendom wavered in the balance, there before the walls of the ancient city of the East. And the wretched Greeks, worn and starved, had already drawn up a capitulation, when word came flying out of the East, a dusty, bloodstained courier on a staggering horse. Out of the East, sudden as a desert-storm, the Tatars had swept, and Sivas, Bayazid's border city, had fallen. That night the shuddering people on the walls of Constantinople saw torches and cressets tossing and moving through the Turkish camp, gleaming on dark hawk-faces and polished armor, but the expected attack did not come, and dawn revealed a great flotilla of boats moving in a steady double stream back and forth across the Bosphorus, bearing the mailed warriors into Asia. The Thunderer's eyes were at last turned eastward.

CHAPTER 4

"The deer runs wild on hill and dale,
The birds fly wild from tree to tree;
But there is neither bread nor kale,
To fend my men and me."

—Battle of *Otterbourne.*

"Here we will camp," said Bayazid, shifting his giant body in the gold-crusted saddle. He glanced back at the long lines of his army, winding beyond sight over the distant hills: over 200,000 fighting men; grim janizaries, spahis glittering in plumes and silver mail, heavy cavalry in silk and steel; and his allies and alien subjects, Greek and Wallachian pikemen, the twenty thousand horsemen of King Peter Lazarus of Serbia, mailed from crown to heel; there were troops of Tatars, too, who had wandered into Asia Minor and been ground into the Ottoman empire with the rest—stocky Kalmucks, who had been on the point of mutiny at the beginning of the march, but had been quieted by a harangue from Donald MacDeesa, in their own tongue.

For weeks the Turkish host had moved eastward on the Sivas road, expecting to encounter the Tatars at any point. They had passed Angora, where the Sultan had established his base-camp; they had crossed the river Halys, or Kizil Irmak, and now were marching through the hill country that lies in the bend of that river which, rising east of Sivas, sweeps southward in a vast half-circle before it bends, west of Kirshehr, northward to the Black Sea.

"Here we camp," repeated Bayazid; "Sivas lies some sixty-five miles to the east. We will send scouts into the city."

"They will find it deserted," predicted Donald, riding at Bayazid's side, and the Sultan scoffed, "Oh gem of wisdom, will the Lame One flee so quickly?"

"He will not flee," answered the Gael. "Remember he can move his host far more quickly than you can. He will take to the hills and fall suddenly upon us when you least expect it."

Bayazid snorted his contempt. "Is he a magician, to flit among the hills with a horde of 150,000 men? Bah! I tell you, he will come along the Sivas road to join battle, and we will crack him like a nutshell."

So the Turkish host went into camp and fortified the hills, and there they waited with growing wrath and impatience for a week. Bayazid's scouts returned with the news that only a handful of Tatars held Sivas. The Sultan roared with rage and bewilderment.

"Fools, have ye passed the Tatars on the road?"

"Nay, by Allah," swore the riders, "they vanished in the night like ghosts, none can say whither. And we have combed the hills between this spot and the city."

"Timour has fled back to his desert," said Peter Lazarus, and Donald laughed.

"When rivers run uphill, Timour will flee," said he; "he lurks somewhere in the hills to the south."

Bayazid had never taken other men's advice, for he had found long ago that his own wit was superior. But now he was puzzled. He had never before fought the desert riders whose secret of victory was mobility and who passed through the land like blown clouds. Then his outriders brought in word that bodies of mounted men had been seen moving parallel to the Turkish right wing.

MacDeesa laughed like a jackal barking. "Now Timour sweeps upon us from the south, as I predicted."

Bayazid drew up his lines and waited for the assault, but it did not come and his scouts reported that the riders had passed on and disappeared. Bewildered for the first time in his career, and mad to come to grips with his illusive foe, Bayazid struck camp and on a forced march reached the Halys river in two days, where he expected to find Timour drawn up to dispute his passage. No Tatar was to be seen. The Sultan cursed in his black beard; were these eastern devils ghosts, to vanish in thin air? He sent riders across the river and they came flying back, splashing recklessly through the shallow water. They had seen the Tatar rear guard. Timour had eluded the whole Turkish army, and was even now marching on Angora! Frothing, Bayazid turned on MacDeesa.

"Dog, what have you to say now?"

"What would you?" the Highlander stood his ground boldly. "You have none but yourself to blame, if Timour has outwitted you. Have you harkened to me in aught, good or bad? I told you Timour would not await your coming, nor did he. I told you he would leave the city and go into the southern hills. And he did. I told you he would fall upon us suddenly, and therein I was mistaken. I did not guess that he would cross the river and elude us. But all else I warned you of has come to pass."

Bayazid grudgingly admitted the truth of the Frank's words, but he was mad with fury. Else he had never sought to overtake the swift-moving horde before it reached Angora. He flung his columns across the river and started on the track of the Tatars. Timour had crossed the river near Sivas, and moving around the outer bend, eluded the Turks on the other side. And now Bayazid followed his road, which swung outward from the river, into the plains where there was little water—and no food, after the horde had swept through with torch and blade.

The Turks marched over a fire-blackened, slaughter-reddened waste. Timour covered the ground in three days, over which Bayazid's columns staggered in a week of forced marching; a hundred miles through the burning, desolated plain, strewn with bare hills that made marching a hell. As the strength of the army lay in its infantry, the cavalry was forced to set its pace with the foot-soldiers, and all stumbled wearily through the clouds of stinging dust that rose from beneath the sore, shuffling feet. Under a burning summer sun they plodded grimly along, suffering fiercely from hunger and thirst.

So they came at last to the plain of Angora, and saw the Tatars installed in the camp they had left, besieging the city. And a roar of desperation went up from the thirst-maddened Turks. Timour had changed the course of the little river which ran through Angora, so that now it ran behind the Tatar lines; the only way to reach it was straight through the desert hordes. The springs and wells of the countryside had been polluted or damaged. For an instant Bayazid sat silent in his saddle, gazing from the Tatar camp to his own long straggling lines, and the marks of suffering and vain wrath in the drawn faces of his warriors. A strange fear tugged at his heart, so unfamiliar he did not recognize the emotion. Victory had always been his; could it ever be otherwise?

CHAPTER 5

"What's yon that follows at my side?—
The foe that ye must fight, my lord,—
That hirples swift as I can ride?—
The shadow of the night, my lord."

—*Kipling.*

On that still summer morning the battle-lines stood ready for the death-grip. The Turks were drawn up in a long crescent, whose tips overlapped the Tatar wings, one of which touched the river and the other an entrenched hill fifteen miles away across the plain.

"Never in all my life have I sought another's advice in war," said Bayazid, "but you rode with Timour six years. Will he come to me?"

Donald shook his head. "You outnumber his host. He will never fling his riders against the solid ranks of your janizaries. He will stand afar off and overwhelm you with flights of arrows. You must go to him."

"Can I charge his horse with my infantry?" snarled Bayazid. "Yet you speak wise words. I must hurl my horse against his—and Allah knows his is the better cavalry."

"His right wing is the weaker," said Donald, a sinister light burning in his eyes. "Mass your strongest horsemen on your left wing, charge and shatter that part of the Tatar host; then let your left wing close in, assailing the main battle of the Amir on the flank, while your janizaries advance from the front. Before the charge the spahis on your right wing may make a feint at the lines, to draw Timour's attention."

Bayazid looked silently at the Gael. Donald had suffered as much as the rest on that fearful march. His mail was white with dust, his lips blackened, his throat caked with thirst.

"So let it be," said Bayazid. "Prince Suleiman shall command the left wing, with the Serbian horse and my own heavy cavalry, supported by the Kalmucks. We will stake all on one charge!"

And so they took up their positions, and no one noticed a flat-faced Kalmuck steal out of the Turkish lines and ride for Timour's camp, flogging his stocky pony like mad. On the left wing was massed the powerful Serbian cavalry and the Turkish heavy horse, with the bow-armed Kalmucks behind. At the head of these rode Donald, for they had clamored for the Frank to lead them against their kin. Bayazid did not intend to match bow-fire with the Tatars, but to drive home a charge that would shatter Timour's lines before the Amir could further outmaneuver him. The Turkish right wing consisted of the spahis; the center of the janizaries and Serbian foot with Peter Lazarus, under the personal command of the Sultan.

Timour had no infantry. He sat with his bodyguard on a hillock behind the lines. Nur ad-Din commanded the right wing of the riders of high Asia, Ak Boga the left, Prince Muhammad the center. With the center were the elephants in their leather trappings, with their battle-towers and archers. Their awesome trumpeting was the only sound along the wide-spread steel-clad Tatar lines as the Turks came on with a thunder of cymbals and kettle-drums.

Like a thunderbolt Suleiman launched his squadrons at the Tatar right wing. They ran full into a terrible blast of arrows, but grimly they swept on, and the Tatar ranks reeled to the shock. Suleiman, cutting a heron-plumed chieftain out of his saddle, shouted in exultation, but even as he did so, behind him rose a guttural roar, "*Ghar! ghar! ghar!* Smite, brothers, for the lord Timour!"

With a sob of rage he turned and saw his horsemen going down in windrows beneath the arrows of the Kalmucks. And in his ear he heard Donald MacDeesa laughing like a madman.

"Traitor!" screamed the Turk. "This is your work—"

The claymore flashed in the sun and Prince Suleiman rolled headless from his saddle.

"One stroke for Nicopolis!" yelled the maddened Highlander. "Drive home your shafts, dog-brothers!"

The stocky Kalmucks yelped like wolves in reply, wheeling away to avoid the scimitars of the desperate Turks, and driving their deadly arrows into the milling ranks at close range. They had endured much from their masters; now was the hour of reckoning. And now the Tatar right wing drove home with a roar; and caught before and behind, the Turkish cavalry buckled and crumpled, whole troops breaking away in headlong flight. At one stroke had been swept away Bayazid's chance to crush his enemy's formation.

As the charge had begun, the Turkish right wing had advanced with a great blare of trumpets and roll of drums, and in the midst of its feint, had been caught by the sudden unexpected charge of the Tatar left. Ak Boga had swept through the light spahis, and losing his head momentarily in the lust of slaughter, he drove them flying before him until pursued and pursuers vanished over the slopes in the distance.

Timour sent Prince Muhammad with a reserve squadron to support the left wing and bring it back, while Nur ad-Din, sweeping aside the remnants of Bayazid's cavalry, swung in a pivot-like movement and thundered against the locked ranks of the janizaries. They held like a wall of iron, and Ak Boga, galloping back from his pursuit of the spahis, smote them on the other flank. And now Timour himself mounted his war-steed, and the center rolled like an iron wave against the staggering Turks. And now the real death-grip came to be.

Charge after charge crashed on those serried ranks, surging on and rolling back like onsweeping and receding waves. In clouds of fire-shot dust the janizaries stood unshaken, thrusting with reddened spears, smiting with dripping ax and notched scimitar. The wild riders swept in like blasting whirlwinds, raking the ranks with the storms of their arrows as they drew and loosed too swiftly for the eye to follow, rushing headlong into the press, screaming and hacking like madmen as their scimitars sheared through buckler, helmet and skull. And the Turks beat them back, overthrowing horse and rider; hacked them down and trampled them under, treading their own dead under foot to close the ranks, until both hosts trod on a carpet of the slain and the hoofs of the Tatar steeds splashed blood at every leap.

Repeated charges tore the Turkish host apart at last, and all over the plain the fight raged on, where clumps of spearmen stood back to back, slaying and dying beneath the arrows and scimitars of the riders from the steppes. Through the clouds of rising dust stalked the elephants trumpeting like Doom, while the archers on their backs rained down blasts of arrows and sheets of fire that withered men in their mail like burnt grain.

All day Bayazid had fought grimly on foot at the head of his men. At his side fell King Peter, pierced by a score of arrows. With a thousand of his janizaries the Sultan held the highest hill upon the plain, and through the blazing hell of that long afternoon he held it still, while his men died beside him. In a hurricane of splintering spears, lashing axes and ripping scimitars, the Sultan's warriors held the victorious Tatars to a gasping deadlock. And then Donald MacDeesa, on foot, eyes glaring like a mad dog's, rushed headlong through the mêlée and smote the Sultan with such hate-driven fury that the crested helmet shattered beneath the claymore's whistling edge and Bayazid fell like a dead man. And over the weary groups of bloodstained defenders rolled the dark tide, and the kettle drums of the Tatars thundered victory.

CHAPTER 6

"The searing glory which hath shone
Amid the jewels of my throne,
Halo of Hell! and with a pain
Not Hell shall make me fear again."

—POE: *Tamerlane.*

The power of the Osmanli was broken, the heads of the emirs heaped before Timour's tent. But the Tatars swept on; at the heels of the flying Turks they burst into Brusa, Bayazid's capital, sweeping the streets with sword and flame. Like a whirlwind they came and like a whirlwind they went, laden with treasures of the palace and the women of the vanished Sultan's seraglio.

Riding back to the Tatar camp beside Nur ad-Din and Ak Boga, Donald MacDeesa learned that Bayazid lived. The stroke which had felled him had only stunned, and the Turk was captive to the Amir he had mocked. MacDeesa cursed; the Gael was dusty and stained with hard riding and harder fighting; dried blood darkened his mail and clotted his scabbard mouth. A red-soaked scarf was bound about his thigh as a rude bandage; his eyes were bloodshot, his thin lips frozen in a snarl of battle-fury.

"By God, I had not thought a bullock could survive that blow. Is he to be crucified—as he swore to deal with Timour thus?"

"Timour gave him good welcome and will do him no hurt," answered the courtier who brought the news. "The Sultan will sit at the feast."

Ak Boga shook his head, for he was merciful except in the rush of battle, but in Donald's ears were ringing the screams of the butchered captives at Nicopolis, and he laughed shortly—a laugh that was not pleasant to hear.

To the fierce heart of the Sultan, death was easier than sitting a captive at the feast which always followed a Tatar victory. Bayazid sat like a grim image, neither speaking nor seeming to hear the crash of the kettle-drums, the roar of barbaric revelry. On his head was the jeweled turban of sovereignty, in his hand the gem-starred scepter of his vanished empire.

He did not touch the great golden goblet before him. Many and many a time had he exulted over the agony of the vanquished, with much less mercy than was now shown him; now the unfamiliar bite of defeat left him frozen.

He stared at the beauties of his seraglio, who, according to Tatar custom, tremblingly served their new masters: black-haired Jewesses with slumberous, heavy-lidded eyes; lithe tawny Circassians and golden-haired Russians; dark-eyed Greek girls and Turkish women with figures like Juno—all naked as the day they were born, under the burning eyes of the Tatar lords.

He had sworn to ravish Timour's wives—the Sultan writhed as he saw the Despina, sister of Peter Lazarus and his favorite, nude like the rest, kneel and in quivering fear offer Timour a goblet of wine. The Tatar absently wove his fingers in her golden locks and Bayazid shuddered as if those fingers were locked in his own heart.

And he saw Donald MacDeesa sitting next to Timour, his stained dusty garments contrasting strangely with the silk-and-gold splendor of the Tatar lords—his savage eyes ablaze, his dark face wilder and more passionate than ever as he ate like a ravenous wolf and drained goblet after goblet of stinging wine. And Bayazid's iron control snapped. With a roar that struck the clamor dumb, the Thunderer lurched upright, breaking the heavy scepter like a twig between his hands and dashing the fragments to the floor.

All eyes turned toward him and some of the Tatars stepped quickly between him and their Amir, who only looked at him impassively.

"Dog and spawn of a dog!" roared Bayazid. "You came to me as one in need and I sheltered you! The curse of all traitors rest on your black heart!"

MacDeesa heaved up, scattered goblets and bowls.

"Traitors?" he yelled. "Is six years so long you forget the headless corpses that molder at Nicopolis? Have you forgotten the ten thousand captives you slew there, naked and with their hands bound? I fought you there with steel; and since I have fought you with guile! Fool, from the hour you marched from Brusa, you were doomed! It was I who spoke softly to the Kalmucks, who hated you; so they were content and seemed willing to serve you. With them I communicated with Timour from the time we first left Angora—sending riders forth secretly or feigning to hunt for antelopes.

"Through me, Timour tricked you—even put into your head the plan of your battle! I caught you in a web of truths, knowing that you would follow your own course, regardless of what I or any one else said. I told you but two lies—when I said I sought revenge on Timour, and when I said the Amir would bide in the hills and fall upon us. Before battle joined I knew what Timour wished, and by my advice led you into a trap. So Timour, who had drawn out the plan you thought part yours and part mine, knew beforehand every move you would make. But in the end, it hinged on me, for it was I who turned the Kalmucks against you, and their arrows in the backs of your horsemen which tipped the scales when the battle hung in the balance.

"I paid high for my vengeance, Turk! I played my part under the eyes of your spies, in your court, every instant, even when my head was reeling with wine. I fought for you against the Greeks and took wounds. In the wilderness beyond the Halys I suffered with the rest. And I would have gone through greater hells to bring you to the dust!"

"Serve well your master as you have served me, traitor," retorted the Sultan. "In the end, Timour-il-leng, you will rue the day you took this adder into your naked hands. Aye, may each of you bring the other down to death!"

"Be at ease, Bayazid," said Timour impassively. "What is written, is written."

"Aye!" answered the Turk with a terrible laugh. "And it is not written that the Thunderer should live a buffoon for a crippled dog! Lame One, Bayazid gives you—hail and farewell!"

And before any could stay him, the Sultan snatched a carving-knife from a table and plunged it to the hilt in his throat. A moment he reeled like a mighty tree, spurting blood, and then crashed thunderously down. All noise was hushed as the multitude stood aghast. A pitiful cry rang out as the young Despina ran forward, and dropping to her knees, drew the lion's head of her grim lord to her naked bosom, sobbing convulsively. But

Timour stroked his beard measuredly and half-abstractedly. And Donald MacDeesa, seating himself, took up a great goblet that glowed crimson in the torchlight, and drank deeply.

CHAPTER 7

"Hath not the same fierce heirdom given
Rome to the Caesar—this to me?"

—POE: *Tamerlane.*

To understand the relationship of Donald MacDeesa to Timour, it is necessary to go back to that day, six years before, when in the turquoise-domed palace at Samarcand the Amir planned the overthrow of the Ottoman.

When other men looked days ahead, Timour looked years; and five years passed before he was ready to move against the Turk, and let Donald ride to Brusa ahead of a carefully trained pursuit. Five years of fierce fighting in the mountain snows and the desert dust, through which Timour moved like a mythical giant, and hard as he drove his chiefs, he drove the Highlander harder. It was as if he studied MacDeesa with the impersonally cruel eyes of a scientist, wringing every ounce of accomplishment from him, seeking to find the limit of man's endurance and valor—the final breaking-point. He did not find it.

The Gael was too utterly reckless to be trusted with hosts and armies. But in raids and forays, in the storming of cities, and in charges of battle, in any action requiring personal valor and prowess, the Highlander was all but invincible. He was a typical fighting-man of European wars, where tactics and strategy meant little and ferocious hand-to-hand fighting much, and where battles were decided by the physical prowess of the champions. In tricking the Turk, he had but followed the instructions given him by Timour.

There was scant love lost between the Gael and the Amir, to whom Donald was but a ferocious barbarian from the outlands of Frankistan. Timour never showered gifts and honors on Donald, as he did upon his Moslem chiefs. But the grim Gael scorned these gauds, seeming to derive his only pleasures from hard fighting and hard drinking. He ignored the formal reverence paid the Amir by his subjects, and in his cups dared beard the somber Tatar to his face, so that the people caught their breath.

"He is a wolf I unleash on my foes," said Timour on one occasion to his lords.

"He is a two-edged blade that might cut the wielder," ventured one of them.

"Not so long as the blade is forever smiting my enemies," answered Timour.

After Angora, Timour gave Donald command of the Kalmucks, who accompanied their kin back into high Asia, and a swarm of restless, turbulent Vigurs. That was his reward: a wider range and a greater capacity for grinding toil and heart-bursting warfare. But Donald made no comment; he worked his slayers into fighting shape, and experimented with various types of saddles and armor, with firelocks—finding them much inferior in actual execution to the bows of the Tatars—and with the latest type of firearm, the cumbrous wheel-lock pistols used by the Arabs a century before they made their appearance in Europe.

Timour hurled Donald against his foes as a man hurls a javelin, little caring whether the weapon be broken or not. The Gael's horsemen would come back bloodstained, dusty and weary, their armor hacked to shreds, their swords notched and blunted, but always with the heads of Timour's foes swinging at their high saddle-peaks. Their savagery, and Donald's own wild ferocity and superhuman strength, brought them repeatedly out of seemingly hopeless positions. And Donald's wild-beast vitality caused him again and again to recover from ghastly wounds, until the iron-thewed Tatars marveled at him.

As the years passed, Donald, always aloof and taciturn, withdrew more and more to himself. When not riding on campaigns, he sat alone in brooding silence in the taverns, or stalked dangerously through the streets, hand on his great sword, while the people slunk softly from in front of him. He had one friend, Ak Boga; but one interest outside of war and carnage. On a raid into Persia, a slim white wisp of a girl had run screaming across the path of the charging squadron and his men had seen Donald bend down and sweep her up into his saddle with one mighty hand. The girl was Zuleika, a Persian dancer.

Donald had a house in Samarcand, and a handful of servants, but only this one girl. She was comely, sensual and giddy. She adored her master in her way, and feared him with a very ecstasy of fear, but was not above secret amours with young soldiers when MacDeesa was away on the wars. Like most Persian women of her caste, she had a capacity for petty intrigue and an inability for keeping her small nose out of affairs which were none of her business. She became a tale-bearer for Shadi Mulkh, the Persian paramour of Khalil, Timour's weak grandson, and thereby indirectly changed the destiny of the world. She was greedy, vain and an outrageous liar, but her hands were soft as drifting snow-flakes when she dressed the wounds of sword and spear on Donald's iron body. He never beat or cursed her, and though he never caressed or wooed her with gentle words as other men might, it was well known that he treasured her above all worldly possessions and honors.

Timour was growing old; he had played with the world as a man plays with a chessboard, using kings and armies for pawns. As a young chief without wealth or power, he had overthrown his Mongol masters, and mastered them in his turn. Tribe after tribe, race after race, kingdom after kingdom he had broken and molded into his growing empire, which stretched from the Gobi to the Mediterranean, from Moscow to Delhi—the mightiest empire the world ever knew. He had opened the doors of the South and East, and through them flowed the wealth of the earth. He had saved Europe from an Asiatic invasion, when he checked the tide of Turkish conquest—a fact of which he neither knew nor cared. He had built cities and he had destroyed cities. He had made the desert blossom like a garden, and he had turned flowering lands into desert. At his command pyramids of skulls had reared up, and lives flowed out like rivers. His helmeted warlords were exalted above the multitudes and nations cried out in vain beneath his grinding heel, like lost women crying in the mountains at night.

Now he looked eastward, where the purple empire of Cathay dreamed away the centuries. Perhaps, with the waning of life's tide, it was the old sleeping home-calling of his race; perhaps he remembered the ancient heroic khans, his ancestors, who had ridden southward out of the barren Gobi into the purple kingdoms.

The Grand Vizier shook his head, as he played at chess with his imperial master. He was old and weary, and he dared speak his mind even to Timour.

"My lord, of what avail these endless wars? You have already subjugated more nations than Genghis Khan or Alexander. Rest in the peace of your conquests and complete the work you have begun in Samarcand. Build more stately palaces. Bring here the philosophers, the artists, the poets of the world—"

Timour shrugged his massive shoulders.

"Philosophy and poetry and architecture are good enough in their way, but they are mist and smoke to conquest, for it is on the red splendor of conquest that all these things rest."

The Vizier played with the ivory pawns, shaking his hoary head.

"My lord, you are like two men—one a builder, the other a destroyer."

"Perhaps I destroy so that I may build on the ruins of my destruction," the Amir answered. "I have never sought to reason out this matter. I only know that I am a conqueror before I am a builder, and conquest is my life's blood."

"But what reason to overthrow this great weak bulk of Cathay?" protested the Vizier. "It will mean but more slaughter, with which you have already crimsoned the earth—more woe and misery, with helpless people dying like sheep beneath the sword."

Timour shook his head, half-absently. "What are their lives? They die anyway, and their existence is full of misery. I will draw a band of iron about the heart of Tatary. With this Eastern conquest I will strengthen my throne, and kings of my dynasty shall rule the world for ten thousand years. All the roads of the world shall lead to Samarcand, and there shall be gathered the wonder and mystery and glory of the world—colleges and libraries and stately mosques—marble domes and sapphire towers and turquoise minarets. But first I shall carry out my destiny—and that is Conquest!"

"But winter draws on," urged the Vizier. "At least wait until spring."

Timour shook his head, unspeaking. He knew he was old; even his iron frame was showing signs of decay. And sometimes in his sleep he heard the singing of Aljai the Dark-eyed, the bride of his youth, dead for more than forty years. So through the Blue City ran the word, and men left their lovemaking and their wine-bibbing, strung their bows, looked to their harness and took up again the worn old road of conquest.

Timour and his chiefs took with them many of their wives and servants, for the Amir intended to halt at Otrar, his border city, and from thence strike into Cathay when the snows melted in the spring. Such of his lords as remained rode with him—war took a heavy toll of Timour's hawks.

As usual Donald MacDeesa and his turbulent rogues led the advance. The Gael was glad to take the road after months of idleness, but he brought Zuleika with him. The years were growing more bitter for the giant Highlander, an outlander among alien races. His wild horsemen worshipped him in their savage way, but he was an alien among them, after all, and they could never understand his inmost thoughts. Ak Boga with his twinkling eyes and jovial laughter had been more like the men Donald had known in his youth, but Ak Boga was dead, his great heart stilled forever by the stroke of an Arab scimitar, and in his growing loneliness Donald more and more sought solace in the Persian girl, who could never understand his strange wayward heart, but who somehow partly filled an aching void in his soul. Through the long lonely nights his hands sought her slim form with a dim formless unquiet hunger even she could dimly sense.

In a strange silence Timour rode out of Samarcand at the head of his long glittering columns and the people did not cheer as of old. With bowed heads and hearts crowded with emotions they could not define, they watched the last conqueror ride forth, and then turned again to their petty lives and commonplace, dreary tasks, with a vague instinctive sense that something terrible and splendid and awesome had gone out of their lives forever.

In the teeth of the rising winter the hosts moved, not with the speed of other times when they passed through the land like windblown clouds. They were two hundred thousand strong and they bore with them herds of spare horses, wagons of supplies and great tent-pavilions.

Beyond the pass men call the Gates of Timour, snow fell, and into the teeth of the blizzard the army toiled doggedly. At last it became apparent that even Tatars could not march in such weather, and Prince Khalil went into winter quarters in that strange town called the Stone City, but Timour plunged on with his own troops. Ice lay three feet deep on the Syr when they crossed, and in the hill-country beyond the going became fiercer, and horses and camels stumbled through the drifts, the wagons lurching and rocking. But the will of Timour drove them grimly onward, and at last they came upon the plain and saw the spires of Otrar gleaming through the whirling snow-wrack.

Timour installed himself and his nobles in the palace, and his warriors went thankfully into winter quarters. But he sent for Donald MacDeesa.

"Ordushar lies in our road," said Timour. "Take two thousand men and storm that city that our road be clear to Cathay with the coming of spring."

When a man casts a javelin he little cares if it splinter on the mark.

Timour would not have sent his valued emirs and chosen warriors on this, the maddest quest he had yet given even Donald. But the Gael cared not; he was more than ready to ride on any adventure which might drown the dim bitter dreams that gnawed deeper and deeper at his heart. At the age of forty MacDeesa's iron frame was unweakened, his ferocious valor undimmed. But at times he felt old in his heart. His thoughts turned more and more back over the black and crimson pattern of his life with its violence and treachery and savagery; its woe and waste and stark futility. He slept fitfully and seemed to hear half-forgotten voices crying in the night. Sometimes it seemed the keening of Highland pipes skirled through the howling winds.

He roused his wolves, who gaped at the command but obeyed without comment, and rode out of Otrar in a roaring blizzard. It was a venture of the damned.

In the palace of Otrar, Timour drowsed on his divan over his maps and charts, and listened drowsily to the everlasting disputes between the women of his household. The intrigues and jealousies of the Samarcand palaces reached to isolated Otrar. They buzzed about him, wearying him to death with their petty spite. As age stole on the iron Amir, the women looked eagerly to his naming of a successor—his queen Sarai Mulkh Khanum; Khan Zade, wife of his dead son Jahangir. Against the queen's claim for her son—and Timour's—Shah Ruhk, was opposed the intrigue of Khan Zade for her son, Prince Khalil, whom the courtesan Shadi Mulkh wrapped about her pink finger.

The Amir had brought Shadi Mulkh with him to Otrar, much against Khalil's will. The Prince was growing restless in the bleak Stone City and hints reached Timour of discord and threats of insubordination. Sarai Khanum came to the Amir, a gaunt weary woman, grown old in wars and grief.

"The Persian girl sends secret messages to Prince Khalil, stirring him up to deeds of folly," said the Great Lady. "You are far from Samarcand. Were Khalil to march thither before you—there are always fools ready to revolt, even against the Lord of Lords."

"At another time," said Timour wearily, "I would have her strangled. But Khalil in his folly would rise against me, and a revolt at this time, however quickly put down, would upset all my plans. Have her confined and closely guarded, so that she can send no more messages."

"This I have already done," replied Sarai Khanum grimly, "but she is clever and manages to get messages out of the palace by means of the Persian girl of the Caphar, lord Donald."

"Fetch this girl," ordered Timour, laying aside his maps with a sigh.

They dragged Zuleika before the Amir, who looked somberly upon her as she groveled whimpering at his feet, and with a weary gesture, sealed her doom—and immediately forgot her, as a king forgets the fly he has crushed.

They dragged the girl screaming from the imperial presence and hurled her upon her knees in a hall which had no windows and only bolted doors. Groveling on her knees she wailed frantically for Donald and screamed for mercy, until terror froze her voice in her pulsing throat, and through a mist of horror she saw the stark half-naked figure and the mask-like face of the grim executioner advancing, knife in hand. . . .

Zuleika was neither brave nor admirable. She neither lived with dignity nor met her fate with courage. She was cowardly, immoral and foolish. But even a fly loves life, and a worm would cry out under the heel that crushed it. And perhaps, in the grim inscrutable books of Fate, even an emperor may not forever trample insects with impunity.

CHAPTER 8

"But I have dreamed a dreary dream,
Beyond the Vale of Skye;
I saw a dead man win a fight,
And I think that man was I."

—*Battle of Otterbourne.*

And at Ordushar the siege dragged on. In the freezing winds that swept down the pass, driving snow in blinding, biting blasts, the stocky Kalmucks and the lean Vigurs strove and suffered and died in bitter anguish. They set scaling-ladders against the walls and struggled upward, and the defenders, suffering no less, speared them, hurled down boulders that crushed the mailed figures like beetles, and thrust the ladders from the walls so that they crashed down, bearing death to men below. Ordushar was actually but a stronghold of the Jat Mongols, set sheer in the pass and flanked by towering cliffs.

Donald's wolves hacked at the frozen ground with frost-bitten raw hands which scarce could hold the picks, striving to sink a mine under the walls. They pecked at the towers while molten lead and weighted javelins fell in a rain upon them; driving their spear-points between the stones, tearing out pieces of masonry with their naked hands. With stupendous toil they had constructed makeshift siege-engines from felled trees and the leather of their harness and woven hair from the manes and tails of their warhorses. The rams battered vainly at the massive stones, the ballistas groaned as they launched tree-trunks and boulders against the towers or over the walls. Along the parapets the attackers fought with the defenders, until their bleeding hands froze to spear-shaft and sword-hilt, and the skin came away in great raw strips. And always, with superhuman fury rising above their agony, the defenders hurled back the attack.

A storming-tower was built and rolled up to the walls, and from the battlements the men of Ordushar poured a drenching torrent of naphtha that sent it up in flame and burnt the men in it, shriveling them in their armor like beetles in a fire. Snow and sleet fell in blinding flurries, freezing to sheets of ice. Dead men froze stiffly where they fell, and wounded men died in their sleeping-furs. There was no rest, no surcease from agony. Days and nights merged into a hell of pain. Donald's men, with tears of suffering frozen on their faces, beat frenziedly against the frosty stone walls, fought with raw hands gripping broken weapons, and died cursing the gods that created them.

The misery inside the city was no less, for there was no more food. At night Donald's warriors heard the wailing of the starving people in the streets. At last in desperation the men of Ordushar cut the throats of their women and children and sallied forth, and the haggard Tatars fell on them weeping with the madness of rage and woe, and in a welter of battle that crimsoned the frozen snow, drove them back through the city gates. And the struggle went hideously on.

Donald used up the last wood in the vicinity to erect another storming-tower higher than the city wall. After that there was no more wood for the fires. He himself stood at the uplifted bridge which was to be lowered to rest on the parapets. He had not spared himself. Day and night he had toiled beside his men, suffering as they had suffered. The tower was rolled to the wall in a hail of arrows that slew half the warriors who had not found shelter behind the thick bulwark. A crude cannon bellowed from the walls, but the clumsy round shot whistled over their heads. The naphtha and Greek fire of the Jats was exhausted. In the teeth of the singing shafts the bridge was dropped.

Drawing his claymore, Donald strode out upon it. Arrows broke on his corselet and glanced from his helmet. Firelocks flashed and bellowed in his face but he strode on unhurt. Lean armored men with eyes like mad dogs' swarmed upon the parapet, seeking to dislodge the bridge, to hack it asunder. Among them Donald sprang, his claymore whistling. The great blade sheared through mail-mesh, flesh and bone, and the struggling clump fell apart. Donald staggered on the edge of the wall as a heavy ax crashed on his shield, and he struck back, cleaving the wielder's spine. The Gael recovered his balance, tossing away his riven shield. His wolves were swarming over the bridge behind him, hurling the defenders from the parapet, cutting them down. Into a swirl of battle Donald strode, swinging his heavy blade. He thought fleetingly of Zuleika, as men in the madness of battle will think of irrelevant things, and it was as if the thought of her had hurt him fiercely under the heart. But it was a spear that had girded through his mail, and Donald struck back savagely; the claymore splintered in his hand and he leaned against the parapet, his face briefly contorted. Around him swept the tides of slaughter as the pent-up fury of his warriors, maddened by the long weeks of suffering, burst all bounds.

CHAPTER 9

"While the red flashing of the light
From clouds that hung, like banners, o'er,
Appeared to my half-closing eye
The pageantry of monarchy."

—POE: *Tamerlane.*

To Timour on his throne in the palace of Otrar came the Grand Vizier. "The survivors of the men sent to the Pass of Ordushar are returning, my lord. The city in the mountains is no more. They bear the lord Donald on a litter, and he is dying."

They brought the litter into Timour's presence, weary, dull-eyed men, with raw wounds tied up with blood-crusted rags, their garments and mail in tatters. They flung before the Amir's feet the golden-scaled corselets of chiefs, and chests of jewels and robes of silk and silver braid; the loot of Ordushar where men had starved among riches. And they set the litter down before Timour.

The Amir looked at the form of Donald. The Highlander was pale, but his sinister face showed no hint of weakness in that wild spirit, his cold eyes gleamed unquenched.

"The road to Cathay is clear," said Donald, speaking with difficulty. "Ordushar lies in smoking ruins. I have carried out your last command."

Timour nodded, his eyes seeming to gaze through and beyond the Highlander. What was a dying man on a litter to the Amir, who had seen so many die? His mind was on the road to Cathay and the purple kingdoms beyond. The javelin had shattered at last, but its final cast had opened the imperial path. Timour's dark eyes burned with strange depths and leaping shadows, as the old fire stole through his blood. Conquest! Outside the winds howled, as if trumpeting the roar of nakars, the clash of cymbals, the deep-throated chant of victory.

"Send Zuleika to me," the dying man muttered. Timour did not reply; he scarcely heard, sitting lost in thunderous visions. He had already forgotten Zuleika and her fate. What was one death in the awesome and terrible scheme of empire.

"Zuleika, where is Zuleika?" the Gael repeated, moving restlessly on his litter. Timour shook himself slightly and lifted his head, remembering.

"I had her put to death," he answered quietly. "It was necessary."

"Necessary!" Donald strove to rear upright, his eyes terrible, but fell back, gagging, and spat out a mouthful of crimson. "You bloody dog, she was mine!"

"Yours or another's," Timour rejoined absently, his mind far away. "What is a woman in the plan of imperial destinies?"

For answer Donald plucked a pistol from among his robes and fired point-blank. Timour started and swayed on his throne, and the courtiers cried out, paralyzed with horror. Through the drifting smoke they saw that Donald lay dead on the litter, his thin lips frozen in a grim smile. Timour sat crumpled on his throne, one hand gripping his breast; through those fingers blood oozed darkly. With his free hand he waved back his nobles.

"Enough; it is finished. To every man comes the end of the road. Let Pir Muhammad reign in my stead, and let him strengthen the lines of the empire I have reared with my hands."

A rack of agony twisted his features. "Allah, that this should be the end of empire!" It was a fierce cry of anguish from his inmost soul. "That I, who have trodden upon kingdoms and humbled sultans, come to my doom because of a cringing trull and a Caphar renegade!" His helpless chiefs saw his mighty hands clench like iron as he held death at bay by the sheer power of his unconquered will. The fatalism of his accepted creed had never found resting-place in his instinctively pagan soul; he was a fighter to the red end.

"Let not my people know that Timour died by the hand of a Caphar," he spoke with growing difficulty. "Let not the chronicles of the ages blazon the name of a wolf that slew an emperor. Ah God, that a bit of dust and metal can dash the Conqueror of the World into the dark! Write, scribe, that this day, by the hand of no man, but by the will of Allah, died Timour, Servant of God."

The chiefs stood about in dazed silence, while the pallid scribe took up parchment and wrote with a shaking hand. Timour's somber eyes were fixed on Donald's still features that seemed to give back his stare, as the dead on the litter faced the dying on the throne. And before the scratching of the quill had ceased, Timour's lion head had sunk upon his mighty chest. And without the wind howled a dirge, drifting the snow higher and higher about the walls of Otrar, even as the sands of oblivion drifted already about the crumbling empire of Timour, the Last Conqueror, Lord of the World.

> Why, if the Soul can fling the Dust aside,
> And naked on the Air of Heaven ride,
> Were't not a Shame—were't not a Shame for him
> In this clay carcase crippled to abide?
>
> 'Tis but a Tent where takes his one day's rest
> A Sultán to the realm of Death addrest;
> The Sultán rises, and the dark Ferrásh
> Strikes, and prepares it for another Guest.
>
> —Rubáiyát of Omar Khayyam.

SOWERS OF THE THUNDER

Iron winds and ruin and flame,
And a Horseman shaking with giant mirth;
Over the corpse-strewn, blackened earth
Death, stalking naked, came
Like a storm-cloud shattering the ships;
Yet the Rider seated high,
Paled at the smile on a dead king's lips,
As the tall white horse went by.

—The Ballad of Baibars

CHAPTER 1

The idlers in the tavern glanced up at the figure framed in the doorway. It was a tall broad man who stood there, with the torch-lit shadows and the clamor of the bazaars at his back. His garments were simple tunic, and short breeches of leather; a camel's-hair mantle hung from his broad shoulders and sandals were on his feet. But belying the garb of the peaceful traveler, a short straight stabbing sword hung at his girdle. One massive arm, ridged with muscles, was outstretched, the brawny hand gripping a pilgrim's staff, as the man stood, powerful legs wide braced, in the doorway. His bare legs were hairy, knotted like tree trunks. His coarse red locks were confined by a single band of blue cloth, and from his square dark face, his strange blue eyes blazed with a kind of reckless and wayward mirth, reflected by the half-smile that curved his thin lips.

His glance passed over the hawk-faced seafarers and ragged loungers who brewed tea and squabbled endlessly, to rest on a man who sat apart at a rough-hewn table, with a wine pitcher. Such a man the watcher in the door had never seen—tall, deep chested, broad shouldered, built with the dangerous suppleness of a panther. His eyes were as cold as blue ice, set off by a mane of golden hair tinted with red; so to the man in the doorway that hair seemed like burning gold. The man at the table wore a light shirt of silvered mail, a long lean sword hung at his hip, and on the bench beside him lay a kite-shaped shield and a light helmet.

The man in the guise of a traveler strode purposefully forward and halted, hands resting on the table across which he smiled mockingly at the other, and spoke in a tongue strange to the seated man, newly come to the East.

The one turned to an idler and asked in Norman French: "What does the infidel say?"

"I said," replied the traveler in the same tongue, "that a man can not even enter an Egyptian inn these days without finding some dog of a Christian under his feet."

As the traveler had spoken the other had risen, and now the speaker dropped his hand to his sword. Scintillant lights flickered in the other's eyes and he moved like a flash of summer lightning. His left hand darted out to lock in the breast of the traveler's tunic, and in his right hand the long sword flashed out. The traveler was caught flat-footed, his sword half clear of its sheath. But the faint smile did not leave his lips and he stared almost childishly at the blade that flickered before his eyes, as if fascinated by its dazzling.

"Heathen dog," snarled the swordsman, and his voice was like the slash of a blade through fabric, "I'll send you to Hell unshriven!"

"What panther whelped you that you move as a cat strikes?" responded the other curiously, as calmly as if his life were not weighing in the balance. "But you took me by surprize. I did not know that a Frank dare draw sword in Damietta."

The Frank glared at him moodily; the wine he had drunk showed in the dangerous gleams that played in his eyes where lights and shadows continuously danced and shifted.

"Who are you?" he demanded.

"Haroum the Traveler," the other grinned. "Put up your steel. I crave pardon for my gibing words. It seems there are Franks of the old breed yet."

With a change of mood the Frank thrust his sword back into its sheath with an impatient clash. Turning back to his bench he indicated table and wine pitcher with a sweeping gesture.

"Sit and refresh yourself; if you are a traveler, you have a tale to tell."

Haroun did not at once comply. His gaze swept the inn and he beckoned the innkeeper, who came grudgingly forward. As he approached the Traveler, the innkeeper suddenly shrank back with a low half-stifled cry. Haroun's eyes went suddenly merciless and he said, "What then, host, do you see in me a man you have known aforetime, perchance?"

His voice was like the purr of a hunting tiger and the wretched innkeeper shivered as with an ague, his dilated eyes fixed on the broad, corded hand that stroked the hilt of the stabbing-sword.

"No, no, master," he mouthed. "By Allah, I know you not—I never saw you before—and Allah grant I never see you again," he added mentally.

"Then tell me what does this Frank here, in mail and wearing a sword," ordered Haroun bruskly, in Turki. "The dog-Venetians are allowed to trade in Damietta as in Alexandria, but they pay for the privilege in humility and insult, and none dares gird on a blade here—much less lift it against a Believer."

"He is no Venetian, good Haroun," answered the innkeeper. "Yesterday he came ashore from a Venetian trading-galley, but he consorts not with the traders or the crew of the infidels. He strides boldly through the streets, wearing steel openly and ruffling against all who would cross him. He says he is going to Jerusalem and could not find a ship bound for any port in Palestine, so came here, intending to travel the rest of the way by land. The Believers have said he is mad, and none molests him."

"Truly, the mad are touched by Allah and given His protection," mused Haroun. "Yet this man is not altogether mad, I think. Bring wine, dog!"

The innkeeper ducked in a deep salaam and hastened off to do the Traveler's bidding. The Prophet's command against strong drink was among other orthodox precepts disobeyed in Damietta where many nations foregathered and Turk rubbed shoulders with Copt, Arab with Sudani.

Haroun seated himself opposite the Frank and took the wine goblet proffered by a servant.

"You sit in the midst of your enemies like a shah of the East, my lord," he grinned. "By Allah, you have the bearing of a king."

"I am a king, infidel," growled the other; the wine he had drunk had touched him with a reckless and mocking madness.

"And where lies your kingdom, *malik?*" The question was not asked in mockery. Haroun had seen many broken kings drifting among the debris that floated Eastward.

"On the dark side of the moon," answered the Frank with a wild and bitter laugh. "Among the ruins of all the unborn or forgotten empires which etch the twilight of the lost ages. Cahal Ruadh O'Donnel, king of Ireland—the name means naught to you, Haroun of the East, and naught to the land which was my birthright. They who were my foes sit in the high seats of power, they who were my vassals lie cold and still, the bats haunt my shattered castles, and already the name of Red Cahal is dim in the memories of men. So—fill up my goblet, slave!"

"You have the soul of a warrior, *malik*. Was it treachery overcame you?"

"Aye, treachery," swore Cahal, "and the wiles of a woman who coiled about my soul until I was as one blind—to be cast out at the end like a broken pawn. Aye, the Lady Elinor de Courcey, with her black hair like midnight shadows on Lough Derg, and the gray eyes of her, like—" he started suddenly, like a man waking from a trance, and his wayward eyes blazed.

"Saints and devils!" he roared. "Who are you that I should spill out my soul to? The wine has betrayed me and loosened my tongue, but I—" He reached for his sword but Haroun laughed.

"I've done you no harm, *malik*. Turn this murderous spirit of yours into another channel. By Erlik, I'll give you a test to cool your blood!"

Rising, he caught up a javelin lying beside a drunken soldier, and striding around the table, his eyes recklessly alight, he extended his massive arm, gripping the shaft close to the middle, point upward.

"Grip the shaft, *malik*," he laughed. "In all my days I have met no one who was man enough to twist a stave out of my hand."

Cahal rose and gripped the shaft so that his clenched fingers almost touched those of Haroun. Then, legs braced wide, arms bent at the elbow, each man exerted his full strength against the other. They were well matched; Cahal was a trifle taller, Haroun thicker of body. It was bear opposed to tiger. Like two statues they stood straining, neither yielding an inch, the javelin almost motionless under the equal forces. Then, with a sudden rending snap, the tough wood gave way and each man staggered, holding half the shaft, which had parted under the terrific strain.

"Hai!" shouted Haroun, his eyes sparkling; then they dulled with sudden doubt.

"By Allah, *malik*," said he, "this is an ill thing! Of two men, one should be master of the other, lest both come to a bad end. Yet this signifies that neither of us will ever yield to the other, and in the end, each will work the other ill."

"Sit down and drink," answered the Gael, tossing aside the broken shaft and reaching for the wine goblet, his dreams of lost grandeur and his anger both apparently forgotten. "I have not been long in the East, but I knew not there were such as you among the paynim. Surely you are not one with the Egyptians, Arabs and Turks I have seen."

"I was born far to the east, among the tents of the Golden Horde, on the steppes of High Asia," said Haroun, his mood changing back to joviality as he flung himself down on his bench. "Ha! I was almost a man grown before I heard of Muhammad—on whom peace! *Hai, bogatyr,* I have been many things! Once I was a princeling of the Tatars—son of the lord Subotai who was right hand to Genghis Khan. Once I was a slave—when the Turkomans drove a raid east and carried off youths and girls from the Horde. In the slave markets of El Kahira I was sold for three pieces of silver, by Allah, and my master gave me to the Bahairiz—the slave-soldiers—because he feared I'd strangle him. Ha! Now I am Haroun the Traveler, making pilgrimage to the holy place. But once, only a few days agone, I was man to Baibars—whom the devil fly away with!"

"Men say in the streets that this Baibars is the real ruler of Cairo," said Cahal curiously; new to the East though he was, he had heard that name oft-repeated.

"Men lie," responded Haroun. "The sultan rules Egypt and Shadjar ad Darr rules the sultan. Baibars is only the general of the Bahairiz—the great oaf!

"I was his man!" he shouted suddenly, with a great laugh, "to come and go at his bidding—to put him to bed—to rise with him—to sit down at meat with him—aye, and to put food and drink into his fool's-mouth. But I have escaped him! Allah, by Allah and by Allah, I have naught to do with this great fool Baibars tonight! I am a free man and the devil may fly away with him and with the sultan, and Shadjar ad Darr and all Saladin's empire! But I am my own man tonight!"

He pulsed with an energy that would not let him be still or silent; he seemed vibrant and joyously mad with the sheer exuberance of life and the huge mirth of living. With gargantuan laughter he smote the table thunderously with his open hand and roared: "By Allah, *malik*, you shall help me celebrate my escape from the great oaf Baibars—whom the devil fly away with! Away with this slop, dogs! Bring kumiss! The Nazarene lord and I intend to hold such a drinking bout as Damietta's inns have not seen in a hundred years!"

"But my master has already emptied a full wine pitcher and is more than half drunk!" clamored the nondescript servant Cahal had picked up on the wharves—not that he cared, but whomever he served, he wished to have the best of any contest, and besides it was his Oriental instinct to intrude his say.

"So!" roared Haroun, catching up a full wine pitcher. "I will not take advantage of any man! See—I quaff this thimbleful that we may start on even terms!" And drinking deeply, he flung down the pitcher empty.

The servants of the inn brought kumiss—fermented mare's milk, in leathern skins, bound and sealed—illegal drink, brought down by the caravans from the lands of the Turkomans, to tempt the sated palates of nobles, and to satisfy the craving of the steppesmen among the mercenaries and the Bahairiz.

Then, goblet for goblet with Haroun, Cahal quaffed the unfamiliar, whitish, acid stuff, and never had the exiled Irish prince seen such a cup-companion as this wanderer. For between enormous drafts, Haroun shook the smoke-stained rafters with giant laughter, and shouted over spicy tales that breathed the very scents of Cairo's merry obscenity and high comedy. He sang Arab love songs that sighed with the whisper of palm leaves and the swish of silken veils, and he roared riding songs in a tongue none in the tavern understood, but which vibrated with the drum of Mongol hoofs and the clashing of swords.

The moon had set and even the clamor of Damietta had ebbed in the darkness before dawn, when Haroun staggered up and clutched reeling at the table for support. A single weary slave stood by, to pour wine. Keeper, servants and guests snored on the floor or had slipped away long before. Haroun shouted a thick-tongued war cry and yelled aloud with the sheer riotousness of his mirth. Sweat stood in beads on his face and the veins of his temples swelled and throbbed from his excesses. His wild wayward eyes danced with joyous deviltry.

"Would you were not a king, *malik!*" he roared, catching up a stout bludgeon. "I would show you cudgel-play! Aye, my blood is racing like a

Turkoman stallion and in good sport I would fain deal strong blows on somebody's pate, by Allah!"

"Then grip your stick, man," answered Cahal reeling up. "Men call me fool, but no man has ever said I was backward where blows were going, be they of steel or wood!"

Upsetting the table, he gripped a leg and wrenched powerfully. There was a splintering of wood, and the rough leg came away in his iron hand.

"Here is my cudgel, wanderer!" roared the Gael. "Let the breaking of heads begin and if the Prophet loves you, he'd best fling his mantle over your skull!"

"Salaam to you, *malik!*" yelled Haroun. "No other king since Malik Ric would take up cudgels with a masterless wanderer!" And with giant laughter, he lunged.

The fight was necessarily short and fierce. The wine they had drunk had made eye and hand uncertain, and their feet unsteady, but it had not robbed them of their tigerish strength. Haroun struck first, as a bear strikes, and it was by luck rather than skill that Cahal partly parried the whistling blow. Even so it fell glancingly above his ear, filling his vision with a myriad sparks of light, and knocking him back against the upset table. Cahal gripped the table edge with his left hand for support and struck back so savagely and swiftly that Haroun could neither duck nor parry. Blood spattered, the cudgel splintered in Cahal's hand and the Traveler dropped like a log, to lie motionless.

Cahal flung aside his cudgel with a motion of disgust and shook his head violently to clear it.

"Neither of us would yield to the other—well, in this I have prevailed—"

He stopped. Haroun lay sprawled serenely and a sound of placid snoring rose on the air. Cahal's blow had laid open his scalp and felled him, but it was the incredible amount of liquor the Tatar had drunk that had caused him to lie where he had fallen. And now Cahal knew that if he did not get out into the cool night air at once, he too would fall senseless beside Haroun.

Cursing himself disgustedly, he kicked his servant awake and gathering up shield, helmet and cloak, staggered out of the inn. Great white clusters of stars hung over the flat roofs of Damietta, reflected in the black lapping waves of the river. Dogs and beggars slept in the dust of the street, and in the black shadows of the crooked alleys not even a thief stole. Cahal swung into the saddle of the horse the sleepy servant brought, and reined his way through the winding silent streets. A cold wind, forerunner of dawn, cleared away the fumes of the wine as he rode out of the tangle of alleys and bazaars. Dawn was not yet whitening the east, but the tang of dawn was in the air.

Past the flat-topped mud huts along the irrigation ditches he rode, past the wells with their long wooden sweeps and deep clumps of palms. Behind him the ancient city slumbered, shadowy, mysterious, alluring. Before him stretched the sands of the Jifar.

CHAPTER 2

The Bedouins did not cut Red Cahal's throat on the road from Damietta to Ascalon. He was preserved for a different destiny and so he rode, careless, and alone except for his ragamuffin servant, across the wastelands, and no barbed arrow or curved blade touched him, though a band of hawk-like riders in floating white khalats harried him the last part of the way and followed him like a wolf pack to the very gates of the Christian outposts.

It was a restless and unquiet land through which Red Cahal rode on his pilgrimage to Jerusalem in the warm spring days of that year 1243. The red-haired prince learned much that was new to him, of the land which had been but a vague haze of disconnected names and events in his mind when he started on his exiled pilgrimage. He had known that the Emperor Frederick II had regained Jerusalem from the infidels without fighting a battle. Now he learned that the Holy City was shared with the Moslems—to whom it likewise was holy; Al Kuds, the Holy, they called it, for from thence, they said, Muhammad ascended to paradise, and there on the last day would he sit in judgment on the souls of men.

And Cahal learned that the kingdom of Outremer was but a shadow of an heroic past. In the north Bohemund VI held Antioch and Tripoli. In the south Christendom held the coast as far as Ascalon, with some inland towns such as Hebron, Bethlehem, and Ramlah. The grim castles of the Templars and of the Knights of St. John loomed like watchdogs above the land and the fierce soldier-monks wore arms day and night, ready to ride to any part of the kingdom threatened by pagan invasion. But how long could that thin line of ramparts and men along the coast stand against the growing pressure of the heathen hinterlands?

In the talk of castle and tavern, as he rode toward Jerusalem, Cahal heard again the name of Baibars. Men said the sultan of Egypt, kin of the great Saladin, was in his dotage, ruled by the girl-slave, Shadjar ad Darr, and that sharing her rule were the war-chiefs, Ae Beg the Kurd, and Baibars the Panther. This Baibars was a devil in human form, men said—a guzzler of wine and a lover of women; yet his wits were as keen as a monk's and his prowess in battle was the subject of many songs among the Arab minstrels. A strong man, and ambitious.

He was generalissimo of the mercenaries, men said, who were the real strength of the Egyptian army—Bahairiz, some called them, others the White Slaves of the River, the memluks. This host was, in the main, composed of Turkish slaves, raised up in its ranks and trained only in the arts of war. Baibars himself had served as a common soldier in the ranks, rising to power by the sheer might of his arm. He could eat a roasted sheep at one meal, the Arab wanderers said, and though wine was forbidden the Faithful, it was well known that he had drunk all his officers under the table. He had been known to break a man's spine in his bare hands in a moment of rage, and when he rode into battle swinging his heavy scimitar, none could stand before him.

And if this incarnate devil came up out of the South with his cutthroats, how could the lords of Outremer stand against him, without the aid that war-torn and intrigue-racked Europe had ceased to send? Spies slipped among the Franks, learning their weaknesses, and it was said that Baibars himself had gained entrance into Bohemund's palace in the guise of a wandering teller-of-tales. He must be in league with the Evil One himself, this Egyptian chief. He loved to go among his people in disguise, it was said, and he ruthlessly slew any man who recognized him. A strange soul, full of wayward whims, yet ferocious as a tiger.

Yet it was not so much Baibars of whom the people talked, nor yet of Sultan Ismail, the Moslem lord of Damascus. There was a threat in the blue mysterious East which overshadowed both these nearer foes.

Cahal heard of a strange new terrible people, like a scourge out of the East—Mongols, or Tartars as the priests called them, swearing they were the veritable demons of Tatary, spoken of by the prophets of old. More than a score of years before they had burst like a sandstorm out of the East, trampling all in their path; Islam had crumpled before them and kings had been dashed into the dust. And as their chief, men named one Subotai, whom Haroun the traveler, Cahal remembered, had claimed as sire.

Then the horde had turned its course and the Holy Land had been spared. The Mongols had drifted back into the limbo of the unknown East with their oxtail standards, their lacquered armor, their kettledrums and terrible bows, and men had almost forgotten them. But now of late years the vultures had circled again in the East, and from time to time news had trickled down through the hills of the Kurds, of the Turkoman clans flying in shattered rout before the yak-tail banners. Suppose the unconquerable Horde should turn southward? Subotai had spared Palestine—but who knew the mind of Mangu Khan, whom the Arab wanderers named the present lord of the nomads?

So the people talked in the dreamy spring weather as Cahal rode to Jerusalem, seeking to forget the past, losing himself in the present; absorbing the spirit and traditions of the country and the people, picking up new languages with the characteristic facility of the Gael.

He journeyed to Hebron, and in the great cathedral of the Virgin at Bethlehem, knelt beside the crypt where candles burned to mark the birthplace of our fair Seigneur Christ. And he rode up to Jerusalem, with its ruined walls and its mullahs calling the muezzin within earshot of the priests chanting beside the Sepulcher. Those walls had been destroyed by the Sultan of Damascus, years before.

Beyond the Via Dolorosa he saw the slender columns of the Al Aksa portals and was told Christian hands first shaped them. He was shown mosques that had once been Christian chapels, and was told that the gilded dome above the mosque of Omar covered a gray rock which was the Muhammadan holy of holies—the rock whence the Prophet ascended to paradise. Aye, and thereon, in the days of Israel, had Abraham stood, and the Ark of the Covenant had rested, and the Temple whence Christ drove the merchants; for the Rock was the pinnacle of Mount Moriah, one of the two mountains on which Jerusalem was built. But now the Moslem Dome of the Rock hid it from Christian view, and dervishes with naked swords stood night and day to bar the way of Unbelievers; though nominally the city was in Christian hands. And Cahal realized how weak the Franks of Outremer had grown.

He rode in the hills about the Holy City and stood on the Mount of Olives where Tancred had stood, nearly a hundred and fifty years before, for his first sight of Jerusalem. And he dreamed deep dim dreams of those old days when men first rode from the West strong with faith and eager with zeal, to found a kingdom of God.

Now men cut their neighbors' throats in the West and cried out beneath the heels of ambitious kings and greedy popes, and in their wars and crying out, forgot that thin frontier where the remnants of a fading glory clung to their slender boundaries.

Through budding spring, hot summer and dreamy autumn, Red Cahal rode—following a blind pilgrimage that led even beyond Jerusalem and whose goal he could not see or guess. Ascalon he tarried in, Tyre, Jaffa and Acre. He was visitor at the castles of the Military Orders. Walter de Brienne offered him a part in the rule of the fading kingdom, but Cahal shook his head and rode on. The throne he had never pressed had been snatched beyond his reach and no other earthly glory would suffice.

And so in the budding dream of a new spring he came to the castle of Renault d'Ibelin beyond the frontier.

CHAPTER 3

The Sieur Renault was a cousin of the powerful crusading family of d'Ibelin which held its grim gray castles on the coast, but little of the fruits of conquest had fallen to him. A wanderer and adventurer, living by his wits and the edge of his sword, he had gotten more hard blows than gold. He was a tall lean man with hawk-eyes and a predatory nose. His mail was worn, his velvet cloak shabby and torn, the gems long gone from hilt of sword and dagger.

And the knight's hold was a haunt of poverty. The dry moat which encircled the castle was filled up in many places; the outer walls were mere heaps of crumbled stone. Weeds grew rank in the courtyard and over the filled-up well.

The chambers of the castle were dusty and bare, and the great desert spiders spun their webs on the cold stones. Lizards scampered across the broken flags and the tramp of mailed feet resounded eerily in the echoing emptiness. No merry villagers bearing grain and wine thronged the barren courts, and no gayly clad pages sang among the dusty corridors. For over half a century the keep had stood deserted, until d'lbelin had ridden across the Jordan to make it a reaver's hold. For the Sieur Renault, in the stress of poverty, had become no more than a bandit chief, raiding the caravans of the Moslems.

And now in the dim dusty tower of the crumbling hold, the knight in his shabby finery sat at wine with his guest.

"The tale of your betrayal is not entirely unknown to me, good sir," said Renault—unbidden, for since that night of drunkenness in Damietta, Cahal had not spoken of his past. "Some word of affairs in Ireland has drifted into this isolated land. As one ruined adventurer to another, I bid you welcome. But I would like to hear the tale from your own lips."

Cahal laughed mirthlessly and drank deeply.

"A tale soon told and best forgotten. I was a wanderer, living by my sword, robbed of my heritage before my birth. The English lords pretended to sympathize with my claim to the Irish throne. If I would aid them against the O'Neills, they would throw off their allegiance to Henry of England—would serve me as my barons. So swore William Fitzgerald and his peers. I am not an utter fool. They had not persuaded me so easily but for the Lady Elinor de Courcey, with her black hair and proud Norman eyes—who feigned love for me. Hell!

"Why draw out the tale? I fought for them—won wars for them. They tricked me and cast me aside. I went into battle for the throne with less than a thousand men. Their bones rot in the hills of Donegal and better had I died there—but my kerns bore me senseless from the field. And then my own clan cast me forth.

"I took the cross—after I cut the throat of William Fitzgerald among his own henchmen. Speak of it no more; my kingdom was clouds and moonmist. I seek forgetfulness—of lost ambition and the ghost of a dead love."

"Stay here and raid the caravans with me," suggested Renault.

Cahal shrugged his shoulders.

"It would not last, I fear. With but forty-five men-at-arms, you can not hold this pile of ruins long. I have seen that the old well is long choked and broken in, and the reservoirs shattered. In case of a siege you would have only the tanks you have built, filled with water you carry from the muddy spring outside the walls. They would last only a few days at most."

"Poverty drives men to desperate deeds," frankly admitted Renault. "Godfrey, first lord of Jerusalem, built this castle for an outpost in the days when his rule extended beyond Jordan. Saladin stormed and partly dismantled it, and since then it has housed only the bat and the jackal. I made it my lair, from whence I raid the caravans which go down to Mecca, but the plunder has been scanty enough.

"My neighbor the Shaykh Suleyman ibn Omad will inevitably wipe me out if I bide here long, though I have skirmished successfully with his riders and beat off a flying raid. He has sworn to hang my head on his tower, driven to madness by my raids on the Mecca pilgrims whom it is his obligation to protect.

"Well, I have another thing in mind. Look, I scratch a map on the table with my dagger-point. Here is this castle; here to the north is El Omad, the stronghold of the Shaykh Suleyman. Now look—far to the east I trace a wandering line—so. That is the great river Euphrates, which begins in the hills of Asia Minor and traverses the whole plain, joining at last with the Tigris and flowing into Bahr el Fars—the Persian Gulf—below Bassorah. Thus—I trace the Tigris.

"Now where I make this mark beside the river Tigris stands Mosul of the Persians. Beyond Mosul lies an unknown land of deserts and mountains, but among those mountains there is a city called Shahazar, the treasure-trove of the sultans. There the lords of the East send their gold and jewels for safekeeping, and the city is ruled by a cult of warriors sworn to safeguard the treasures. The gates are kept bolted night and day, and no caravans pass out of the city. It is a secret place of wealth and pleasure and the Moslems seek to keep word of it from Christian ears. Now it is my mind to desert this ruin and ride east in quest of that city!"

Cahal smiled in admiration of the splendid madness, but shook his head.

"If it is as well guarded as you, say, how could a handful of men hope to take it, even if they win through the hostile country which lies between?"

"Because a handful of Franks *has* taken it," retorted d'Ibelin. "Nearly half a century ago the adventurer Cormac FitzGeoffrey raided Shahazar among the mountains and bore away untold plunder. What he did, another can do. Of course, it is madness; the chances are all that the Kurds will cut our throats before we ever see the banks of the Euphrates. But we will ride swiftly—and then, the Moslems may be so engaged with the Mongols, a small, hard-riding band might slip through. We will ride ahead of the news of our coming, and smite Shahazar as a whirlwind smites. Lord Cahal, shall we sit supine until Baibars comes up out of Egypt and cuts all our throats, or shall we cast the dice of chance to loot the eagle's eyrie under the nose of Moslem and Mongol alike?"

Cahal's cold eyes gleamed and he laughed aloud as the lurking madness in his soul responded to the madness of the proposal. His hard hand smote against the brown palm of Renault d'Ibelin.

"Doom hovers over all Outremer, and Death is no grimmer met on a mad quest than in the locked spears of battle! East we ride to the Devil knows what doom!"

The sun had scarce set when Cahal's ragged servant, who had followed him faithfully through all his previous wanderings, stole away from the ruined walls and rode toward Jordan, flogging his shaggy pony hard. The madness of his master was no affair of his and life was sweet, even to a Cairo gutter-waif.

The first stars were blinking when Renault d'Ibelin and Red Cahal rode down the slope at the head of the men-at-arms. A hard-bitten lot these were, lean taciturn fighters, born in Outremer for the most part—a few veterans of Normandy and the Rhineland who had followed wandering lords into the Holy Land and had remained. They were well armed—clad in chain-mail shirts and steel caps, bearing kite-shaped shields. They rode fleet Arab horses and tall Turkoman steeds, and led horses followed. It was the capture of a number of fine steeds which had crystallized the idea of the raid in Renault's mind.

D'Ibelin had long learned the lesson of the East—swift marches that went ahead of the news of the raid, and depended on the quality of the mounts. Yet he knew the whole plan was madness. Cahal and Renault rode into the unknown land and far in the east the vultures circled endlessly.

CHAPTER 4

The bearded watcher on the tower above the gates of El Omad shaded his hawk-eyes. In the east a dust cloud grew and out of the cloud a black dot came flying. And the lean Arab knew it was a lone horseman, riding hard. He shouted a warning, and in an instant other lean, hawk-eyed figures were at his side, brown fingers toying with bowstring and cane-shafted spear. They watched the approaching figure with the intentness of men born to feud and raid.

"A Frank," grunted one, "and on a dying horse."

They watched tensely as the lone rider dipped out of sight in a dry wadi, came into view again on the near side, clattered reelingly across the dusty level and drew rein beneath the gate. A lean hand drew shaft to ear, but a word from the first watcher halted the archer. The Frank below had half-climbed, half-fallen from his reeling horse, and now he staggered to the gate and smote against it resoundingly with his mailed fist.

"By Allah and by Allah!" swore the bearded watcher in wonder. "The Nazarene is mad!" He leaned over the battlement and shouted: "Oh, dead man, what wouldst thou at the gate of El Omad?"

The Frank looked up with eyes glazed from thirst and the burning winds of the desert. His mail was white with the drifting dust, with which likewise his lips were parched and caked. He spoke with difficulty.

"Open the gates, dog, lest ill befall you!"

"It is Kizil Malik—the Red King—whom men call The Mad," whispered an archer. "He rode with the lord Renault, the shepherds say. Hold him in play while I fetch the Shaykh."

"Art thou weary of life, Nazarene," called the first speaker, "that thou comest to the gate of thine enemy?"

"Fetch the lord of the castle, dog," roared the Gael. "I parley not with menials—and my horse is dying."

The tall lean form of Shaykh Suleyman ibn Omad loomed among the guardsmen and the old chief swore in his beard.

"By Allah, this is a trap of some sort. Nazarene, what do ye here?"

Cahal licked his blackened lips with a dry tongue.

"When the wild dogs run, panther and buffalo flee together," he said. "Doom rushes from the east on Moslem and Christian alike. I bring you warning—call in your vassals and make fast your gates, lest another rising sun find you sleeping among the charred embers of your hold. I claim the courtesy due a perishing traveler—and my horse is dying."

"It is no trap," growled the Shaykh in his beard. "The Frank has a tale—there has been a harrying in the east and perchance the Mongols are upon us—open the gates, dogs, and let him in."

Through the opened gates Cahal unsteadily led his drooping steed, and his first words gained him esteem among the Arabs.

"See to my horse," he mumbled, and willing hands complied.

Cahal stumbled to a horse block and sank down, his head in his hands. A slave gave him a flagon of water and he drank avidly. As he set down the flagon he was aware that the Shaykh had come from the tower and stood before him. Suleyman's keen eyes ran over the Gael from head to foot, noting the lines of weariness on his face, the dust that caked his mail, the fresh dints on helmet and shield—black dried blood was caked thick about the mouth of his scabbard, showing he had sheathed his sword without pausing to cleanse it.

"You have fought hard and fled swiftly," concluded Suleyman aloud.

"Aye, by the Saints!" laughed the prince. "I have fled for a night and a day and a night without rest. This horse is the third which has fallen under me—"

"Whom do you flee?"

"A horde that must have ridden up from the dim limbo of Hell! Wild riders with tall fur caps and the heads of wolves on their standards."

"Allah il Allah!" swore Suleyman. "Kharesmians!—flying before the Mongols!"

"They were apparently fleeing some greater horde," answered Cahal. "Let me tell the tale swiftly—the Sieur Renault and I rode east with all his men, seeking the fabled city of Shahazar—"

"So that was the quest!" interrupted Suleyman. "Well, I was preparing to sweep down and stamp out that robbers' nest when divers herdsmen brought me word that the bandits had ridden away swiftly in the night like the thieves they were. I could have ridden after, but knew that Christians riding eastward but rode to their doom—and none can alter the will of Allah."

"Aye," grinned Cahal wolfishly, "east to our doom we rode, like men riding blind into the teeth of a storm. We slashed our way through the lands of the Kurds and crossed the Euphrates. Beyond, far to the east, we saw smoke and flame and the wheeling of many vultures, and Renault said the Turkomans fought the Horde. But we met no fugitives and I wondered then—I wonder not now. The slayers rode over them like a wave out of the night and none was left to flee.

"Like men riding to death in a dream, we rode into the onrushing storm and the suddenness of its coming was like a thunderbolt. A sudden drum of hoofs over a ridge and they were upon us—hundreds of them, a swarm of outriders scouting ahead of the horde. There was no chance to flee—our men died where they stood."

"And the Sieur Renault?" asked the Shaykh.

"Dead!" said Cahal. "I saw a curved blade cleave his helmet and his skull."

"Allah be merciful and save his soul from the hellfire of unbelievers!" piously exclaimed Suleyman, who had sworn to kill the luckless adventurer on sight.

"He took toll before he fell," grimly answered the Gael. "By God, the heathen lay like ripe grain beneath our horses' hoofs before the last man fell. I alone hacked my way through."

The Shaykh, grown old in warfare, visualized the scene that lay behind that simple sentence—the swarming, howling, fur-clad horsemen with their barbaric war cries, and Red Cahal riding like a wind of Death through that maelstrom of flashing blades, his sword singing in his hand as horse and rider went down before him.

"I outstripped the pursuers," said Cahal, "and as I rode over a hill I looked back and saw the great black mass of the horde swarming like locusts over the land, filling the sky with the clamor of their kettledrums. The Turkomans had risen behind us as we had raced through their lands, and now the desert was alive with horsemen—but the whole east was aflame and the tribesmen had no time to hunt down a single rider. They were faced with a stronger foe. So I won through.

"My horse fell under me, but I stole a steed from a herd watched by a Turkoman boy. When it could do no more, I took a mount from a wandering Kurd who rode up, thinking to loot a dying traveler. And now I say to you, whom men dub the Watcher of the Trail—beware, lest these demons from the east ride over your ruins as they have ridden over the corpses of the Turkomans. I do not think they'll lay siege—they are like wolves ranging the steppes; they strike and pass on. But they ride like the wind. They have crossed the Euphrates. Behind me last night the sky was red as blood. Hard as I have ridden, they must be close on my heels."

"Let them come," grimly answered the Arab. "El Omad has held out against Nazarene, Kurd and Turk—for a hundred years no foe has set foot within these walls. *Malik*, this is a time when Christian and Moslem should join hands. I thank you for your warning, and beg you to aid me in holding the walls."

But Cahal shook his head.

"You will not need my help, and I have other work to do. It was not to save my worthless life that I have ridden three noble steeds to death—otherwise I had left my body beside Renault d'Ibelin. I must ride on; Jerusalem is in the path of these devils, with its ruined walls and scanty guard."

Suleyman paled and plucked his beard.

"Al Kuds! These pagan dogs will slay Christian and Muhammadan alike, and desecrate the holy places!"

"And so," Cahal rose stiffly, "I must on to warn them. So swiftly have these Kharesmians come that no word of their coming can have gone into

Palestine. On me alone the burden of warning lies. Give me a fleet horse and let me go."

"You can do no more," objected Suleyman. "You are foredone—an hour more and you would drop senseless from the saddle. I will send one of my men instead—"

Cahal shook his head. "The duty is mine. Yet I will sleep an hour—one small hour can make no great difference. Then I will fare on."

"Come to my couch," urged Suleyman, but the hardy Gael shook his head.

"This has been my couch before," said he, and flinging himself down on the scanty grass of the courtyard, he drew his cloak about him and fell into the deep sleep of utter exhaustion. Yet he slept but an hour when he awoke of his own accord. Food and wine were placed before him and he drank and ate ravenously. His features were still drawn and haggard, but in his short rest he had drawn upon hidden springs of endurance. An iron man in an age of iron, he added to his physical ruggedness a dynamic nerve-energy that carried him beyond himself and upheld him after more stolid men had dropped by the wayside.

As he reined out of the gates on a swift Arab steed, the watchmen shouted and pointed to the east where a pillar of smoke billowed up against the hot blue sky. The Shaykh flung up his arm in salute as Cahal rode toward Jerusalem at a swinging gallop that ate up the miles.

Bedouins in their black felt tents gaped at him; herdsmen leaning on their staves stiffened at his shout. A rising drum of hoofs, the wave of a mailed arm, a shouted warning, then the dwindling hoofbeats—behind him the frenzied people snatched up their belongings and fled shrieking to places of shelter or hiding.

CHAPTER 5

The moon was setting as Cahal splashed through the calm waters of the Jordan, flecked with the mirrored stars. The sun was rising when his horse fell at the gate of Jerusalem that opens on the Damascus road. Cahal staggered up, half-dead himself, and gazing at the crumbling ruins of the shattered walls, he groaned aloud. On foot he hurried forward and a group of placid Syrians watched him curiously. A bearded Flemish man-at-arms came forward, trailing his pike. Cahal snatched a wine-flask that hung at the soldier's girdle and emptied it at one draft.

"Lead me to the patriarch," he gasped throatily. "Doom rides on swift hoofs to Jerusalem—ha!"

From the people a thin cry of wonder and fear had gone up—Cahal wheeled and felt fear constrict his throat. Again in the east he saw flying flame and drifting smoke—the gigantic tracks of the destroying horde.

"They have crossed the Jordan!" he cried. "Saints of God, when did men born of women ride so madly? They spurn the very wind—curst be the weakness that made me waste a single hour—"

The words died in his throat as he looked at the ruined walls. Truly, an hour more or less could have no significance in that doomed city.

Cahal hurried through the streets with the soldier, and he saw that already the word had spread like wildfire. Jews in their blue shubas ran about howling; in the streets and on the housetops women wrung their white hands and wailed. Tall Syrians bound their belongings on donkeys and formed the nucleus of a disorderly horde that streamed out of the western gates staggering under bundles of household goods. The city crouched trembling and dazed with terror under the threat rising in the east. What horde was sweeping upon them they did not know, nor care; death is death, whoever the dealer.

Some cried out that the Tartars were upon them and both Moslem and Nazarene shook. Cahal found the patriarch bewildered and helpless. With a handful of soldiers, how could he defend the wallless city? He was ready to give up his life in the vain attempt; he could do no more. The mullahs rallied their people, and for the first time in all history Moslem and Christian joined forces to defend the city that was holy to both. The great mass of the people fled into the mosques or the cathedrals, or crouched resignedly in the streets, dumbly awaiting the stroke. Men cried on Jehovah and on Allah, and some prophesied a miracle that should deliver the Holy City. But in the merciless blue sky no flaming sword appeared, only the smoke of the pillaging, the flame of the slaughter, and at last the dust clouds of the riders.

The patriarch had bunched his pitiful force of men-at-arms, knights, armed pilgrims and Moslems, at the Damascus Gate. Useless to man the ruined walls. There they would face the horde and give up their lives, without hope and without fear.

Cahal, his weariness half-forgotten in the drunkenness of anticipated battle, reined beside the patriarch on the great red stallion that had been given him, and cried out suddenly at the sight of a tall, broad man on a rangy Turkish bay.

"Haroun, by all the Saints!"

The other turned toward him and Cahal wavered. Was this Haroun? The fellow was clad in the mail shirt and peaked helmet of a Turkish soldier. On his brawny right arm he bore a round spiked buckler and at his belt hung a long broad scimitar, heavier by pounds than the average Moslem blade. Moreover, Haroun had been clean-shaven and this man wore the fierce curving mustachios of the Turk. Yet the build of him—that square dark face—those blazing blue eyes—

"By the Saints, Haroun," said Cahal heartily, "what do you here?"

"Allah blast me if I be any Haroun," answered the soldier in a deep growling voice. "I am Akbar the Soldier, come to Al Kuds on pilgrimage. You have mistaken me for another."

Cahal frowned. The voice was not even that of Haroun, yet surely in all the world there was not such another pair of eyes. He shrugged his shoulders.

"Well, it is of no moment—where are you going?"

For the man had reined about.

"To the hills!" answered the soldier. "We can do no good by dying here—best come with me. From the dust, it is a whole horde that is riding upon us."

"Flee without striking a blow? Not I!" snapped Cahal. "Go, if you fear."

Akbar swore loudly. "By Allah and by Allah! A man had better place his head beneath an elephant's tread than call me coward! I'll stand my ground as long as any Nazarene!"

Cahal turned away shortly, irritated by the fellow's manner and by his boasting. Yet for all the soldier's wrath, it seemed to the Gael that a vagrant twinkle lighted his fierce eyes as though he shook with inward mirth. Then Cahal forgot him. A wail went up from the housetops where the helpless people watched their oncoming doom. The horde had swept into sight, up from the hazes of the Jordan's gorge.

The skies shook with the clamor of the kettledrums; the earth trembled with the thunder of the hoofs. The headlong speed of the yelling fiends numbed the minds of their victims. From the steppes of high Asia these barbarians had fled before the Mongols like thistledown flying before the wind. Drunken with the blood of slaughtered tribes, ten thousand strong they surged on Jerusalem, where thousands of helpless folk knelt shuddering.

Cahal saw anew the hideous figures which had haunted his half-delirious dreams as he swayed in the saddle on that long flight: tall rangy steeds on which crouched the broad forms of the riders in wolfskins and mail—square dark faces, eyes glaring like mad dogs' from beneath high fur caps or peaked helmets; standards with the heads of wolves, panthers and bears.

Headlong they swept down the Damascus road—leaping their horses over the broken walls, crowding through the ruined gates at breakneck speed—and headlong they smote the clump of defenders which spurred to meet them—smote them, broke them, shattered them, trampled them down and under, and over their mangled bodies, struck the heart of the doomed city.

Red hell reigned rampant in the streets of Jerusalem, where helpless men, women and children ran screaming before the slayers who rode them down, howling like wolves, spitting babes on their lances and holding them on high like gory standards. Under the frenzied hoofs pitiful forms fell writhing and blood flooded the gutters. Dark blood-stained hands tore the garments from shrieking girls and lance-butts shattered doors and windows behind which cowered terrified prey. All objects of worth were ripped from their places and screams of agony rose to the smoke-fouled heavens as the victims were tortured with steel and fire to make them give up their pitiful treasures. Death stalked howling through the streets of Jerusalem and men blasphemed their gods as they died.

In the first irresistible flood of that charge, such defenders as were not instantly ridden down had been torn apart and swept back in utter confusion. The weight of the impact had swept Red Cahal's steed away as on the crest of a flood, and he found himself reining about in a narrow alley, where he had been tossed as a bit of driftwood is flung into a back-eddy by a rushing tide. He had lost sight of the patriarch and had no doubt that he lay among the trampled dead before the Damascus Gate.

His sword was red to the hilt, his soul ablaze with the battle-lust, his brain sick with fury and horror as the cries of the butchered city smote on his ears.

"I'll leave my corpse before the Sepulcher," he growled, and wheeling, spurred up the alley. He raced down a narrow winding street and emerged upon the Via Dolorosa just as the first Kharesmian came flying along it, scimitar dripping crimson. The red stallion's shoulder brushed the barbarian's stirrup and Cahal's sword flashed like a sunburst. The Kharesmian's head leaped from his shoulders on an arch of crimson and the Gael yelped with murderous exultation.

And now came another riding like the wind, and Cahal saw it was Akbar. The soldier reined in and shouted, "Well, good sir, are you still determined to sacrifice both our lives?"

"Your life is your own—my life is mine!" roared Cahal, eyes blazing.

He saw that a group of horsemen had ridden up to the Sepulcher from another street and were dismounting, shouting in their barbaric tongue, spattering the holy stones with blood-drops from their blades. In a red mist of fury Cahal smote them as an avalanche smites the pines. His whistling sword cleft buckler and helmet, severing necks and splitting skulls; under the hammering hoofs of his screaming charger, men rolled with smashed heads. And even in his madness Cahal was aware that he was not alone. Akbar had charged after him; his great voice roared above the clamor and the heavy scimitar in his left hand crashed through mail and flesh and bone.

The men before the Sepulcher lay in a silent gory heap when Cahal reined back and shook the bloody mist from his eyes. Akbar roared in a strange tongue and smote him thunderously on the shoulders.

"*Bodga, bogatyr*!" he roared, his eyes dancing, and no longer Cahal doubted that he was Haroun. "You fight like a hero, by Erlik! But come, *malik*—you have offered a noble sacrifice to your God and He'll hardly blame you for saving yourself now. Thunder of Allah, man, we can not fight ten thousand!"

"Ride on," answered Cahal, shaking the red drops from his blade. "Here I die."

"Well," laughed Akbar, "if you wish to throw away your life here where it will do no good—that's your affair! The heathen may thank you, but your brothers scarcely will, when the raiders smite them suddenly! The horsemen are all dead or hemmed in the alleys. Only you and I escaped that charge. Who will carry the news of the raid to the Frankish barons?"

"You speak truth," said Cahal shortly. "Let us go."

The pair wheeled away and galloped down the street just as a howling horde came flying up the other end. Beyond the shattered walls Cahal looked back to see a mounting flame. He hid his face in his hands.

"Wounds of God!" he groaned. "They are burning the Sepulcher!"

"And defiling the Al Aksa mosque too, I doubt not," said Akbar tranquilly. "Well, that which is written will come to pass, and no man may escape his fate. All things pass away, yes, even the Holy of Holies."

Cahal shook his head, soul-sick. They rode through toiling bands of fugitives who screamed and caught at their stirrups, but Cahal steeled his heart. If he was to bear warning to the barons, he could not be burdened by helpless ones.

The roar of pillage and slaughter faded into the distance; only the smoke stood up among the hills, mute witness of the horror. Akbar laughed gustily.

"By Allah!" he swore, smiting his saddlebow, "these Kharesmians are woundy fighters! They ride like Tatars and slay like Turks! Right well would I lead them into battle! I had rather fight beside them than against them."

Cahal made no reply. His strange companion seemed to him like a faun, a soulless fantastic being full of titanic laughter at all human things—a creature outside the boundaries of men's dreams and reverences.

Akbar spoke abruptly. "Here our roads part for a space, *malik*; your road lies to Ascalon—mine to El Kahira."

"Why to Cairo, Akbar, or Haroun, or whatever your name is?" asked Cahal.

"Because I have business with that great oaf, Baibars, whom the devil fly away with!" yelled Akbar, and his shout of laughter floated back above the hoof-beats.

It was hours later when Cahal, pushing his horse as hard as he dared, met the travelers—a slender knight in full mail and vizored helmet, with a single attendant, a big carle with a rough red beard, who wore a horned helmet and a shirt of scale-mail and bore a heavy ax. Something slumbering stirred in Cahal as he looked on that fierce bluff face, and he reined in.

"Man, where have I seen you before?"

The fierce frosty eyes met him levelly.

"By Odin, that I can't say. I'm Wulfgar the Dane and this is my master."

Cahal glanced at the silent knight with his plain shield. Through the bars of the vizor, shadowed eyes looked at him—great God! A shock went through Cahal, leaving him bewildered and shaken with a thousand racing chaotic thoughts. He leaned forward, striving to peer through the lowered vizor, and the knight drew back with an almost womanish gesture of rebuke. Cahal reddened.

"I crave your pardon, sir," he said. "I did not intend this seeming rudeness."

"My master has taken a vow not to speak or reveal his features until he has accomplished his penance," broke in the rough Dane. "He is known as the Masked Knight. We journey to Jerusalem."

Sorrowfully Cahal shook his head.

"No Christian may ride thither. The paynim from the outer steppes have swept over the walls and the Holy of Holies lies in smoking ruins."

The Dane's bearded mouth gaped.

"Jerusalem—taken?" he mouthed stupidly. "Why, good sir, that can not be! How would God allow his Holy City to fall into the hands of the infidels?"

"I know not," said Cahal bitterly. "The ways of God and His infinite mercy are past my knowledge—but the streets of Jerusalem run with the blood of His people and the Sepulcher is black with the flames of the heathen."

Perplexed, the Dane tugged at his red beard and glanced at his master, sitting image-like in the saddle.

"By Odin," he growled, "what are we to do now?"

"There is but one thing to be done," answered Cahal. "Ride back to Ascalon and give warning. I was going thither, but if you will do this thing, I will seek Walter de Brienne. Tell the Seneschal of Ascalon that Jerusalem has fallen to heathen Turks of the outer steppes, known as Kharesmians, who number some ten thousand men. Bid him arm for war—and let no grass grow under your horses' hoofs in going."

And Cahal reined aside and took the road for Jaffa.

CHAPTER 6

Cahal found Walter de Brienne in Ramlah, brooding in the White Mosque over the sepulcher of Saint George. Fainting with weariness the Gael told his tale in a few stark bare words, and even they seemed to drag leaden and lifeless from his blackened lips. He was but dimly aware that men led him into a house and laid him on a couch. And there he slept the sun around.

He woke to a deserted city. Horror-stricken, the people of Ramlah had gathered up their belongings and fled along the road to Jaffa, crying that the end of the world was come. But Walter de Brienne had ridden north, leaving a single man-at-arms to bid Cahal follow him to Acre. The Gael rode through the hollow-echoing streets, feeling like a ghost in a dead city. The western gates swung idly open and a spear lay on the worn flags, as if the watch had dropped their weapons and fled in a sudden panic.

Cahal rode through the fields of date-palms and groves of figtrees hugging the shadow of the wall, and out on the plain he overtook staggering crowds of frantic folk burdened with their goods and crying with weariness and thirst. When the fugitives saw Cahal they screamed with fear to know if the slayers were upon them. He shook his head, pushing through. It seemed logical to him that the Kharesmians would sweep on to the sea, and their path might well take them by Ramlah. But as he rode he scanned the horizon behind him and saw neither smoke-rack nor dust cloud.

He left the Jaffa road with its hurrying throngs, and swung north. Already the tale had passed like wildfire from mouth to mouth. The villages were deserted as the folk thronged to the coast towns or retired into towers on the heights. Christian Outremer stood with its back to the sea, facing the onrushing menace out of the East.

Cahal rode into Acre, where the waning powers of Outremer were already gathering—hawk-eyed knights in worn mail—the barons with their wolfish men-at-arms. Sultan Ismail of Damascus had sent swift emissaries urging an alliance—which had been quickly accepted. Knights of St. John from their great grim Krak des Chevaliers, Templars with their red skull-caps and untrimmed beards rode in from all parts of the kingdom—the grim silent watchdogs of Outremer.

Survivors had drifted into Ascalon and Jaffa—lame, weary folk, a bare handful who had escaped the torch and sword and survived the hardships of the flight. They told tales of horror. Seven thousand Christians, mostly women and children, had perished in the sack of Jerusalem. The Holy Sepulcher had been blackened by flame, the altars of the city shattered, the shrines burned with fire. Moslem had suffered with Christian. The patriarch was among the fugitives—saved from death by the valor and faithfulness of a nameless Rhinelander man-at-arms, who hid a cruel wound until he said, "Yonder be the towers of Ascalon, master, and since you have no more need o' me, I'll lie me down and sleep, for I be sore weary." And he died in the dust of the road.

And word came of the Kharesmian horde; they had not tarried long in the broken city, but swept on, down through the deserts of the south, to Gaza, where they lay encamped at last after their long drift. And pregnant, mysterious hints floated up from the blue web of the South, and de Brienne sent for Cahal O'Donnel.

"Good sir," said the baron, "my spies tell me that a host of memluks is advancing from Egypt. Their object is obvious—to take possession of the city the Kharesmians left desolate. But what else? There are hints of an alliance between the memluks and the nomads. If this be the case, we may as well be shriven before we go into battle, for we can not stand against both hosts.

"The men of Damascus cry out against the Kharesmians for befouling holy places—Moslem as well as Christian—but these memluks are of Turkish blood, and who knows the mind of Baibars, their master?

"Sir Cahal, will you ride to Baibars and parley with him? You saw with your own eyes the sack of Jerusalem and can tell him the truth of how the pagans befouled Al Aksa as well as the Sepulcher. After all, he is a Moslem. At least learn if he means to join hands with these devils.

"Tomorrow, when the cohorts of Damascus come up, we advance southward to go against the foe ere he can come against us. Ride you ahead of the host as emissary under a flag of truce, with as many men as you wish."

"Give me the flag," said Cahal. "I'll ride alone."

He rode out of the camp before sunset on a palfrey, bearing the flag of peace and without his sword. Only a battle-ax hung at his saddlebow as a precaution against bandits who respected no flag, as he rode south through a half-deserted land. He guided his course by the words of the wandering Arab herdsmen who knew all things that went on in the land. And beyond Ascalon he learned that the host had crossed the Jifar and was encamped to the southeast of Gaza. The close proximity to the Kharesmians made him wary and he swung far to the east to avoid any scouts of the pagans who might be combing the countryside. He had no trust in the peace-token as a safeguard against the barbarians.

He rode, in a dreamy twilight, into the Egyptian camp which lay about a cluster of wells a bare league from Gaza. Misgivings smote him as he noted their arms, their numbers, their evident discipline. He dismounted, displaying the peace-gonfalcon and his empty sword-belt. The wild memluks in their silvered mail and heron feathers swarmed about him in sinister silence, as if minded to try their curved blades on his flesh, but they escorted him to a spacious silk pavilion in the midst of the camp.

Black slaves with wide-tipped scimitars stood ranged about the entrance and from within a great voice—strangely familiar—boomed a song.

"This is the pavilion of the amir, even Baibars the Panther, *Caphar,*" growled a bearded Turk, and Cahal said as haughtily as if he sat on his lost throne amid his gallaglachs, "Lead me to your lord, dog, and announce me with due respect."

The eyes of the gaudily clad ruffian fell sullenly, and with a reluctant salaam he obeyed. Cahal strode into the silken tent and heard the memluk boom: "The lord Kizil Malik, emissary from the barons of Palestine!"

In the great pavilion a single huge candle on a lacquered table shed a golden light; the chiefs of Egypt sprawled about on silken cushions, quaffing the forbidden wine. And dominating the scene, a tall broad figure in voluminous silken trousers, satin vest, a broad cloth-of-gold girdle—without a doubt Baibars, the ogre of the South. And Cahal caught his breath—that coarse red hair—that square dark face—those blazing blue eyes—

"I bid you welcome, lord *Caphar,*" boomed Baibars. "What news do you bring?"

"You were Haroun the Traveler," said Cahal slowly, "and at Jerusalem you were Akbar the Soldier."

Baibars rocked with laughter.

"By Allah!" he roared, "I bear a scar on my head to this day as a relic of that night's bout in Damietta! By Allah, you gave me a woundy clout!"

"You play your parts like a mummer," said Cahal. "But what reason for these deceptions?"

"Well," said Baibars, "I trust no spy but myself, for one thing. For another it makes life worth living. I did not lie when I told you that night in Damietta that I was celebrating my escape from Baibars. By Allah, the affairs of the world weigh heavily on Baibars' shoulders, but Haroun the Traveler, he is a mad and merry rogue with a free mind and a roving foot. I play the mummer and escape from myself, and try to be true to each part—so long as I play it. Sit ye and drink!"

Cahal shook his head. All his carefully thought out plans of diplomacy fell away, futile as dust. He struck straight and spoke bluntly and to the point.

"A word and my task is done, Baibars," he said. "I come to find whether you mean to join hands with the pagans who desecrated the Sepulcher—and Al Aksa."

Baibars drank and considered, though Cahal knew well that the Tatar had already made up his mind, long before.

"Al Kuds is mine for the taking," he said lazily. "I will cleanse the mosques—aye, by Allah, the Kharesmians shall do the work, most piously. They'll make good Moslems. And winged war-men. With them I sow the thunder—who reaps the tempest?"

"Yet you fought against them at Jerusalem," Cahal reminded bitterly.

"Aye," frankly admitted the amir, "but there they would have cut my throat as quick as any Frank's. I could not say to them: 'Hold, dogs, I am Baibars!'"

Cahal bowed his lion-like head, knowing the futility of arguing.

"Then my work is done; I demand safe-conduct from your camp."

Baibars shook his head, grinning. "Nay, *malik*, you are thirsty and weary. Bide here as my guest."

Cahal's hand moved involuntarily toward his empty girdle. Baibars was smiling but his eyes glittered between narrowed lids and the slaves about him half-drew their scimitars.

"You'd keep me prisoner despite the fact that I am an ambassador?"

"You came without invitation," grinned Baibars. "I ask no parley. Di Zaro!"

A tall lank Venetian in black velvet stepped forward.

"Di Zaro," said Baibars in a jesting voice, "the *malik* Cahal is our guest. Mount ye and ride like the devil to the host of the Franks. There say that Cahal sent you secretly. Say that the lord Cahal is twisting that great fool Baibars about his finger, and pledges to keep him aloof from the battle."

The Venetian grinned bleakly and left the tent, avoiding Cahal's smoldering eyes. The Gael knew that the trade-lusting Italians were often in secret league with the Moslems, but few stooped so low as this renegade.

"Well, Baibars," said Cahal with a shrug of his shoulders, "since you must play the dog, there is naught I can do. I have no sword."

"I'm glad of that," responded Baibars candidly. "Come, fret not. It is but your misfortune to oppose Baibars and his destiny. Men are my tools—at the Damascus Gate I knew that those red-handed riders were steel to forge into a Moslem sword. By Allah, *malik*, if you could have seen me riding like the wind into Egypt—marching back across the Jifar without pausing to rest! Riding into the camp of the pagans with mullahs shouting the advantages of Islam! Convincing their wild Kuran Shah that his only safety lay in conversion and alliance!

"I do not fully trust the wolves, and have pitched my camp apart from them—but when the Franks come up, they will find our hordes joined for battle—and should be horribly surprized, if that dog di Zaro does his work well!"

"Your treachery makes me a dog in the eyes of my people," said Cahal bitterly.

"None will call you traitor," said Baibars serenely, "because soon all will cease to be. Relics of an outworn age, I will rid the land of them. Be at ease!"

He extended a brimming goblet and Cahal took it, sipped at it absently, and began to pace up and down the pavilion, as a man paces in worry and despair. The memluks watched him, grinning surreptitiously.

"Well," said Baibars, "I was a Tatar prince, I was a slave, and I will be a prince again. Kuran Shah's shaman read the stars for me—and he says that if I win the battle against the Franks, I will be sultan of Egypt!"

The amir was sure of his chiefs, thought Cahal, to thus flaunt his ambition openly. The Gael said, "The Franks care not who is sultan of Egypt."

"Aye, but battles and the corpses of men are stairs whereby I climb to fame. Each war I win clinches my hold on power. Now the Franks stand in my path; I will brush them aside. But the shaman prophesied a strange thing—that a dead man's sword will deal me a grievous hurt when the Franks come up against us—"

From the corner of his eye Cahal saw that his apparently aimless strides had taken him close to the table on which stood the great candle. He lifted the goblet toward his lips, then with a lightning flick of his wrist, dashed the wine onto the flame. It sputtered and went out, plunging the tent into total darkness. And simultaneously Cahal ripped a hidden dirk from under his arm and like a steel spring released, bounded toward the place where he knew Baibars sat. He catapulted into somebody in the dark and his dirk hummed and sank home. A death scream ripped the clamor and the Gael wrenched the blade free and sprang away. No time for another stroke. Men yelled and fell over each other and steel clanged wildly. Cahal's crimsoned blade ripped a long slit in the silk of the tent-wall and he sprang into the outer starlight where men were shouting and running toward the pavilion.

Behind him a bull-like bellowing told the Gael that his blindly stabbing dirk had found some other flesh than Baibars'. He ran swiftly toward the horse-lines, leaping over taut tent-ropes, a shadow among a thousand racing figures. A mounted sentry came galloping through the confusion, firelight gleaming on his drawn scimitar. As a panther leaps Cahal sprang, landing behind the saddle. The memluk's startled yell broke in a gurgle as the keen dirk crossed his throat.

Flinging the corpse to the earth, the Gael quieted the snorting, plunging steed and reined it away. Like the wind he rode through the swarming camp and the free air of the desert struck his face. He gave the Arab horse the rein and heard the clamor of pursuit die away behind him. Somewhere to the north lay the slowly advancing host of the Christians, and Cahal rode north. He hoped to overtake the Venetian on the road, but the other had too long a start. Men who rode for Baibars rode with a flowing rein.

The Franks were breaking camp at dawn when a Venetian rode headlong into their lines, gasping a tale of escape and flight, and demanding to see de Brienne.

Within the baron's half-dismantled tent, di Zaro gasped: "The lord Cahal sent me, *seigneur*—he holds Baibars in parley. He gives his word that the memluks will not join the Kharesmians, and urges you to press forward—"

Outside a clatter of hoofs split the din—a lone rider whose flying hair was like a veil of blood against the crimson of dawn. At de Brienne's tent the hard-checked steed slid to its haunches. Cahal leaped to the earth and rushed in like an avenging blast. Di Zaro cried out and paled, frozen by his doom—till Cahal's dirk split his heart and the Venetian rolled, an earthen-faced corpse, to Walter de Brienne's feet. The baron sprang up, bewildered.

"Cahal! What news, in God's name?"

"Baibars joins arms with the pagans," answered Cahal.

De Brienne bowed his head.

"Well—no man can ask to live forever."

CHAPTER 7

Through the drear gray dusty desert the host of Outremer crawled southward. The black and white standard of the Templars floated beside the cross of the patriarch, and the black banners of Damascus billowed in the faintly stirring air. No king led them. The Emperor Frederick claimed the kingship of Jerusalem and he skulked in Sicily, plotting against the pope. De Brienne had been chosen to lead the barons and he shared his command with Al Mansur el Haman, warlord of Damascus.

They went into camp within sight of the Moslem outposts, and all night the wind that blew up from the south throbbed with the beat of drums and the clash of cymbals. Scouts reported the movements of the Kharesmian horde, and that the memluks had joined them.

In the gray light of dawn Red Cahal came from his tent fully armed. On all sides the host was moving, striking tents and buckling armor. In the illusive light Cahal saw them moving like phantoms—the tall patriarch, shriving and blessing; the giant form of the Master of the Temple among his grim war-dogs; the heron-feathered gold helmet of Al Mansur. And he stiffened as he saw a slim mailed shape moving through the swarm, followed close by a rough figure with ax on shoulder. Bewildered, he shook his head—why did his heart pound so strangely at sight of that mysterious Masked Knight? Of whom did the slim youth remind him, and of what dim bitter memories? He felt as one plunged into a web of illusion.

And now a familiar figure fell upon Cahal and embraced him.

"By Allah!" swore Shaykh Suleyman ibn Omad, "but for thee I had slept in the ruins of my keep! They came like the wind, those dogs, but they found the gates closed, the archers on the walls—and after one assault, they passed on to easier prey! Ride with me this day, my son!"

Cahal assented, liking the lean hearty old desert hawk. And so it was in the glittering, plume-helmeted ranks of Damascus the Gael rode to battle.

In the dawn they moved forward, no more than twelve thousand men to meet the memluks and nomads—fifteen thousand warriors, not counting light-armed irregulars. In the center of the right wing the Templars held their accustomed place, in advance of the rest; five hundred grim iron men, flanked on one side by the Knights of St. John and the Teutonic Knights, some three hundred in all; and on the other by the handful of barons with the patriarch and his iron mace. The combined forces of their men-at-arms did not exceed seven thousand. The rest of the host consisted of the cavalry of Damascus, in the center of the army, and the warriors of the amir of Kerak who held the left wing—lean hawk-faced Arabs better at raiding than at fighting pitched battles.

Now the desert blackened ahead of them with the swarms of their foes, and the drums throbbed and bellowed. The warriors of Damascus sang and chanted, but the men of the Cross were silent, like men riding to a known doom. Cahal, riding beside Al Mansur and Shaykh Suleyman, let his gaze sweep down those grim gray-mailed ranks, and found that which he sought. Again his heart leaped curiously at the sight of the slim Masked Knight, riding close to the patriarch. Close at the knight's side bobbed the horned helmet of the Dane. Cahal cursed, bewilderedly.

And now both hosts advanced, the dark swarms of the desert riders moving ahead of the ordered ranks of the memluks. The Kharesmians trotted forward in some formation, and Cahal saw the Crusaders close their ranks to meet the charge, without slackening their even pace. The wild riders struck in the rowels and the dark swarm rolled swiftly across the sands; then suddenly they shifted as a crafty swordsman shifts. Wheeling in perfect order they swept past the front of the knights and bursting into a headlong run, thundered down on the banners of Damascus.

The trick, born in the brain of Baibars, took the whole allied host by surprize. The Arabs yelled and prepared to meet the onset, but they were bewildered by the mad fury and numbing speed of that charge.

Riding like madmen the Kharesmians bent their heavy bows and shot from the saddle, and clouds of feathered shafts hummed before them. The leather bucklers and light mail of the Arabs were useless against those whistling missiles, and along the Damascus front warriors fell like ripe grain. Al Mansur was screaming commands for a countercharge, but in the teeth of that deadly blast the dazed Arabs milled helplessly, and in the midst of the confusion, the charge crashed into their lines. Cahal saw again the broad squat figures, the wild dark faces, the madly hacking scimitars—broader and heavier than the light Damascus blades. He felt again the irresistible concussion of the Kharesmian charge.

His great red stallion staggered to the impact and a whistling blade shivered on his shield. He stood up in his stirrups, slashing right and left, and felt mail-mesh part under his edge, saw headless corpses drop from their saddles. Up and down the line the blades were flashing like spray in the sun and the Damascus ranks were breaking and melting away. Man to man, the Arabs might have held fast; but dazed and outnumbered, that demoralizing rain of arrows had begun the rout that the curved swords completed.

Cahal, hurled back with the rest, vainly striving to hold his ground as he slashed and thrust, heard old Suleyman ibn Omad cursing like a fiend beside him as his scimitar wove a shining wheel of death about his head.

"Dogs and sons of dogs!" yelled the old hawk. "Had ye stood but a moment, the day had been yours! By Allah, pagan, will ye press me close?—So! Ha! Now carry your head to Hell in your hand! Ho, children, rally to me and the lord Cahal! My son, keep at my side. The fight is already lost and we must hack clear."

Suleyman's hawks reined in about him and Cahal, and the compact little knot of desperate men slashed through, riding down the snarling wolfish shapes that barred their path, and so rode out of the red frenzy of the mêlée into the open desert. The Damascus clans were in full flight, their black banners streaming ingloriously behind them. Yet there was no shame to be attached to them. That unexpected charge had simply swept them away, like a shattered dam before a torrent.

On the left wing the amir of Kerak was giving back, his ranks crumbling before the singing arrows and flying blades of tribesmen. So far the memluks had taken no part in the battle, but now they rode forward and Cahal saw the huge form of Baibars galloping into the fray, beating the howling nomads from their flying prey and reforming their straggling lines. The wolfskin-clad riders swung about and trotted across the sands, reinforced by the memluks in their silvered mail and heron-feathered helmets. So suddenly had the storm burst that before the Franks could wheel their ponderous lines to support the center, their Arab allies were broken and flying. But the men of the Cross came doggedly onward.

"Now the real death-grip," grunted Suleyman, "with but one possible end. By Allah, my head was not made to dangle at a pagan's saddlebow. The road to the desert is open to us—ha, my son, are you mad?"

For Cahal wheeled away, jerking his rein from the clutching hand of the protesting Shaykh. Across the corpse-littered plain he galloped toward the gray-steel ranks that swept inexorably onward. Riding hard, he swept into line just as the oliphants trumpeted for the onset. With a deep-throated roar the knights of the Cross charged to meet the onrushing hordes through a barbed and feathered cloud. Heads down, grimly facing the singing shafts that could not check them, the knights swept on in their last charge. With an earthquake shock the two hosts crashed together, and this time it was the Kharesmian horde which staggered.

The long lances of the Templars ripped their foremost line to shreds and the great chargers of the Crusaders overthrew horse and rider. Close on the heels of the warrior-monks thundered the rest of the Christian host, swords flashing. Dazed in their turn, the wild riders in their wolfskins reeled backward, howling and plying their deadly blades. But the long swords of the Europeans hacked through iron mesh and steel plate, to split skulls and bosoms. Squat corpses choked the ground under their horses' hoofs, as deep into the heart of the disorganized horde the knights slashed, and the yells of the tribesmen changed to howls of dismay as the whole battle-mass surged backward.

And now Baibars, seeing the battle tremble in the balance, deployed swiftly, skirted the ragged edge of the mêlée and hurled his memluks like a thunderbolt at the back of the Crusaders. The fresh, unwearied Bahairiz struck home, and the Franks found themselves hemmed in on all sides, as the wavering Kharesmians stiffened and with a fresh resurge of confidence renewed the fight.

Leaguered all about, the Christians fell fast, but even in dying they took bitter toll. Back to back, in a slowly shrinking ring facing outward, about a rocky knoll on which was planted the patriarch's cross, the last host of Outremer made its last stand.

Until the red stallion fell dying, Red Cahal fought in the saddle, and then he joined the ring of men on foot. In the berserk fury that gripped him, he felt not the sting of wounds. Time faded in an eternity of plunging bodies and frantic steel; of chaotic, wild figures that smote and died. In a red maze he saw a gold-mailed figure roll under his sword, and knew, in a brief passing flash of triumph, that he had slain Kuran Shah, khan of the horde. And remembering Jerusalem, he ground the dying face under his mailed heel. And the grim fight raged on. Beside Cahal fell the grim Master of the Temple, the Seneschal of Ascalon, the lord of Acre. The thin ring of defenders staggered beneath the repeated charges; blood blinded them, the heat of the sun smote fierce upon them, they were choked with dust and maddened with wounds. Yet with broken swords and notched axes they smote, and against that iron ring Baibars hurled his slayers again and again, and again and again he saw his hordes stagger back broken.

The sun was sinking toward the horizon when, foaming with rage that for once drowned his gargantuan laughter, he launched an irresistible charge upon the dying handful that tore them apart and scattered their corpses over the plain.

Here and there single knights or weary groups, like the drift of a storm, were ridden down by the chanting riders who swarmed the plain.

Cahal O'Donnel walked dazedly among the dead, the notched and crimsoned sword trailing in his weary hand. His helmet was gone, his arms and legs gashed, and from a deep wound beneath his hauberk, blood trickled sluggishly.

And suddenly his head jerked up.

"Cahal! Cahal!"

He drew an uncertain hand across his eyes. Surely the delirium of battle was upon him. But again the voice rose, in agony.

"Cahal!"

He was close to a boulder-strewn knoll where the dead lay thick. Among them lay Wulfgar the Dane, his unshaven lip a-snarl, his red beard tilted truculently, even in death. His mighty hand still gripped his ax, notched and clotted red, and a gory heap of corpses beneath him gave mute evidence of his berserk fury.

"Cahal!"

The Gael dropped to his knees beside the slender figure of the Masked Knight. He lifted off the helmet—to reveal a wealth of unruly black tresses—gray eyes luminous and deep. A choked cry escaped him.

"Saints of God! Elinor! I dream—this is madness—"

The slender mailed arms groped about his neck. The eyes misted with growing blindness. Through the pliant links of the hauberk blood seeped steadily.

"You are not mad, Red Cahal," she whispered. "You do not dream. I am come to you at last—though I find you but in death. I did you a deathly wrong—and only when you were gone from me forever did I know I loved you. Oh, Cahal, we were born under a blind unquiet star—both seeking goals of fire and mist. I loved you—and knew it not until I lost you. You were gone—and I knew not where.

"The Lady Elinor de Courcey died then, and in her place was born the Masked Knight. I took the Cross in penance. Only one faithful servitor knew my secret—and rode with me—to the ends of the earth—"

"Aye," muttered Cahal, "I remember him now—even in death he was faithful."

"When I met you among the hills below Jerusalem," she whispered faintly, "my heart tore at its strings to burst from my bosom and fall in the dust at your feet. But I dared not reveal myself to you. Ah, Cahal, I have done bitter penance! I have died for the Cross this day, like a knight. But I ask not forgiveness of God. Let Him do with me as He will—but oh, it is forgiveness of you I crave, and dare not ask!"

"I freely forgive you," said Cahal heavily. "Fret no more about it, girl; it was but a little wrong, after all. Faith, all things and the deeds and dreams of men are fleeting and unstable as moon-mist, even the world which has here ended."

"Then kiss me," she gasped, fighting hard against the onrushing darkness.

Cahal passed his arm under her shoulders, lifting her to his blackened lips. With a convulsive effort she stiffened half-erect in his arms, her eyes blazing with a strange light.

"The sun sets and the world ends!" she cried. "But I see a crown of red gold on your head, Red Cahal, and I shall sit beside you on at throne of glory! Hail, Cahal, chief of Uland; hail, Cahal Ruadh, *ard-ri na Eireann*—"

She sank back, blood starting from her lips. Cahal eased her to the earth and rose like a man in a dream. He turned toward the low slope and staggered with a passing wave of dizziness. The sun was sinking toward the desert's rim. To his eyes the whole plain seemed veiled in a mist of blood through which vague phantasmal figures moved in ghostly pageantry. A chaotic clamor rose like the acclaim to a king, and it seemed to him that all the shouts merged into one thunderous roar: *"Hail, Cahal Ruadh, ard-ri na Eireann!"*

He shook the mists from his brain and laughed. He strode down the slope, and a group of hawklike riders swept down upon him with a swift rattle of hoofs. A bow twanged and an iron arrowhead smashed through his mail. With a laugh he tore it out and blood flooded his hauberk. A lance thrust at his throat and he caught the shaft in his left hand, lunging upward. The gray sword's point rent through the rider's mail, and his death-scream was still echoing when Cahal stepped aside from the slash of a scimitar and hacked off the hand that wielded it. A spear-point bent on the links of his mail and the lean gray sword leaped like a serpent-stroke, splitting helmet and head, spilling the rider from the saddle.

Cahal dropped his point to the earth and stood with bare head thrown back, as a gleaming clump of horsemen swept by. The foremost reined his white horse back on its haunches with a shout of laughter. And so the victor faced the vanquished. Behind Cahal the sun was setting in a sea of blood, and his hair, floating in the rising breeze, caught the last glints of the sun, so that it seemed to Baibars the Gael wore a misty crown of red gold.

"Well, *malik*," laughed the Tatar, "they who oppose the destiny of Baibars lie under my horses' hoofs, and over them I ride up the gleaming stair of empire!"

Cahal laughed and blood started from his lips. With a lion-like gesture he threw up his head, flinging high his sword in kingly salute.

"Lord of the East!" his voice rang like a trumpet-call, "welcome to the fellowship of kings! To the glory and the witch-fire, the gold and the moon-mist, the splendor and the death! Baibars, a king hails thee!"

And he leaped and struck as a tiger leaps. Not Baibars' stallion that screamed and reared, not his trained swordsmen, not his own quickness could have saved the memluk then. Death alone saved him—death that took the Gael in the midst of his leap. Red Cahal died in midair and it was a corpse that crashed against Baibars' saddle—a falling sword in a dead hand, that, the momentum of the blow completing its arc, scarred Baibar's forehead and split his eyeball.

His warriors shouted and reined forward. Baibars slumped in the saddle, sick with agony, blood gushing from between the fingers that gripped his wound. As his chiefs cried out and sought to aid him, he lifted his head and saw, with his single, pain-dimmed eye, Red Cahal lying dead at his horse's feet. A smile was on the Gael's lips, and the gray sword lay in shards beside him, shattered, by some freak of chance, on the stones as it fell beside the wielder.

"A hakim, in the name of Allah," groaned Baibars. "I am a dead man."

"Nay, you are not dead, my lord," said one of his memluk chiefs. "It is the wound from the dead man's sword and it is grievous enough, but bethink you: here has the host of the Franks ceased to be. The barons are all taken or slain and the Cross of the patriarch has fallen. Such of the Kharesmians as live are ready to serve you as their new lord—since Kizil Malik slew their khan. The Arabs have fled and Damascus lies helpless before you—and Jerusalem is ours! You will yet be sultan of Egypt."

"I have conquered," answered Baibars, shaken for the first time in his wild life, "but I am half-blind—and of what avail to slay men of that breed? They will come again and again and again, riding to death like a feast because of the restlessness of their souls, through all the centuries. What though we prevail this little Now? They are a race unconquerable, and at last, in a year or a thousand years, they will trample Islam under their feet and ride again through the streets of Jerusalem."

And over the red field of battle night fell shuddering.

THE LION OF TIBERIAS

1

The battle in the meadowlands of the Euphrates was over, but not the slaughter. On that bloody field where the Caliph of Bagdad and his Turkish allies had broken the onrushing power of Doubeys ibn Sadaka of Hilla and the desert, the steel-clad bodies lay strewn like the drift of a storm. The great canal men called the Nile, which connected the Euphrates with the distant Tigris, was choked with the bodies of the tribesmen, and survivors were panting in flight toward the white walls of Hilla which shimmered in the distance above the placid waters of the nearer river. Behind them the mailed hawks, the Seljuks, rode down the fleeing, cutting the fugitives from their saddles. The glittering dream of the Arab emir had ended in a storm of blood and steel, and his spurs struck blood as he rode for the distant river.

Yet at one spot in the littered field the fight still swirled and eddied, where the emir's favorite son, Achmet, a slender lad of seventeen or eighteen, stood at bay with one companion. The mailed riders swooped in, struck and reined back, yelling in baffled rage before the lashing of the great sword in this man's hands. His was a figure alien and incongruous, his red mane contrasting with the black locks about him no less than his dusty gray mail contrasted with the plumed burnished headpieces and silvered hauberks of the slayers. He was tall and powerful, with a wolfish hardness of limbs and frame that his mail could not conceal. His dark, scarred face was moody, his blue eyes cold and hard as the blue steel whereof Rhineland gnomes forge swords for heroes in northern forests.

Little of softness had there been in John Norwald's life. Son of a house ruined by the Norman conquest, this descendant of feudal thanes had only memories of wattle-thatched huts and the hard life of a man-at-arms, serving for poor hire barons he hated. Born in north England, the ancient Danelagh, long settled by blue-eyed vikings, his blood was neither Saxon nor Norman, but Danish, and the grim unbreakable strength of the blue

North was his. From each stroke of life that felled him, he rose fiercer and more unrelenting. He had not found existence easier in his long drift East which led him into the service of Sir William de Montserrat, seneschal of a castle on the frontier beyond Jordan.

In all his thirty years, John Norwald remembered but one kindly act, one deed of mercy; wherefore he now faced a whole host, desperate fury nerving his iron arms.

It had been Achmet's first raid, whereby his riders had trapped de Montserrat and a handful of retainers. The boy had not shrunk from the swordplay, but the savagery that butchers fallen foes was not his. Writhing in the bloody dust, stunned and half-dead, John Norwald had dimly seen the lifted scimitar thrust aside by a slender arm, and the face of the youth bending above him, the dark eyes filled with tears of pity.

Too gentle for the age and his manner of life, Achmet had made his astounded warriors take up the wounded Frank and bring him with them. And in the weeks that passed while Norwald's wounds healed, he lay in Achmet's tent by an oasis of the Asad tribes, tended by the lad's own *hakim*. When he could ride again, Achmet had brought him to Hilla. Doubeys ibn Sadaka always tried to humor his son's whims, and now, though muttering pious horror in his beard, he granted Norwald his life. Nor did he regret it, for in the grim Englishman he found a fighting-man worth any three of his own hawks.

John Norwald felt no tugging of loyalty toward de Montserrat, who had fled out of the ambush leaving him in the hands of the Moslems, nor toward the race at whose hands he had had only hard knocks all his life. Among the Arabs he found an environment congenial to his moody, ferocious nature, and he plunged into the turmoil of desert feuds, forays and border wars as if he had been born under a Bedouin black felt tent instead of a Yorkshire thatch. Now, with the failure of ibn Sadaka's thrust at Bagdad and sovereignty, the Englishman found himself once more hemmed in by chanting foes, mad with the tang of blood. About him and his youthful comrade swirled the wild riders of Mosul; the mailed hawks of Wasit and Bassorah, whose lord, Zenghi Imad ed din, had that day outmaneuvered ibn Sadaka and slashed his shining host to pieces.

On foot among the bodies of their warriors, their backs to a wall of dead horses and men, Achmet and John Norwald beat back the onslaught. A heron-feathered emir reined in his Turkoman steed, yelling his war-cry, his house-troops swirling in behind him.

"Back, boy; leave him to me!" grunted the Englishman, thrusting Achmet behind him. The slashing scimitar struck blue sparks from his basinet and his great sword dashed the Seljuk dead from his saddle. Bestriding the chieftain's body, the giant Frank lashed up at the shrieking swordsmen who spurred in, leaning from their saddles to swing their blades. The curved sabers shivered on his shield and armor, and his long sword crashed through bucklers, breastplates, and helmets, cleaving flesh and splintering bones, littering corpses at his iron-sheathed feet. Panting and howling the survivors reined back.

Then a roaring voice made them glance quickly about, and they fell back as a tall, strongly built horseman rode through them and drew rein before the grim Frank and his slender companion. John Norwald for the first time stood face to face with Zenghi esh Shami, Imad ed din, governor of Wasit and warden of Basorah, whom men called the Lion of Tiberias, because of his exploits at the siege of Tiberias.

The Englishman noted the breadth of the mighty steel-clad shoulders, the grip of the powerful hands on rein and sword-hilt; the blazing magnetic blue eyes, setting off the ruthless lines of the dark face. Under the thin black lines of the mustaches the wide lips smiled, but it was the merciless grin of the hunting panther.

Zenghi spoke and there was at the back of his powerful voice a hint of mockery or gargantuan mirth that rose above wrath and slaughter.

"Who are these paladins that they stand among their prey like tigers in their den, and none is found to go against them? Is it Rustem whose heel is on the necks of my emirs—or only a renegade Nazarene? And the other, by Allah, unless I am mad, it is the cub of the desert wolf! Are you not Achmet ibn Doubeys?"

It was Achmet who answered; for Norwald maintained a grim silence, watching the Turk through slit eyes, fingers locked on his bloody hilt.

"It is so, Zenghi esh Shami," answered the youth proudly, "and this is my brother at arms, John Norwald. Bid your wolves ride on, oh prince. Many of them have fallen. More shall fall before their steel tastes our hearts."

Zenghi shrugged his mighty shoulders, in the grip of the mocking devil that lurks at the heart of all the sons of high Asia.

"Lay down your weapons, wolf-cub and Frank. I swear by the honor of my clan, no sword shall touch you."

"I trust him not," growled John Norwald. "Let him come a pace nearer and I'll take him to Hell with us."

"Nay," answered Achmet. "The prince keeps his word. Lay down your sword, my brother. We have done all men might do. My father the emir will ransom us."

He tossed down his scimitar with a boyish sigh of unashamed relief, and Norwald grudgingly laid down his broadsword.

"I had rather sheathe it in his body," he growled.

Achmet turned to the conqueror and spread his hands.

"Oh, Zenghi—" he began, when the Turk made a quick gesture, and the two prisoners found themselves seized and their hands bound behind them with thongs that cut the flesh.

"There is no need of that, prince," protested Achmet. "We have given ourselves into your hands. Bid your men loose us. We will not seek to escape."

"Be silent, cub!" snapped Zenghi. The Turk's eyes still danced with dangerous laughter, but his face was dark with passion. He reined nearer. "No sword shall touch you, young dog," he said deliberately. "Such was my word, and I keep my oaths. No blade shall come near you, yet the vultures shall pluck your bones tonight. Your dog-sire escaped me, but you shall not escape, and when men tell him of your end, he will tear his locks in anguish."

Achmet, held in the grip of the powerful soldiers, looked up, paling, but answered without a quaver of fear.

"Are you then a breaker of oaths, Turk?"

"I break no oath," answered the lord of Wasit. "A whip is not a sword."

His hand came up, gripping a terrible Turkoman scourge, to the seven rawhide thongs of which bits of lead were fastened. Leaning from his saddle as he struck, he brought those metal-weighted thongs down across the boy's face with terrible force. Blood spurted and one of Achmet's eyes was half torn from its socket. Held helpless, the boy could not evade the blows Zenghi rained upon him. But not a whimper escaped him, though his features turned to a bloody, raw, ghastly and eyeless ruin beneath the ripping strokes that shredded the flesh and splintered the bones beneath. Only at last a low animal-like moaning drooled from his mangled lips as he hung senseless and dying in the hands of his captors.

Without a cry or a word John Norwald watched, while the heart in his breast shriveled and froze and turned to ice that naught could touch or thaw or break. Something died in his soul and in its place rose an elemental spirit unquenchable as frozen fire and bitter as hoarfrost.

The deed was done. The mangled broken horror that had been Prince Achmet iby Doubeys was cast carelessly on a heap of dead, a touch of life still pulsing through the tortured limbs. On the crimson mask of his features fell the shadow of vulture wings in the sunset. Zenghi threw aside the dripping scourge and turned to the silent Frank. But when he met the burning eyes of his captive, the smile faded from the prince's lips and the taunts died unspoken. In those cold, terrible eyes the Turk read hate beyond common conception—a monstrous, burning, almost tangible thing, drawn up from the lower pits of Hell, not to be dimmed by time or suffering.

The Turk shivered as from a cold unseen wind. Then he regained his composure. "I give you life, infidel," said Zenghi, "because of my oath. You have seen something of my power. Remember it in the long dreary years when you shall regret my mercy, and howl for death. And know that as I serve you, I will serve all Christendom. I have come into Outremer and left their castles desolate; I have ridden eastward with the heads of their chiefs swinging at my saddle. I will come again, not as a raider but as a conqueror. I will sweep their hosts into the sea. Frankistan shall howl for her dead kings, and my horses shall stamp in the citadels of the infidel; for on this field I set my feet on the glittering stairs that lead to empire."

"This is my only word to you, Zenghi, dog of Tiberias," answered the Frank in a voice he did not himself recognize. "In a year, or ten years, or twenty years, I will come again to you, to pay this debt."

"Thus spake the trapped wolf to the hunter," answered Zenghi, and turning to the memluks who held Norwald, he said, "Place him among the unransomed captives. Take him to Bassorah and see that he is sold as a galley-slave. He is strong and may live for four or five years."

The sun was setting in crimson, gloomy and sinister for the fugitives who staggered toward the distant towers of Hilla that the setting sun tinted in blood. But the land was as one flooded with the scarlet glory of imperial pageantry to the Caliph who stood on a hillock, lifting his voice to Allah who had once more vindicated the dominance of his chosen viceroy, and saved the sacred City of Peace from violation.

"Verily, verily, a young lion has risen in Islam, to be as a sword and shield to the Faithful, to revive the power of Muhammad, and to confound the infidels!"

2

Prince Zenghi was the son of a slave, which was no great handicap in that day, when the Seljuk emperors, like the Ottomans after them, ruled through slave generals and satraps. His father, Ak Sunkur, had held high posts under the sultan Melik Shah, and as a young boy Zenghi had been taken under the special guidance of that war-hawk Kerbogha of Mosul. The young eagle was not a Seljuk; his sires were Turks from beyond the Oxus, of that people which men later called Tatars. Men of this blood were rapidly becoming the dominant factor in western Asia, as the empire of the Seljuks, who had enslaved and trained them in the art of ruling, began to crumble. Emirs were stirring restlessly under the relaxing yoke of the sultans. The Seljuks were reaping the yield of the seeds of the feudal system they had sown, and among the jealous sons of Melik Shah there was none strong enough to rebuild the crumbling lines.

So far the fiefs, held by feudal vassals of the sultans, were at least nominally loyal to the royal masters, but already there was beginning the slow swirling upheaval that ultimately reared kingdoms on the ruins of the old empire. The driving impetus of one man advanced this movement more than anything else—the vital dynamic power of Zenghi esh Shami—Zenghi the Syrian, so called because of his exploits against the Crusaders in Syria. Popular legendry has passed him by, to exalt Saladin who followed and overshadowed him; yet he was the forerunner of the great Moslem heroes who were to shatter the Crusading kingdoms, and but for him the shining deeds of Saladin might never have come to pass.

In the dim and misty pageantry of phantoms that move shadow-like through those crimson years, one figure stands out clear and bold-etched—a figure on a rearing black stallion, the black silken cloak flowing from his mailed shoulders, the dripping scimitar in his hand. He is Zenghi, son of the pagan nomads, the first of a glittering line of magnificent conquerors before whom the iron men of Christendom reeled—Nur-ad-din, Saladin, Baibars, Kalawun, Bayazid—aye, and Subotai, Genghis Khan, Hulagu, Tamerlane, and Suleiman the Great.

In 1124 the fall of Tyre to the Crusaders marked the high tide of Frankish power in Asia. Thereafter the hammer-strokes of Islam fell on a waning sovereignty. At the time of the battle of the Euphrates the kingdom of Outremer extended from Edessa in the north to Ascalon in the south, a distance of some five hundred miles. Yet it was in few places more than fifty miles broad, from east to west, and walled Moslem towns were within a day's ride of Christian keeps. Such a condition could not exist forever. That it existed as long as it did was owing partly to the indomitable valor of the cross-wearers, and partly to the lack of a strong leader among the Moslems.

In Zenghi such a leader was found. When he broke ibn Sadaka he was thirty-eight years of age, and had held his fief of Wasit but a year. Thirty-six was the minimum age at which the sultans allowed a man to hold a governorship, and most notables were much older when they were so honored than was Zenghi. But the honor only whetted his ambition.

The same sun that shone mercilessly on John Norwald, stumbling along in chains on the road that led to the galley's bench, gleamed on Zenghi's gilded mail as he rode north to enter the service of the sultan Muhammad at Hamadhan. His boast that his feet were set on the stairs of fame was no idle one. All orthodox Islam vied in honoring him.

To the Franks who had felt his talons in Syria, came faint tidings of that battle beside the Nile canal, and they heard other word of his growing power. There came tidings of a dispute between sultan and Caliph, and of Zenghi turning against his former master, riding into Bagdad with the banners of Muhammad. Honors rained like stars on his turban, sang the Arab minstrels. Warden of Bagdad, governor of Irak, prince of el Jezira, Atabeg of Mosul—on up the glittering stairs of power rode Zenghi, while the Franks ignored the tidings from the East with the perverse blindness of their race—until Hell burst along their borders and the roar of the Lion shook their towers.

Outposts and castles went up in flames, and Christian throats felt the knife edge, Christian necks the yoke of slavery. Outside the walls of doomed Athalib, Baldwin, king of Jerusalem, saw his picked chivalry swept broken and flying into the desert. Again at Barin the Lion drove Baldwin and his Damascene allies headlong in flight, and when the Emperor of Byzantium himself, John Comnene, moved against the victorious Turk, he found himself chasing a desert wind that turned unexpectedly and slaughtered his stragglers, and harried his lines until life was a burden and a stone about his royal neck. John Comnene decided that his Moslem neighbors were no more to be despised than his barbaric Frankish allies, and before he sailed away from the Syrian coast he held secret parleys with Zenghi that bore crimson fruit in later years. His going left the Turk free to move against his eternal enemies, the Franks. His objective was Edessa, northernmost stronghold of the Christians, and one of the most powerful of their cities. But like a crafty swordsman he blinded his foes by feints and gestures.

Outremer reeled before his blows. The land was filled with the chanting of the riders, the twang of bows, and the whine of swords. Zenghi's hawks swept through the land and their horses hoofs spattered blood on the standards of kings. Walled castles toppled in flame, sword-hacked corpses strewed the valleys, dark hands knotted in the yellow tresses of screaming women, and the lords of the Franks cried out in wrath and pain. Up the glittering stairs of empire rode Zenghi on his black stallion, his scimitar dripping in his hand, stars jeweling his turban.

And while he swept the land like a storm, and hurled down barons to make drinking-cups of their skulls and stables of their palaces, the galley-slaves, whispering to one another in their eternal darkness where the oars clacked everlastingly and the lap of the waves was a symphony of slow madness, spoke of a red-haired giant who never spoke, and whom neither labor, nor starvation, nor the dripping lash, nor the drag of the bitter years could break.

The years passed, glittering, star-strewn, gilt-spangled years to the rider in the shining saddle, to the lord in the golden-domed palace; black, silent, bitter years in the creaking, reeking, rat-haunted darkness of the galleys.

3

"He rides on the wind with the stars in his hair;
Like Death falls his shadow on castles and towns;
And the kings of the Caphars cry out in despair,
For the hoofs of his stallion have trampled their crowns."

Thus sang a wandering Arab minstrel in the tavern of a little outpost village which stood on the ancient—and now little-traveled—road from Antioch to Aleppo. The village was a cluster of mud huts huddling about a castle-crowned hill. The population was mongrel—Syrians, Arabs, mixed breeds with Frankish blood in their veins.

Tonight a representative group was gathered in the inn—native laborers from the fields; a lean Arab herdsman or two; French men-at-arms in worn leather and rusty mail, from the castle on the hill; a pilgrim wandered off his route to the holy places of the south; the ragged minstrel. Two figures held the attention of casual lookers-on. They sat on opposite sides of a rudely carved table, eating meat and drinking wine, and they were evidently strangers to each other, since no word passed between them, though each glanced surreptitiously at the other from time to time.

Both were tall, hard limbed and broad shouldered, but there the resemblance ended. One was clean-shaven, with a hawk-like predatory face from which keen blue eyes gleamed coldly. His burnished helmet lay on the bench beside him with the kite-shaped shield, and his mail coif was pushed back, revealing a mass of red-gold hair. His armor gleamed with gilt-work and silver chasing, and the hilt of his broadsword sparkled with jewels.

The man opposite him seemed drab by comparison, with his dusty gray chain mail and worn sword-hilt untouched by any gleam of gem or gold. His square-cut tawny mane was matched by a short beard which masked the strong lines of jaw and chin.

The minstrel finished his song with an exultant clash of the strings, and eyed his audience half in insolence, half in uneasiness.

"And thus, masters," he intoned, one eye on possible alms, the other on the door. "Zenghi, prince of Wasit, brought his memluks up the Tigris on boats to aid the sultan Muhammad who lay encamped about the walls of Bagdad. Then, when the Caliph saw the banners of Zenghi, he said, 'Lo, now is come up against me the young lion who overthrew ibn Sadaka for me; open the gates, friends, and throw yourselves on his mercy, for there is none found to stand before him.' And it was done, and the sultan gave to Zenghi all the land of el Jezira.

"Gold and power flowed through his fingers. Mosul, his capital, which he found a waste of ruins, he made to bloom as roses blossom by an oasis. Kings trembled before him but the poor rejoiced, for he shielded them from the sword. His servants looked on him as upon God. Of him it is told that he gave a slave a husk to hold, and not for a year did he ask for it. Then when he demanded it, lo, the man gave it into his hands, wrapped in a napkin, and for his diligence Zenghi gave him command of a castle. For though the Atabeg is a hard master, yet he is just to True Believers."

The knight in the gleaming mail flung the minstrel a coin.

"Well sung, pagan!" he cried in a harsh voice that sounded the Norman-French words strangely. "Know you the song of the sack of Edessa?"

"Aye, my lord," smirked the minstrel, "and with the favor of your lordships I will essay it."

"Your head shall roll on the floor first," spoke the other knight suddenly in a voice deep and somber with menace. "It is enough that you praise the dog Zenghi in our teeth. No man sings of his butcheries at Edessa, beneath a Christian roof in my presence."

The minstrel blenched and gave back, for the cold gray eyes of the Frank were grim. The knight in the ornate mail looked at the speaker curiously, no resentment in his reckless dancing eyes.

"You speak as one to whom the subject is a sore one, friend," said he.

The other fixed his somber stare on his questioner, but made no reply save a slight shrug of his mighty mailed shoulders as he continued his meal.

"Come," persisted the stranger, "I meant no offense. I am newly come to these parts—I am Sir Roger d'Ibelin, vassal to the king of Jerusalem. I have fought Zenghi in the south, when Baldwin and Anar of Damascus made alliance against him, and I only wished to hear the details of the taking of Edessa. By God, there were few Christians who escaped to bear the tale."

"I crave pardon for my seeming discourtesy," returned the other. "I am Miles du Courcey, in the service of the prince of Antioch. I was in Edessa when it fell.

"Zenghi came up from Mosul and laid waste the Diyar Bekr, taking town after town from the Seljuks. Count Joscelin de Courtenay was dead, and the rule was in the hands of that sluggard, Joscelin II. In the late fall of the year Zenghi laid siege to Amid, and the count bestirred himself—but only to march away to Turbessel with all his household.

"We were left at Edessa with the town in charge of fat Armenian merchants who gripped their moneybags and trembled in fear of Zenghi, unable to overcome their swinish avarice enough to pay the mongrel mercenaries Joscelin had left to defend the city.

"Well, as anyone might know, Zenghi left Amid and marched against us as soon as word reached him that the poor fool Joscelin had departed. He reared his siege engines over against the walls, and day and night hurled assaults against the gates and towers, which had never fallen had we had the proper force to man them.

"But to give them their due, our wretched mercenaries did well. There was no rest or ease for any of us; day and night the ballistas creaked, stones and beams crashed against the towers, arrows blinded the sky in their whistling clouds, and Zenghi's chanting devils swarmed up the walls. "We beat them back until our swords were broken, our mail hung in bloody tatters, and our arms were dead with weariness. For a month we kept Zenghi at bay, waiting for Count Joscelin, but he never came.

"It was on the morning of December 23rd that the rams and engines made a great breach in the outer wall, and the Moslems came through like a river bursting through a dam. The defenders died like flies along the broken ramparts, but human power could not stem that tide. The memluks rode into the streets and the battle became a massacre. The Turkish sword knew no mercy. Priests died at their altars, women in their courtyards, children at their play. Bodies choked the streets, the gutters ran crimson, and through it all rode Zenghi on his black stallion like a phantom of Death."

"Yet you escaped?"

The cold gray eyes became more somber.

"I had a small band of men-at-arms. When I was dashed senseless from my saddle by a Turkish mace, they took me up and rode for the western gate. Most of them died in the winding streets, but the survivors brought me to safety. When I recovered my senses the city lay far behind me.

"But I rode back." The speaker seemed to have forgotten his audience. His eyes were distant, withdrawn; his bearded chin rested on his mailed fist; he seemed to be speaking to himself. "Aye, I had ridden into the teeth of Hell itself. But I met a servant, fallen death-stricken among the straggling fugitives, and ere he died he told me that she whom I sought was dead—struck down by a memluk's scimitar."

Shaking his iron-clad shoulders he roused himself as from a bitter revelry. His eyes grew cold and hard again; the harsh timbre re-entered his voice.

"Two years have seen a great change in Edessa I hear. Zenghi rebuilt the walls and has made it one of his strongest holds. Our hold on the land is crumbling and tearing away. With a little aid, Zenghi will surge over Outremer and obliterate all vestiges of Christendom."

"That aid may come from the north," muttered a bearded man-at-arms. "I was in the train of the barons who marched with John Comnene when Zenghi outmaneuvered him. The emperor has no love for us."

"Bah! He is at least a Christian," laughed the man who called himself d'Ibelin, running his restless fingers through his clustering golden locks.

Du Courcey's cold eyes narrowed suddenly as they rested on a heavy golden ring of curious design on the other's finger, but he said nothing.

Heedless of the intensity of the Norman's stare, d'Ibelin rose and tossed a coin on the table to pay his reckoning. With a careless word of farewell to the idlers he rose and strode out of the inn with a clanking of armor. The men inside heard him shouting impatiently for his horse. And Sir Miles du Courcey rose, took up shield and helmet, and followed.

The man known as d'Ibelin had covered perhaps a half-mile, and the castle on the hill was but a faint bulk behind him, gemmed by a few points of light, when a drum of hoofs made him wheel with a guttural oath that was not French. In the dim starlight he made out the form of his recent inn companion, and he laid hand on his jeweled hilt. Du Courcey drew up beside him and spoke to the grimly silent figure.

"Antioch lies the other way, good sir. Perhaps you have taken the wrong road by mischance. Three hours' ride in this direction will bring you into Saracen territory."

"Friend," retorted the other, "I have not asked your advice concerning my road. Whether I go east or west is scarcely your affair."

"As vassal to the prince of Antioch it is my affair to inquire into suspicious actions within his domain. When I see a man traveling under false pretenses, with a Saracen ring on his finger, riding by night toward the border, it seems suspicious enough for me to make inquiries."

"I can explain my actions if I see fit," bruskly answered d'Ibelin, "but these insulting accusations I will answer at the sword's point. What mean you by false pretensions?"

"You are not Roger d'Ibelin. You are not even a Frenchman."

"No?" a sneer rasped in the other's voice as he slipped his sword from its sheath.

"No. I have been to Constantinople, and seen the northern mercenaries who serve the Greek emperor. I can not forget your hawk face. You are John Comnene's spy—Wulfgar Edric's son, a captain in the Varangian Guard."

A wild beast snarl burst from the masquerader's lips and his horse screamed and leaped convulsively as he struck in the spurs, throwing all his frame behind his sword arm as the beast plunged. But du Courcey was too seasoned a fighter to be caught so easily. With a wrench of his rein he brought his steed round, rearing. The Varangian's frantic horse plunged past, and the whistling sword struck fire from the Norman's lifted shield. With a furious yell the fierce Norman wheeled again to the assault, and the horses reared together while the swords of their riders hissed, circled in flashing arcs, and fell with ringing clash on mail-links or shield.

The men fought in grim silence, save for the panting of straining effort, but the clangor of their swords awoke the still night and sparks flew as from a blacksmith's anvil. Then with a deafening crash a broadsword shattered a helmet and splintered the skull within. There followed a loud clash of armor as the loser fell heavily from his saddle. A riderless horse galloped away, and the conqueror, shaking the sweat from his eyes, dismounted and bent above the motionless steel-clad figure.

4

On the road that leads south from Edessa to Rakka, the Moslem host lay encamped, the lines of gay-colored pavilions spread out in the plains. It was a leisurely march, with wagons, luxurious equipment, and whole households with women and slaves. After two years in Edessa the Atabeg of Mosul was returning to his capital by the way of Rakka. Fires glimmered in the gathering dusk where the first stars were peeping; lutes twanged and voices were lifted in song and laughter about the cooking pots.

Before Zenghi, playing at chess with his friend and chronicler, the Arab Ousama of Sheyzar, came the eunuch Yaruktash, who salaamed low and in his squeaky voice intoned, "Oh, Lion of Islam, an emir of the infidels desires audience with thee—the captain of the Greeks who is called Wulfgar Edric's son. The chief Il-Ghazi and his memluks came upon him, riding alone, and would have slain him but he threw up his arm and on his hand they saw the ring thou gavest the emperor as a secret sign for his messengers."

Zenghi tugged his gray-shot black beard and grinned, well pleased. "Let him be brought before me." The slave bowed and withdrew.

To Ousama, Zenghi said, "Allah, what dogs are these Christians, who betray and cut one another's throats for the promise of gold or land!"

"Is it well to trust such a man?" queried Ousama. "If he will betray his kind, he will surely betray you if he may."

"May I eat pork if I trust him," retorted Zenghi, moving a chessman with a jeweled finger. "As I move this pawn I will move the dog-emperor of the Greeks. With his aid I will crack the kings of Outremer like nutshells. I have promised him their seaports, and he will keep his promises until he thinks his prizes are in his hands. Ha! Not towns but the sword-edge I will give him. What we take together shall be mine, nor will that suffice me. By Allah, not Mesopotamia, nor Syria, nor all Asia Minor is enough! I will cross the Hellespont! I will ride my stallion through the palaces on the Golden Horn! Frankistan herself shall tremble before me!"

The impact of his voice was like that of a harsh-throated trumpet, almost stunning the hearers with its dynamic intensity. His eyes blazed, his fingers knotted like iron on the chessboard.

"You are old, Zenghi," warned the cautious Arab. "You have done much. Is there no limit to your ambitions?"

"Aye!" laughed the Turk. "The horn of the moon and the points of the stars! Old? Eleven years older than thyself, and younger in spirit than thou wert ever. My thews are steel, my heart is fire, my wits keener even than on the day I broke ibn Sadaka beside the Nile and set my feet on the shining stairs of glory! Peace, here comes the Frank."

A small boy of about eight years of age, sitting cross-legged on a cushion near the edge of the dais whereon lay Zenghi's divan, had been staring up in rapt adoration. His fine brown eyes sparkled as Zenghi spoke of his ambition, and his small frame quivered with excitement, as if his soul had taken fire from the Turk's wild words. Now he looked at the entrance of the pavilion with the others, as the memluks entered with the visitor between them, his scabbard empty. They had taken his weapons outside the royal tent.

The memluks fell back and ranged themselves on either side of the dais, leaving the Frank in an open space before their master. Zenghi's keen eyes swept over the tall form in its glittering gold-worked mail, took in the clean-shaven face with its cold eyes, and rested on the Koran-inscribed ring on the man's finger.

"My master, the emperor of Byzantium," said the Frank in Turki, "sends thee greeting, oh Zenghi, Lion of Islam."

As he spoke he took in the details of the impressive figure, clad in steel, silk and gold, before him; the strong dark face, the powerful frame which, despite the years, betokened steel-spring muscles and unquenchable vitality; above all the Atabeg's eyes, gleaming with unperishable youth and innate fierceness.

"And what said thy master, oh Wulfgar?" asked the Turk.

"He sends thee this letter," answered the Frank, drawing forth a packet and proffering it to Yaruktash, who in turn, and on his knees, delivered it to Zenghi. The Atabeg perused the parchment, signed in the Emperor's unmistakable hand and sealed with the royal Byzantine seal. Zenghi never dealt with underlings, but always with the highest power of friends or foes.

"The seals have been broken," said the Turk, fixing his piercing eyes on the inscrutable countenance of the Frank. "Thou hast read?"

"Aye. I was pursued by men of the prince of Antioch, and fearing lest I be seized and searched, I opened the missive and read it, so that if I were forced to destroy it lest it fall into enemy hands, I could repeat the message to thee by word of mouth."

"Let me hear, then, if thy memory be equal to thy discretion," commanded the Atabeg.

"As thou wilt. My master says to thee, 'Concerning that which hath passed between us, I must have better proof of thy good faith. Wherefore do thou send me by this messenger, who, though unknown to thee, is a man to be trusted, full details of thy desires and good proof of the aid thou hast promised us in the proposed movement against Antioch. Before I put to sea I must know that thou art ready to move by land, and there must be binding oaths between us.' And the missive is signed with the emperor's own hand."

The Turk nodded; a mirthful devil danced in his blue eyes.

"They are his very words. Blessed is the monarch who boasts such a vassal. Sit ye upon that heap of cushions; meat and drink shall be brought to you."

Calling Yaruktash, Zenghi whispered in his ear. The eunuch started, stared, and then salaamed and hastened from the pavilion. Slaves brought food and the forbidden wine in golden vessels, and the Frank broke his fast with unfeigned relish. Zenghi watched him inscrutably and the glittering memluks stood like statues of burnished steel.

"You came first to Edessa?" asked the Atabeg.

"Nay. When I left my ship at Antioch I set forth for Edessa, but I had scarce crossed the border when a band of wandering Arabs, recognizing your ring, told me you were on the march for Rakka, thence to Mosul. So I turned aside and rode to cut your line of march, and my way being made clear for me by virtue of the ring which all your subjects know, I was at last met by the chief Il-Ghazi who escorted me thither."

Zenghi nodded his leonine head slowly.

"Mosul calls me. I go back to my capital to gather my hawks, to brace my lines. When I return I will sweep the Franks into the sea with the aid of—thy master.

"But I forget the courtesy due a guest. This is the prince Ousama of Sheyzar, and this child is the son of my friend Nejm-ed-din, who saved my army and my life when I fled from Karaja the Cup-bearer—one of the few foes who ever saw my back. His father dwells at Baalbekk, which I gave him to rule, but I have taken Yusef with me to look on Mosul. Verily, he is more to me than my own sons. I have named him Salah-ed-din, and he shall be a thorn in the flesh of Christendom."

At this instant Yaruktash entered and whispered in Zenghi's ear, and the Atabeg nodded.

As the eunuch withdrew, Zenghi turned to the Frank. The Turk's manner had changed subtly. His lids drooped over his glittering eyes and a faint hint of mockery curled his bearded lips.

"I would show you one whose countenance you know of old," said he.

The Frank looked up in surprize.

"Have I a friend in the hosts of Mosul?"

"You shall see!" Zenghi clapped his hands, and Yaruktash, appearing at the door of the pavilion grasping a slender white wrist, dragged the owner into view and cast her from him so that she fell to the carpet almost at the Frank's feet. With a terrible cry he started up, his face deathly.

"Ellen! My God! Alive!"

"Miles!" she echoed his cry, struggling to her knees. In a mist of stupefaction he saw her white arms outstretched, her pale face framed in the golden hair which fell over the white shoulders the scanty *harim* garb left bare. Forgetting all else he fell to his knees beside her, gathering her into his arms.

"Ellen! Ellen de Tremont! I had scoured the world for you and hacked a path through the legions of Hell itself—but they said you were dead. Musa, before he died at my feet, swore he saw you lying in your blood among the corpses of your servants in your courtyard."

"Would God it had been so!" she sobbed, her golden head against his steel-clad breast. "But when they cut down my servants I fell among the bodies in a swoon, and their blood stained my garments; so men thought me dead. It was Zenghi himself who found me alive, and took me—" She hid her face in her hands.

"And so, Sir Miles du Courcey," broke in the sardonic voice of the Turk, "you have found a friend among the Mosuli! Fool! My senses are keener than a whetted sword. Think you I did not know you, despite your clean-shaven face? I saw you too often on the ramparts of Edessa, hewing down my memluks. I knew you as soon as you entered. What have you done with the real messenger?"

Grimly Miles disengaged himself from the girl's clinging arms and rose, facing the Atabeg. Zenghi likewise rose, quick and lithe as a great panther, and drew his scimitar, while from all sides the heron-feathered memluks began to edge in silently. Miles' hand fell away from his empty scabbard and his eyes rested for an instant on something close to his feet—a curved knife, used for carving fruit, and lying there forgotten, half-hidden under a cushion.

"Wulfgar Edric's son lies dead among the trees on the Antioch road," said Miles grimly. "I shaved off my beard and took his armor and the ring the dog bore."

"The better to spy on me," quoth Zenghi.

"Aye." There was no fear in Miles du Courcey. "I wished to learn the details of the plot you hatched with John Comnene, and to obtain proofs of his treachery and your ambitions to show to the lords of Outremer."

"I deduced as much," smiled Zenghi. "I knew you, as I said. But I wished you to betray yourself fully; hence the girl, who has spoken your name with weeping many times in the years of her captivity."

"It was an unworthy gesture and one in keeping with your character," said Miles somberly. "Yet I thank you for allowing me to see her once more, and to know that she is alive whom I thought long dead."

"I have done her great honor," answered Zenghi laughing. "She has been in my *harim* for two years."

Miles' grim eyes only grew more somber, but the great veins swelled almost to bursting along his temples. At his feet the girl covered her face with her white hands and wept silently. The boy on the cushion looked about uncertainly, not understanding. Ousama's fine eyes were touched with pity. But Zenghi grinned broadly. Such scenes were like wine to the Turk, shaking inwardly with the gargantuan laughter of his breed.

"You shall bless me for my bounty, Sir Miles," said Zenghi. "For my kingly generosity you shall give praise. Lo, the girl is yours! When I tear you between four wild horses tomorrow, she shall accompany you to Hell on a pointed stake—ha!"

Like a striking cobra Miles du Courcey had moved. Snatching the knife from beneath the cushion he leaped—not at the guarded Atabeg on the divan, but at the child on the edge of the dais. Before any could stop him, he caught up the boy Saladin with one hand, and with the other pressed the curved edge to his throat.

"Back, dogs!" His voice cracked with mad triumph. "Back, or I send this heathen spawn to Hell!"

Zenghi, his face livid, yelled a frenzied order, and the memluks fell back. Then while the Atabeg stood trembling and uncertain, at a loss for the first and only time of his whole wild career, du Courcey backed toward the door, holding his captive, who neither cried out nor struggled. The contemplative brown eyes showed no fear, only a fatalistic resignation of a philosophy beyond the owner's years.

"To me, Ellen!" snapped the Norman, his somber despair changed to dynamic action. "Out of the door behind me—back dogs, I say!"

Out of the pavilion he backed, and the memluks who ran up, sword in hand, stopped short as they saw the imminent peril of their lord's favorite. Du Courcey knew that the success of his action depended on speed. The surprize and boldness of his move had taken Zenghi off guard, that was all. A group of horses stood near by, saddled and bridled, always ready for the Atabeg's whim, and du Courcey reached them with a single long stride, the grooms falling back from his threat.

"Into a saddle, Ellen!" he snapped, and the girl, who had followed him like one in a daze, reacting mechanically to his orders, swung herself up on the nearest mount. Quickly he followed suit and cut the tethers that held their mounts. A bellow from inside the tent told him Zenghi's momentarily scattered wits were working again, and he dropped the child unhurt into the sand. His usefulness was past, as a hostage. Zenghi, taken by surprize, had instinctively followed the promptings of his unusual affection for the child, but Miles knew that with his ruthless reason dominating him again, the Atabeg would not allow even that affection to stand in the way of their recapture.

The Norman wheeled away, drawing Ellen's steed with him, trying to shield her with his own body from the arrows which were already whistling about them. Shoulder to shoulder they raced across the wide open space in front of the royal pavilion, burst through a ring of fires, floundered for an instant among tent-pegs, cords and scurrying yelling figures, then struck the open desert flying and heard the clamor die out behind them.

It was dark, clouds flying across the sky and drowning the stars. With the clatter of hoofs behind them, Miles reined aside from the road that led westward, and turned into the trackless desert. Behind them the hoof-beats faded westward. The pursuers had taken the old caravan road, supposing the fugitives to be ahead of them.

"What now, Miles?" Ellen was riding alongside, and clinging to his iron-sheathed arm as if she feared he might fade suddenly from her sight.

"If we ride straight for the border they will have us before dawn," he answered. "But I know this land as well as they—I have ridden all over it of old in foray and war with the counts of Edessa; so I know that Jabar Kal'at lies within our reach to the southwest. The commander of Jabar is a nephew of Muin-ed-din Anar, who is the real ruler of Damascus, and who, as perhaps you know, has made a pact with the Christians against Zenghi, his old rival. If we can reach Jabar, the commander will give us shelter and food, and fresh horses and an escort to the border."

The girl bowed her head in acquiescence. She was still like one dazed. The light of hope burned too feebly in her soul to sting her with new pangs. Perhaps in her captivity she had absorbed some of the fatalism of her masters. Miles looked at her, drooping in the saddle, humble and silent, and thought of the picture he retained of a saucy, laughing beauty, vibrant with vitality and mirth. And he cursed Zenghi and his works with sick fury. So through the night they rode, the broken woman and the embittered man, handiworks of the Lion who dealt in swords and souls and human hearts, and whose victims, living and dead, filled the land like a blight of sorrow, agony and despair.

All night they pressed forward as fast as they dared, listening for sounds that would tell them the pursuers had found their trail, and in the dawn, which lit the helmets of swift-following horsemen, they saw the towers of Jabar rising above the mirroring waters of the Euphrates. It was a strong keep, guarded with a moat that encircled it, connecting with the river at either end. At their hail the commander of the castle appeared on the wall, and a few words sufficed to cause the drawbridge to be lowered. It was not a moment too soon. As they clattered across the bridge, the drum of hoofs was in their ears, and as they passed through the gates, arrows fell in a shower about them.

The leader of the pursuers reined his rearing steed and called arrogantly to the commander on the tower. "Oh man, give up these fugitives, lest thy blood quench the embers of thy keep!"

"Am I then a dog that you speak to me thus?" queried the Seljuk, clutching his beard in passion. "Begone, or my archers will feather thy carcass with fifty shafts."

For answer the memluk laughed jeeringly and pointed to the desert. The commander paled. Far away the sun glinted on a moving ocean of steel. His practiced eye told him that a whole army was on the march.

"Zenghi has turned from his march to hunt down a pair of fleeing jackals," called the memluk mockingly. "Great honor he has done them, marching hard on their spoor all night. Send them out, oh fool, and my master will ride on in peace."

"Let it be as Allah wills," said the Seljuk, recovering his poise. "But the friends of my uncle have thrown themselves into my hands, and may shame rest on me and mine if I give them to the butcher."

Nor did he alter his resolution when Zenghi himself, his face dark with passion as the cloak that flowed from his steel-clad shoulders, sat his stallion beneath the towers and called: "Oh man, by receiving mine enemy thou hast forfeited thy castle and thy life. Yet I will be merciful. Send out those who fled and I will allow thee to march out unharmed with thy women and retainers. Persist in this madness and I will burn thee like a rat in thy castle."

"Let it be as Allah wills," repeated the Seljuk philosophically, and in an undertone spoke quietly to a crouching archer, "Drive quickly a shaft through yon dog."

The arrow glanced harmlessly from Zenghils breastplate and the Atabeg galloped out of range with a shout of mocking laughter. Now began the siege of Jabar Kal'at, unsung and unglorified, yet in the course of which the dice of Fate were cast.

Zenghi's riders laid waste the surrounding countryside and drew a cordon about the castle through which no courier could steal to ride for aid. While the emir of Damascus and the lords of Outremer remained in ignorance of what was taking place beyond the Euphrates, their ally waged his unequal battle.

By nightfall the wagons and siege engines came up, and Zenghi set to his task with the skill of long practice. The Turkish sappers dammed up the moat at the upper end, despite the arrows of the defenders, and filled up the drained ditch with earth and stone. Under cover of darkness they sank mines beneath the towers. Zenghi's ballistas creaked and crashed and huge rocks knocked men off the walls like tenpins or smashed through the roof of the towers. His rams gnawed and pounded at the walls, his archers plied the turrets with their arrows everlastingly, and on scaling-ladders and storming-towers his memluks moved unceasingly to the onset. Food waned in the castle's larders; the heaps of dead grew larger, the rooms became full of wounded men, groaning and writhing.

But the Seljuk commander did not falter on the path his feet had taken. He knew that he could not now buy safety from Zenghi, even by giving up his guests; to his credit, he never even considered giving them up. Du Courcey knew this, and though no word of the matter was spoken between them, the commander had evidence of the Norman's fierce gratitude. Miles showed his appreciation in actions, not words—in the fighting on the walls, in the slaughter in the gates, in the long night-watches on the towers; with whirring sword-strokes that clove bucklers and peaked helmets, that cleft spines and severed necks and limbs and shattered skulls; by the casting down of scaling-ladders when the clinging Turks howled as they crashed to their death, and their comrades cried out at the terrible strength in the Frank's naked hands. But the rams crunched, the arrows sang, the steel tides surged on again and again, and the haggard defenders dropped one by one until only a skeleton force held the crumbling walls of Jabar Kal'at.

5

In his pavilion little more than a bowshot from the beleaguered walls, Zenghi played chess with Ousama. The madness of the day had given way to the brooding silence of night, broken only by the distant cries of wounded men in delirium.

"Men are my pawns, friend," said the Atabeg. "I turn adversity into triumph. I had long sought an excuse to attack Jabar Kal'at, which will make a strong outpost against the Franks once I have taken it and repaired the dents I have made, and filled it with my memluks. I knew my captives would ride hither; that is why I broke camp and took up the march before my scouts found their tracks. It was their logical refuge. I will have the castle and the Franks, which last is most vital. Were the Caphars to learn now of my intrigue with the emperor, my plans might well come to naught. But they will not know until I strike. Du Courcey will never bear news to them. If he does not fall with the castle, I will tear him between wild horses as I promised, and the infidel girl shall watch, sitting on a pointed stake."

"Is there no mercy in your soul, Zenghi?" protested the Arab.

"Has life shown mercy to me save what I wrung forth by the sword?" exclaimed Zenghi, his eyes blazing in a momentary upheaval of his passionate spirit. "A man must smite or be smitten—slay or be slain. Men are wolves, and I am but the strongest wolf of the pack. Because they fear me, men crawl and kiss my sandals. Fear is the only emotion by which they may be touched."

"You are a pagan at heart, Zenghi," sighed Ousama.

"It may be," answered the Turk with a shrug of his shoulders. "Had I been born beyond the Oxus and bowed to yellow Erlik as did my grandsire, I had been no less Zenghi the Lion. I have spilled rivers of gore for the glory of Allah, but I have never asked mercy or favor of Him. What care the gods if a man lives or dies? Let me live deep, let me know the sting of wine in my palate, the wind in my face, the glitter of royal pageantry, the bright madness of slaughter—let me burn and sting and tingle with the madness of life and living, and I quest not whether Muhammad's paradise, or Erlik's frozen hell, or the blackness of empty-oblivion lies beyond."

As if to give point to his words, he poured himself a goblet of wine and looked interrogatively at Ousama. The Arab, who had shuddered at Zenghi's blasphemous words, drew back in pious horror. The Atabeg emptied the goblet, smacking his lips loudly in relish, Tatar-fashion.

"I think Jabar Kal'at will fall tomorrow," he said. "Who has stood against me? Count them, Ousama—there was ibn Sadaka, and the Caliph, and the Seljuk Timurtash, and the sultan Dawud, and the king of Jerusalem, and the count of Edessa. Man after man, city after city, army after army, I broke them and brushed them from my path."

"You have waded through a sea of blood," said Ousama. "You have filled the slave-markets with Frankish girls, and the deserts with the bones of Frankish warriors. Nor have you spared your rivals among the Moslems."

"They stood in the way of my destiny," laughed the Turk, "and that destiny is to be sultan of Asia! As I will be. I have welded the swords of Irak, el Jezira, Syria and Roum, into a single blade. Now with the aid of the Greeks, all Hell can not save the Nazarenes. Slaughter? Men have seen naught; wait until I ride into Antioch and Jerusalem, sword in hand!"

"Your heart is steel," said the Arab. "Yet I have seen one touch of tenderness in you—your affection for Nejm-ed-din's son, Yusef. Is there a like touch of repentance in you? Of all your deeds, is there none you regret?"

Zenghi played with a pawn in silence, and his face darkened.

"Aye," he said slowly. "It was long ago, when I broke ibn Sadaka beside the lower reaches of this very river. He had a son, Achmet, a girl-faced boy. I beat him to death with my riding-scourge. It is the one deed I could wish undone. Sometimes I dream of it."

Then with an abrupt "Enough!" he thrust aside the board, scattering the chessmen. "I would sleep," said he, and throwing himself on his cushion-heaped divan, he was instantly locked in slumber. Ousama went quietly from the tent, passing between the four giant memluks in gilded mail who stood with wide-tipped scimitars at the pavilion door.

In the castle of Jabar, the Seljuk commander held counsel with Sir Miles du Courcey. "My brother, for us the end of the road has come. The walls are crumbling, the towers leaning to their fall. Shall we not fire the castle, cut the throats of our women and children, and go forth to die like men in the dawn?"

Sir Miles shook his head. "Let us hold the walls for one more day. In a dream I saw the banners of Damascus and of Antioch marching to our aid."

He lied in a desperate attempt to bolster up the fatalistic Seljuk. Each followed the instinct of his kind, and Miles was to cling with teeth and nails to the last vestige of life until the bitter end. The Seljuk bowed his head.

"If Allah wills, we will hold the walls for another day."

Miles thought of Ellen, into whose manner something of the old vibrant spirit was beginning to steal faintly again, and in the blackness of his despair no light gleamed from earth or heaven. The finding of her had stung to life a heart long frozen; now in death he must lose her again. With the taste of bitter ashes in his mouth he bent his shoulders anew to the burden of life.

In his tent Zenghi moved restlessly. Alert as a panther, even in sleep, his instinct told him that someone was moving stealthily near him. He woke and sat up glaring. The fat eunuch Yaruktash halted suddenly, the wine jug halfway to his lips. He had thought Zenghi lay helplessly drunk when he stole into the tent to filch the liquor he loved. Zenghi snarled like a wolf, his familiar devil rising in his brain.

"Dog! Am I a fat merchant that you steal into my tent to guzzle my wine? Begone! Tomorrow I will see to you!"

Cold sweat beaded Yaruktash's sleek hide as he fled from the royal pavilion. His fat flesh quivered with agonized anticipation of the sharp stake which would undoubtedly be his portion. In a day of cruel masters, Zenghi's name was a byword of horror among slaves and servitors.

One of the memluks outside the tent caught Yaruktash's arm and growled, "Why flee you, gelding?"

A great flare of light rose in the eunuch's brain, so that he gasped at its grandeur and audacity. Why remain here to be impaled, when the whole desert was open before him, and here were men who would protect him in his flight?

"Our lord discovered me drinking his wine," he gasped. "He threatens me with torture and death."

The memluks laughed appreciatively, their crude humor touched by the eunuch's fright. Then they started convulsively as Yaruktash added, "You too are doomed. I heard him curse you for not keeping better watch, and allowing his slaves to steal his wine."

The fact that they had never been told to bar the eunuch from the royal pavilion meant nothing to the memluks, their wits frozen with sudden fear. They stood dumbly, incapable of coherent thought, their minds like empty jugs ready to be filled with the eunuch's guile. A few whispered words and they slunk away like shadows on Yaruktash's heels, leaving the pavilion unguarded.

The night waned. Midnight hovered and was gone. The moon sank below the desert hills in a welter of blood. From dreams of imperial pageantry Zenghi again awoke, to stare bewilderedly about the dim-lit pavilion. Without, all was silence that seemed suddenly tense and sinister. The prince lay in the midst of ten thousand armed men; yet he felt suddenly apart and alone, as if he were the last man left alive on a dead world. Then he saw that he was not alone. Looking somberly down on him stood a strange and alien figure. It was a man, whose rags did not hide his gaunt limbs, at which Zenghi stared appalled. They were gnarled like the twisted branches of ancient oaks, knotted with masses of muscle and thews, each of which stood out distinct, like iron cables. There was no soft flesh to lend symmetry or to mask the raw savagery of sheer power. Only years of incredible labor could have produced this terrible monument of muscular over-development. White hair hung about the great shoulders, a white beard fell upon the mighty breast. His terrible arms were folded, and he stood motionless as a statue looking down upon the stupefied Turk. His features were gaunt and deep-lined, as if cut by some mad artist's chisel from bitter, frozen rock.

"Avaunt!" gasped Zenghi, momentarily a pagan of the steppes. "Spirit of evil—ghost of the desert—demon of the hills—I fear you not!"

"Well may you speak of ghosts, Turk!" The deep hollow voice woke dim memories in Zenghi's brain. "I am the ghost of a man dead twenty years, come up from darkness deeper than the darkness of Hell. Have you forgotten my promise, Prince Zenghi?"

"Who are you?" demanded the Turk.

"I am John Norwald."

"The Frank who rode with ibn Sadaka? Impossible!" ejaculated the Atabeg. "Twenty-three years ago I doomed him to the rower's bench. What galley-slave could live so long?"

"I lived," retorted the other. "Where others died like flies, I lived. The lash that scarred my back in a thousand overlying patterns could not kill me, nor starvation, nor storm, nor pestilence, nor battle. The years have been long, Zenghi esh Shami, and the darkness deep and full of mocking voices and haunting faces. Look at my hair, Zenghi—white as hoarfrost, though I am eight years younger than yourself. Look at these monstrous talons that were hands, these knotted limbs—they have driven the weighted oars for many a thousand leagues through storm and calm. Yet I lived, Zenghi, even when my flesh cried out to end the long agony. When I fainted on the oar, it was not ripping lash that roused me to life anew, but the hate that would not let me die. That hate has kept the soul in my tortured body for twenty-three years, dog of Tiberias. In the galleys I lost my youth, my hope, my manhood, my soul, my faith and my God. But my hate burned on, a flame that nothing could quench.

"Twenty years at the oars, Zenghi! Three years ago the galley in which I then toiled crashed on the reefs off the coast of India. All died but me, who, knowing my hour had come, burst my chains with the strength and madness of a giant, and gained the shore. My feet are yet unsteady from the shackles and the galley-bench, Zenghi, though my arms are strong beyond the belief of man. I have been on the road from India for three years. But the road ends here."

For the first time in his life Zenghi knew fear that froze his tongue to his palate and turned the marrow in his bones to ice.

"Ho, guards!" he roared. "To me, dogs!"

"Call louder, Zenghi!" said Norwald in his hollow resounding voice. "They hear thee not. Through thy sleeping host I passed like the Angel of Death, and none saw me. Thy tent stood unguarded. Lo, mine enemy, thou art delivered into my hand, and thine hour has come!"

With the ferocity of desperation Zenghi leaped from his cushions, whipping out a dagger, but like a great gaunt tiger the Englishman was upon him, crushing him back on the divan. The Turk struck blindly, felt the blade sink deep into the other's side; then as he wrenched the weapon free to strike again, he felt an iron grip on his wrist, and the Frank's right hand locked on his throat, choking his cry.

As he felt the inhuman strength of his attacker, blind panic swept the Atabeg. The fingers on his wrist did not feel like human bone and flesh and sinew. They were like the steel jaws of a vise that crushed through flesh and muscle. Over the inexorable fingers that sank into his bull-throat, blood trickled from skin torn like rotten cloth. Mad with the torture of strangulation, Zenghi tore at the wrist with his free hand, but he might have been wrenching at a steel bar welded to his throat. The massed muscles of Norwald's left arm knotted with effort, and with a sickening snap Zenghi's wrist bones gave way. The dagger fell from his nerveless hand, and instantly Norwald caught it up and sank the point into the Atabeg's breast.

The Turk released the arm that prisoned his throat, and caught the knife-wrist, but all his desperate strength could not stay the inexorable thrust. Slowly, slowly, Norwald drove home the keen point, while the Turk writhed in soundless agony. Approaching through the mists which veiled his glazing sight, Zenghi saw a face, raw, torn and bleeding. And then the dagger-point found his heart and visions and life ended together.

Ousama, unable to sleep, approached the Atabeg's tent, wondering at the absence of the guardsmen. He stopped short, an uncanny fear prickling the short hairs at the back of his neck, as a form came from the pavilion. He made out a tall white-bearded man, clad in rags. The Arab stretched forth a hand timidly, but dared not touch the apparition. He saw that the figure's hand was pressed against its left side, and blood oozed darkly from between the fingers.

"Where go you, old man?" stammered the Arab, involuntarily stepping back as the white-bearded stranger fixed weird blazing eyes upon him.

"I go back to the void which gave me birth," answered the figure in a deep ghostly voice, and as the Arab stared in bewilderment, the stranger passed on with slow, certain, unwavering steps, to vanish in the darkness.

Ousama ran into Zenghi's tent—to halt aghast at sight of the Atabeg's body lying stark among the torn silks and bloodstained cushions of the royal divan.

"Alas for kingly ambitions and high visions!" exclaimed the Arab. "Death is a black horse that may halt in the night by any tent, and life is more unstable than the foam on the sea! Woe for Islam, for her keenest sword is broken! Now may Christendom rejoice, for the Lion that roared against her lies lifeless!"

Like wildfire ran through the camp the word of the Atabeg's death, and like chaff blown on the winds his followers scattered, looting the camp as they fled. The power that had welded them together was broken, and it was every man for himself, and the plunder to the strong.

The haggard defenders on the walls, lifting their notched stumps of blades for the last death-grapple, gaped as they saw the confusion in the camp, the running to and fro, the brawling, the looting and shouting, and at last the scattering over the plain of emirs and retainers alike. These hawks lived by the sword, and they had no time for the dead, however regal. They turned their steeds aside to seek a new lord, in a race for the strongest.

Stunned by the miracle, not yet understanding the cast of Fate that had saved Jabar Kal'at and Outremer, Miles du Courcey stood with Ellen and their Seljuk friend, staring down on a silent and abandoned camp, where the torn deserted tent flapped idly in the morning breeze above the bloodstained body that had been the Lion of Tiberias.

THE SHADOW OF THE VULTURE

"Are the dogs dressed and gorged?"

"Aye, Protector of the Faithful."

"Then let them crawl into the Presence."

So they brought the envoys, pallid from months of imprisonment, before the canopied throne of Suleyman the Magnificent, Sultan of Turkey, and the mightiest monarch in an age of mighty monarchs. Under the great purple dome of the royal chamber gleamed the throne before which the world trembled—gold-paneled, pearl-inlaid. An emperor's wealth in gems was sewn into the silken canopy from which depended a shimmering string of pearls ending a frieze of emeralds which hung like a halo of glory above Suleyman's head. Yet the splendor of the throne was paled by the glitter of the figure upon it, bedecked in jewels, the aigrette feather rising above the diamonded white turban. About the throne stood his nine viziers, in attitudes of humility, and warriors of the imperial bodyguard ranged the dais—Solaks in armor, black and white and scarlet plumes nodding above the gilded helmets.

The envoys from Austria were properly impressed—the more so as they had had nine weary months for reflection in the grim Castle of the Seven Towers that overlooks the Sea of Marmora. The head of the embassy choked down his choler and cloaked his resentment in a semblance of submission—a strange cloak on the shoulders of Habordansky, general of Ferdinand, Archduke of Austria. His rugged head bristled incongruously from the flaming silk robes presented him by the contemptuous Sultan, as he was brought before the throne, his arms gripped fast by stalwart Janizaries. Thus were foreign envoys presented to the sultans, ever since that red day by Kossova when Milosh Kabilovitch, knight of slaughtered Serbia, had slain the conqueror Murad with a hidden dagger.

The Grand Turk regarded Habordansky with scant favor. Suleyman was a tall, slender man, with a thin down-curving nose and a thin straight mouth, the resolution of which his drooping mustachios did not soften. His narrow outward-curving chin was shaven. The only suggestion of weakness was in the slender, remarkably long neck, but that suggestion was belied by the hard lines of the slender figure, the glitter of the dark eyes. There was more than a suggestion of the Tatar about him—rightly so, since he was no more the son of Selim the Grim, than of Hafsza Khatun, princess of Crimea. Born to the purple, heir to the mightiest military power in the world, he was crested with authority and cloaked in pride that recognized no peer beneath the gods.

Under his eagle gaze old Habordansky bent his head to hide the sullen rage in his eyes. Nine months before, the general had come to Stamboul representing his master, the Archduke, with proposals for truce and the disposition of the iron crown of Hungary, torn from the dead king Louis' head on the bloody field of Mohacz, where the Grand Turk's armies opened the road to Europe. There had been another emissary before him—Jerome Lasczky, the Polish count palatine. Habordansky, with the bluntness of his breed, had claimed the Hungarian crown for his master, rousing Suleyman's ire. Lasczky had, like a suppliant, asked on his bended knees that crown for his countrymen at Mohacz.

To Lasczky had been given honor, gold and promises of patronage, for which he had paid with pledges abhorrent even to his avaricious soul—selling his ally's subjects into slavery, and opening the road through the subject territory to the very heart of Christendom.

All this was made known to Habordansky, frothing with fury in the prison to which the arrogant resentment of the Sultan had assigned him. Now Suleyman looked contemptuously at the staunch old general, and dispensed with the usual formality of speaking through the mouthpiece of the Grand Vizier. A royal Turk would not deign to admit knowledge of any Frankish tongue, but Habordansky understood Turki. The Sultan's remarks were brief and without preamble.

"Say to your master that I now make ready to visit him in his own lands, and that if he fails to meet me at Mohacz or at Pesth, I will meet him beneath the walls of Vienna."

Habordansky bowed, not trusting himself to speak. At a scornful wave of the imperial hand, an officer of the court came forward and bestowed upon the general a small gilded bag containing two hundred ducats. Each member of his retinue, waiting patiently at the other end of the chamber, under the spears of the Janizaries, was likewise so guerdoned. Habordansky mumbled thanks, his knotty hands clenched about the gift with unnecessary vigor. The Sultan grinned thinly, well aware that the ambassador would have hurled the coins into his face, had he dared. He half-lifted his hand, in token of dismissal, then paused, his eyes resting on the group of men who composed the general's suite—or rather, on one of these men. This man was the tallest in the room, strongly built, wearing his Turkish gift-garments clumsily. At a gesture from the Sultan he was brought forward in the grasp of the soldiers.

Suleyman stared at him narrowly. The Turkish vest and voluminous khalat could not conceal the lines of massive strength. His tawny hair was close-cropped, his sweeping yellow mustaches drooping below a stubborn chin. His blue eyes seemed strangely clouded; it was as if the man slept on his feet, with his eyes open.

"Do you speak Turki?" The Sultan did the fellow the stupendous honor of addressing him directly. Through all the pomp of the Ottoman court there remained in the Sultan some of the simplicity of Tatar ancestors.

"Yes, your majesty," answered the Frank.

"Who are you?"

"Men name me Gottfried von Kalmbach."

Suleyman scowled and unconsciously his fingers wandered to his shoulder, where, under his silken robes, he could feel the outlines of an old scar.

"I do not forget faces. Somewhere I have seen yours—under circumstances that etched it into the back of my mind. But I am unable to recall those circumstances."

"I was at Rhodes," offered the German.

"Many men were at Rhodes," snapped Suleyman.

"Aye." agreed von Kalmbach tranquilly. "De l'Isle Adam was there."

Suleyman stiffened and his eyes glittered at the name of the Grand Master of the Knights of Saint John, whose desperate defense of Rhodes had cost the Turk sixty thousand men. He decided, however, that the Frank was not clever enough for the remark to carry any subtle thrust, and dismissed the embassy with a wave. The envoys were backed out of the Presence and the incident was closed. The Franks would be escorted out of Stamboul, and to the nearest boundaries of the empire. The Turk's warning would be carried posthaste to the Archduke, and soon on the heels of that warning would come the armies of the Sublime Porte.

Suleyman's officers knew that the Grand Turk had more in mind than merely establishing his puppet Zapolya on the conquered Hungarian throne. Suleyman's ambitions embraced all Europe—that stubborn Frankistan which had for centuries sporadically poured forth hordes chanting and pillaging into the East, whose illogical and wayward peoples had again and again seemed ripe for Moslem conquest, yet who had always emerged, if not victorious, at least unconquered.

It was the evening of the morning on which the Austrian emissaries departed that Suleyman, brooding on his throne, raised his lean head and beckoned his Grand Vizier Ibrahim, who approached with confidence. The Grand Vizier was always sure of his master's approbation; was he not cup-companion and boyhood comrade of the Sultan? Ibrahim had but one rival in his master's favor—the red-haired Russian girl, Khurrem the Joyous, whom Europe knew as Roxelana, whom slavers had dragged from her father's house in Rogatino to be the Sultan's *harim* favorite.

"I remember the infidel at last," said Suleyman. "Do you recall the first charge of the knights at Mohacz?"

Ibrahim winced slightly at the allusion.

"Oh, Protector of the Pitiful, is it likely that I should forget an occasion on which the divine blood of my master was spilt by an unbeliever?"

"Then you remember that thirty-two knights, the paladins of the Nazarenes, drove headlong into our array, each having pledged his life to cut down our person. By Allah, they rode like men riding to a wedding, their great horses and long lances overthrowing all who opposed them, and their plate-armor turned the finest steel. Yet they fell as the firelocks spoke until only three were left in the saddle—the knight Marczali and two companions. These paladins cut down my Solaks like ripe grain, but Marczali and one of his companions fell—almost at my feet.

"Yet one knight remained, though his vizored helmet had been torn from his head and blood started from every joint in his armor. He rode full at me, swinging his great two-handed sword, and I swear by the beard of the Prophet, death was so nigh me that I felt the burning breath of Azrael on my neck!

"His sword flashed like lightning in the sky, and glancing from my casque, whereby I was half-stunned so that blood gushed from my nose, rent the mail on my shoulder and gave me this wound, which irks me yet when the rains come. The Janizaries who swarmed around him cut the hocks of his horse, which brought him to earth as it went down, and the remnants of my Solaks bore me back out of the mêlée. Then the Hungarian host came on, and I saw not what became of the knight. But today I saw him again."

Ibrahim started with an exclamation of incredulity.

"Nay, I could not mistake those blue eyes. How it is I know not, but the knight that wounded me at Mohacz was this German, Gottfried von Kalmbach."

"But, Defender of the Faith," protested Ibrahim, "the heads of those dog-knights were heaped before thy royal pavilion—"

"And I counted them and said nothing at the time, lest men think I held thee in blame," answered Suleyman. "There were but thirty-one. Most were so mutilated I could tell little of the features. But somehow the infidel escaped, who gave me this blow. I love brave men, but our blood is not so common that an unbeliever may with impunity spill it on the ground for the dogs to lap up. See ye to it."

Ibrahim salaamed deeply and withdrew. He made his way through broad corridors to a blue-tiled chamber whose gold-arched windows looked out on broad galleries, shaded by cypress and plane-trees, and cooled by the spray of silvery fountains. There at his summons came one Yaruk Khan, a Crim Tatar, a slant-eyed impassive figure in harness of lacquered leather and burnished bronze.

"Dog-brother," said the Vizier, "did thy koumiss-clouded gaze mark the tall German lord who served the emir Habordansky—the lord whose hair is tawny as a lion's mane?"

"Aye, *noyon*, he who is called Gombuk."

"The same. Take a *chambul* of thy dog-brothers and go after the Franks. Bring back this man and thou shalt be rewarded. The persons of envoys are sacred, but this matter is not official," he added cynically.

"To hear is to obey!" With a salaam as profound as that accorded to the Sultan himself, Yaruk Khan backed out of the presence of the second man of the empire.

He returned some days later, dusty, travel-stained, and without his prey. On him Ibrahim bent an eye full of menace, and the Tatar prostrated himself before the silken cushions on which the Grand Vizier sat, in the blue chamber with the gold-arched windows.

"Great khan, let not thine anger consume thy slave. The fault was not mine, by the beard of the Prophet."

"Squat on thy mangy haunches and bay out the tale," ordered Ibrahim considerately.

"Thus it was, my lord," began Yaruk Khan. "I rode swiftly, and though the Franks and their escort had a long start, and pushed on through the night without halting, I came up with them the next midday. But lo, Gombuk was not among them, and when I inquired after him, the paladin Habordansky replied only with many great oaths, like to the roaring of a cannon. So I spoke with various of the escort who understood the speech of these infidels, and learned what had come to pass. Yet I would have my lord remember that I only repeat the words of the Spahis of the escort, who are men without honor and lie like—"

"Like a Tatar," said Ibrahim.

Yaruk Khan acknowledged the compliment with a wide dog-like grin, and continued. "This they told me. At dawn Gombuk drew horse away from the rest, and the emir Habordansky demanded of him the reason. Then Gombuk laughed in the manner of the Franks—huh! huh! huh!—so. And Gombuk said, 'The devil of good your service has done me, so I cool my heels for nine months in a Turkish prison. Suleyman has given us safe conduct over the border and I am not compelled to ride with you.' 'You dog,' said the emir, 'there is war in the wind and the Archduke has need of your sword.' 'Devil eat the Archduke,' answered Gombuk; 'Zapolya is a dog because he stood aside at Mohacz, and let us, his comrades, be cut to pieces, but Ferdinand is a dog too. When I am penniless I sell him my sword. Now I have two hundred ducats and these robes which I can sell to any Jew for a handful of silver, and may the devil bite me if I draw sword for any man while I have a penny left. I'm for the nearest Christian tavern, and you and the Archduke may go to the devil.' Then the emir cursed him with many great curses, and Gombuk rode away laughing, huh! huh! huh!, and singing a song about a cockroach named—"

"Enough!" Ibrahim's features were dark with rage. He plucked savagely at his beard, reflecting that in the allusion to Mohacz, von Kalmbach had practically clinched Suleyman's suspicion. That matter of thirty-one heads when there should have been thirty-two was something no Turkish sultan would be likely to overlook. Officials had lost positions and their own heads over more trivial matters. The manner in which Suleyman had acted showed his almost incredible fondness and consideration for his Grand Vizier, but Ibrahim, vain though he was, was shrewd and wished no slightest shadow to come between him and his sovereign.

"Could you not have tracked him down, dog?" he demanded.

"By Allah," swore the uneasy Tatar, "he must have ridden on the wind. He crossed the border hours ahead of me, and I followed him as far as I dared—"

"Enough of excuses," interrupted Ibrahim. "Send Mikhal Oglu to me."

The Tatar departed thankfully. Ibrahim was not tolerant of failure in any man.

The Grand Vizier brooded on his silken cushions until the shadow of a pair of vulture wings fell across the marble-tiled floor, and the lean figure he had summoned bowed before him. The man whose very name was a shuddering watchword of horror to all western Asia was soft-spoken and moved with the mincing ease of a cat, but the stark evil of his soul showed in his dark countenance, gleamed in his narrow slit eyes. He was the chief of the Akinji, those wild riders whose raids spread fear and desolation throughout all lands beyond the Grand Turk's borders. He stood in full armor, a jeweled helmet on his narrow head, the wide vulture wings made fast to the shoulders of his gilded chain-mail hauberk. Those wings spread wide in the wind when he rode, and under their pinions lay the shadows of death and destruction. It was Suleyman's scimitar-tip, the most noted slayer of a nation of slayers, who stood before the Grand Vizier.

"Soon you will precede the hosts of our master into the lands of the infidel," said Ibrahim. "It will be your order, as always, to strike and spare not. You will waste the fields and the vineyards of the Caphars, you will burn their villages, you will strike down their men with arrows, and lead away their wenches captive. Lands beyond our line of march will cry out beneath your heel."

"That is good hearing, Favored of Allah," answered Mikhal Oglu in his soft courteous voice.

"Yet there is an order within the order," continued Ibrahim, fixing a piercing eye on the Akinji. "You know the German, von Kalmbach?"

"Aye—Gombuk as the Tatars call him."

"So. This is my command—whoever fights or flees, lives or dies—this man must not live. Search him out wherever he lies, though the hunt carry you to the very banks of the Rhine. When you bring me his head, your reward shall be thrice its weight in gold."

"To hear is to obey, my lord. Men say he is the vagabond son of a noble German family, whose ruin has been wine and women. They say he was once a Knight of Saint John, until cast forth for guzzling and—"

"Yet do not underrate him," answered Ibrahim grimly. "Sot he may be, but if he rode with Marczali, he is not to be despised. See thou to it!"

"There is no den where he can hide from me, oh Favored of Allah," declared Mikhal Oglu, "no night dark enough to conceal him, no forest thick enough. If I bring you not his head, I give him leave to send you mine."

"Enough!" Ibrahim grinned and tugged at his beard, well pleased. "You have my leave to go."

The sinister vulture-winged figure went springily and silently from the blue chamber, nor could Ibrahim guess that he was taking the first steps in a feud which should spread over years and far lands, swirling in dark tides to draw in thrones and kingdoms and red-haired women more beautiful than the flames of hell.

2

In a small thatched hut in a village not far from the Danube, lusty snores resounded where a figure reclined in state on a ragged cloak thrown over a heap of straw. It was the paladin Gottfried von Kalmbach who slept the sleep of innocence and ale. The velvet vest, voluminous silken trousers, khalat and shagreen boots, gifts from a contemptuous sultan, were nowhere in evidence. The paladin was clad in worn leather and rusty mail. Hands tugged at him, breaking his sleep, and he swore drowsily.

"Wake up, my lord! Oh, wake, good knight—good pig—good dog-soul—will you wake, then?"

"Fill my flagon, host," mumbled the slumberer. "Who?—what? May the dogs bite you, Ivga! I've not another asper—not a penny. Go off like a good lass and let me sleep."

The girl renewed her tugging and shaking.

"Oh dolt! Rise! Gird on your spit! There are happenings forward!"

"Ivga," muttered Gottfried, pulling away from her attack, "take my burganet to the Jew. He'll give you enough for it to get drunk again."

"Fool!" she cried in despair. "It isn't money I want! The whole east is aflame, and none knows the reason thereof!"

"Has the rain ceased?" asked von Kalmbach, taking some interest in the proceedings at last.

"The rain ceased hours ago. You can only hear the drip from the thatch. Put on your sword and come out into the street. The men of the village are all drunk on your last silver, and the women know not what to think or do. Ah!"

The exclamation was broken from her by the sudden upleaping of a weird illumination which shone through the crevices of the hut. The German got unsteadily to his feet, quickly girt on the great two-handed sword and stuck his dented burganet on his cropped locks. Then he followed the girl into the straggling street. She was a slender young thing, barefooted, clad only in a short tunic-like garment, through the wide rents of which gleamed generous expanses of white flesh.

There seemed no life or movement in the village. Nowhere showed a light. Water dripped steadily from the eaves of the thatched roofs. Puddles in the muddy streets gleamed black. Wind sighed and moaned eerily through the black sodden branches of the trees which pressed in bulwarks of darkness about the little village, and in the southeast, towering higher into the leaden sky, rose the lurid crimson glow that set the dank clouds to smoldering. The girl Ivga cringed close to the tall German, whimpering.

"I'll tell you what it is, my girl," said he, scanning the glow. "It's Suleyman's devils. They've crossed the river and they're burning the villages. Aye, I've seen glares like that in the sky before. I've expected him before now, but these cursed rains we've had for weeks must have held him back. Aye, it's the Akinji, right enough, and they won't stop this side of Vienna. Look you, my girl, go quickly and quietly to the stable behind the hut and bring me my gray stallion. We'll slip out like mice from between the devil's fingers. The stallion will carry us both, easily."

"But the people of the village!" she sobbed, wringing her hands.

"Eh, well," he said, "God rest them; the men have drunk my ale valiantly and the women have been kind—but horns of Satan, girl, the gray nag won't carry a whole village!"

"Go you!" she returned. "I'll stay and die with my people!"

"The Turks won't kill you," he answered. "They'll sell you to a fat old Stamboul merchant who'll beat you. I won't stay to be cut open, and neither shall you—"

A terrible scream from the girl cut him short and he wheeled at the awful terror in her flaring eyes. Even as he did so, a hut at the lower end of the village sprang into flames, the sodden material burning slowly. A medley of screams and maddened yells followed the cry of the girl. In the sluggish light figures danced and capered wildly. Gottfried, straining his eyes in the shadows, saw shapes swarming over the low mud wall which drunkenness and negligence had left unguarded.

"Damnation!" he muttered. "The accursed ones have ridden ahead of their fire. They've stolen on the village in the dark—come on, girl!"

But even as he caught her white wrist to drag her away, and she screamed and fought against him like a wild thing, mad with fear, the mud wall crashed at the point nearest them. It crumpled under the impact of a score of horses, and into the doomed village reined the riders, distinct in the growing light. Huts were flaring up on all hands, screams rising to the dripping clouds as the invaders dragged shrieking women and drunken men from their hovels and cut their throats. Gottfried saw the lean figures of the horsemen, the firelight gleaming on their burnished steel; he saw the vulture wings on the shoulders of the foremost. Even as he recognized Mikhal Oglu, he saw the chief stiffen and point.

"At him, dogs!" yelled the Akinji, his voice no longer soft, but strident as the rasp of a drawn saber. "It is Gombuk! Five hundred aspers to the man who brings me his head!"

With a curse von Kalmbach bounded for the shadows of the nearest hut, dragging the screaming girl with him. Even as he leaped he heard the twang of bowstrings, and the girl sobbed and went limp in his grasp. She sank down at his feet, and in the lurid glare he saw the feathered end of an arrow quivering under her heart. With a low rumble he turned toward his assailants as a fierce bear turns at bay. An instant he stood, head out-thrust truculently, sword gripped in both hands; then, as a bear gives back from the onset of the hunters, he turned and fled about the hut, arrows whistling about him and glancing from the rings of his mail. There were no shots; the ride through that dripping forest had dampened the powder-flasks of the raiders.

Von Kalmbach quartered about the back of the hut, mindful of the fierce yells behind him, and gained the shed behind the hut he had occupied, wherein he stabled his gray stallion. Even as he reached the door, someone snarled like a panther in the semi-dark and cut viciously at him. He parried the stroke with the lifted sword and struck back with all the power of his broad shoulders. The great blade glanced stunningly from the Akinji's polished helmet and rent through the mail links of his hauberk, tearing arm from shoulder. The Muhammadan sank down with a groan, and the German sprang over his prostrate form. The gray stallion, wild with fear and excitement, neighed shrilly and reared as his master sprang on his back. No time for saddle or bridle. Gottfried dug his heels into the quivering flanks and the great steed shot through the door like a thunderbolt, knocking men right and left like tenpins. Across the firelit open space between the burning huts he raced, clearing crumpled corpses in his stride, splashing his rider from heel to head as he thrashed through the puddles.

The Akinji made after the flying rider, loosing their shafts and giving tongue like hounds. Those mounted spurred after him, while those who had entered the village on foot ran through the broken wall for their horses.

Arrows flickered about Gottfried's head as he put his steed at the only point open to him—the unbroken western wall. It was touch and go, for the footing was tricky and treacherous and never had the gray stallion attempted such a leap. Gottfried held his breath as he felt the great body beneath him gathering and tensing in full flight for the desperate effort; then with a volcanic heave of mighty thews the stallion rose in the air and cleared the barrier with scarce an inch to spare. The pursuers yelled in amazement and fury, and reined back. Born horsemen though they were, they dared not attempt that breakneck leap. They lost time seeking gates and breaks in the wall, and when they finally emerged from the village, the black, dank, whispering, dripping forest had swallowed up their prey.

Mikhal Oglu swore like a fiend and leaving his lieutenant Othman in charge with instructions to leave no living human being in the village, he pressed on after the fugitive, following the trail, by torches, in the muddy mold, and swearing to run him down, if the road led under the very walls of Vienna.

3

Allah did not will it that Mikhal Oglu should take Gottfried von Kalmbach's head in the dark, dripping forest. He knew the country better than they, and in spite of their zeal, they lost his trail in the darkness. Dawn found Gottfried riding through terror-stricken farmlands, with the flame of a burning world lighting the east and south. The country was thronged with fugitives, staggering under pitiful loads of household goods, driving bellowing cattle, like people fleeing the end of the world. The torrential rains that had offered false promise of security had not long stayed the march of the Grand Turk.

With a quarter-million followers he was ravaging the eastern marches of Christendom. While Gottfried had loitered in the taverns of isolated villages, drinking up the Sultan's bounty, Pesth and Buda had fallen, the German soldiers of the latter having been slaughtered by the Janizaries, after promises of safety sworn by Suleyman, whom men named the Generous.

While Ferdinand and the nobles and bishops squabbled at the Diet of Spires, the elements alone seemed to war for Christendom. Rain fell in torrents, and through the floods that changed plains and forest-bed to dank morasses, the Turks struggled grimly. They drowned in raging rivers, and lost great stores of ammunition, ordnance and supplies when boats capsized, bridges gave way, and wagons mired. But on they came, driven by the implacable will of Suleyman, and now in September, 1529, over the ruins of Hungary, the Turk swept on Europe, with the Akinji—the Sackmen—ravaging the land like the drift ahead of a storm.

This in part Gottfried learned from the fugitives as he pushed his weary stallion toward the city which was the only sanctuary for the panting thousands. Behind him the skies flamed red and the screams of butchered victims came dimly down the wind to his ears. Sometimes he could even make out the swarming black masses of wild horsemen. The wings of the vulture beat horrifically over that butchered land and the shadows of those great wings fell across all Europe. Again the destroyer was riding out of the blue mysterious East as his brothers had ridden before him—Attila—Subotai—Bayazid—Muhammad the Conqueror. But never before had such a storm risen against the West.

Before the waving vulture wings the road thronged with wailing fugitives; behind them it ran red and silent, strewn with mangled shapes that cried no more. The killers were not a half-hour behind him when Gottfried von Kalmbach rode his reeling stallion through the gates of Vienna. The people on the walls had heard the wailing for hours, rising awfully on the wind, and now afar they saw the sun flicker on the points of lances as the horsemen rode in amongst the masses of fugitives toiling down from the hills into the plain which girdles the city. They saw the play of naked steel like sickles among ripe grain.

Von Kalmbach found the city in turmoil, the people swirling and screaming about Count Nikolas Salm, the seventy-year-old warhorse who commanded Vienna, and his aides, Roggendrof, Count Nikolas Zrinyi and Paul Bakics. Salm was working with frantic haste, leveling houses near the walls and using their material to brace the ramparts, which were old and unstable, nowhere more than six feet thick, and in many places crumbling and falling down. The outer palisade was so frail it bore the name of Stadtzaun—city hedge.

But under the lashing energy of Count Salm, a new wall twenty feet high was thrown up from the Stuben to the Karnthner Gate. Ditches interior to the old moat were dug, and ramparts erected from the drawbridge to the Salz Gate. Roofs were stripped of shingles, to lessen the chances of fire, and paving was ripped up to soften the impact of cannonballs.

The suburbs had been deserted, and now they were fired lest they give shelter to the besiegers. In the process, which was carried out in the very teeth of the oncoming Sackmen, conflagrations broke out in the city and added to the delirium. It was all hell and bedlam turned loose, and in the midst of it, five thousand wretched noncombatants, old men and women, and children, were ruthlessly driven from the gates to shift for themselves, and their screams, as the Akinjis swooped down, maddened the people within the walls. These hellions were arriving by thousands, topping the skylines, and sweeping down on the city in irregular squadrons, like vultures gathering about a dying camel. Within an hour after the first swarm had appeared, not one Christian remained alive outside the gates, except those bound by long ropes to the saddle-peaks of their captors and forced to run at full speed or be dragged to death. The wild riders swirled about the walls, yelling and loosing their shafts. Men on the towers recognized the dread Mikhal Oglu by the wings on his cuirass, and noted that he rode from one heap of dead to another, avidly scanning each corpse in turn, pausing to glare questioningly at the battlements.

Meanwhile, from the west, a band of German and Spanish troops cut their way through a cordon of Sackmen and marched into the streets to the accompaniment of frenzied cheers, Philip the Palgrave at their head.

Gottfried von Kalmbach leaned on his sword and watched them pass in their gleaming breastplates and plumed crested helmets, with long matchlocks on their shoulders and two-handed swords strapped to their steel-clad backs. He was a curious contrast in his rusty chain-mail, old-fashioned harness picked up here and there and slovenly pieced together—he seemed like a figure out of the past, rusty and tarnished, watching a newer, brighter generation go by. Yet Philip saluted him, with a glance of recognition, as the shining column swung past.

Von Kalmbach started toward the walls, where the gunners were firing frugally at the Akinji, who showed some disposition to climb upon the bastions on lariats thrown from their saddles. But on the way he heard that Salm was impressing nobles and soldiers in the task of digging moats and rearing new earthworks, and in great haste he took refuge in a tavern, where he bullied the host, a knock-kneed and apprehensive Wallachian, into giving him credit, and rapidly drank himself into a state where no one would have considered asking him to do work of any kind.

Shots, shouts and screams reached his ears, but he paid scant heed. He knew that the Akinji would strike and pass on, to ravage the country beyond. He learned from the tavern talk that Salm had 20,000 pikemen, 2,000 horsemen and 1,000 volunteer citizens to oppose Suleyman's hordes, together with seventy guns—cannons, demi-cannons and culverins. The news of the Turks' numbers numbed all hearts with dread—all but von Kalmbach's. He was a fatalist in his way. But he discovered a conscience in ale, and was presently brooding over the people the miserable Viennese had driven forth to perish. The more he drank the more melancholy he became, and maudlin tears dripped from the drooping ends of his mustaches.

At last he rose unsteadily and took up his great sword, muzzily intent on challenging Count Salm to a duel because of the matter. He bellowed down the timid importunities of the Wallachian and weaved out on the street. To his groggy sight the towers and spires cavorted crazily; people jostled him, knocking him aside as they ran about aimlessly. Philip the Palgrave strode by clanking in his armor, the keen dark faces of his Spaniards contrasting with the square, florid countenances of the Lanzknechts.

"Shame upon you, von Kalmbach!" said Philip sternly. "The Turk is upon us, and you keep your snout shoved in an ale-pot!"

"Whose snout is in what ale-pot?" demanded Gottfried, weaving in an erratic half-circle as he fumbled at his sword. "Devil bite you, Philip, I'll rap your pate for that—"

The Palgrave was already out of sight, and eventually Gottfried found himself on the Karnthner Tower, only vaguely aware of how he had got there. But what he saw sobered him suddenly. The Turk was indeed upon Vienna. The plain was covered with his tents, thirty thousand, some said, and swore that from the lofty spire of Saint Stephen's cathedral a man could not see their limits. Four hundred of his boats lay on the Danube, and Gottfried heard men cursing the Austrian fleet which lay helpless far upstream, because its sailors, long unpaid, refused to man the ships. He also heard that Salm had made no reply at all to Suleyman's demand to surrender.

Now, partly as a gesture, partly to awe the Caphar dogs, the Grand Turk's array was moving in orderly procession before the ancient walls before settling down to the business of the siege. The sight was enough to awe the stoutest. The low-swinging sun struck fire from polished helmet, jeweled saber-hilt and lance-point. It was as if a river of shining steel flowed leisurely and terribly past the walls of Vienna.

The Akinji, who ordinarily formed the vanguard of the host, had swept on, but in their place rode the Tatars of Crimea, crouching on their high-peaked, short-stirruped saddles, their gnome-like heads guarded by iron helmets, their stocky bodies with bronze breastplates and lacquered leather. Behind them came the Azabs, the irregular infantry, Kurds and Arabs for the most part, a wild, motley horde. Then their brothers, the Delis, the Madcaps, wild men on tough ponies fantastically adorned with fur and feathers. The riders wore caps and mantles of leopard skin; their unshorn hair hung in tangled strands about their high shoulders, and over their matted beards their eyes glared the madness of fanaticism and bhang.

After them came the real body of the army. First the beys and emirs with their retainers—horsemen and footmen from the feudal fiefs of Asia Minor. Then the Spahis, the heavy cavalry, on splendid steeds. And last of all the real strength of the Turkish empire—the most terrible military organization in the world—the Janizaries. On the walls men spat in black fury, recognizing kindred blood. For the Janizaries were not Turks. With a few exceptions, where Turkish parents had smuggled their offspring into the ranks to save them from the grinding life of a peasant, they were sons of Christians—Greeks, Serbs, Hungarians—stolen in infancy and raised in the ranks of Islam, knowing but one master—the Sultan; but one occupation—slaughter.

Their beardless features contrasted with those of their Oriental masters. Many had blue eyes and yellow mustaches. But all their faces were stamped with the wolfish ferocity to which they had been reared. Under their dark blue cloaks glinted fine mail, and many wore steel skull-caps under their curious, high-peaked hats from which depended a white sleeve-like piece of cloth, and through which was thrust a copper spoon. Long bird-of-paradise plumes likewise adorned these strange headpieces.

Besides scimitars, pistols and daggers, each Janizary bore a matchlock, and their officers carried pots of coals for the lighting of the matches. Up and down the ranks scurried the dervishes, clad only in kalpaks of camel-hair and green aprons fringed with ebony beads, exhorting the Faithful. Military bands, the invention of the Turk, marched with the columns, cymbals clashing, lutes twanging. Over the flowing sea the banners tossed and swayed—the crimson flag of the Spahis, the white banner of the Janizaries with its two-edged sword worked in gold, and the horse-tail standards of the rulers—seven tails for the Sultan, six for the Grand Vizier, three for the Agha of the Janizaries. So Suleyman paraded his power before despairing Caphar eyes.

But von Kalmbach's gaze was centered on the groups that labored to set up the ordnance of the Sultan. And he shook his head in bewilderment.

"Demi-culverins, sakers, and falconets!" he grunted. "Where the devil's all the heavy artillery Suleyman's so proud of?"

"At the bottom of the Danube!" A Hungarian pikeman grinned fiercely and spat as he answered. "Wulf Hagen sank that part of the Soldan's flotilla. The rest of his cannon and cannon royal, they say, were mired because of the rains."

A slow grin bristled Gottfried's mustache.

"What was Suleyman's word to Salm?"

"That he'd eat breakfast in Vienna day after tomorrow—the 29th."

Gottfried shook his head ponderously.

4

The siege commenced, with the roaring of cannons, the whistling of arrows, and the blasting crash of matchlocks. The Janizaries took possession of the ruined suburbs, where fragments of walls gave them shelter. Under a screen of irregulars and a volley of arrow-fire, they advanced methodically just after dawn.

On a gun-turret on the threatened wall, leaning on his great sword and meditatively twisting his mustache, Gottfried von Kalmbach watched a Transylvanian gunner being carried off the wall, his brains oozing from a hole in his head; a Turkish matchlock had spoken too near the walls. The field-pieces of the Sultan were barking like deep-toned dogs, knocking chips off the battlements. The Janizaries were advancing, kneeling, firing, reloading as they came on. Bullets glanced from the crenelles and whined off venomously into space. One flattened against Gottfried's hauberk, bringing an outraged grunt from him. Turning toward the abandoned gun, he saw a colorful, incongruous figure bending over the massive breech.

It was a woman, dressed as von Kalmbach had not seen even the dandies of France dressed. She was tall, splendidly shaped, but lithe. From under a steel cap escaped rebellious tresses that rippled red gold in the sun over her compact shoulders. High boots of Cordovan leather came to her mid-thighs, which were cased in baggy breeches. She wore a shirt of fine Turkish mesh-mail tucked into her breeches. Her supple waist was confined by a flowing sash of green silk, into which were thrust a brace of pistols and a dagger, and from which depended a long Hungarian saber. Over all was carelessly thrown a scarlet cloak.

This surprizing figure was bending over the cannon, sighting it in a manner betokening more than a passing familiarity, at a group of Turks who were wheeling a carriage-gun just within range.

"Eh, Red Sonya!" shouted a man-at-arms, waving his pike. "Give 'em hell, my lass!"

"Trust me, dog-brother," she retorted as she applied the glowing match to the vent. "But I wish my mark was Roxelana's—"

A terrific detonation drowned her words and a swirl of smoke blinded every one on the turret, as the terrific recoil of the overcharged cannon knocked the firer flat on her back. She sprang up like a spring rebounding and rushed to the embrasure, peering eagerly through the smoke, which clearing, showed the ruin of the gun crew. The huge ball, bigger than a man's head, had smashed full into the group clustered about the saker, and now they lay on the torn ground, their skulls blasted by the impact, or their bodies mangled by the flying iron splinters from their shattered gun. A cheer went up from the towers, and the woman called Red Sonya yelled with a sincere joy and did the steps of a Cossack dance.

Gottfried approached, eying in open admiration the splendid swell of her bosom beneath the pliant mail, the curves of her ample hips and rounded limbs. She stood as a man might stand, booted legs braced wide apart, thumbs hooked into her girdle, but she was all woman. She was laughing as she faced him, and he noted with fascination the dancing sparkling lights and changing colors of her eyes. She raked back her rebellious locks with a powder-stained hand and he wondered at the clear pinky whiteness of her firm flesh where it was unstained.

"Why did you wish for the Sultana Roxelana for a target, my girl?" he asked.

"Because she's my sister, the slut!" answered Sonya.

At that instant a great cry thundered over the walls and the girl started like a wild thing, ripping out her blade in a long flash of silver in the sun.

"That bellow!" she cried. "The Janizaries—"

Gottfried was already on his way to the embrasures. He too had heard before the terrible soul-shaking shout of the charging Janizaries. Suleyman meant to waste no time on the city that barred him from helpless Europe. He meant to crush its frail walls in one storm. The bashi-bazouki, the irregulars, died like flies to screen the main advance, and over heaps of their dead, the Janizaries thundered against Vienna. In the teeth of cannonade and musket volley they surged on, crossing the moats on scaling-ladders laid across, bridge-like. Whole ranks went down as the Austrian guns roared, but now the attackers were under the walls and the cumbrous balls whirred over their heads, to work havoc in the rear ranks.

The Spanish matchlock men, firing almost straight down, took ghastly toll, but now the ladders gripped the walls, and the chanting madmen surged upward. Arrows whistled, striking down the defenders. Behind them the Turkish field-pieces boomed, careless of injury to friend as well as foe. Gottfried, standing at an embrasure, was overthrown by a sudden terrific impact. A ball had smashed the merlon, braining half a dozen defenders.

Gottfried rose, half-stunned, out of the debris of masonry and huddled corpses. He looked down into an uprushing waste of snarling, impassioned faces, where eyes glared like mad dogs' and blades glittered like sunbeams on water. Bracing his feet wide, he heaved up his great sword and lashed down. His jaw jutted out, his mustache bristled. The five-foot blade caved in steel caps and skulls, lashing through uplifted bucklers and iron shoulder-pieces. Men fell from the ladders, their nerveless fingers slipping from the bloody rungs.

But they swarmed through the breach on either side of him. A terrible cry announced that the Turks had a foothold on the wall. But no man dared leave his post to go to the threatened point. To the dazed defenders it seemed that Vienna was ringed by a glittering, tossing sea that roared higher and higher about the doomed walls.

Stepping back to avoid being hemmed in, Gottfried grunted and lashed right and left. His eyes were no longer cloudy; they blazed like blue balefire. Three Janizaries were down at his feet; his broadsword clanged in a forest of slashing scimitars. A blade splintered on his basinet, filling his eyes with fire-shot blackness. Staggering, he struck back and felt his great blade crunch home. Blood jetted over his hands and he tore his sword clear. Then with a yell and a rush someone was at his side and he heard the quick splintering of mail beneath the madly flailing strokes of a saber that flashed like silver lightning before his clearing sight.

It was Red Sonya who had come to his aid, and her onslaught was no less terrible than that of a she-panther. Her strokes followed each other too quickly for the eye to follow; her blade was a blur of white fire, and men went down like ripe grain before the reaper. With a deep roar Gottfried strode to her side, bloody and terrible, swinging his great blade. Forced irresistibly back, the Moslems wavered on the edge of the wall, then leaped for the ladders or fell screaming through empty space.

Oaths flowed in a steady stream from Sonya's red lips and she laughed wildly as her saber sang home and blood spurted along the edge. The last Turk on the battlement screamed and parried wildly as she pressed him; then dropping his scimitar, his clutching hands closed desperately on her dripping blade. With a groan he swayed on the edge, blood gushing from his horribly cut fingers.

"Hell to you, dog-soul!" she laughed. "The devil can stir your broth for you!"

With a twist and a wrench she tore away her saber, severing the wretch's fingers; with a moaning cry he pitched backward and fell headlong.

On all sides the Janizaries were falling back. The field-pieces, halted while the fighting went on upon the walls, were booming again, and the Spaniards, kneeling at the embrasures, were returning the fire with their long matchlocks.

Gottfried approached Red Sonya, who was cleansing her blade, swearing softly.

"By God, my girl," said he, extending a huge hand, "had you not come to my aid, I think I'd have supped in Hell this night. I thank—"

"Thank the devil!" retorted Sonya rudely, slapping his hand aside. "The Turks were on the wall. Don't think I risked my hide to save yours, dog-brother!"

And with a scornful flirt of her wide coattails, she swaggered off down the battlements, giving back promptly and profanely the rude sallies of the soldiers. Gottfried scowled after her, and a Lanzknecht slapped him jovially on the shoulder.

"Eh, she's a devil, that one! She drinks the strongest head under the table and outswears a Spaniard. She's no man's light o' love. Cut—slash—death to you, dog-soul! There's her way."

"Who is she, in the devil's name?" growled von Kalmbach.

"Red Sonya from Rogatino—that's all we know. Marches and fights like a man—God knows why. Swears she's sister to Roxelana, the Soldan's favorite. If the Tatars who grabbed Roxelana that night had got Sonya, by Saint Piotr! Suleyman would have had a handful! Let her alone, sir brother; she's a wildcat. Come and have a tankard of ale."

The Janizaries, summoned before the Grand Vizier to explain why the attack failed after the wall had been scaled at one place, swore they had been confronted by a devil in the form of a red-headed woman, aided by a giant in rusty mail. Ibrahim discounted the woman, but the description of the man woke a half-forgotten memory in his mind. After dismissing the soldiers, he summoned the Tatar, Yaruk Khan, and dispatched him up-country to demand of Mikhal Oglu why he had not sent a certain head to the royal tent.

5

Suleyman did not eat his breakfast in Vienna on the morning of the 29th. He stood on the height of Semmering, before his rich pavilion with its gold-knobbed pinnacles and its guard of five hundred Solaks, and watched his light batteries pecking away vainly at the frail walls; he saw his irregulars wasting their lives like water, striving to fill the fosse, and he saw his sappers burrowing like moles, driving mines and counter-mines nearer and nearer the bastions.

Within the city there was little ease. Night and day the walls were manned. In their cellars the Viennese watched the faint vibrations of peas on drumheads that betrayed the sounds of digging in the earth. They told of Turkish mines burrowing under the walls, and sank their counter-mines, accordingly. Men fought no less fiercely under the earth than above.

Vienna was the one Christian island in a sea of infidels. Night by night men watched the horizons burning where the Akinji yet scoured the agonized land. Occasionally word came from the outer world—slaves escaping from the camp to slipping into the city. Always their news was fresh horror. In Upper Austria less than a third of the inhabitants were left alive; Mikhal Oglu was outdoing himself. And the people said that it was evident the vulture-winged one was looking for one in particular. His slayers brought men's heads and heaped them high before him; he avidly searched among the grisly relics, then, apparently in fiendish disappointment, drove his devils to new atrocities.

These tales, instead of paralyzing the Austrians with dread, fired them with the mad fury of desperation. Mines exploded, breaches were made and the Turks swarmed in, but always the desperate Christians were there before them, and in the choking, blind, wild-beast madness of hand-to-hand fighting they paid in part the red debt they owed.

September dwindled into October; the leaves turned brown and yellow on Wiener Wald, and the winds blew cold. The watchers shivered at night on the walls that whitened to the bite of the frost; but still the tents ringed the city; and still Suleyman sat in his magnificent pavilion and glared at the frail barrier that barred his imperial path. None but Ibrahim dared speak to him; his mood was black as the cold nights that crept down from the northern hills. The wind that moaned outside his tent seemed a dirge for his ambitions of conquest.

Ibrahim watched him narrowly, and after a vain onset that lasted from dawn till midday, he called off the Janizaries and bade them retire into the ruined suburbs and rest. And he sent a bowman to shoot a very certain shaft into a very certain part of the city, where certain persons were waiting for just such an event.

No more attacks were made that day. The field-pieces, which had been pounding at the Karnthner Gate for days, were shifted northward, to hammer at the Burg. As an assault on that part of the wall seemed imminent, the bulk of the soldiery was shifted there. But the onslaught did not come, though the batteries kept up a steady fire, hour after hour. Whatever the reason, the soldiers gave thanks for the respite; they were dizzy with fatigue, mad with raw wounds and lack of sleep.

That night the great square, the Am-Hof market, seethed with soldiers, while civilians looked on enviously. A great store of wine had been discovered hidden in the cellars of a rich Jewish merchant, who hoped to reap triple profit when all other liquor in the city was gone. In spite of their officers, the half-crazed men rolled the great hogsheads into the square and broached them. Salm gave up the attempt to control them. Better drunkenness, growled the old warhorse, than for the men to fall in their tracks from exhaustion. He paid the Jew from his own purse. In relays the soldiers came from the walls and drank deep.

In the glare of cressets and torches, to the accompaniment of drunken shouts and songs, to which the occasional rumble of a cannon played a sinister undertone, von Kalmbach dipped his basinet into a barrel and brought it out brimful and dripping. Sinking his mustache into the liquid, he paused as his clouded eyes, over the rim of the steel cap, rested on a strutting figure on the other side of the hogshead. Resentment touched his expression. Red Sonya had already visited more than one barrel. Her burganet was thrust sidewise on her rebellious locks, her swagger was wilder, her eyes more mocking.

"Ha!" she cried scornfully. "It's the Turk-killer, with his nose deep in the keg, as usual! Devil bite all topers!"

She consistently thrust a jeweled goblet into the crimson flood and emptied it at a gulp. Gottfried stiffened resentfully. He had had a tilt with Sonya already, and he still smarted.

"Why should I even look at you, in your ragged harness and empty purse," she had mocked, "when even Paul Bakics is mad for me? Go along, guzzler, beer-keg!"

"Be damned to you," he had retorted. "You needn't be so high, just because your sister is the Soldan's mistress—"

At that she had flown into an awful passion, and they had parted with mutual curses. Now, from the devil in her eyes, he saw that she intended making things further uncomfortable for him.

"Hussy!" he growled. "I'll drown you in this hogshead."

"Nay, you'll drown yourself first, boar-pig!" she shouted amid a roar of rough laughter. "A pity you aren't as valiant against the Turks as you are against the wine-butts!"

"Dogs bite you, slut!" he roared. "How can I break their heads when they stand off and pound us with cannon balls? Shall I throw my dagger at them from the wall?"

"There are thousands just outside," she retorted in the madness induced by drink and her own wild nature, "if any had the guts to go to them."

"By God!" the maddened giant dragged out his great sword. "No baggage can call *me* coward, sot or not! I'll go out upon them, if never a man follow me!"

Bedlam followed his bellow; the drunken temper of the crowd was fit for such madness. The nearly empty hogsheads were deserted as men tipsily drew sword and reeled toward the outer gates. Wulf Hagen fought his way into the storm, buffeting men right and left, shouting fiercely, "Wait, you drunken fools! Don't surge out in this shape! Wait—" They brushed him aside, sweeping on in a blind senseless torrent.

Dawn was just beginning to tip the eastern hills. Somewhere in the strangely silent Turkish camp a drum began to throb. Turkish sentries stared wildly and loosed their matchlocks in the air to warn the camp, appalled at the sight of the Christian horde pouring over the narrow drawbridge, eight thousand strong, brandishing swords and ale tankards. As they foamed over the moat a terrific explosion rent the din, and a portion of the wall near the Karnthner Gate seemed to detach itself and rise into the air. A great shout rose from the Turkish camp, but the attackers did not pause.

They rushed headlong into the suburbs, and there they saw the Janizaries, not rousing from slumber, but fully clad and armed, being hurriedly drawn up in charging lines. Without pausing, they burst headlong into the half-formed ranks. Far outnumbered, their drunken fury and velocity was yet irresistible. Before the madly thrashing axes and lashing broadswords, the Janizaries reeled back dazed and disordered. The suburbs became a shambles where battling men, slashing and hewing at one another, stumbled on mangled bodies and severed limbs. Suleyman and Ibrahim, on the height of Semmering, saw the invincible Janizaries in full retreat, streaming out toward the hills.

In the city the rest of the defenders were working madly to repair the great breach the mysterious explosion had torn in the wall. Salm gave thanks for that drunken sortie. But for it, the Janizaries would have been pouring through the breach before the dust settled.

All was confusion in the Turkish camp. Suleyman ran to his horse and took charge in person, shouting at the Spahis. They formed ranks and swung down the slopes in orderly squadrons. The Christian warriors, still following their fleeing enemies, suddenly awakened to their danger. Before them the Janizaries were still falling back, but on either flank the horsemen of Asia were galloping to cut them off. Fear replaced drunken recklessness. They began to fall back, and the retreat quickly became a rout. Screaming in blind panic they threw away their weapons and fled for the drawbridge. The Turks rode them down to the water's edge, and tried to follow them across the bridge, into the gates which were opened for them. And there at the bridge Wulf Hagen and his retainers met the pursuers and held them hard. The flood of the fugitives flowed past him to safety; on him the Turkish tide broke like a red wave. He loomed, a steel-clad giant, in a waste of spears.

Gottfried von Kalmbach did not voluntarily quit the field, but the rush of his companions swept him along the tide of flight, blaspheming bitterly. Presently he lost his footing and his panic-stricken comrades stampeded across his prostrate frame. When the frantic heels ceased to drum on his mail, he raised his head and saw that he was near the fosse, and naught but Turks about him. Rising, he ran lumberingly toward the moat, into which he plunged unexpectedly, looking back over his shoulder at a pursuing Moslem.

He came up floundering and spluttering, and made for the opposite bank, splashing water like a buffalo. The blood-mad Muhammadan was close behind him—an Algerian corsair, as much at home in water as out. The stubborn German would not drop his great sword, and burdened by his mail, just managed to reach the other bank, where he clung, utterly exhausted and unable to lift a hand in defense as the Algerian swirled in, dagger gleaming above his naked shoulder. Then someone swore heartily on the bank hard by. A slim hand thrust a long pistol into the Algerian's face; he screamed as it exploded, making a ghastly ruin of his head. Another slim, strong hand gripped the sinking German by the scruff of his mail.

"Grab the bank, fool!" gritted a voice, indicative of great effort. "I can't heave you up alone; you must weigh a ton. Pull, dolt, pull!"

Blowing, gasping and floundering, Gottfried half-clambered, was half lifted, out of the moat. He showed some disposition to lie on his belly and retch, what of the dirty water he had swallowed, but his rescuer urged him to his feet.

"The Turks are crossing the bridge and the lads are closing the gates against them—haste, before we're cut off."

Inside the gate Gottfried stared about, as if waking from a dream.

"Where's Wulf Hagen? I saw him holding the bridge."

"Lying dead among twenty dead Turks," answered Red Sonya.

Gottfried sat down on a piece of fallen wall, and because he was shaken and exhausted, and still mazed with drink and blood-lust, he sank his face in his huge hands and wept. Sonya kicked him disgustedly.

"Name o' Satan, man, don't sit and blubber like a spanked schoolgirl. You drunkards had to play the fool, but that can't be mended. Come—let's go to the Walloon's tavern and drink ale."

"Why did you pull me out of the moat?" he asked.

"Because a great oaf like you never can help himself. I see you need a wise person like me to keep life in that hulking frame."

"But I thought you despised me!"

"Well, a woman can change her mind, can't she?" she snapped.

Along the walls the pikemen were repelling the frothing Moslems, thrusting them off the partly repaired breach. In the royal pavilion Ibrahim was explaining to his master that the devil had undoubtedly inspired that drunken sortie just at the right moment to spoil the Grand Vizier's carefully laid plans. Suleyman, wild with fury, spoke shortly to his friend for the first time.

"Nay, thou hast failed. Have done with thine intrigues. Where craft has failed, sheer force shall prevail. Send a rider for the Akinji; they are needed here to replace the fallen. Bid the hosts to the attack again."

6

The preceding onslaughts were naught to the storm that now burst on Vienna's reeling walls. Night and day the cannons flashed and thundered. Bombs burst on roofs and in the streets. When men died on the walls there was none to take their places. Fear of famine stalked the streets and the darker fear of treachery ran black-mantled through the alleys. Investigation showed that the blast that had rent the Karnthner wall had not been fired from without. In a mine tunneled from an unsuspected cellar inside the city, a heavy charge of powder had been exploded beneath the wall. One or two men, working secretly, might have done it. It was now apparent that the bombardment of the Burg had been merely a gesture to draw attention away from the Karnthner wall, to give the traitors an opportunity to work undiscovered.

Count Salm and his aides did the work of giants. The aged commander, fired with superhuman energy, trod the walls, braced the faltering, aided the wounded, fought in the breaches side by side with the common soldiers, while death dealt his blows unsparingly.

But if death supped within the walls, he feasted full without. Suleyman drove his men as relentlessly as if he were their worst foe.

Plague stalked among them, and the ravaged countryside yielded no food. The cold winds howled down from the Carpathians and the warriors shivered in their light Oriental garb. In the frosty nights the hands of the sentries froze to their matchlocks. The ground grew hard as flint and the sappers toiled feebly with blunted tools. Rain fell, mingled with sleet, extinguishing matches, wetting powder, turning the plain outside the city to a muddy wallow, where rotting corpses sickened the living.

Suleyman shuddered as with an ague, as he looked out over the camp. He saw his warriors, worn and haggard, toiling in the muddy plain like ghosts under the gloomy leaden skies. The stench of his slaughtered thousands was in his nostrils. In that instant it seemed to the Sultan that he looked on a gray plain of the dead, where corpses dragged their lifeless bodies to an outworn task, animated only by the ruthless will of their master. For an instant the Tatar in his veins rose above the Turk and he shook with fear. Then his lean jaws set. The walls of Vienna staggered drunkenly, patched and repaired in a score of places. How could they stand?

"Sound for the onslaught. Thirty thousand aspers to the first man on the walls!"

The Grand Vizier spread his hands helplessly. "The spirit is gone out of the warriors. They can not endure the miseries of this icy land."

"Drive them to the walls with whips," answered Suleyman, grimly. "This is the gate to Frankistan. It is through it we must ride the road to empire."

Drums thundered through the camp. The weary defenders of Christendom rose up and gripped their weapons, electrified by the instinctive knowledge that the death-grip had come.

In the teeth of roaring matchlocks and swinging broadswords, the officers of the Sultan drove the Moslem hosts. Whips cracked and men cried out blasphemously up and down the lines. Maddened, they hurled themselves at the reeling walls, riddled with great breaches, yet still barriers behind which desperate men could crouch. Charge after charge rolled on over the choked fosse, broke on the staggering walls, and rolled back, leaving its wash of dead. Night fell unheeded, and through the darkness, lighted by blaze of cannon and flare of torches, the battle raged. Driven by Suleyman's terrible will, the attackers fought throughout the night, heedless of all Moslem tradition.

Dawn rose as on Armageddon. Before the walls of Vienna lay a vast carpet of steel-clad dead. Their plumes waved in the wind. And across the corpses staggered the hollow-eyed attackers to grapple with the dazed defenders.

The steel tides rolled and broke, and rolled on again, till the very gods must have stood aghast at the giant capacity of men for suffering and enduring. It was the Armageddon of races—Asia against Europe. About the walls raved a sea of Eastern faces—Turks, Tatars, Kurds, Arabs, Algerians, snarling, screaming, dying before the roaring matchlocks of the Spaniards, the thrust of Austrian pikes, the strokes of the German Lanzknechts, who swung their two-handed swords like reapers mowing ripe grain. Those within the walls were no more heroic than those without, stumbling among fields of their own dead.

To Gottfried von Kalmbach, life had faded to a single meaning—the swinging of his great sword. In the wide breach by the Karnthner Tower he fought until time lost all meaning. For long ages maddened faces rose snarling before him, the faces of devils, and scimitars flashed before his eyes everlastingly. He did not feel his wounds, nor the drain of weariness. Gasping in the choking dust, blind with sweat and blood, he dealt death like a harvest, dimly aware that at his side a slim, pantherish figure swayed and smote—at first with laughter, curses and snatches of song, later in grim silence.

His identity as an individual was lost in that cataclysm of swords. He hardly knew it when Count Salm was death-stricken at his side by a bursting bomb. He was not aware when night crept over the hills, nor did he realize at last that the tide was slackening and ebbing. He was only dimly aware that Nikolas Zrinyi tore him away from the corpse-choked breach, saying, "God's name, man, go and sleep. We've beaten them off—for the time being, at least."

He found himself in a narrow, winding street, all dark and forsaken. He had no idea of how he had got there, but seemed vaguely to remember a hand on his elbow, tugging, guiding. The weight of his mail pulled at his sagging shoulders. He could not tell if the sound he heard were the cannon fitfully roaring, or a throbbing in his own head. It seemed there was someone he should look for—someone who meant a great deal to him. But all was vague. Somewhere, sometime, it seemed long, long ago, a sword-stroke had cleft his basinet. When he tried to think he seemed to feel again the impact of that terrible blow, and his brain swam. He tore off the dented head-piece and cast it into the street.

Again the hand was tugging at his arm. A voice urged, "Wine, my lord—drink!"

Dimly he saw a lean, black-mailed figure extending a tankard. With a gasp he caught at it and thrust his muzzle into the stinging liquor, gulping like a man dying of thirst. Then something burst in his brain. The night filled with a million flashing sparks, as if a powder magazine had exploded in his head. After that, darkness and oblivion.

He came slowly to himself, aware of a raging thirst, an aching head, and an intense weariness that seemed to paralyze his limbs. He was bound hand and foot, and gagged. Twisting his head, he saw that he was in a small bare dusty room, from which a winding stone stair led up. He deduced that he was in the lower part of the tower.

Over a guttering candle on a crude table stooped two men. They were both lean and hook-nosed, clad in plain black garments—Asiatics, past doubt. Gottfried listened to their low-toned conversation. He had picked up many languages in his wanderings. He recognized them—Tshoruk and his son Rhupen, Armenian merchants. He remembered that he had seen Tshoruk often in the last week or so, ever since the domed helmets of the Akinji had appeared in Suleyman's camp. Evidently the merchant had been shadowing him, for some reason. Tshoruk was reading what he had written on a bit of parchment.

"My lord, though I blew up the Karnthner wall in vain, yet I have news to make my lord's heart glad. My son and I have taken the German, von Kalmbach. As he left the wall, dazed with fighting, we followed, guiding him subtly to the ruined tower whereof you know, and giving him drugged wine, bound him fast. Let my lord send the emir Mikhal Oglu to the wall by the tower, and we will give him into thy hands. We will bind him on the old mangonel and cast him over the wall like a tree trunk."

The Armenian took up an arrow and began to bind the parchment about the shaft with light silver wire.

"Take this to the roof, and shoot it toward the mantlet, as usual," he began, when Rhupen exclaimed, "Hark!" and both froze, their eyes glittering like those of trapped vermin—fearful yet vindictive.

Gottfried gnawed at the gag; it slipped. Outside he heard a familiar voice. "Gottfried! Where the devil are you?"

His breath burst from him in a stentorian roar. "Hey, Sonya! Name of the devil! Be careful, girl—"

Tshoruk snarled like a wolf and struck him savagely on the head with a scimitar hilt. Almost instantly, it seemed, the door crashed inward. As in a dream Gottfried saw Red Sonya framed in the doorway, pistol in hand. Her face was drawn and haggard; her eyes burned like coals. Her basinet was gone, and her scarlet cloak. Her mail was hacked and red-clotted, her boots slashed, her silken breeches splashed and spotted with blood.

With a croaking cry Tshoruk ran at her, scimitar lifted. Before he could strike, she crashed down the barrel of the empty pistol on his head, felling him like an ox. From the other side Rhupen slashed at her with a curved Turkish dagger. Dropping the pistol, she closed with the young Oriental. Moving like someone in a dream, she bore him irresistibly backward, one hand gripping his wrist, the other his throat. Throttling him slowly, she inexorably crashed his head again and again against the stones of the wall, until his eyes rolled up and set. Then she threw him from her like a sack of loose salt.

"God!" she muttered thickly, reeling an instant in the center of the room, her hands to her head. Then she went to the captive and sinking stiffly to her knees, cut his bonds with fumbling strokes that sliced his flesh as well as the cords.

"How did you find me?" he asked stupidly, clambering stiffly up.

She reeled to the table and sank down in a chair. A flagon of wine stood at her elbow and she seized it avidly and drank. Then she wiped her mouth on her sleeve and surveyed him wearily but with renewed life.

"I saw you leave the wall and followed. I was so drunk from the fighting I scarce knew what I did. I saw those dogs take your arm and lead you into the alleys, and then I lost sight of you. But I found your burganet lying outside in the street, and began shouting for you. What the hell's the meaning of this?"

She picked up the arrow, and blinked at the parchment fastened to it. Evidently she could read the Turkish characters, but she scanned it half a dozen times before the meaning became apparent to her exhaustion-numbed brain. Then her eyes flickered dangerously to the men on the floor. Tshoruk sat up, dazedly feeling the gash in his scalp; Rhupen lay retching and gurgling on the floor.

"Tie them up, brother," she ordered, and Gottfried obeyed. The victims eyed the woman much more apprehensively than him.

"This missive is addressed to Ibrahim, the Wezir," she said abruptly. "Why does he want Gottfried's head?"

"Because of a wound he gave the Sultan at Mohacz," muttered Tshoruk uneasily.

"And you, you lower-than-a-dog," she smiled mirthlessly, "you fired the mine by the Karnthner! You and your spawn are the traitors among us." She drew and primed a pistol. "When Zrinyi learns of you," she said, "your end will be neither quick nor sweet. But first, you old swine, I'm going to give myself the pleasure of blowing out your cub's brains before your eyes—"

The older Armenian gave a choking cry. "God of my fathers, have mercy! Kill me—torture me—but spare my son!"

At that instant a new sound split the unnatural quiet—a great peal of bells shattered the air.

"What's this?" roared Gottfried, groping wildly at his empty scabbard.

"The bells of Saint Stephen!" cried Sonya. "They peal for victory!"

She sprang for the sagging stair and he followed her up the perilous way. They came out on a sagging shattered roof, on a firmer part of which stood an ancient stone-casting machine, relic of an earlier age, and evidently recently repaired. The tower overlooked an angle of the wall, at which there were no watchers. A section of the ancient glacis, and a ditch interior the main moat, coupled with a steep natural pitch of the earth beyond, made the point practically invulnerable. The spies had been able to exchange messages here with little fear of discovery, and it was easy to guess the method used. Down the slope, just within long arrow-shot, stood up a huge mantlet of bullhide stretched on a wooden frame, as if abandoned there by chance. Gottfried knew that message-laden arrows were loosed from the tower roof into this mantlet. But just then he gave little thought to that. His attention was riveted on the Turkish camp. There a leaping glare paled the spreading dawn; above the mad clangor of the bells rose the crackle of flames, mingled with awful screams.

"The Janizaries are burning their prisoners," said Red Sonya.

"Judgment Day in the morning," muttered Gottfried, awed at the sight that met his eyes.

From their eyrie the companions could see almost all of the plain. Under a cold gray leaden sky, tinged a somber crimson with dawn, it lay strewn with Turkish corpses as far as the sight would carry. And the hosts of the living were melting away. From Semmering the great pavilion had vanished. The other tents were now coming down fast. Already the head of the long column was out of sight, moving into the hills through the cold dawn. Snow began falling in light swift flakes.

The Janizaries were glutting their mad disappointment on their helpless captives, hurling men, women and children living into the flames they had kindled under the somber eyes of their master, the monarch men called the Magnificent, the Merciful. All the time the bells of Vienna clanged and thundered as if their bronze throats would burst.

"They shot their bolt last night," said Red Sonya. "I saw their officers lashing them, and heard them cry out in fear beneath our swords. Flesh and blood could stand no more. Look!" She clutched her companion's arm. "The Akinji will form the rear-guard."

Even at that distance they made out a pair of vulture wings moving among the dark masses; the sullen light glimmered on a jeweled helmet. Sonya's powder-stained hands clenched so that the pink, broken nails bit into the white palms, and she spat out a Cossack curse that burned like vitriol.

"There he goes, the bastard that made Austria a desert! How easily the souls of the butchered folk ride on his cursed winged shoulders! Anyway, old warhorse, he didn't get your head."

"While he lives it'll ride loose on my shoulders," rumbled the giant.

Red Sonya's keen eyes narrowed suddenly. Seizing Gottfried's arm, she hurried downstairs. They did not see Nikolas Zrinyi and Paul Bakics ride out of the gates with their tattered retainers, risking their lives in sorties to rescue prisoners. Steel clashed along the line of march, and the Akinji retreated slowly, fighting a good rear-guard action, balking the headlong courage of the attackers by their very numbers. Safe in the depths of his horsemen, Mikhal Oglu grinned sardonically. But Suleyman, riding in the main column, did not grin. His face was like a death-mask.

Back in the ruined tower, Red Sonya propped one booted foot on a chair, and cupping her chin in her hand, stared into the fear-dulled eyes of Tshoruk.

"What will you give for your life?"

The Armenian made no reply.

"What will you give for the life of your whelp?"

The Armenian started as if stung. "Spare my son, princess," he groaned. "Anything—I will pay—I will do anything."

She threw a shapely booted leg across the chair and sat down.

"I want you to bear a message to a man."

"What man?"

"Mikhal Oglu."

He shuddered and moistened his lips with his tongue.

"Instruct me; I obey," he whispered.

"Good. We'll free you and give you a horse. Your son shall remain here as hostage. If you fail us, I'll give the cub to the Viennese to play with—"

Again the old Armenian shuddered.

"But if you play squarely, we'll let you both go free, and my pal and I will forget about this treachery. I want you to ride after Mikhal Oglu and tell him—"

* * *

Through the slush and driving snow, the Turkish column plodded slowly. Horses bent their heads to the blast; up and down the straggling lines camels groaned and complained, and oxen bellowed pitifully. Men stumbled through the mud, leaning beneath the weight of their arms and equipment. Night was falling, but no command had been given to halt. All day the retreating host had been harried by the daring Austrian cuirassiers who darted down upon them like wasps, tearing captives from their very hands.

Grimly rode Suleyman among his Solaks. He wished to put as much distance as possible between himself and the scene of his first defeat, where the rotting bodies of thirty thousand Muhammadans reminded him of his crushed ambitions. Lord of western Asia he was; master of Europe he could never be. Those despised walls had saved the Western world from Moslem dominion, and Suleyman knew it. The rolling thunder of the Ottoman power re-echoed around the world, paling the glories of Persia and Mogul India. But in the West the yellow-haired Aryan barbarian stood unshaken. It was not written that the Turk should rule beyond the Danube.

Suleyman had seen this written in blood and fire, as he stood on Semmering and saw his warriors fall back from the ramparts, despite the flailing lashes of their officers. It had been to save his authority that he gave the order to break camp—it burned his tongue like gall, but already his soldiers were burning their tents and preparing to desert him. Now in darkly brooding silence he rode, not even speaking to Ibrahim.

In his own way Mikhal Oglu shared their savage despondency. It was with a ferocious reluctance that he turned his back on the land he had ruined, as a half-glutted panther might be driven from its prey. He recalled with satisfaction the blackened, corpse-littered wastes—the screams of tortured men—the cries of girls writhing in his iron arms; recalled with much the same sensations the death-shrieks of those same girls in the blood-fouled hands of his killers.

But he was stung with the disappointment of a task undone—for which the Grand Vizier had lashed him with stinging word. He was out of favor with Ibrahim. For a lesser man that might have meant a bowstring. For him it meant that he would have to perform some prodigious feat to reinstate himself. In this mood he was dangerous and reckless as a wounded panther.

Snow fell heavily, adding to the miseries of the retreat. Wounded men fell in the mire and lay still, covered by a growing white mantle. Mikhal Oglu rode among his rearmost ranks, straining his eyes into the darkness. No foe had been sighted for hours. The victorious Austrians had ridden back to their city.

The columns were moving slowly through a ruined village, whose charred beams and crumbling fire-seared walls stood blackly in the falling snow. Word came back down the lines that the Sultan would pass on through and camp in a valley which lay a few miles beyond.

The quick drum of hoofs back along the way they had come caused the Akinji to grip their lances and glare slit-eyed into the flickering darkness. They heard but a single horse, and a voice calling the name of Mikhal Oglu. With a word the chief stayed a dozen lifted bows, and shouted in return. A tall, gray stallion loomed out of the flying snow, a black-mantled figure crouched grotesquely atop of it.

"Tshoruk! You Armenian dog! What in the name of Allah—"

The Armenian rode close to Mikhal Oglu and whispered urgently in his ear. The cold bit through the thickest garments. The Akinji noted that Tshoruk was trembling violently. His teeth chattered and he stammered in his speech. But the Turk's eyes blazed at the import of his message.

"Dog, do you lie?"

"May I rot in hell if I lie!" A strong shudder shook Tshoruk and he drew his kaftan close about him. "He fell from his horse, riding with the cuirassiers to attack the rear-guard, and lies with a broken leg in a deserted peasant's hut some three miles back—alone except for his mistress Red Sonya, and three or four Lanzknechts, who are drunk on wine they found in the deserted camp."

Mikhal Oglu wheeled his horse with sudden intent.

"Twenty men to me!" he barked. "The rest ride on with the main column. I go after a head worth its weight in gold. I'll overtake you before you go in camp."

Othman caught his jeweled rein." Are you mad, to ride back now? The whole country will be on our heels—"

He reeled in his saddle as Mikhal Oglu slashed him across the mouth with his riding whip. The chief wheeled away, followed by the men he had designated. Like ghosts they vanished into the spectral darkness.

Othman sat his horse uncertainly, looking after them. The snow shafted down, the wind sobbed drearily among the bare branches. There was no sound except the receding noises of the trudging column. Presently these ceased. Then Othman started. Back along the way they had come, he heard a distant reverberation, a roar as of forty or fifty matchlocks speaking together. In the utter silence which followed, panic came upon Othman and his warriors. Whirling away they fled through the ruined village after the retreating horde.

7

None noticed when night fell on Constantinople, for the splendor of Suleyman made night no less glorious than day. Through gardens that were riots of blossoms and perfume, cressets twinkled like myriad fireflies. Fireworks turned the city into a realm of shimmering magic, above which the minarets of five hundred mosques rose like towers of fire in an ocean of golden foam. Tribesmen on Asian hills gaped and marveled at the blaze that pulsed and glowed afar, paling the very stars. The streets of Stamboul were thronged with crowds in the attire of holiday and rejoicing. The million lights shone on jeweled turban and striped khalat—on dark eyes sparkling over filmy veils—on shining palanquins borne on the shoulders of huge ebony-skinned slaves.

All that splendor centered in the Hippodrome, where in lavish pageants the horsemen of Turkistan and Tatary competed in breathtaking races with the riders of Egypt and Arabia, where warriors in glittering mail spilled one another's blood on the sands, where swordsmen were matched against wild beasts, and lions were pitted against tigers of Bengal and boars from northern forests. One might have deemed the imperial pageantry of Rome revived in Eastern garb.

On a golden throne, set upon lapis lazuli pillars, Suleyman reclined, gazing on the splendors, as purple-togaed Caesars had gazed before him. About him bowed his viziers and officers, and the ambassadors from foreign courts—Venice, Persia, India, the khanates of Tatary. They came—including the Venetians—to congratulate him on his victory over the Austrians. For this grand fête was in celebration of that victory, as set forth in a manifesto under the Sultan's hand, which stated, in part, that the Austrians having made submission and sued for pardon on their knees, and the German realms being so distant from the Ottoman empire, "the Faithful would not trouble to clean out the fortress (Vienna), or purify, improve, and put it in repair." Therefore the Sultan had accepted the submission of the contemptible Germans, and left them in possession of their paltry "fortress"!

Suleyman was blinding the eyes of the world with the blaze of his wealth and glory, and striving to make himself believe that he had actually accomplished all he had intended. He had not been beaten on the field of open battle; he had set his puppet on the Hungarian throne; he had devastated Austria; the markets of Stamboul and Asia were full of Christian slaves. With this knowledge he soothed his vanity, ignoring the fact that thirty thousand of his subjects rotted before Vienna, and that his dreams of European conquest had been shattered.

Behind the throne shone the spoils of war—silken and velvet pavilions, wrested from the Persians, the Arabs, the Egyptian memluks; costly tapestries, heavy with gold embroidery. At his feet were heaped the gifts and tributes of subject and allied princes. There were vests of Venetian velvet, golden goblets crusted with jewels from the courts of the Grand Moghul, ermine-lined kaftans from Erzeroum, carven jade from Cathay, silver Persian helmets with horse-hair plumes, turban-cloths, cunningly sewn with gems, from Egypt, curved Damascus blades of watered steel, matchlocks from Kabul worked richly in chased silver, breastplates and shields of Indian steel, rare furs from Mongolia. The throne was flanked on either hand by a long rank of youthful slaves, made fast by golden collars to a single, long silver chain. One file was composed of young Greek and Hungarian boys, the other of girls; all clad only in plumed headpieces and jeweled ornaments intended to emphasize their nudity.

Eunuchs in flowing robes, their rotund bellies banded by cloth-of-gold sashes, knelt and offered the royal guests sherbets in gemmed goblets, cooled with snow from the mountains of Asia Minor. The torches danced and flickered to the roars of the multitudes. Around the courses swept the horses, foam flying from their bits; wooden castles reeled and went up in flames as the Janizaries clashed in mock warfare. Officers passed among the shouting people, tossing showers of copper and silver coins amongst them. None hungered or thirsted in Stamboul that night except the miserable Caphar captives. The minds of the foreign envoys were numbed by the bursting sea of splendor, the thunder of imperial magnificence. About the vast arena stalked trained elephants, almost covered with housings of gold-worked leather, and from the jeweled towers on their backs, fanfares of trumpets vied with the roar of the throngs and the bellowing of lions. The tiers of the Hippodrome were a sea of faces, all turning toward the jeweled figure on the shining throne, while thousands of tongues wildly thundered his acclaim.

As he impressed the Venetian envoys, Suleyman knew he impressed the world. In the blaze of his magnificence, men would forget that a handful of desperate Caphars behind rotting walls had closed his road to empire. Suleyman accepted a goblet of the forbidden wine, and spoke aside to the Grand Vizier, who stepped forth and lifted his arms.

"Oh, guests of my master, the Padishah forgets not the humblest in the hour of rejoicing. To the officers who led his hosts against the infidels, he has made rare gifts. Now he gives two hundred and forty thousand ducats to be distributed among the common soldiers, and likewise to each Janizary he gives a thousand aspers."

In the midst of the roar that went up, a eunuch knelt before the Grand Vizier, holding up a large round package, carefully bound and sealed. A folded piece of parchment, held shut by a red seal, accompanied it. The attention of the Sultan was attracted.

"Oh, friend, what has thou there?"

Ibrahim salaamed. "The rider of the Adrianople post delivered it, oh Lion of Islam. Apparently it is a gift of some sort from the Austrian dogs. Infidel riders, I understand, gave it into the hands of the border guard, with instructions to send it straightway to Stamboul."

"Open it," directed Suleyman, his interest roused. The eunuch salaamed to the floor, then began breaking the seals of the package. A scholarly slave opened the accompanying note and read the contents, written in a bold yet feminine hand:

To the Soldan Suleyman and his Wezir Ibrahim and to the hussy Roxelana we who sign our names below send a gift in token of our immeasurable fondness and kind affection.

Sonya of Rogatino, and Gottfried von Kalmbach

Suleyman, who had started up at the name of his favorite, his features suddenly darkening with wrath, gave a choking cry, which was echoed by Ibrahim. The eunuch had torn the seals of the bale, disclosing what lay within. A pungent scent of herbs and preservative spices filled the air, and the object, slipping from the horrified eunuch's hands, tumbled among the heaps of presents at Suleyman's feet, offering a ghastly contrast to the gems, gold and velvet bales. The Sultan stared down at it and in that instant his shimmering pretense of triumph slipped from him; his glory turned to tinsel and dust. Ibrahim tore at his beard with a gurgling, strangling sound, purple with rage.

At the Sultan's feet, the features frozen in a death-mask of horror, lay the severed head of Mikhal Oglu, Vulture of the Grand Turk.

GATES OF EMPIRE

The clank of the sour sentinels on the turrets, the gusty uproar of the Spring winds, were not heard by those who reveled in the cellar of Godfrey de Courtenay's castle; and the noise these revelers made was bottled up deafeningly within the massive walls.

A sputtering candle lighted those rugged walls, damp and uninviting, flanked with wattled casks and hogsheads over which stretched a veil of dusty cobwebs. From one barrel the head had been knocked out, and leathern drinking-jacks were immersed again and again in the foamy tide, in hands that grew increasingly unsteady.

Agnes, one of the serving wenches, had stolen the massive iron key to the cellar from the girdle of the steward; and rendered daring by the absence of their master, a small but far from select group were making merry with characteristic heedlessness of the morrow.

Agnes, seated on the knee of the varlet Peter, beat erratic time with a jack to a ribald song both were bawling in different tunes and keys. The ale slopped over the rim of the wobbling jack and down Peter's collar, a circumstance he was beyond noticing.

The other wench, fat Marge, rolled on her bench and slapped her ample thighs in uproarious appreciation of a spicy tale just told by Giles Hobson. This individual might have been the lord of the castle from his manner, instead of a vagabond rapscallion tossed by every wind of adversity. Tilted back on a barrel, booted feet propped on another, he loosened the belt that girdled his capacious belly in its worn leather jerkin, and plunged his muzzle once more into the frothing ale.

"Giles, by Saint Withold his beard," quoth Marge, "madder rogue never wore steel. The very ravens that pick your bones on the gibbet tree will burst their sides a-laughing. I hail ye—prince of all bawdy liars!"

She flourished a huge pewter pot and drained it as stoutly as any man in the realm.

At this moment another reveler, returning from an errand, came into the scene. The door at the head of the stairs admitted a wobbly figure in close-fitting velvet. Through the briefly opened door sounded noises of the night—slap of hangings somewhere in the house, sucking and flapping in the wind that whipped through the crevices; a faint disgruntled hail from a watchman on a tower. A gust of wind whooped down the stair and set the candle to dancing.

Guillaume, the page, shoved the door shut and made his way with groggy care down the rude stone steps. He was not so drunk as the others, simply because, what of his extreme youth, he lacked their capacity for fermented liquor.

"What's the time, boy?" demanded Peter.

"Long past midnight," the page answered, groping unsteadily for the open cask. "The whole castle is asleep, save for the watchmen. But I heard a clatter of hoofs through the wind and rain; methinks 'tis Sir Godfrey returning."

"Let him return and be damned!" shouted Giles, slapping Marge's fat haunch resoundingly. "He may be lord of the keep, but at present we are keepers of the cellar! More ale! Agnes, you little slut, another song!"

"Nay, more tales!" clamored Marge. "Our mistress's brother, Sir Guiscard de Chastillon, has told grand tales of Holy Land and the infidels, but by Saint Dunstan, Giles' lies outshine the knight's truths!"

"Slander not a—hic!—holy man as has been on pilgrimage and Crusade," hiccuped Peter. "Sir Guiscard has seen Jerusalem and foughten beside the King of Palestine—how many years?"

"Ten year come May Day, since he sailed to Holy Land," said Agnes. "Lady Eleanor had not seen him in all that time, till he rode up to the gate yesterday morn. Her husband, Sir Godfrey, never has seen him."

"And wouldn't know him?" mused Giles; "nor Sir Guiscard him?"

He blinked, raking a broad hand through his sandy mop. He was drunker than even he realized. The world spun like a top and his head seemed to be dancing dizzily on his shoulders. Out of the fumes of ale and a vagrant spirit, a madcap idea was born.

A roar of laughter burst gustily from Giles' lips. He reeled upright, spilling his jack in Marge's lap and bringing a burst of rare profanity from her. He smote a barrelhead with his open hand, strangling with mirth.

"Good lack!" squawked Agnes. "Are you daft, man?"

"A jest!" The roof reverberated to his bull's bellow. "Oh, Saint Withold, a jest! Sir Guiscard knows not his brother-in-law, and Sir Godfrey is now at the gate. Hark ye!"

Four heads, bobbing erratically, inclined toward him as he whispered as if the rude walls might hear. An instant's bleary silence was followed by boisterous guffaws. They were in the mood to follow the maddest course suggested to them. Only Guillaume felt some misgivings, but he was swept away by the alcoholic fervor of his companions.

"Oh, a devil's own jest!" cried Marge, planting a loud, moist kiss on Giles' ruddy cheek. "On, rogues, to the sport!"

"En avant!" bellowed Giles, drawing his sword and waving it unsteadily, and the five weaved up the stairs, stumbling, blundering, and lurching against one another. They kicked open the door, and shortly were running erratically up the wide hall, giving tongue like a pack of hounds.

The castles of the Twelfth Century, fortresses rather than mere dwellings, were built for defense, not comfort.

The hall through which the drunken band was hallooing was broad, lofty, windy, strewn with rushes, now but faintly lighted by the dying embers in a great ill-ventilated fireplace. Rude, sail-like hangings along the walls rippled in the wind that found its way through. Hounds, sleeping under the great table, woke yelping as they were trodden on by blundering feet, and added their clamor to the din.

This din roused Sir Guiscard de Chastillon from dreams of Acre and the sun-drenched plains of Palestine. He bounded up, sword in hand, supposing himself to be beset by Saracen raiders, then realized where he was. But events seemed to be afoot. A medley of shouts and shrieks clamored outside his door, and on the stout oak panels boomed a rain of blows that bade fair to burst the portal inward. The knight heard his name called loudly and urgently.

Putting aside his trembling squire, he ran to the door and cast it open. Sir Guiscard was a tall gaunt man, with a great beak of a nose and cold grey eyes. Even in his shirt he was a formidable figure. He blinked ferociously at the group limned dimly in the glow from the coals at the other end of the hall. There seemed to be women, children, a fat man with a sword.

This fat man was bawling: "Succor, Sir Guiscard, succor! The castle is forced, and we are all dead men! The robbers of Horsham Wood are within the hall itself!"

Sir Guiscard heard the unmistakable tramp of mailed feet, saw vague figures coming into the hall—figures on whose steel the faint light gleamed redly. Still mazed by slumber, but ferocious, he went into furious action.

Sir Godfrey de Courtenay, returning to his keep after many hours of riding through foul weather, anticipated only rest and ease in his own castle. Having vented his irritation by roundly cursing the sleepy grooms who shambled up to attend his horses, and were too bemused to tell him of his guest, he dismissed his men-at-arms and strode into the donjon, followed by his squires and the gentlemen of his retinue. Scarcely had he entered when the devil's own bedlam burst loose in the hall. He heard a wild stampede of feet, crash of overturned benches, baying of dogs, and an uproar of strident voices, over which one bull-like bellow triumphed.

Swearing amazedly, he ran up the hall, followed by his knights, when a ravening maniac, naked but for a shirt, burst on him, sword in hand, howling like a werewolf.

Sparks flew from Sir Godfrey's basinet beneath the madman's furious strokes, and the lord of the castle almost succumbed to the ferocity of that onslaught before he could draw his own sword. He fell back, bellowing for his men-at-arms. But the madman was yelling louder than he, and from all sides swarmed other lunatics in shirts who assailed Sir Godfrey's dumfounded gentlemen with howling frenzy.

The castle was in an uproar—lights flashing up, dogs howling, women screaming, men cursing, and over all the clash of steel and the stamp of mailed feet.

The conspirators, sobered by what they had raised, scattered in all directions, seeking hiding-places—all except Giles Hobson. His state of intoxication was too magnificent to be perturbed by any such trivial scene. He admired his handiwork for a space; then, finding swords flashing too close to his head for comfort, withdrew, and following some instinct, departed for a hiding-place known to him of old. There he found with gentle satisfaction that he had all the time retained a cobwebbed bottle in his hand. This he emptied, and its contents, coupled with what had already found its way down his gullet, plunged him into extinction for an amazing period. Tranquilly he snored under the straw, while events took place above and around him, and matters moved not slowly.

There in the straw Friar Ambrose found him just as dusk was falling after a harassed and harrying day. The friar, ruddy and well paunched, shook the unpenitent one into bleary wakefulness.

"The saints defend us!" said Ambrose. "Up to your old tricks again! I thought to find you here. They have been searching the castle all day for you; they searched these stables, too. Well that you were hidden beneath a very mountain of hay."

"They do me too much honor," yawned Giles. "Why should they search for me?"

The friar lifted his hands in pious horror.

"Saint Denis is my refuge against Sathanas and his works! Is it not known how you were the ringleader in that madcap prank last night that pitted poor Sir Guiscard against his sister's husband?"

"Saint Dunstan!" quoth Giles, expectorating dryly. "How I thirst! Were any slain?"

"No, by the providence of God. But there is many a broken crown and bruised rib this day. Sir Godfrey nigh fell at the first onset, for Sir Guiscard is a woundy swordsman. But our lord being in full armor, he presently dealt Sir Guiscard a shrewd cut over the pate, whereby blood did flow in streams, and Sir Guiscard blasphemed in a manner shocking to hear. What had then chanced, God only knows, but Lady Eleanor, awakened by the noise, ran forth in her shift, and seeing her husband and her brother at swords' points, she ran between them and bespoke them in words not to be repeated. Verily, a flailing tongue hath our mistress when her wrath is stirred.

"So understanding was reached, and a leech was fetched for Sir Guiscard and such of the henchmen as had suffered scathe. Then followed much discussion, and Sir Guiscard had recognized you as one of those who banged on his door. Then Guillaume was discovered hiding, as from a guilty conscience, and he confessed all, putting the blame on you. Ah me, such a day as it has been!

"Poor Peter in the stocks since dawn, and all the villeins and serving-wenches and villagers gathered to clod him—they but just now left off, and a sorry sight he is, with nose a-bleeding, face skinned, an eye closed, and broken eggs in his hair and dripping over his features. Poor Peter!

"And as for Agnes, Marge and Guillaume, they have had whipping enough to content them all a lifetime. It would be hard to say which of them has the sorest posterior. But it is you, Giles, the masters wish. Sir Guiscard swears that only your life will anyways content him."

"Hmmmm," ruminated Giles. He rose unsteadily, brushed the straw from his garments, hitched up his belt and stuck his disreputable bonnet on his head at a cocky angle.

The friar watched him gloomily. "Peter stocked, Guillaume birched, Marge and Agnes whipped—what should be your punishment?"

"Methinks I'll do penance by a long pilgrimage," said Giles.

"You'll never get through the gates," predicted Ambrose.

"True," sighed Giles. "A friar may pass at will, where an honest man is halted by suspicion and prejudice. As further penance, lend me your robe."

"My robe?" exclaimed the friar. "You are a fool—"

A heavy fist *clunked* against his fat jaw, and he collapsed with a whistling sigh.

A few minutes later a lout in the outer ward, taking aim with a rotten egg at the dilapidated figure in the stocks, checked his arm as a robed and hooded shape emerged from the stables and crossed the open space with slow steps. The shoulders drooped as from a weight of weariness, the head was bent forward; so much so, in fact, that the features were hidden by the hood.

"The lout doffed his shabby cap and made a clumsy leg.

"God go wi' 'ee, good faither," he said.

"Pax vobiscum, my son," came the answer, low and muffled from the depths of the hood.

The lout shook his head sympathetically as the robed figure moved on, unhindered, in the direction of the postern gate.

"Poor Friar Ambrose," quoth the lout. "He takes the sin o' the world so much to heart; there 'ee go, fair bowed down by the wickedness o' men."

He sighed, and again took aim at the glum countenance that glowered above the stocks.

Through the blue glitter of the Mediterranean wallowed a merchant galley, clumsy, broad in the beam. Her square sail hung limp on her one thick mast. The oarsmen, sitting on the benches which flanked the waist deck on either side, tugged at the long oars, bending forward and heaving back in machine-like unison. Sweat stood out on their sun-burnt skin, their muscles rolled evenly. From the interior of the hull came a chatter of voices, the complaint of animals, a reek as of barnyards and stables. This scent was observable some distance to leeward. To the south the blue waters spread out like molten sapphire. To the north, the gleaming sweep was broken by an island that reared up white cliffs crowned with dark green. Dignity, cleanliness and serenity reigned over all, except where that smelly, ungainly tub lurched through the foaming water, by sound and scent advertising the presence of man.

Below the waist-deck passengers, squatted among bundles, were cooking food over small braziers. Smoke mingled with a reek of sweat and garlic. Horses, penned in a narrow space, whinnied wretchedly. Sheep, pigs and chickens added their aroma to the smells.

Presently, amidst the babble below decks, a new sound floated up to the people above—members of the crew, and the wealtheir passengers who shared the *patrono's* cabin. The voice of the *patrono* came to them, strident with annoyance, answered by a loud rough voice with an alien accent.

The Venetian captain, prodding among the butts and bales of the cargo, had discovered a stowaway—a fat, sandy-haired man in worn leather, snoring bibulously among the barrels.

Ensued an impassioned oratory in lurid Italian, the burden of which at last focused in a demand that the stranger pay for his passage.

"Pay?" echoed that individual, running thick fingers through unkempt locks. "What should I pay with, Thin-shanks? Where am I? What ship is this? Where are we going?"

"This is the *San Stefano,* bound for Cyprus from Palermo."

"Oh, yes," muttered the stowaway. "I remember. I came aboard at Palermo—lay down beside a wine cask between the bales—"

The *patrono* hastily inspected the cask and shrieked with new passion.

"Dog! You've drunk it all!"

"How long have we been at sea?" demanded the intruder.

"Long enough to be out of sight of land," snarled the other. "Pig, how can a man lie drunk so long—"

"No wonder my belly's empty," muttered the other. "I've lain among the bales, and when I woke, I'd drink till I fell asleep again. Hmmm!"

"Money!" clamored the Italian. "Bezants for your fare!"

"Bezants!" snorted the other. "I haven't a penny to my name."

"Then overboard you go," grimly promised the *patrono.* "There's no room for beggars aboard the *San Stefano.*"

That struck a spark. The stranger gave vent to a warlike snort and tugged at his sword.

"Throw me overboard into all that water? Not while Giles Hobson can wield blade. A freeborn Englishman is as good as any velvet-breeched Italian. Call your bullies and watch me bleed them!"

From the deck came a loud call, strident with sudden fright. "Galleys off the starboard bow! Saracens!"

A howl burst from the *patrono's* lips and his face went ashy. Abandoning the dispute at hand, he wheeled and rushed up on deck. Giles Hobson followed and gaped about him at the anxious brown faces of the rowers, the frightened countenances of the passengers—Latin priests, merchants and pilgrims. Following their gaze, he saw three long low galleys shooting across the blue expanse toward them. They were still some distance away, but the people on the *San Stefano* could hear the faint clash of cymbals, see the banners stream out from the mast heads. The oars dipped into the blue water, came up shining silver.

"Put her about and steer for the island!" yelled the *patrono.* "If we can reach it, we may hide and save our lives. The galley is lost—and all the cargo! Saints defend me!" He wept and wrung his hands, less from fear than from disappointed avarice.

The *San Stefano* wallowed cumbrously about and waddled hurriedly toward the white cliffs jutting in the sunlight. The slim galleys came up, shooting through the waves like water snakes. The space of dancing blue between the *San Stefano* and the cliffs narrowed, but more swiftly narrowed the space between the merchant and the raiders. Arrows began to arch through the air and patter on the deck. One struck and quivered near Giles Hobson's boot, and he gave back as if from a serpent. The fat Englishman mopped perspiration from his brow. His mouth was dry, his head throbbed, his belly heaved. Suddenly he was violently seasick.

The oarsmen bent their backs, gasped, heaved mightily, seeming almost to jerk the awkward craft out of the water. Arrows, no longer arching, raked the deck. A man howled; another sank down without a word. An oarsman flinched from a shaft through his shoulder, and faltered in his stroke. Panic-stricken, the rowers began to lose rhythm. The *San Stefano* lost headway and rolled more wildly, and the passengers sent up a wail. From the raiders came yells of exultation. They separated in a fan-shaped formation meant to envelop the doomed galley.

On the merchant's deck the priests were shriving and absolving.

"Holy Saints grant me—" gasped a gaunt Pisan, kneeling on the boards—convulsively he clasped the feathered shaft that suddenly vibrated in his breast, then slumped sidewise and lay still.

An arrow thumped into the rail over which Giles Hobson hung, quivered near his elbow. He paid no heed. A hand was laid on his shoulder.

Gagging, he turned his head, lifted a green face to look into the troubled eyes of a priest.

"My son, this may be the hour of death; confess your sins and I will shrive you."

"The only one I can think of," gasped Giles miserably, "is that I mauled a priest and stole his robe to flee England in."

"Alas, my son," the priest began, then cringed back with a low moan. He seemed to bow to Giles; his head inclining still further, he sank to the deck. From a dark welling spot on his side jutted a Saracen arrow.

Giles gaped about him; on either hand a long slim galley was sweeping in to lay the *San Stefano* aboard. Even as he looked, the third galley, the one in the middle of the triangular formation, rammed the merchant ship with a deafening splintering of timber. The steel beak cut through the bulwarks, rending apart the stern cabin. The concussion rolled men off their feet. Others, caught and crushed in the collision, died howling awfully. The other raiders ground alongside, and their steel-shod prows sheared through the banks of oars, twisting the shafts out of the oarsmen's hands, crushing the ribs of the wielders.

The grappling hooks bit into the bulwarks, and over the rail came dark naked men with scimitars in their hands, their eyes blazing. They were met by a dazed remnant who fought back desperately.

Giles Hobson fumbled out his sword, strode groggily forward. A dark shape flashed at him out of the mêlée. He got a dazed impression of glittering eyes, and a curved blade hissing down. He caught the stroke on his sword, staggering from the spark-showering impact. Braced on wide straddling legs, he drove his sword into the pirate's belly. Blood and entrails gushed forth, and the dying corsair dragged his slayer to the deck with him in his throes.

Feet booted and bare stamped on Giles Hobson as he strove to rise. A curved dagger hooked at his kidneys, caught in his leather jerkin and ripped the garment from hem to collar. He rose, shaking the tatters from him. A dusky hand locked in his ragged shirt, a mace hovered over his head. With a frantic jerk, Giles pitched backward, to a sound of rending cloth, leaving the torn shirt in his captor's hand. The mace met empty air as it descended, and the wielder went to his knees from the wasted blow. Giles fled along the blood-washed deck, twisting and ducking to avoid struggling knots of fighters.

A handful of defenders huddled in the door of the forecastle. The rest of the galley was in the hands of the triumphant Saracens. They swarmed over the deck, down into the waist. The animals squealed piteously as their throats were cut. Other screams marked the end of the women and children dragged from their hiding-places among the cargo.

In the door of the forecastle the bloodstained survivors parried and thrust with notched swords. The pirates hemmed them in, yelping mockingly, thrusting forward their pikes, drawing back, springing in to hack and slash.

Giles sprang for the rail, intending to dive and swim for the island. A quick step behind him warned him in time to wheel and duck a scimitar. It was wielded by a stout man of medium height, resplendent in silvered chain-mail and chased helmet, crested with egret plumes.

Sweat misted the fat Englishman's sight; his wind was short; his belly heaved, his legs trembled. The Moslem cut at his head. Giles parried, struck back. His blade clanged against the chief's mail. Something like a white-hot brand seared his temple, and he was blinded by a rush of blood. Dropping his sword, he pitched head-first against the Saracen, bearing him to the deck. The Moslem writhed and cursed, but Giles' thick arms clamped desperately about him.

Suddenly a wild shout went up. There was a rush of feet across the deck. Men began to leap over the rail, to cast loose the boarding-irons. Giles' captive yelled stridently, and men raced across the deck toward him. Giles released him, ran like a bulky cat along the bulwarks, and scrambled up over the roof of the shattered poop cabin. None heeded him. Men naked but for *tarboushes* hauled the mailed chieftain to his feet and rushed him across the deck while he raged and blasphemed, evidently wishing to continue the contest. The Saracens were leaping into their own galleys and pushing away. And Giles, crouching on the splintered cabin roof, saw the reason.

Around the western promontory of the island they had been trying to reach, came a squadron of great red *dromonds,* with battle-castles rearing at prow and stern. Helmets and spearheads glittered in the sun. Trumpets blared, drums boomed. From each masthead streamed a long banner bearing the emblem of the Cross.

From the survivors aboard the *San Stefano* rose a shout of joy. The galleys were racing southward. The nearest *dromond* swung ponderously alongside, and brown faces framed in steel looked over the rail.

"Ahoy, there!" rang a stern-voiced command. "You are sinking; stand by to come aboard."

Giles Hobson started violently at that voice. He gaped up at the battle-castle towering above the *San Stefano.* A helmeted head bent over the bulwark, a pair of cold grey eyes met his. He saw a great beak of a nose, a scar seaming the face from the ear down the rim of the jaw.

Recognition was mutual. A year had not dulled Sir Guiscard de Chastillon's resentment.

"So!" The yell rang bloodthirstily in Giles Hobson's ears. "At last I have found you, rogue—"

Giles wheeled, kicked off his boots, ran to the edge of the roof. He left it in a long dive, shot into the blue water with a tremendous splash. His head bobbed to the surface, and he struck out for the distant cliffs in long pawing strokes.

A mutter of surprize rose from the *dromond,* but Sir Guiscard smiled sourly.

"A bow, varlet," he commanded.

It was placed in his hands. He nocked the arrow, waited until Giles' dripping head appeared again in a shallow trough between the waves. The bowstring twanged, the arrow flashed through the sunlight like a silver beam. Giles Hobson threw up his arms and disappeared. Nor did Sir Guiscard see him rise again, though the knight watched the waters for some time.

To Shawar, vizier of Egypt, in his palace in el-Fustat, came a gorgeously robed eunuch who, with many abased supplications, as the due of the most powerful man in the caliphate, announced: "The Emir Asad ed din Shirkuh, lord of Emesa and Rahba, general of the armies of Nour ed din, Sultan of Damascus, has returned from the ships of el Ghazi with a Nazarene captive, and desires audience."

A nod of acquiescence was the vizier's only sign, but his slim white fingers twitched at his jewel-encrusted white girdle—sure evidence of mental unrest.

Shawar was an Arab, a slim, handsome figure, with the keen dark eyes of his race. He wore the silken robes and pearl-sewn turban of his office as if he had been born to them—instead of to the black felt tents from which his sagacity had lifted him.

The Emir Shirkuh entered like a storm, booming forth his salutations in a voice more fitted for the camp than for the council chamber. He was a powerfully built man of medium height, with a face like a hawk's. His *khalat* was of watered silk, worked with gold thread, but like his voice, his hard body seemed more fitted for the harness of war than the garments of peace. Middle age had dulled none of the restless fire in his dark eyes.

With him was a man whose sandy hair and wide blue eyes contrasted incongruously with the voluminous bag trousers, silken *khalat* and turned-up slippers which adorned him.

"I trust that Allah granted you fortune upon the sea, *ya khawand*?" courteously inquired the vizier.

"Of a sort," admitted Shirkuh, casting himself down on the cushions. "We fared far, Allah knows, and at first my guts were like to gush out of my mouth with the galloping of the ship, which went up and down like a foundered camel. But later Allah willed that the sickness should pass."

"We sank a few wretched pilgrims' galleys and sent to Hell the infidels therein—which was good, but the loot was wretched stuff. But look ye, lord vizier, did you ever see a Caphar like to this man?"

The man returned the vizier's searching stare with wide guileless eyes.

"Such as he I have seen among the Franks of Jerusalem," Shawar decided.

Shirkuh grunted and began to munch grapes with scant ceremony, tossing a bunch to his captive.

"Near a certain island we sighted a galley," he said, between mouthfuls, "and we ran upon it and put the folk to the sword. Most of them were miserable fighters, but this man cut his way clear and would have sprung overboard had I not intercepted him. By Allah, he proved himself strong as a bull! My ribs are yet bruised from his hug.

"But in the midst of the mêlée up galloped a herd of ships full of Christian warriors, bound—as we later learned—for Ascalon; Frankish adventurers seeking their fortune in Palestine. We put the spurs to our galleys, and as I looked back I saw the man I had been fighting leap overboard and swim toward the cliffs. A knight on a Nazarene ship shot an arrow at him and he sank, to his death, I supposed.

"Our water butts were nearly empty. We did not run far. As soon as the Frankish ships were out of sight over the skyline, we beat back to the island for fresh water. And we found, fainting on the beach, a fat, naked, red-haired man whom I recognized as he whom I had fought. The arrow had not touched him; he had dived deep and swum far under the water.

But he had bled much from a cut I had given him on the head, and was nigh dead from exhaustion.

"Because he had fought me well, I took him into my cabin and revived him, and in the days that followed he learned to speak the speech we of Islam hold with the accursed Nazarenes. He told me that he was a bastard son of the king of England, and that enemies had driven him from his father's court, and were hunting him over the world. He swore the king his father would pay a mighty ransom for him, so I make you a present of him. For me, the pleasure of the cruise is enough. To you shall go the ransom the *malik* of England pays for his son. He is a merry companion who can tell a tale, quaff a flagon, and sing a song as well as any man I have ever known."

Shawar scanned Giles Hobson with new interest. In that rubicund countenance he failed to find any evidence of royal parentage, but reflected that few Franks showed royal lineage in their features: ruddy, freckled, light-haired, the western lords looked much alike to the Arab.

He turned his attention again to Shirkuh, who was of more importance than any wandering Frank, royal or common. The old war-dog, with shocking lack of formality, was humming a Kurdish war song under his breath as he poured a goblet of Shiraz wine—the Shiite rulers of Egypt were no stricter in their morals than were their Mameluke successors.

Apparently Shirkuh had no thought in the world except to satisfy his thirst, but Shawar wondered what craft was revolving behind that bluff exterior. In another man Shawar would have despised the Emir's restless vitality as an indication of an inferior mentality. But the Kurdish right-hand man of Nour ed din was no fool. The vizier wondered if Shirkuh had embarked on that wild-goose chase with el Ghazi's corsairs merely because his restless energy would not let him be quiet, even during a visit to the caliph's court, or if there was a deeper meaning behind his voyaging. Shawar always looked for hidden motives, even in trivial things. He had reached his position by ignoring no possibility of intrigue. Moreover, events were stirring in the womb of Destiny in that early spring of 1167 A.D.

Shawar thought of Dirgham's bones rotting in a ditch near the chapel of Sitta Nefisa, and he smiled and said: "A thousand thanks for your gifts, my lord. In return a jade goblet filled with pearls shall be carried to your chamber. Let this exchange of gifts symbolize the everlasting endurance of our friendship."

"Allah fill thy mouth with gold, lord," boomed Shirkuh, rising; "I go to drink wine with my officers, and tell them lies of my voyagings. Tomorrow I ride for Damascus. Allah be with thee!"

"And with thee, *ya khawand*."

After the Kurd's springy footfalls had ceased to rustle the thick carpets of the halls, Shawar motioned Giles to sit beside him on the cushions.

"What of your ransom?" he asked, in the Norman French he had learned through contact with the Crusaders.

"The king my father will fill this chamber with gold," promptly answered Giles. "His enemies have told him I was dead. Great will be the joy of the old man to learn the truth."

So saying, Giles retired behind a wine goblet and racked his brain for bigger and better lies. He had spun this fantasy for Shirkuh, thinking to make himself sound too valuable to be killed. Later—well, Giles lived for today, with little thought of the morrow.

Shawar watched, in some fascination, the rapid disappearance of the goblet's contents down his prisoner's gullet.

"You drink like a French baron," commented the Arab.

"I am the prince of all topers," answered Giles modestly—and with more truth than was contained in most of his boastings.

"Shirkuh, too, loves wine," went on the vizier. "You drank with him?"

"A little. He wouldn't get drunk, lest we sight a Christian ship. But we emptied a few flagons. A little wine loosens his tongue."

Shawar's narrow dark head snapped up; that was news to him.

"He talked? Of what?"

"Of his ambitions."

"And what are they?" Shawar held his breath.

"To be Caliph of Egypt," answered Giles, exaggerating the Kurd's actual words, as was his habit. Shirkuh had talked wildly, though rather incoherently.

"Did he mention me?" demanded the vizier.

"He said he held you in the hollow of his hand," said Giles, truthfully, for a wonder.

Shawar fell silent; somewhere in the palace a lute twanged and a black girl lifted a weird whining song of the South. Fountains splashed silverly, and there was a flutter of pigeons' wings.

"If I send emissaries to Jerusalem his spies will tell him," murmured Shawar to himself. "If I slay or constrain him, Nour ed din will consider it cause for war."

He lifted his head and stared at Giles Hobson.

"You call yourself king of topers; can you best the Emir Shirkuh in a drinking-bout?"

"In the palace of the king, my father," said Giles, "in one night I drank fifty barons under the table, the least of which was a mightier toper than Shirkuh."

"Would you win your freedom without ransom?"

"Aye, by Saint Withold!"

"You can scarcely know much of Eastern politics, being but newly come into these parts. But Egypt is the keystone of the arch of empire. It is coveted by Amalric, king of Jerusalem, and Nour ed din, sultan of Damascus. Ibn Ruzzik, and after him Dirgham, and after him, I, have played one against the other. By Shirkuh's aid I overthrew Dirgham; by Amalric's aid, I drove out Shirkuh. It is a perilous game, for I can trust neither.

"Nour ed din is cautious. Shirkuh is the man to fear. I think he came here professing friendship in order to spy me out, to lull my suspicions. Even now his army may be moving on Egypt.

"If he boasted to you of his ambitions and power, it is a sure sign that he feels secure in his plots. It is necessary that I render him helpless for a few hours; yet I dare not do him harm without true knowledge of whether his hosts are actually on the march. So this is your part."

Giles understood and a broad grin lit his ruddy face, and he licked his lips sensuously.

Shawar clapped his hands and gave orders, and presently, at request, Shirkuh entered, carrying his silk-girdled belly before him like an emperor of India.

"Our royal guest," purred Shawar, "has spoken of his prowess with the wine-cup. Shall we allow a Caphar to go home and boast among his people that he sat above the Faithful in anything? Who is more capable of humbling his pride than the Mountain Lion?"

"A drinking-bout?" Shirkuh's laugh was gusty as a sea blast. "By the beard of Muhammad, it likes me well! Come, Giles ibn Malik, let us to the quaffing!"

A procession began, of slaves bearing golden vessels brimming with sparkling nectar. . . .

During his captivity on el Ghazi's galley, Giles had become accustomed to the heady wine of the East. But his blood was boiling in his veins, his head was singing, and the gold-barred chamber was revolving to his dizzy gaze before Shirkuh, his voice trailing off in the midst of an incoherent song, slumped sidewise on his cushions, the gold beaker tumbling from his fingers.

Shawar leaped into frantic activity. At his clap Sudanese slaves entered, naked giants with gold earrings and silk loinclouts.

"Carry him into the alcove and lay him on a divan," he ordered. "Lord Giles, can you ride?"

Giles rose, reeling like a ship in a high wind.

"I'll hold to the mane," he hiccuped. "But why should I ride?"

"To bear my message to Amalric," snapped Shawar. "Here it is, sealed in a silken packet, telling him that Shirkuh means to conquer Egypt, and offering him payment in return for aid. Amalric distrusts me, but he will listen to one of the royal blood of his own race, who tells him of Shirkuh's boasts."

"Aye," muttered Giles groggily, "royal blood; my grandfather was a horse-boy in the royal stables."

"What did you say?" demanded Shawar, not understanding, then went on before Giles could answer. "Shirkuh has played into our hands. He will lie senseless for hours, and while he lies there, you will be riding for Palestine. He will not ride for Damascus tomorrow; he will be sick of overdrunkenness. I dared not imprison him, or even drug his wine. I dare make no move until I reach an agreement with Amalric. But Shirkuh is safe for the time being, and you will reach Amalric before he reaches Nour ed din. Haste!"

In the courtyard outside sounded the clink of harness, the impatient stamp of horses. Voices blurred in swift whispers. Footfalls faded away through the halls. Alone in the alcove, Shirkuh unexpectedly sat upright. He shook his head violently, buffeted it with his hands as if to clear away the clinging cobwebs. He reeled up, catching at the arras for support. But his beard bristled in an exultant grin. He seemed bursting with a triumphant whoop he could scarcely restrain. Stumblingly he made his way to a gold-barred window. Under his massive hands the thin gold rods twisted and buckled. He tumbled through, pitching headfirst to the ground in the midst of a great rose bush. Oblivious of bruises and scratches, he rose, careening like a ship on a tack, and oriented himself. He was in a broad garden; all about him waved great white blossoms; a breeze shook the palm leaves, and the moon was rising.

None halted him as he scaled the wall, though thieves skulking in the shadows eyed his rich garments avidly as he lurched through the deserted streets.

By devious ways he came to his own quarters and kicked his slaves awake.

"Horses, Allah curse you!" His voice crackled with exultation.

Ali, his captain of horse, came from the shadows.

"What now, lord?"

"The desert and Syria beyond!" roared Shirkuh, dealing him a terrific buffet on the back. "Shawar has swallowed the bait! Allah, how drunk I am! The world reels—but the stars are mine!

"That bastard Giles rides to Amalric—I heard Shawar give him his instructions as I lay in feigned slumber. We have forced the vizier's hand! Now Nour ed din will not hesitate, when his spies bring him news from Jerusalem of the marching of the iron men! I fumed in the caliph's court, checkmated at every turn by Shawar, seeking a way. I went into the galleys of the corsairs to cool my brain, and Allah gave into my hands a red-haired tool! I filled the lord Giles full of 'drunken' boastings, hoping he would repeat them to Shawar, and that Shawar would take fright and send for Amalric—which would force our overly cautious sultan to act. Now follow marching and war and the glutting of ambition. But let us ride, in the devil's name!"

A few minutes later the Emir and his small retinue were clattering through the shadowy streets, past gardens that slept, a riot of color under the moon, lapping six-storied palaces that were dreams of pink marble and lapis lazuli and gold.

At a small, secluded gate, a single sentry bawled a challenge and lifted his pike.

"Dog!" Shirkuh reined his steed back on its haunches and hung over the Egyptian like a silk-clad cloud of death. "It is Shirkuh, your master's guest!"

"But my orders are to allow none to pass without written order, signed and sealed by the vizier," protested the soldier. "What shall I say to Shawar—"

"You will say naught," prophesied Shirkuh. "The dead speak not."

His scimitar gleamed and fell, and the soldier crumpled, cut through helmet and head.

"Open the gate, Ali," laughed Shirkuh. "It is Fate that rides tonight—Fate and Destiny!"

In a cloud of moon-bathed dust they whirled out of the gate and over the plain. On the rocky shoulder of Mukattam, Shirkuh drew rein to gaze back over the city, which lay like a legendary dream under the moonlight, a waste of masonry and stone and marble, splendor and squalor merging in the moonlight, magnificence blent with ruin. To the south the dome of Imam Esh Shafi'y shone beneath the moon; to the north loomed up the gigantic pile of the Castle of El Kahira, its walls carved blackly out of the white moonlight. Between them lay the remains and ruins of three capitals of Egypt; palaces with their mortar yet undried reared beside crumbling walls haunted only by bats.

Shirkuh laughed, and yelled with pure joy. His horse reared and his scimitar glittered in the air.

"A bride in cloth-of-gold! Await my coming, oh Egypt, for when I come again, it will be with spears and horsemen, to seize ye in my hands!"

Allah willed it that Amalric, king of Jerusalem, should be in Darum, personally attending to the fortifying of that small desert outpost, when the envoys from Egypt rode through the gates. A restless, alert and wary king was Amalric, bred to war and intrigue.

In the castle hall the Egyptian emissaries salaamed before him like corn bending before a wind, and Giles Hobson, grotesque in his dusty silks and white turban, louted awkwardly and presented the sealed packet of Shawar.

Amalric took it with his own hands and read it, striding absently up and down the hall, a gold-maned lion, stately, yet dangerously supple.

"What talk is this of royal bastards?" he demanded suddenly, staring at Giles, who was nervous but not embarrassed.

"A lie to cozen the paynim, your majesty," admitted the Englishman, secure in his belief that the Egyptians did not understand Norman French. "I am no illegitimate of the blood, only the honest-born younger son of a baron of the Scottish marches."

Giles did not care to be kicked into the scullery with the rest of the varlets. The nearer the purple, the richer the pickings. It seemed safe to assume that the king of Jerusalem was not over-familiar with the nobility of the Scottish border.

"I have seen many a younger son who lacked coat-armor, war-cry and wealth, but was none the less worthy," said Amalric. "You shall not go unrewarded. Messer Giles, know you the import of this message?"

"The wazeer Shawar spoke to me at some length," admitted Giles.

"The ultimate fate of Outremer hangs in the balance," said Amalric. "If the same man holds both Egypt and Syria, we are caught in the jaws of the vise. Better for Shawar to rule in Egypt, than Nour ed din. We march for Cairo. Would you accompany the host?"

"In sooth, lord," began Giles, "it has been a wearisome time—"

"True," broke in Amalric. "'Twere better that you ride on to Acre and rest from your travels. I will give you a letter for the lord commanding there. Sir Guiscard de Chastillon will give you service—"

Giles started violently.

"Nay, Lord," he said hurriedly, "duty calls, and what are weary limbs and an empty belly beside duty? Let me go with you and do my devoir in Egypt!"

"Your spirit likes me well, Messer Giles," said Amalric with an approving smile. "Would that all the foreigners who come adventuring in Outremer were like you."

"And they were," quietly murmured an immobile-faced Egyptian to his mate, "not all the wine-vats of Palestine would suffice. We will tell a tale to the vizier concerning this liar."

But lies or not, in the grey dawn of a young spring day, the iron men of Outremer rode southward, with the great banner billowing over their helmeted heads, and their spear-points coldly glinting in the dim light.

There were not many; the strength of the Crusading kingdoms lay in the quality, not the quantity, of their defenders. Three hundred and seventy-five knights took the road to Egypt: nobles of Jerusalem, barons whose castles guarded the eastern marches, Knights of Saint John in their white surcoats, grim Templars, adventurers from beyond the sea, their skins yet ruddy from the cold sun of the north.

With them rode a swarm of Turcoples, Christianized Turks, wiry men on lean ponies. After the horsemen lumbered the wagons, attended by the rag-and-tag camp followers, the servants, ragamuffins and trolls that tag after any host. With shining, steel-sheathed, banner-crowned van, and rear trailing out into picturesque squalor, the army of Jerusalem moved across the land.

The dunes of the Jifar knew again the tramp of shod horses, the clink of mail. The iron men were riding again the old road of war, the road their fathers had ridden so oft before them.

Yet when at last the Nile broke the monotony of the level land, winding like a serpent feathered with green palms, they heard the strident clamor of cymbals and *nakirs,* and saw egret feathers moving among gay-striped pavilions that bore the colors of Islam. Shirkuh had reached the Nile before them, with seven thousand horsemen.

Mobility was always an advantage possessed by the Moslems. It took time to gather the cumbrous Frankish host, time to move it.

Riding like a man possessed, the Mountain Lion had reached Nor ed din, told his tale, and then, with scarcely a pause, had raced southward again with the troops he had held in readiness since the first Egyptian campaign. The thought of Amalric in Egypt had sufficed to stir Nour ed din to action. If the Crusaders made themselves masters of the Nile, it meant the eventual doom of Islam.

Shirkuh's was the dynamic vitality of the nomad. Across the desert by Wadi el Ghizlan he had driven his riders until even the tough Seljuks reeled in their saddles. Into the teeth of a roaring sandstorm he had plunged, fighting like a madman for each mile, each second of time. He had crossed the Nile at Atfih, and now his riders were regaining their breath, while Shirkuh watched the eastern skyline for the moving forest of lances that would mark the coming of Amalric.

The king of Jerusalem dared not attempt a crossing in the teeth of his enemies; Shirkuh was in the same case. Without pitching camp, the Franks moved northward along the river bank. The iron men rode slowly, scanning the sullen stream for a possible crossing.

The Moslems broke camp and took up the march, keeping pace with the Franks. The *fellaheen,* peeking from their mud huts, were amazed by the sight of two hosts moving slowly in the same direction without hostile demonstration, with the river between.

So they came at last into sight of the towers of El Kahira.

The Franks pitched their camp close to the shores of Birket el Habash, near the gardens of el Fustat, whose six-storied houses reared their flat roofs among oceans of palms and waving blossoms. Across the river Shirkuh encamped at Gizeh, in the shadow of the scornful colossus reared by cryptic monarchs forgotten before his ancestors were born.

Matters fell at a deadlock. Shirkuh, for all his impetuosity, had the patience of the Kurd, imponderable as the mountains which bred him. He was content to play a waiting game, with the broad river between him and the terrible swords of the Europeans.

Shawar waited on Amalric with pomp and parade and the clamor of *nakirs,* and he found the lion as wary as he was indomitable. Two hundred thousand *dinars* and the caliph's hand on the bargain, that was the price he demanded for Egypt. And Shawar knew he must pay. Egypt slumbered as she had slumbered for a thousand years, inert alike under the heel of Macedonian, Roman, Arab, Turk or Fatimid. The *fellah* toiled in his field, and scarcely knew to whom he paid his taxes. There was no land of Egypt: it was a myth, a cloak for a despot. Shawar was Egypt; Egypt was Shawar; the price of Egypt was the price of Shawar's head.

So the Frankish ambassadors went to the hall of the caliph.

Mystery ever shrouded the person of the Incarnation of Divine Reason. The spiritual center of the Shiite creed moved in a maze of mystic inscrutability, his veil of supernatural awe increasing as his political power was usurped by plotting viziers. No Frank had ever seen the caliph of Egypt.

Hugh of Caesarea and Geoffrey Fulcher, Master of the Templars, were chosen for the mission, blunt war-dogs, grim as their own swords. A group of mailed horsemen accompanied them.

They rode through the flowering gardens of el Fustat, past the chapel of Sitta Nefisa where Dirgham had died under the hands of the mob; through winding streets which covered the ruins of el Askar and el Katai; past the Mosque of Ibn Tulun, and the Lake of the Elephant, into the teeming streets of El Mansuriya, the quarter of the Sudanese, where weird native citterns twanged in the houses, and swaggering black men, gaudy in silk and gold, stared childishly at the grim horsemen.

At the Gate Zuweyla the riders halted, and the Master of the Temple and the lord of Caesarea rode on, attended by only one man—Giles Hobson. The fat Englishman wore good leather and chain-mail, and a sword at his thigh, though the portly arch of his belly somewhat detracted from his war-like appearance. Little thought was being taken in those perilous times of royal bastards or younger sons; but Giles had won the approval of Hugh of Caesarea, who loved a good tale and a bawdy song.

At Zuweyla gate Shawar met them with pomp and pageantry and escorted them through the bazaars and the Turkish quarter where hawk-like men from beyond the Oxus stared and silently spat. For the first time, Franks in armor were riding through the streets of El Kahira.

At the gates of the Great East Palace the ambassadors gave up their swords, and followed the vizier through dim tapestry-hung corridors and gold arched doors where tongueless Sudanese stood like images of black silence, sword in hand. They crossed an open court bordered by fretted arcades supported by marble columns; their iron-clad feet rang on mosaic paving. Fountains jetted their silver sheen into the air, peacocks spread their iridescent plumage, parrots fluttered on gold threads. In broad halls jewels glittered for eyes of birds wrought of silver or gold. So they came at last to the vast audience room, with its ceiling of carved ebony and ivory. Courtiers in silks and jewels knelt facing a broad curtain heavy with gold and sewn with pearls that gleamed against its satin darkness like stars in a midnight sky.

Shawar prostrated himself thrice to the carpeted floor. The curtains were swept apart, and the wondering Franks gazed on the gold throne, where, in robes of white silk, sat al Adhid, Caliph of Egypt.

They saw a slender youth, dark almost to negroid, whose hands lay limp, whose eyes seemed already shadowed by ultimate sleep. A deadly weariness clung about him, and he listened to the representations of his vizier as one who heeds a tale too often told.

But a flash of awakening came to him when Shawar suggested, with extremest delicacy, that the Franks wished his hand upon the pact. A visible shudder passed through the room. Al Adhid hesitated, then extended his gloved hand. Sir Hugh's voice boomed through the breathless hall.

"Lord, the good faith of princes is naked; troth is not clothed."

All about came a hissing intake of breath. But the Caliph smiled, as at the whims of a barbarian, and stripping the glove from his hand, laid his slender fingers in the bear-like paw of the Crusader.

All this Giles Hobson observed from his discreet position in the background. All eyes were centered on the group clustered about the golden throne. From near his shoulder a soft hiss reached Giles' ear. Its feminine note brought him quickly about, forgetful of kings and caliphs. A heavy tapestry was drawn slightly aside, and in the sweet-smelling gloom, a slender white hand waved invitingly. Another scent made itself evident, a luring perfume, subtle yet unmistakable.

Giles turned silently and pulled aside the tapestry, straining his eyes in the semidarkness. There was an alcove behind the hangings, and a narrow corridor meandering away. Before him stood a figure whose vagueness did not conceal its lissomeness. A pair of eyes glowed and sparkled at him, and his head swam with the power of that diabolical perfume.

He let the tapestry fall behind him. Through the hangings the voices in the throne room came vague and muffled.

The woman spoke not; her little feet made no sound on the thickly carpeted floor over which he stumbled. She invited, yet retreated; she beckoned, yet she withheld herself. Only when, baffled, he broke into earnest profanity, she admonished him with a finger to her lips and a warning: "Sssssh!"

"Devil take you, wench!" he swore, stopping short. "I'll follow you no more. What manner of game is this, anyway? If you don't want to deal with me, why did you wave at me? Why do you beckon and then run away? I'm going back to the audience hall and may the dogs bite your—"

"Wait!" The voice was liquid sweet.

She glided close to him, laying her hands on his shoulders. What light there was in the winding tapestried corridor was behind her, outlining her supple figure through her filmy garments. Her flesh shone like dim ivory in the purple gloom.

"I could love you," she whispered.

"Well, what detains you?" he demanded uneasily.

"Not here; follow me." She glided out of his groping arms and drifted ahead of him, a lithely swaying ghost among the velvet hangings.

He followed, burning with impatience and questing not at all for the reason of the whole affair, until she came out into an octagonal chamber, almost as dimly lighted as had been the corridor. As he pushed after her, a hanging slid over the opening behind him. He gave it no heed. Where he was he neither knew nor cared. All that was important to him was the supple figure that posed shamelessly before him, veilless, naked arms uplifted and slender fingers intertwined behind her nape over which fell a mass of hair that was like black burnished foam.

He stood struck dumb with her beauty. She was like no other woman he had ever seen; the difference was not only in her dark eyes, her dusky tresses, her long *kohl*-tinted lashes, or the warm ivory of her roundly slender limbs. It was in every glance, each movement, each posture, that made voluptuousness an art. Here was a woman cultured in the arts of pleasure, a dream to madden any lover of the fleshpots of life. The English, French and Venetian women he had nuzzled seemed slow, stolid, frigid beside this vibrant image of sensuality. A favorite of the Caliph! The implication of the realization sent the blood pounding suffocatingly through his veins. He panted for breath.

"Am I not fair?" Her breath, scented with the perfume that sweetened her body, fanned his face. The soft tendrils of her hair brushed against his cheek. He groped for her, but she eluded him with disconcerting ease. "What will you do for me?"

"Anything!" he swore ardently, and with more sincerity than he usually voiced the vow.

His hand closed on her wrist and he dragged her to him; his other arm bent about her waist, and the feel of her resilient flesh made him drunk. He pawed for her lips with his, but she bent supplely backward, twisting her head this way and that, resisting him with unexpected strength; the lithe pantherish strength of a dancing-girl. Yet even while she resisted him, she did not repulse him.

"Nay," she laughed, and her laughter was the gurgle of a silver fountain; "first there is a price!"

"Name it, for the love of the Devil!" he gasped. "Am I a frozen saint? I can not resist you forever!" He had released her wrist and was pawing at her shoulder straps.

Suddenly she ceased to struggle; throwing both arms about his thick neck, she looked into his eyes. The depths of hers, dark and mysterious, seemed to drown him; he shuddered as a wave of something akin to fear swept over him.

"You are high in the council of the Franks!" she breathed. "We know you disclosed to Shawar that you are a son of the English king. You came with Amalric's ambassadors. You know his plans. Tell what I wish to know, and I am yours! What is Amalric's next move?"

"He will build a bridge of boats and cross the Nile to attack Shirkuh by night," answered Giles without hesitation.

Instantly she laughed, with mockery and indescribable malice, struck him in the face, twisted free, sprang back, and cried out sharply. The next moment the shadows were alive with rushing figures as from the tapestries leaped naked black giants.

Giles wasted no time in futile gestures toward his empty belt. As great dusky hands fell on him, his massive fist smashed against bone, and the Negro dropped with a fractured jaw. Springing over him, Giles scudded across the room with unexpected agility. But to his dismay he saw that the doorways were hidden by the tapestries. He groped frantically among the hangings; then a brawny arm hooked throttlingly about his throat from behind, and he felt himself dragged backward and off his feet. Other hands snatched at him, woolly heads bobbed about him, white eyeballs and teeth glimmered in the semi-darkness. He lashed out savagely with his foot and caught a big black in the belly, curling him up in agony on the floor. A thumb felt for his eye and he mangled it between his teeth, bringing a whimper of pain from the owner. But a dozen pairs of hands lifted him, smiting and kicking. He heard a grating, sliding noise, felt himself swung up violently and hurled downward—a black opening in the floor rushed up to meet him. An ear-splitting yell burst from him, and then he was rushing headlong down a walled shaft, up which sounded the sucking and bubbling of racing water.

He hit with a tremendous splash and felt himself swept irresistibly onward. The well was wide at the bottom. He had fallen near one side of it, and was being carried toward the other in which, he had light enough to see as he rose blowing and snorting above the surface, another black orifice gaped. Then he was thrown with stunning force against the edge of that opening, his legs and hips were sucked through but his frantic fingers, slipping from the mossy stone lip, encountered something and clung on. Looking wildly up, he saw, framed high above him in the dim light, a cluster of woolly heads rimming the mouth of the well. Then abruptly all light was shut out as the trap was replaced, and Giles was conscious only of utter blackness and the rustle and swirl of the racing water that dragged relentlessly at him.

This, Giles knew, was the well into which were thrown foes of the Caliph. He wondered how many ambitious generals, plotting viziers, rebellious nobles and importunate *harim* favorites had gone whirling through that black hole to come into the light of day again only floating as carrion on the bosom of the Nile. It was evident that the well had been sunk into an underground flow of water that rushed into the river, perhaps miles away.

Clinging there by his fingernails in the dank rushing blackness, Giles Hobson was so frozen with horror that it did not even occur to him to call on the various saints he ordinarily blasphemed. He merely hung on to the irregularly round, slippery object his hands had found, frantic with fear of being torn away and whirled down that black slimy tunnel, feeling his arms and fingers growing numb with the strain, and slipping gradually but steadily from their hold.

His last ounce of breath went from him in a wild cry of despair, and—miracle of miracles—it was answered. Light flooded the shaft, a light dim and gray, yet in such contrast with the former blackness that it momentarily dazzled him. Someone was shouting, but the words were unintelligible amidst the rush of the black waters. He tried to shout back, but he could only gurgle. Then, mad with fear lest the trap should shut again, he achieved an inhuman screech that almost burst his throat.

Shaking the water from his eyes and craning his head backward, he saw a human head and shoulders blocked in the open trap far above him. A rope was dangling down toward him. It swayed before his eyes, but he dared not let go long enough to seize it. In desperation, he mouthed for it, gripped it with his teeth, then let go and snatched, even as he was sucked into the black hole. His numbed fingers slipped along the rope. Tears of fear and helplessness rolled down his face. But his jaws were locked desperately on the strands, and his corded neck muscles resisted the terrific strain.

Whoever was on the other end of the rope was hauling like a team of oxen. Giles felt himself ripped bodily from the clutch of the torrent. As his feet swung clear, he saw, in the dim light, that to which he had been clinging: a human skull, wedged somehow in a crevice of the slimy rock.

He was drawn rapidly up, revolving like a pendant. His numbed hands clawed stiffly at the rope, his teeth seemed to be tearing from their sockets. His jaw muscles were knots of agony, his neck felt as if it were being racked.

Just as human endurance reached its limit, he saw the lip of the trap slip past him, and he was dumped on the floor at its brink.

He groveled in agony, unable to unlock his jaws from about the hemp. Someone was massaging the cramped muscles with skilful fingers, and at last they relaxed with a stream of blood from the tortured gums. A goblet of wine was pressed to his lips and he gulped it loudly, the liquid slopping over and spilling on his slime-smeared mail. Someone was tugging at it, as if fearing lest he injure himself by guzzling, but he clung on with both hands until the beaker was empty. Then only he released it, and with a loud gasping sigh of relief, looked up into the face of Shawar. Behind the vizier were several giant Sudani, of the same type as those who had been responsible for Giles' predicament.

"We missed you from the audience hall," said Shawar. "Sir Hugh roared treachery, until a eunuch said he saw you follow a woman slave off down a corridor. Then the lord Hugh laughed and said you were up to your old tricks, and rode away with the lord Geoffrey. But I knew the peril you ran in dallying with a woman in the Caliph's palace; so I searched for you, and a slave told me he had heard a frightful yell in this chamber. I came, and entered just as a black was replacing the carpet above the trap. He sought to flee, and died without speaking." The vizier indicated a sprawling form that lay near, head lolling on half-severed neck. "How came you in this state?"

"A woman lured me here," answered Giles, "and set blackamoors upon me, threatening me with the well unless I revealed Amalric's plans."

"What did you tell her?" The vizier's eyes burned so intently on Giles that the fat man shuddered slightly and hitched himself further away from the yet open trap.

"I told them nothing! Who am I to know the king's plans, anyway? Then they dumped me into that cursed hole, though I fought like a lion and maimed a score of the rogues. Had I but had my trusty sword—"

At a nod from Shawar the trap was closed, the rug drawn over it. Giles breathed a sigh of relief. Slaves dragged the corpse away.

The vizier touched Giles' arm and led the way through a corridor concealed by the hangings.

"I will send an escort with you to the Frankish camp. There are spies of Shirkuh in this palace, and others who love him not, yet hate me. Describe me this woman—the eunuch saw only her hand."

Giles groped for adjectives, then shook his head.

"Her hair was black, her eyes moonfire, her body alabaster."

"A description that would fit a thousand women of the Caliph," said the vizier. "No matter; get you gone, for the night wanes and Allah only knows what morn will bring."

The night was indeed late as Giles Hobson rode into the Frankish camp surrounded by Turkish *memluks* with drawn sabres. But a light burned in Amalric's pavilion, which the wary monarch preferred to the palace offered him by Shawar; and thither Giles went, confident of admittance as a teller of lusty tales who had won the king's friendship.

Amalric and his barons were bent above a map as the fat man entered, and they were too engrossed to notice his entry, or his bedraggled appearance.

"Shawar will furnish us men and boats," the king was saying; "they will fashion the bridge, and we will make the attempt by night—"

An explosive grunt escaped Giles' lips, as if he had been hit in the belly.

"What, Sir Giles the Fat!" exclaimed Amalric, looking up; "are you but now returned from your adventuring in Cairo? You are fortunate still to have head on your shoulders. Eh—what ails you, that you sweat and grow pale? Where are you going?"

"I have taken an emetic," mumbled Giles over his shoulder.

Beyond the light of the pavilion he broke into a stumbling run. A tethered horse started and snorted at him. He caught the rein, grasped the saddle peak; then, with one foot in the stirrup, he halted. Awhile he meditated; then at last, wiping cold sweat beads from his face, he returned with slow and dragging steps to the king's tent.

He entered unceremoniously and spoke forthwith: "Lord, is it your plan to throw a bridge of boats across the Nile?"

"Aye, so it is," declared Amalric.

Giles uttered a loud groan and sank down on a bench, his head in his hands. "I am too young to die!" he lamented. "Yet I must speak, though my reward be a sword in the belly. This night Shirkuh's spies trapped me into speaking like a fool. I told them the first lie that came into my head—and Saint Withold defend me, I spoke the truth unwittingly. I told them you meant to build a bridge of boats!"

A shocked silence reigned. Geoffrey Fulcher dashed down his cup in a spasm of anger. "Death to the fat fool!" he swore, rising.

"Nay!" Amalric smiled suddenly. He stroked his golden beard. "Our foe will be expecting the bridge, now. Good enough. Hark ye!"

And as he spoke, grim smiles grew on the lips of the barons, and Giles Hobson began to grin and thrust out his belly, as if his fault had been virtue, craftily devised.

All night the Saracen host had stood at arms; on the opposite bank fires blazed, reflected from the rounded walls and burnished roofs of el Fustat. Trumpets mingled with the clang of steel. The Emir Shirkuh, riding up and down the bank along which his mailed hawks were ranged, glanced toward the eastern sky, just tinged with dawn. A wind blew out of the desert.

There had been fighting along the river the day before, and all through the night drums had rumbled and trumpets blared their threat. All day Egyptians and naked Sudani had toiled to span the dusky flood with boats chained together, end to end. Thrice they had pushed toward the western bank, under the cover of their archers in the barges, only to falter and shrink back before the clouds of Turkish arrows. Once the end of the boat bridge had almost touched the shore, and the helmeted riders had spurred their horses into the water to slash at the shaven heads of the workers. Skirkuh had expected an onslaught of the knights across the frail span, but it had not come. The men in the boats had again fallen back, leaving their dead floating in the muddily churning wash.

Shirkuh decided that the Franks were lurking behind walls, saving themselves for a supreme effort, when their allies should have completed the bridge. The opposite bank was clustered with swarms of naked figures, and the Kurd expected to see them begin the futile task once more.

As dawn whitened the desert, there came a rider who rode like the wind, sword in hand, turban unbound, blood dripping from his beard.

"Woe to Islam!" he cried. "The Franks have crossed the river!"

Panic swept the Moslem camp; men jerked their steeds from the river bank, staring wildly northward. Only Shirkuh's bull-like voice kept them from flinging away their swords and bolting.

The Emir's profanity was frightful. He had been fooled and tricked. While the Egyptians held his attention with their useless labor, Amalric and the iron men had marched northward, crossed the prongs of the Delta in ships, and were now hastening vengefully southward. The Emir's spies had had neither time nor opportunity to reach him. Shawar had seen to that.

The Mountain Lion dared not await attack in this unsheltered spot. Before the sun was well up, the Turkish host was on the march; behind them the rising light shone on spear-points that gleamed in a rising cloud of dust.

This dust irked Giles Hobson, riding behind Amalric and his councilors. The fat Englishman was thirsty; dust settled greyly on his mail; gnats bit him, sweat got into his eyes, and the sun, as it rose, beat mercilessly on his basinet; so he hung it on his saddle peak and pushed back his linked coif, daring sunstroke. On either side of him leather creaked and worn mail clinked. Giles thought of the ale-pots of England, and cursed the man whose hate had driven him around the world.

And so they hunted the Mountain Lion up the valley of the Nile, until they came to el Baban, The Gates, and found the Saracen host drawn up for battle in the gut of the low sandy hills.

Word came back along the ranks, putting new fervor into the knights. The clatter of leather and steel seemed imbued with new meaning. Giles put on his helmet and rising in his stirrups, looked over the iron-clad shoulders in front of him.

To the left were the irrigated fields on the edge of which the host was riding. To the right was the desert. Ahead of them the terrain was broken by the hills. On these hills and in the shallow valleys between, bristled the banners of the Turks, and their *nakirs* blared. A mass of the host was drawn up in the plain between the Franks and the hills.

The Christians had halted: three hundred and seventy-five knights, plus half a dozen more who had ridden all the way from Acre and reached the host only an hour before, with their retainers. Behind them, moving with the baggage, their allies halted in straggling lines: a thousand Turcoples, and some five thousand Egyptians, whose gaudy garments outshone their courage.

"Let us ride forward and smite those on the plain," urged one of the foreign knights, newly come to the East.

Amalric scanned the closely massed ranks and shook his head. He glanced at the banners that floated among the spears on the slopes on either flank where the kettledrums clamored.

"That is the banner of Saladin in the center," he said. "Shirkuh's house troops are on yonder hill. If the center expected to stand, the Emir would be there. No, messers, I think it is their wish to lure us into a charge. We will wait their attack, under cover of the Turcoples' bows. Let them come to us; they are in a hostile land, and must push the war."

The rank and file had not heard his words. He lifted his hand, and thinking it preceded an order to charge, the forest of lances quivered and sank in rest. Amalric, realizing the mistake, rose in his stirrups to shout his command to fall back, but before he could speak, Giles' horse, restive, shouldered that of the knight next to him. This knight, one of those who had joined the host less than an hour before, turned irritably; Giles looked into a lean beaked face, seamed by a livid scar.

"Ha!" Instinctively the ogre caught at his sword.

Giles' action was also instinctive. Everything else was swept out of his mind at the sight of that dread visage which had haunted his dreams for more than a year. With a yelp he sank his spurs into his horse's belly. The beast neighed shrilly and leaped, blundering against Amalric's warhorse. That high-strung beast reared and plunged, got the bit between its teeth, broke from the ranks and thundered out across the plain.

Bewildered, seeing their king apparently charging the Saracen host single-handed, the men of the Cross gave tongue and followed him. The plain shook as the great horses stampeded across it, and the spears of the iron-clad riders crashed splinteringly against the shields of their enemies.

The movement was so sudden it almost swept the Moslems off their feet. They had not expected a charge so instantly to follow the coming up of the Christians. But the allies of the knights were struck by confusion. No orders had been given, no arrangement made for battle. The whole host was disordered by that premature onslaught. The Turcoples and Egyptians wavered uncertainly, drawing up about the baggage wagons.

The whole first rank of the Saracen center went down, and over their mangled bodies rode the knights of Jerusalem, swinging their great swords. An instant the Turkish ranks held; then they began to fall back in good order, marshaled by their commander, a slender, dark, self-contained young officer, Salah ed din, Shirkuh's nephew.

The Christians followed. Amalric, cursing his mischance, made the best of a bad bargain, and so well he plied his trade that the harried Turks cried out on Allah and turned their horses' heads from him.

Back into the gut of the hills the Saracens retired, and turning there, under cover of slope and cliff, darkened the air with their shafts. The headlong force of the knights' charge was broken in the uneven ground, but the iron men came on grimly, bending their helmeted heads to the rain.

Then on the flanks, kettledrums roared into fresh clamor. The riders of the right wing, led by Shirkuh, swept down the slopes and struck the horde which clustered loosely about the baggage train. That charge swept the unwarlike Egyptians off the field in headlong flight. The left wing began to close in to take the knights on the flank, driving before it the troops of the Turcoples. Amalric, hearing the kettledrums behind and on either side of him as well as in front, gave the order to fall back, before they were completely hemmed in.

To Giles Hobson it seemed the end of the world. He was deafened by the clang of swords and the shouts. He seemed surrounded by an ocean of surging steel and billowing dust clouds. He parried blindly and smote blindly, hardly knowing whether his blade cut flesh or empty air. Out of the defiles horsemen were moving, chanting exultantly. A cry of *"Yala-l-Islam!"* rose above the thunder—Saladin's war-cry, that was in later years to ring around the world. The Saracen center was coming into the battle again.

Abruptly the press slackened, broke; the plain was filled with flying figures. A strident ululation cut the din. The Turcoples' shafts had stayed the Saracens' left wing just long enough to allow the knights to retreat through the closing jaws of the vise. But Amalric, retreating slowly, was cut off with a handful of knights. The Turks swirled about him, screaming in exultation, slashing and smiting with mad abandon. In the dust and confusion the ranks of the iron men fell back, unaware of the fate of their king.

Giles Hobson, riding through the field like a man in a daze, came face to face with Guiscard de Chastillon.

"Dog!" croaked the knight. "We are doomed, but I'll send you to Hell ahead of me!"

His sword went up, but Giles leaned from his saddle and caught his arm. The fat man's eyes were bloodshot; he licked his dust-stained lips. There was blood on his sword, and his helmet was dinted.

"Your selfish hate and my cowardice has cost Amalric the field this day," Giles croaked. "There he fights for his life; let us redeem ourselves as best we may."

Some of the glare faded from de Chastillon's eyes; he twisted about, stared at the plumed heads that surged and eddied about a cluster of iron helmets; and he nodded his steel-clad head.

They rode together into the mêlée. Their swords hissed and crackled on mail and bone. Amalric was down, pinned under his dying horse. Around him whirled the eddy of battle, where his knights were dying under a sea of hacking blades.

Giles fell rather than jumped from his saddle, gripped the dazed king and dragged him clear. The fat Englishman's muscles cracked under the strain, a groan escaped his lips. A Seljuk leaned from the saddle, slashed at Amalric's unhelmeted head. Giles bent his head, took the blow on his own crown; his knees sagged and sparks flashed before his eyes. Guiscard de Chastillon rose in his stirrups, swinging his sword with both hands. The blade crunched through mail, gritted through bone. The Seljuk dropped, shorn through the spine. Giles braced his legs, heaved the king up, slung him over his saddle.

"Save the king!" Giles did not recognize that croak as his own voice.

Geoffrey Fulcher loomed through the crush, dealing great strokes. He seized the rein of Giles' steed; half a dozen reeling, blood-dripping knights closed about the frantic horse and its stunned burden. Nerved to desperation they hacked their way clear. The Seljuks swirled in behind them to be met by Guiscard de Chastillon's flailing blade.

The waves of wild horsemen and flying blades broke on him. Saddles were emptied and blood spurted. Giles rose from the red-splashed ground among the lashing hoofs. He ran in among the horses, stabbing at bellies and thighs. A sword stroke knocked off his helmet. His blade snapped under a Seljuk's ribs.

Guiscard's horse screamed awfully and sank to the earth. His grim rider rose, spurting blood at every joint of his armor. Feet braced wide on the blood-soaked earth, he wielded his great sword until the steel wave washed over him and he was hidden from view by waving plumes and rearing steeds.

Giles ran at a heron-feathered chief, gripped his leg with his naked hands. Blows rained on his coif, bringing fire-shot darkness, but he hung grimly on. He wrenched the Turk from his saddle, fell with him, groping for his throat. Hoofs pounded about him, a steed shouldered against him, knocking him rolling in the dust. He clambered painfully to his feet, shaking the blood and sweat from his eyes. Dead men and dead horses lay heaped in a ghastly pile about him.

A familiar voice reached his dulled ears. He saw Shirkuh sitting his white horse, gazing down at him. The Mountain Lion's beard bristled in a grin.

"You have saved Amalric," said he, indicating a group of riders in the distance, closing in with the retreating host; the Saracens were not pressing the pursuit too closely. The iron men were falling back in good order. They were defeated, not broken. The Turks were content to allow them to retire unmolested.

"You are a hero, Giles ibn Malik," said Shirkuh.

Giles sank down on a dead horse and dropped his head in his hands. The marrow of his legs seemed turned to water, and he was shaken with a desire to weep.

"I am neither a hero nor the son of a king," said Giles. "Slay me and be done with it."

"Who spoke of slaying?" demanded Shirkuh. "I have just won an empire in this battle, and I would quaff a goblet in token of it. Slay you? By Allah, I would not harm a hair of such a stout fighter and noble toper. You shall come and drink with me in celebration of a kingdom won when I ride into El Kahira in triumph."

www.ingramcontent.com/pod-product-compliance
Lightning Source LLC
Chambersburg PA
CBHW030817310726
48980CB00006B/526/J
9780809515509